A Brief Madness

Also by Karisha Kalʻeeʻay

Waiting to Know You

Through a partnership with Carbonfund.org, Karisha Kalʻeeʻay has calculated her carbon footprint arising from energy usage, commuting, and business travel and has offset that by investing in Carbonfund.org's third-party certified carbon reduction projects.

**SAMPLE
NOT FOR RESALE**

A
Brief
Madness

A Novel

Karisha Kal'ee'ay

A Brief Madness is a work of fiction. Names, characters, places, organizations, and incidents are either products of the writer's imagination or are used fictitiously. Any resemblance to actual events, locales, or persons, living or dead, is entirely coincidental.

Copyright © 2011 by Karisha Kalʻeeʻay

All rights reserved. Published in the United States by Linden House Publishing, Grand Rapids, Michigan. No part of this book may be reproduced or utilized in any form or by any means, electronic or mechanical, including information storage and retrieval systems, without permission in writing from the publisher or author, except in the case of a reviewer, who may quote brief passages embodied in critical articles or in a review.

Library of Congress Control Number: 2010941941
Kalʻeeʻay, Karisha

ISBN 978-0-9845464-4-2

PRINTED IN THE UNITED STATES OF AMERICA

First Edition

Linden House Publishing

For Melba the Storyteller,
who inspired me with her tales, outlasted Irene by seven years,
married Earl (the kindest person I've ever known),
and produced three more raconteurs to entertain us all:
my dad (who wed my wonderful mother)
and my sisters, Shaylona and Trishelle

A Brief Madness

Part One

1

The elevator never stops on any other floor.

She would have chosen the stairs for her solitary travels if she had known. For a while there were mistakes: the doors slid open and impassive faces stared until they shut again, or a person would mime forgetfulness and bustle away calling, "Don't wait."

To prevent such mishaps, Ember hasn't altered her schedule for seven months. It is rarely lonely since socializing in the elevator was never something she looked forward to, and most days there are thoughts to occupy her mind for the scant six floors.

Today she has the memories of women's voices in her head: Her dead husband's ex-wife on the answering machine, and the best friend of the last murdered girl, reminiscing ghoulishly on a television interview show about the claustrophobic victim never wearing anything around her neck.

Because of these, Ember shared a rather hurtful memory with her group this evening:

Her husband told her that he had identified the unfortunate flaw of a seemingly perfect marriage. "It has forced upon me the lonely cognizance that no one, not even my beloved spouse, can ever understand everything about me."

She took it personally, but the habit of helping him edit was ingrained. She immediately suggested a new version: "It has led to the lonely realization that no one, not even my beloved spouse, can ever understand everything about me."

"You're so quick," he said fondly. "It's not as dramatic."

"It's not as pompous. And if it's true, why don't you explain yourself better?" she had asked, but he was already wandering away—probably back to his desk to write his great thought down (she found it months afterward in one of his diaries).

He leaned only his head into the room a few minutes later to clarify that by "understand" he meant "internally process into love and acceptance."

"Richard!" she shouted before he disappeared. "Who will you be giving those words to?"

He didn't answer.

She had her own interpretation: he had decided she was incapable of comprehending his complexities.

He had a mustache then, and its albino hairs stood up and out against his hard dark skin. The hair on his head was shades richer and thin but not thinning, so that his tanned skull showed through. The blond strands had gone mostly white the way the baby photographs he kept in two well-organized albums showed his skin once was.

He was so familiar to her by then that she thought of all this only later, seeing him frozen against the wall in her memory.

Ember provided the quote to her grief group as if it were her own, and then asked if anyone else felt that way about marriage. Not surprisingly, one disturbingly curious attendee said he had, which added to her malicious enjoyment when she announced that it was Richard's feeling he had just related to.

Nothing like sharing the deeply intimate mental state of a serial killer.

Now as soon as she locks the door and drops her purse, she goes into Richard's office and picks up the diary where she found the phrase after his death. He was worried about all his unshared thoughts and feelings dying with him so had been planning for his own biography, which he often mentioned he hoped would be written by one of his former students.

Her grieving group isn't made up of the loved ones of serial killers, however, and the moderator let the implications of what Ember had said build for only a moment before leading the discussion to someone else.

Or perhaps it had just seemed that way. Perhaps she was being a little paranoid and underestimating her fellow grievers, who were instead silent out of respect.

And perhaps the stares during their break, as two or three eager gossips chatted to a new attendee, were really directed at a funny stain on the wall above her head.

This is her third group, and she has been with it for about four months. The first was for the loved ones of the victims of violent crimes. That was awkward. She was then misdirected to a meeting for the family members of suicides. Now she is part of General Bereavement.

She thinks there should be a subcategory called "Grieving with Betrayal." It wouldn't be limited to relatives of murderers (although there must be plenty that could use the support) but open to anyone who discovered something unbearable about her loved one when it was too late for questions or confrontation.

General Bereavement isn't set up to deal with complicated situations. Most of the attendees wish they could say "I love you" one more time, whereas Ember wants answers and a chance to shout recriminations.

"Maybe 'Grieving with Anger' would be more appropriate," she murmurs to herself.

In group there are rare outbursts of "some people deserve to die" directed toward her and usually followed by heavy tears. Jill, the moderator, takes such people aside and explains, "Just because Ember's husband was who he was doesn't mean she feels any less—and maybe it's even more painful for her since all her memories have become tarnished." Jill gave the same speech to the group at Ember's first meeting, after it became clear that people recognized her from the news.

The worst is when someone accuses her of knowing what Richard was up to all along—or even helping him. That happened a lot in the beginning, not so much in group but on television . . . in the world. She thinks the police were suspicious. After all, the alleged serial killer had been her husband.

Her now very dead husband.

The phone rings, and she is sure it's the ex-wife again. Vicky's message this morning sounded urgent but didn't provide any information beyond "I must speak with you as soon as possible" followed by four different telephone numbers and the layout of a complicated schedule. The mobile phone would be muted between such and such hours, but her secretary was available until three when Vicky would be at her boyfriend's restaurant . . . She was still talking as Ember left the house.

They haven't spoken at all since Richard's death. From newspaper stories Ember knows Vicky took thirteen-year-old Bridgett to France right afterward to avoid the media.

"Ember? Hello?"

"Yes."

"Hi, this is Vicky Andres. I left you a message earlier today?"

"Yes."

"Mrs. Dayle—Frances Dayle called me yesterday. Has she called you yet? She wants us all to go to Georgia before she sells the house?"

"I've never met her."

"She would like to meet you."

Richard told her before their wedding that she could never meet his mother, who didn't approve of him marrying a Japanese woman. Ember had never described herself that way; only her father was one-third Japanese, and a second generation American besides.

"Did you know she, uh, felt like this?" Ember had asked, confused as to why Richard thought to label her so inaccurately.

"She's always lived in the South," Richard told her. "You know Southerners, they hate everyone."

"Then why did you tell her I was Japanese?"

"It was your last name. She asked."

"That's pretty perceptive for a racist Southerner," Ember had said, and they hadn't discussed it again.

"She refused to meet me when Richard was alive. She didn't contact us once. Now she expects me to fly to the South on her whim and take more of the blame for her son's eccentricities?"

"Eccentricities? I don't—what do you have against the South? That's where I'm from."

"Richard's mom is racist. After hearing my last name she disapproved of the marriage."

"What? God, I didn't—Richard was lying. Richard told you that, right? I mean, there's no other way you could get such an idea." Vicky sighs an ex-wife sigh.

"Bridgett and I are in California. Let me call Mrs.—Frances and straighten this out. Can we meet somewhere this evening?"

Vicky has a house in Glendale that she owns with her boyfriend, the head chef at some restaurant Ember has never visited.

"I'm not sure . . . why don't you call me back in an hour?"

They agree, but Ember supposes Vicky will show up unannounced to find her lonesome and clearly unencumbered self.

The phone rings again, and expecting Vicky she answers with a flat, "What."

"Um—Is this Ember?"

"Yes it is."

"This is Frances Dayle."

Ember's surprise causes bland pleasantries to flow into her mouthpiece. Frances' voice is deep and warm with a light drawl. Can this be the bitter, shriveled cliché Ember has always imagined? She doesn't appear in any of Richard's photographs after he turned twelve, the same year his father died of a heart attack.

"I'm sorry to bother you. Have you spoken with Victy yet?"

Vicky's real name is Victor, shortened to Victy in her hometown only. She described the horror of it to Ember the first time they met as she was dropping Bridgett off for a weekend visit. She spoke in such a quick, nervous ramble that Ember almost liked her, despite her treatment of Richard.

"How could he have been killing women?"

The anguish in her voice shocks her more than the awareness that she muttered aloud—probably because talking to herself is becoming increasingly common.

There is a long silence, during which she holds the receiver very close to her head, and then: "God, Ember, I don't know."

Without any communication between them, Frances Dayle hired a publicist to deal with the media for Ember after the latter yelled at one reporter over the phone, "It's the fucking *mother* who's at fault when the son kills women. Contact her."

She still receives the stray interview request on her new line, but after so many months of "No thank you" to any question or comment, most of them have given up. By phone, that is. She's considered very photogenic, so if a new detail surfaces they are often waiting for her with cameras somewhere around town.

"I think you know." Ember is not sure if she expects Frances to admit she was an abusive parent or that he was kidnapped and tortured as a child, but the woman has to give her something.

"He was born that way." His mother takes a loud breath. "If possible, he was born that way."

And she hangs up the phone.

2

When Richard Earle Dayle was five his mother had a miscarriage. Believing it best to raise her son with scientific fact in the place of religious superstition, Frances explained why he wasn't going to have the baby sister his father had rashly promised.

"It is very difficult to be born," she told her blond brown boy as he slyly stuck his thumb in his mouth to see if she would notice and snatch it away. "The fetus must be strong and healthy. If it never grows up to become a baby outside mama, that means it was probably sick and wouldn't have lived anyway."

"Scott was born," he mumbled around his plump thumb. Scott lived across the street; his mother and Frances exchanged babysitting favors. He was younger than Richard and severely disabled, incapable of doing anything for himself. Scott's parents both worked full time to employ a nanny with nursing credentials, but they often needed extra assistance, which they received from other parents in the neighborhood.

Frances was ready for the Scott question: "Scott is a very strong little boy, but even so, he might not live very much longer. Our baby wasn't as strong as Scott, so it was natural for her to die before being born. She was so little she didn't even look like a person yet." She was annoyed with herself for using biased pronouns; they didn't know if it would have been a girl. They knew nothing, it was a simple miscarriage—or it would have been if her husband weren't so sentimental. She should have waited to tell even him she was pregnant until at least three months had passed; she hadn't understood how desperately he wanted another child.

Scott was napping at home when he died at sixteen months. Richard was there at the time but didn't seem adversely affected. Frances thought it was healthy for him to learn about death at an early age. It was the only useful purpose of pets, she had always maintained, but had too much dislike for domesticated animals to teach her child that way.

After his death Scott's nanny left for another job, but she showed up back in town three months later to speak with Frances.

"It's so nice to see you again, Angie," Frances said at the door, hoping the poor girl wasn't in need of employment.

"I have something to tell you," Angie said, without noticing Frances' gesture inviting her in. She continued without remembering to breathe, "Richard was sitting on a pillow on Scott's head when I went into the room. When Scott died. I told his parents but they said I must have been mistaken, the boys were just playing, Richard was a rambunctious kid and he loved Scott—anyway, Scott didn't have long to live, they said, and if anything, it was a game gone wrong. They told me Richard didn't know how to deal with babies and that you and Thad had always been such close friends to them. But—I thought you should know, to be careful, in case you have another child." Angie took a gasping breath. There were tears in her eyes, and she blinked powerfully to keep them there. "I have to go now."

"Thank you," Frances said politely, an icicle slowly forming from her chest down to her abdomen. I am cold, she thought, trying to focus on that. I am cold all over. I am cold, cold, cold.

"Who's there, Mama?" Richard asked. He had listened to the conversation at the door and wondered what would happen now. He knew that making Scott die had been very bad, and he might even be spanked like the one time he hid under the Buick and the police were called, and then his mom almost ran him over when she started the car to go search. But he had been tired of having Scott around all the time, especially since most sick people died before they were born like they were supposed to.

"That was Angie. Do you remember her?"

"Yes. Scott's nanny."

Frances shut the door and took Richard's hand, leading him into the dining room. She lifted her son onto a chair and then sat facing him.

"Do you remember when Scott died?"

"Yes."

"Will you tell me what happened?" Now the ice was a round lake in the bottom of her stomach. She wanted to throw up the large breakfast they had just eaten.

"I don't remember. Everyone was calling the ambulance and trying CPR."

"Did you like Scott, Richard?"

"I told you. He just laid there. He wasn't as much fun as Todd and Darren."

"Remember when you said that bad word in front of Scott, and he repeated it to his parents?" Scott didn't have a large vocabulary, but he was attracted to the sound of "shit," which Richard had overheard at school. Richard became inordinately upset when scolded by Scott's parents, and convincing him to apologize was an exhausting ordeal.

"Yes, Scott was a tattletale."

Frances had always been proud of her son's ability to articulate what he was feeling. She hadn't tutored him any differently than the other children in the neighborhood but took credit for his advancement. Now she wondered why it was so easy for her to believe with no evidence that he had killed someone.

"Little children," she thought, "don't have the ability to commit intentional murder."

"Did you hurt Scott?" Frances asked calmly. She was even able to produce a smile that she hoped wasn't too frightening.

It convinced Richard, who was eager to tell someone what he had done. "I put the pillow on his head but it didn't hurt him. I tried to have him sit up against the bars of his crib but he fell and then sort of started to cry, so I tried to make him quiet. Then he was quiet, but I sat on the pillow to see what would happen. Angie came in and threw me on the floor. My arm was all black and green."

"Why didn't you tell me," Frances asked flatly through the balloon around her head.

Richard had lost interest and was leaving the room. Frances suspected he hadn't blamed Angie for his bruised arm because if confronted, she would tell on him. His normal procedure was to show his mom, who kissed each injury and praised the big, tough guy he was.

Frances thought over every parenting choice she had made that was different than what the neighbors did and wondered: Was that what made him evil?

For the next ten years Richard received intense psychiatric counseling. At thirteen he was hospitalized for raping a girl and his treatment increased. Never again did he attempt rape, nor did he again kill anyone of the male gender. He was released permanently at fifteen, considered cured.

As a child he didn't invent any imaginary friends or pets, but when in counseling he had the thought that if he did have one, no other person would ever need to know. He could create and destroy it in his head, without breaking any laws or worrying about being caught. That was a plan he forgot for twenty-eight years, remembering a few days before he died of a heart attack while burying his last two victims.

3

"Failure, failure, failure, failure, failure." Horace mutters the word as he types it over and over into his computer's Internet search engine. This isn't the first time he has investigated failure—then he had enjoyed the excited suspicion that no data would be forthcoming. Certainly he wasn't so egotistically alienated that he didn't recognize failure as universal; he had merely hoped it wouldn't appear in a forum of mass-mediated information.

That was long ago.

During his first painful search, failure seemed to invoke a great deal of creativity in the rest of the world, as it was the name of a heavy metal band, a theatre production, two movies, and both a country-western and a blues song—all of which materialized on his screen. Far more distressing were the two published books invoking the same title: one work of fiction and one of self-help. It is a search he has tried repeatedly throughout the years, but today's experiment is to see if repetition will yield different results.

The room feels drafty, and Horace is disturbed by bursts of chilled air, which are typical, combined with the new sensation of a rather weak high-pitched voice singing his name from somewhere in the lower regions of the building. This must be an unpleasant fantasy as he isn't expecting any visitors, and even if one did show up, he or she would probably ring the ornate and rather obvious doorbell which is wired to trumpet the first few lines of "O Christmas Tree" into every room of the house.

Horace considers this doorbell the prime reason he is living in a gutted-out dump of a building rather than supporting himself in relative luxury with the profits of a thriving rental operation. His grandfather, Willy-B, bought the large, aged house because it reminded him of his childhood home. He planned to create an old-fashioned boardinghouse-like apartment complex. A manager would be hired to cook supper and take care of minor plumbing problems, and Willy-B was lucky to find two culinary arts students willing to do just that for a place to live and grocery bill reimbursement.

Willy-B refused to have the doorbell disconnected from the bedrooms, so whenever anyone rang it, the jarring frivolity was inescapable. The doorbell was masterfully constructed and would have been expensive to dismantle—many tenants tried unsuccessfully to destroy its connection to their rooms—but that wasn't Willy-B's reason for keeping it. He wanted a sense of family in his boardinghouse and thought the music would bring great cheer to everyone.

He didn't live there.

Willy-B was too rich and too old; he never saw the failure of his final project. He left it in his will to his youngest grandson, imagining it was quite equal to the corporations and land passed on to the others. Horace assumed Willy was in the throes of dementia, and he tried not to be too bitter about it.

Willy-B wasn't his blood-related grandfather. Like most of the grandchildren in this highly infertile family, Horace and his sister are adopted. They have the same mother, who they found almost accidentally after they were told of her existence at seventeen and twenty-two. Their birth mother had sex for money with their dad, then carried the results and handed them off for a much larger payment. No father was named on their birth certificates, but both times they were almost immediately adopted by their birth father and his wife: Bruce Jean and Betty Greene.

Horace's sister Lilac jokingly said the saddest thing about their parent's divorce (which took place soon after their mom found out these details) was that their names were so perfect together.

Betty and Bruce were only separated for two months. Everyone was relieved when they remarried. And although what Bruce did was undeniably foolish, it was clear he had done it for Betty; if he had enjoyed the two encounters with the prostitute, he thankfully kept those details to himself.

Willy-B was Betty's father and the sire of five other sterile offspring. Lilac insists that she, coincidentally, shares this trait, although their birth mother told Horace rather naughtily that Lilac's husband could be wearing a condom every time and the poor girl would never know.

Horace receives what is at the moment his only income from Lilac and her husband Trese. They pay all his bills and give him a very small allowance, just until he "writes that best seller."

"Horace Hooo-race." He continues to hear his name as the search engine freezes up while revealing a cure for failure of the sexual variety. He decides to go downstairs and accost whoever is interrupting his most productive time of day for writing. He's an artist, damn it.

The entryway is unlocked, and it seems that a person with the stubbornness to set his awkward name to melody (despite the inability to carry a tune) would have investigated further. For him to hear the feminine-sounding voice at all, she must have at least taken the initiative to push open the door and stick her head through.

Perhaps she is frightened by the ornately decorated bowling balls and pins that sit on a shelf lining the entire expanse of the room. These are Horace's mementos of what Betty felt was her one shameful moment of parental neglect.

At nine years old, Horace joined a youth bowling league midseason. Betty already had tickets to a Batten Cole concert (a band that made its start in her high school gymnasium) for the same night as the tournament. Everyone, including Horace, insisted she go to the concert, so she did.

Horace made three strikes in a row, then on his way to the bathroom was attacked by his own team's former strike champion, Mike. Horace's left arm was broken, but he also gained the timely, if not permanent, reputation as a tough guy since Mike appeared worse off with a black eye and swollen nose. Horace had never been involved in a fight before and he loved it, only retiring from the sport of physical confrontation a year later when he knocked two of another schoolmate's bottom teeth out and had to get a job to pay for the replacements.

Betty, however, felt that she should have been there to both prevent the altercation and see her son's halted winning streak. The bowling-related shelfware was to show Horace how proud she was of his three strikes, making the topic one of lasting embarrassment to him, as he still wishes he could complete something else successfully enough to overshadow that stupid game of decades ago.

"What in the world," Horace mutters aloud on viewing his bowling collection. Half of it—more than half—has disappeared.

"Ho-race." He backs into the hallway as a small sexless person creeps through the partially cracked door and picks up an especially heavy black ball engraved with gold Chinese characters.

"Yes?" he asks quietly.

The creature gasps and twirls around to face him, still firmly clutching the object against its chest.

"I'm Horace," he says pleasantly.

"Oh. Horace." It is a woman saying his name as if she has just tasted something surprisingly pleasant. She has large eyes that he can only describe as blue, although that isn't quite correct, and a stocking cap pulled low over hair and ears. Her cheekbones are sharp and her lips chapped. "You aren't at all how I imagined. The woman outside said you were named *Horace* and ran a motel."

"What woman outside?"

"Do I like to bowl? No, not really. I haven't been for years." There is a pause while she stares at the ball in her arms.

"Why don't you bring the other stuff back in. I mean, you are stealing from me, aren't you?"

Her eyes drift up to the ceiling then shoot down to pinpoint his face. "I'll be honest with you: Yes. I didn't think anyone was home."

"I should turn you in." He sighs. "But if you bring everything back..."

She puts the bowling ball down, and he follows her outside. The back of a white van is open and holds the rest of his collection.

"Horace Jean-Greene?" The tall woman sitting on the lawn next to the driveway looks familiar, and he's impressed that she said his name correctly. His sister is Lilac Greene-Jean (switching the order of the names had been a parental whim), and few people can make any sense of the difference.

She stands and puts a hand out to shake but doesn't introduce herself. "Your cleaning person told me that you would be back soon; I had no idea you were home. I have some guests coming to town and was interested in renting rooms for a week or so. Do you have any available?"

Horace assumes she is being polite, not sarcastic. When the town's surprisingly successful culinary arts school closed down, movement to the area almost stopped. No one knew how the single turgid little motel had remained open as long as it did, until five or six years ago when the building was condemned.

"I've knocked down all the walls on the top floor, but I guess they can use the rooms downstairs. There are—let's see, five decent ones."

Horace needs the money, but he isn't sure what to request. Also, the place hasn't been cleaned in far too long. He wipes down the kitchen and the upstairs bathrooms now and then, but that's about it.

"They will need three rooms. Are there bathrooms attached?"

"No, there's just one in that downstairs area."

"Victy won't be happy about that although she could always stay with her parents."

"Victy Andres?" Horace asks. At Frances' nod he laughs. "Wow, I haven't seen her since—" He suddenly remembers that this woman was Richard's mom.

"Yes, you were Brett's friend, weren't you?"

Horace is eight or nine years younger than Richard but knew him because Brett always wanted to work on the Dayle lawn instead of play. They were given endless goodies, and Richard treated them like soldiers with the fate of the world in their dirty hands.

"Yes, we were good friends. We lost touch during college though. Do you know—?"

"No, his parents moved away some time ago. I think Brett lives in Atlanta."

They are quiet for a moment.

The thief comes out for another bowling ball. She lifts it from the back without even glancing at them and carries it slowly into the house.

"She was taking those *to* her van when I arrived," Frances comments without much curiosity.

"Yes," Horace says. "She's new."

4

Frances didn't mention traveling to Georgia. Ember decides to call Jill from her grief group.

They have never met outside the counseling venue, which varies from the stage in a high school auditorium to a claustrophobic furry-carpeted room in a church, but they talk on the phone often. Jill called Ember unexpectedly one day, after other members of the group had been particularly harsh, and started describing the divorce she was going through—mainly focusing on how escaping the confines of marriage would improve her sex life.

Ember had never thought of the counselor becoming a friend, but lately she has determined that Jill doesn't concern herself with codes of conduct. Despite the hints for more information on Richard, it's easy to redirect the conversation back to Jill's life. So far Ember has been successful in learning much more than she has told: Jill has a PhD in psychology but runs the group sessions as court-induced community service. She killed an old man in a drunk driving accident. He was a violent alcoholic and a preacher of doom to all he encountered on the sidewalk. The night he died he was jaywalking in the dark wearing black, and Jill claimed she would most likely have hit him while completely sober. But she also insisted (with much slurring of words) that she stopped drinking forever that night for a couple of reasons: one, she didn't want to end up an alcoholic jaywalking in the middle of the night, and two, if she ever again hit someone behaving carelessly, she didn't want to be punished.

Jill's community service requirements are legion, but she isn't on probation and wasn't given any jail time. It helped that none of the dead man's family appeared to tell the judge just what they were missing without him in their lives. Jill said it was "proof that all humans aren't equal under the law." After that phrase had been uttered between them they were both quiet for a long time, and then Ember became fairly certain Jill was asleep, so she hung up the phone.

It is only since becoming her confidante that Ember has developed the fear that the group might not have the power to improve or change anything. Before they got to know each other, Ember saw Jill as thoroughly professional and inspiring.

Still, Ember trusts Jill to help with her current problem, and as soon as they are both on the phone describes Vicky's intent to visit, receiving a satisfyingly defensive "What does she want?" in response.

"Something about his mom—whom I've never even met. I don't know what she wants. I was just wondering if you're busy?"

Jill pauses. Then, "One moment, please," and there is silence until, "Do you mind if I don't come alone? I'm with a woman and man from our group. You remember Tony and Irene?"

Then she is gone and presumably on her way, bringing two strangers that Ember can't identify and probably wouldn't like if she could.

Grievers can be so unpleasant.

5

"That was Ember Oto," Jill says significantly after hanging up the phone. All her movements are precise and heavy here in her office at night, unlike her brisk manner during group.

Irene smells something sour as Jill spins slowly around in her chair. The scent is unpleasantly familiar. When facing them again, Jill lifts one bare foot up onto her desk.

In a state of hungry ecstasy Irene notices that Tony has missed the point of the phone call: they will be meeting that woman from group. The one he made an unsuccessful attempt at spying on, loitering outside the ornate iron fence in front of her condominium complex. The one who snubbed them coldly just this afternoon when Tony tried to say he understood exactly what she meant—or as it turned out, what her husband meant. They were fascinated by this Ember and talked of her often at home in their apartment without television—Tony had thrown it down the stairs when Irene wouldn't abandon her program. He had wanted her to go with him to stare at the transvestite prostitutes along Santa Monica Boulevard, but they spent the evening cleaning up the mess instead.

Irene already feels that Tony's new hormones are making him violent, now watching him watch Jill she sees they are giving him a sex drive as well. He is staring at Jill's huge, ugly, pink-chipped polish-adorned toes instead of winking and jabbing his faithful roommate with the excitement of going to visit the home of a serial killer.

6

Ember is absorbed in the search for suitable drinking containers when the intercom buzzes. She lets out a tiny squeal, what Richard called her third-dimension shriek.

On the day she accepted that her husband had really done what they said, she broke all the glasses. There were only about twenty, so she drank something from each to prolong the process. Then the plates and bowls were sacrificed during the unofficial posthumous media trial that went on for many months—the dishes became shards in one day.

The first round of destruction led to the awkward "glass in the ass" situation. How she ended up with slivers of it in her right butt cheek she will never be sure. When she recovered the rhyme seemed too good to ignore, although she doesn't have a social life and therefore can't turn the story into a humorous anecdote.

At the time she was of great interest to the media and certainly not up to visiting the emergency room for assistance. With many drunken tears she crouched awkwardly, looked over her shoulder at the full-length mirror, and jabbed herself with tweezers. Finally she stretched out on the floor, facedown, and slept for a few hours. That was the start of her obsession with being unconscious.

After awaking on her back, she found two of the pieces had popped out on their own—at least she never saw them again—and the other was retrievable with one minor, albeit bloody, gouging from her fine-tipped tweezers.

As for cups, she still has three plastic containers and a few thick, chipped ceramic mugs.

She pushes the answer button and shouts her "Hello?" since the system isn't working well. A few months ago the property manager sent around a memo suggesting they change to a phone service, but this was apparently voted down at the last meeting. Even though she no longer attends, it's nice to know she still thinks like the rest of the tenants.

"Ms. Oto, it's Sammy. You have some people here to see you. Ms. Jill Patternini—"

"Send them up please, Sammy."

Sammy has worked at the building for over thirteen years, starting about the time Richard moved in, two years before Ember arrived. He is also the only person here who has spoken to her supportively since Richard's death, and she believes he remains completely convinced of her husband's innocence.

"If only we all had the faith of an old, loyal doorman," she mutters, staring out the peephole.

"Ms. Oto," he told her once (she doesn't think he remembers her first name), "your Richard was not the man they talk about on the news. I would've married him off to my own daughter." Another time he grabbed her arm a bit too hard and whispered, "We'd of let him babysit our grandkids, you unnerstand?"

"That is the cutest little fat man," Jill says as Ember opens the door.

"You mean Sammy?"

"I saw a ring, so he probably lives in that oxymoron called 'happily married.'" She walks in, boldly curious.

Ember smiles weakly at Jill's two companions. They shake her hand without eye contact and scurry inside. The "Tony" she thought was a "Toni" until last week although she's surprised to see long, wispy chin hairs. A "he" trying to be a "she," or the other way around? The third person is a tiny lady inches below five-feet tall. She is slightly stooped about the shoulders and very slender in a sweater and nicely pressed slacks. Tony is sexlessly casual, but Jill has on a tight dress cut short on her heavy legs and low between her breasts.

Ember feels rescued and hopes Vicky will appear.

"Let's go to the sitting room," she murmurs. Then she tells her little lie: "I was cleaning and didn't have a chance to change. Sit down, and I'll run get dressed."

As she walks slowly to the bedroom she wonders what they think about her beautiful apartment. She won't be showing anyone Richard's office or their bedroom with the pretty bathroom attached, but the front door opens onto a large tiled area checkered with green and white glazed porcelain all the way to the balcony—this always impressed their friends.

When she reaches her room she moves even more reluctantly. She is planning to eavesdrop but has never stopped fearing what she might hear. Richard bugged the sitting and living room before she knew him. In a small safe-like box cut into the bedroom wall there is a receiver attached to headphones. During parties they would take turns sneaking away to move the dial on the receiver, as if it were a radio, to listen to each one of the six bugs. It was fun, but they both knew the purpose of the technology was Richard's paranoia. She never heard anything negative, but he wouldn't say why he stopped inviting two men from the faculty at his school.

She pulls her outfit off quickly and grabs a button-up blouse and black jeans. Placing the headphones on her ears, she dresses as she listens, her heart thumping loudly in her throat. She rolls the dial to 46.1, which is the frequency for the bug in the frame of the volcano painting above Jill's seat. Richard replaced all the microphones with new ones not long before he died, so she no longer has to switch back and forth to different areas of the room to attain the gist of any conversation.

"—and see all this cute peachy facial hair?" someone says.

She hears laughter and then the same voice, probably the older woman: "He used to be so placid and wilted and—"

Something else is muttered, and then there is more laughter.

"But now he cheerfully breaks things! He's taken up boxing and is getting all these muscles—yes, he's still long and sleek, but—"

"So you had to do how many months?"

"Almost eight."

"Instead of the usual three?" Jill asks.

"Three's really the minimum for the injections, but I was pretty upset about having to wait so long."

"What a difference a month of them has made."

"Are you going to continue grief counseling?" It's Jill again.

"I have to, so they'll know I want it for the right reasons."

"Well, we're glad to have you," Jill says warmly. "But now that you're officially diagnosed as a transsexual—"

Ember's pants are zipped up, and she catches her hair taking off the headphones.

They stop talking when she enters the room. "Would anyone like something to drink?"

"Do you have any beer?" Jill asks.

"No, but I have some very old wine." She is going through Richard's valuable little collection without appreciation.

"That'll do."

"There are a couple of bottles on the counter. Anyone else?"

"Just water," the other two say at the same time. They look at each other and snicker.

She gestures for them to follow her. "The dining room and kitchen," she announces.

"This is a huge place," Jill says. "It's bigger than my house. Do you live on the whole floor?"

"Yes, it's the same upstairs, but the five levels below are split."

"I love Pasadena," Jill continues. "If I didn't have a house all paid for I'd move here in a second."

Jill smiles when handed her mug. The two giggly conspirators are given purified tap water in plastic cups. Ember leans back against the counter and folds her arms under her breasts.

The phone rings, and she groans internally at the thought that Vicky might be calling before coming over.

"Hello," she says as the intercom buzzes. "One moment." She pushes the receiver against her chest and walks to the wall to yell to Sammy.

"A Vicky and Bridgett Andres—"

"Send them up. Thank you, Sammy."

"Hello," she repeats into the phone.

"I wonder if you have a comment on Cammy Hollingsworth's interview with *Bright and Focused* this morning?"

"No, thank you." She hangs up and moves to the door, remembering her surprised relief that the interview hadn't resulted in anyone waiting for her as she left work. One call on a Friday isn't bad though; a dozen newsworthy happenings over the weekend will cause her to be forgotten by Monday.

"Vicky. Hi, Bridgett!" Richard's daughter has turned fourteen since Ember last saw her and is taller than her mom. Ember feels suddenly sick as she prevents herself from blurting out that Bridgett looks just like her father. Her heart won't slow down until Bridgett gives her an awkward hug. They laugh that the teenager is up to her chin.

Ember was almost exactly the same height as Richard at five eleven. He didn't admit that he hated her being a tad taller than him, but it improved his posture, as when they first met he had the tendency to let his shoulders slump down. By his death he had unconsciously developed a high, squared-off way of carrying himself.

Spending all her time around her flower-fairy mother is causing Bridgett to adopt the same drooping habit.

They are both very blond with short wispy hair, but pale where Richard was so dark. Together the three were a remarkably attractive family. Ember wishes she could take a picture of Bridgett with Richard now.

Jill is coming toward them with a take-charge expression; Ember introduces her quickly without mentioning how they know each other. She has momentarily forgotten the name of the other woman from group.

Neither of the newcomers is thirsty, so it's back to the sitting room. Vicky is glaring with what Ember assumes to be a silent request to send the visitors away, which she blithely ignores.

It is silent, after all.

Ember hasn't recently been around so many women at once outside group, and she feels an unexpected craving for male companionship—not counting the hairy supermodel, Tony.

Jill finally introduces Tony and Irene, then focuses on Vicky. Bridgett gives Ember her sly look that means she is going into the bedroom to eavesdrop; the girl was dramatically sworn to secrecy before being told about the wired rooms a few years ago, after Ember insisted that it would help them bond. Richard didn't want to have any more children, so he let his second wife take control of raising Bridgett while she was with them, hoping that would satisfy any maternal impulses. Now Ember is relieved she didn't have a baby, especially a son.

She can't figure out what Vicky might be telling her daughter to explain the situation surrounding Richard's death; maybe the truth has been avoided altogether.

"You guys were visiting Jill?" Ember asks Tony and Irene, hoping they will carry the conversation from there.

Tony nods.

Ember can't remember anything about their reasons for being in the grief group. Their stories must not have made an impact.

Vicky's voice rises, and they all turn to her. "We're only in California for a few days, and I have some urgent family issues to discuss with Ember."

"What a wonderfully rude woman," Ember thinks. "As if his ex-wife has any claim on my time."

Jill looks at Ember, who shrugs slightly. "I didn't know you and Ember were related."

"She married my ex-husband," Vicky says. "Our mother-in-law is selling her family home in Georgia and would like us all to gather there one last time."

"Except I've never even been there before. I've never even met my mother-in-law." Ember is embarrassed by how childishly defiant she sounds. "I've never even spoken with her over the phone until today." Too late she catches that she repeated the word "even," something Richard would surely have noticed.

She feels lonely when no one else does.

"In eight years?"

"She didn't want Richard to marry a Japanese woman," Ember says somewhat proudly, ignoring Irene's ghoulish knowledge of her marriage.

"That's what *Richard* claimed." Vicky is triumphant. "I spoke to Frances after she called you, and she said she had *no idea* you were part Japanese."

"You're Japanese?" Tony asks.

"My dad is Japanese and Polynesian. My mom's European." Everyone inspects her for a moment. "My parents were so excited when I was born with black hair that they gave me the middle name Akiko, Japanese for 'Fall's child'—I was born in August.

"Now no one can tell I'm Asian. Although I'm closer than my siblings, who are blondish and freckled."

Bridgett is standing in the doorway, and she says a little defensively: "Grandma has a kimono and the book *Tales of a Geisha*. She said she wanted to bind her feet when she was a girl because they were so big. Until she learned that binding made them rot, I mean."

"That's an ancient *Chinese* custom," Vicky corrects quickly. "And a horrible one at that."

"And *Tales of a Geisha* was written by a white man," Irene adds.

"But it's a wonderful book," Ember assures the embarrassed girl.

"Bridgett, sweetie, will you grab that bottle of wine off the counter for me?" Jill asks.

Bridgett looks to her mom, who is glaring at Jill, and then leaves the room.

"I wish I had a daughter like that," Jill says.

"Ember." Vicky is impatient. "Frances would like you to visit."

"I see no reason for it."

"OK. Fine. We'd better be going. Bridgett!"

There is the sound of glass breaking.

"I'll see what happened," Ember says as Vicky rises.

Bridgett is staring at the huge wine bottle in pieces on the floor. Another scar for the kitchen tile. Ember is surprised the girl isn't crying.

"Can I spend the night here?" Bridgett asks. "I have to talk to you about something."

"Did you break that bottle on purpose?"

"I heard Mom saying we had to leave, and I didn't know what to do. Then it was broken. It wasn't a plan or anything."

"Clean it up."

Ember feels frightened. If Richard's daughter spends the night, she will lock her bedroom door.

7

When Richard held the publication party for the third volume in his biographical series on Dwight Eisenhower, he invited the entire history department from Pasadena City College, where he had taught for thirteen years.

The president of the college wrote the introduction to Richard's book, despite the author secretly desiring a flashier name. He liked to pacify people now and then—particularly before inciting their irritation, as he was planning to do the upcoming term. Not by dying in the graveyard of his own creation, which wasn't to happen for six more years, but with an unusual curriculum that he hoped would cause dissension.

There were only three colleagues that Richard regularly included in his social life, but at this party he overheard a conversation that ended his friendship with two of them.

He had maneuvered a couple of Ember's coworkers next to the gas fireplace prior to excusing himself, but before adjusting the receiver he was distracted by a discussion between his colleagues on 53.2, the microphone for the table in the living room. Howard also belonged to the history department, while Devon taught general business and Minorities in Business.

Richard was already a little wary of these men. They had yet to mention that they were on the college-sponsored committee promoting women's self-defense classes. Usually all three made such decisions together, and he wondered why this time they didn't think he would be interested. He had given them several openings to the subject, and although they hadn't reacted suspiciously, it still bothered him.

"Tanaka's back and asking about Ember."

"You tell Richard?"

"I mentioned it. I'll tell Ember another time."

"Is he still considering a move?"

"Nope. No date tonight?"

"Her kid's sick."

Richard took the headphones off and punched the wall just hard enough to bruise his knuckles.

He and Tanaka had been roommates at Stanford, and it was while sitting in on his friend's beginning Japanese class that he met Ember. She had graduated from the University of Colorado three years earlier and wanted to see if she had an affinity for the language of her Japanese ancestors.

Richard concluded that if his coworkers were on Tanaka's side after he had been married to Ember for two years, on top of not mentioning the self-defense class, then they were dangerous enemies indeed. While he didn't invite them into his home again, he stayed casually involved in their lives for monitoring purposes.

He never found out that neither Howard nor Devon had personally taken the initiative to join the self-defense committee. Howard's teaching assistant had put his name on the list of supporters, and Devon's wife, the head of the nursing program, had added him when the sheet went around the departments.

While Ember noted but didn't mind the absence of Howard (sensitively pompous) or Devon (who had an embarrassingly loud wife), Richard missed the two men for the rest of his life.

8

Ember expects instructions from Vicky before Bridgett is allowed to spend the night, but all her guests leave together. Then she worries over the tearful, hopeless discussion she's sure to have with Bridgett, something with pain and healing and nostalgia . . . but the girl is asleep on the couch by the time everyone else has gone.

Ember knows the child will wake up uncomfortable in her tennis shoes and training bra. Her skinny little legs are still crossed as if she were sitting just fine until she fell over.

Bridgett has three cavities already, so Ember places a wrapped toothbrush on the counter of the bathroom next to a tube of toothpaste.

Since Bridgett normally sleeps in the family room when she stays over, Ember places a pile of blankets and pillows next to one of the couches in there. She leaves the hall light on and at the last minute remembers the nightgown and underwear Bridgett keeps in the laundry room. She puts those on top of the pillows.

Ember no longer feels the ridiculous need to lock her bedroom door, and she is grateful she didn't when she wakes up at three in the morning with Bridgett in her nightgown snoring evenly next to her. Richard was a snorer too, and after using the toilet the familiar sound lulls her back to sleep.

9

"We need this time alone, beautiful."

Vicky has her face pressed against Carl's chest, which smells of flour. After his shower he put on the same shirt he wore to make bread that morning, knowing she likes the scent although they tease each other often over whether flour really has one.

"For a cook you sure don't use that most important of senses very often," she says irritably when he tries to raise the affectionate argument today.

Vicky changes the subject back to her worry over leaving Bridgett. "I don't know anything about Ember."

"It can't be worse than letting her stay with a murderer."

Vicky knows Carl, with his dark sense of humor, can't resist. She wants to be mad or shocked but finds herself giggling, and soon it's hysteria with tears soaking her cheeks.

"I'm sorry, I'm sorry," Carl repeats softly, rocking her slightly in his arms. She doesn't think he is though; his chest vibrates now and then, and she is certain he's laughing. It's not the first time since Richard's death that she has let herself experience senseless emotional release, so she doubts its long-term benefits even as she feels a deep shudder of relief. Heavy exhaustion pulls her eyelids. Yet when Carl lowers her gently onto the bed her brain starts to gnaw once again at painfully worn scenarios, and she knows she won't be able to sleep.

Carl's sigh brushes her face, and she slowly opens her eyes just enough to see him through her lashes.

"You're thinking again, aren't you? Maybe—I guess you were right, you need those pills." He pauses. "Unless you're just being stubborn."

She tries to smile but can't. For a week Carl's nagging has kept her off the sleeping pills, but after over seven months with the medication her body can't seem to remember its natural rhythm.

"Let's have sex."

"Do you really want to?" Hope is mixed with doubt.

She isn't sure her tormented body feels interest. Maybe she just brought it up out of past habit. "A natural sleep drug."

"Hmm, I think the doctor would approve of that."

He pulls the blanket off her and pushes up her long shirt. The air is unpleasantly chilly and she decides she could sleep now, she truly could, if he would just leave her alone.

His tongue is too persistent and it makes her angry that it finds the right places to force her to react. He holds down her kicking legs. "You just needed your pussy licked, didn't you?" He teases softly and kisses her stomach. He climbs up, his mouth wet and smelling too strongly of her, and then he's easing inside although she hadn't noticed him remove his clothes.

Suddenly everything is all right. She doesn't even hear herself make the sounds of no-child-present sex, but Carl does and it is over too fast. She's asleep before he is.

10

Frances supposes her promise to rent rooms in the old boardinghouse that Willy B's grandson owns was hasty. There aren't any hotels of salubrious reputation nearby though, and she cannot have them stay in this house with her.

She has been forgetting things lately. Not details like where she put the keys or in which drawer the silverware is—those particulars are still blissfully automatic. But more important things, like being human and sad and guilty. She has forgotten her loss of interest in sex and feels desires that haven't bothered her for years. Sometimes she thinks she is becoming very light and will float away even on the heavy, wet breezes of this humid spring.

It is some type of dementia, she is sure. A typical old-age insanity that will be categorized and assigned medication when she is eventually forced to see a doctor. But for now she doesn't want to know, as for long moments she is happier than she has ever been.

The house might be harder or easier to sell because of the bodies that were found in the backyard a few months ago. After Richard's death the ground was torn up. Although by then she could have told them just where to look, she wanted to appear ignorant rather than complicit.

One of Richard's counselors when he was fourteen suggested he take up a hobby like gardening to teach him the value of life. It was also something he could have power over and might find relaxing. Frances told him he could take care of as much or as little of the yard as he wished. He designed the entire two acres, front and back, then hired younger neighborhood boys to maintain the bushes and grass while he focused on a twelve-by-twelve-foot vegetable garden at the furthest right-hand corner in the back.

Frances made all the children that stepped onto the property report to her first, and then she would call their homes after they left to make sure they had returned. She was endlessly baking sweets to ensure that the kids didn't try to avoid her. Despite her fame as a cook (which she considered exaggerated), she didn't delight in the activity.

The parents never felt better than when their children were at the Dayle's house. They were watched, exercised, and fed; Richard, a natural teacher, filled them with interesting nature facts that they repeated at night to Mom and Dad.

Scott's parents had produced a healthy son two years after their first one died, and they loved to have him spend time with Richard as well. They would tell Brett about what a special friend Richard had been to Scott, and Brett grew up thinking of him as a replacement older brother.

"What stupidity," Frances would mutter after she sent Brett with his cookies into the yard. She was terrified that Richard would one day react to how much the two brothers looked alike, as if Scott's features and coloring had been to blame.

That Richard had never killed animals was always reassuring to the psychologists, but Frances wasn't sure they were right in assuming it meant anything. He had such a disinterest in nonhuman creatures; they didn't exist for him. If an animal bothered him enough, who knew what he might do.

Finally she went to Dr. Filler at the Grangage Pediatric Psychiatric Hospital for children under eighteen. He had been Richard's first therapist, and although he had moved into an administrative position and stopped seeing patients regularly, Frances remembered how fully he had embraced them.

"Perhaps it would be best if you spoke with Scott's parents first to make sure they confirm the babysitter's suspicions. She might have been confused or even a troublemaker. And your memory of Richard's reaction could have become corrupted."

To a shocked Frances this meant that if Richard had always been an innocent child, all the counseling had led to him becoming a rapist, perhaps as revenge against her, a woman, for forcing the treatment on him.

"I think you've forgotten that your initial evaluation of Richard showed that he knew the difference between right and wrong but chose wrong in the situation with Scott," Frances said a little desperately. "What about the rape?"

"All I'm saying is that Richard seems fine now, and it would be a pity to bring up an old situation based on hearsay."

After working with Richard, Dr. Filler had written an award-winning paper based on precisely what he later called hearsay: the possibility of infantile criminality disconnected from survival needs. Thinking the doctor had since lost his mind, Frances murmured politely and left. She was fairly certain he didn't remember Richard at all, despite his current position being the result of the environmental versus genetic study he developed from the paper.

"Anne said what to you?" Scott's mom, Alicia, asked in horror.

Frances had waited until Alicia's husband Adam was gone because his jolly hugging and tendency for tears discomforted her.

"Angie."

"What?"

"Her name was Angie."

"Oh, sorry. All these 'A' names, I can hardly keep track. Listen, maybe Richard *was* playing a little rough. He treated Scott like a normal kid, which we all appreciated. We didn't even see what happened, and Angie was always overprotective. It wasn't worth mentioning and upsetting everyone. If it was anything, it was an accident."

"I just feel responsible. I don't want Brett near my house because if anything happened—to—to him—" Frances pretended to cry, thinking it the only way to get the gravity of what she was saying across to this woman.

"Oh, that little brat, Angie." Alicia started to cry herself. "I can't believe this has been on your mind . . . Richard is the most considerate child in the world. We all talk about how grateful we are to have your family in our town. When your Thad died no one could understand why it had to happen to such good people. There's nothing a little five-year-old boy could've done to our Scott that the good Lord didn't intend."

Frances was sure that if a good Lord existed there were many happenings he didn't intend, but she wasn't interested in a theological discussion. Earlier she had considered ways to ask for Angie's last name, but that was impossible now.

Scott's dad showed up at her door that night with rolls that his wife had baked. They were lumpy in some places and flat in others, but Frances absently started to eat the one handed to her.

"I won't come in. Alicia told me what was worrying you. I feel terrible about that nanny girl. I mean, she did a really good job with Scott, but Richard—I think she felt bad that he had enough energy for both kids when Scott couldn't share any. That's how much she loved our boy, cared about him nearly as much as us."

"What was her name again?"

"Angie."

"Oh yeah. Angie Hollander—"

"No, no. That's Ed's ex-wife. Angie—um, it was a color. Gray! Yes, Gray. She always said she wished her last name had some color to it. That was a joke of hers. We get Christmas cards from her. Alicia says she flirted with me and usually throws them out pretty quick, but it's the memory of our Scott that really rankles."

Adam was the friendliest person Frances knew, and married to the most jealous, but he always linked his wife's reactions to more noble emotions.

"She lives in Atlanta now."

Frances couldn't believe she had forgotten to ask. "Did she change her last name?"

"No, the guy is a Brown. Can you believe that? She decided to stay Gray. Their names are how they met too. It was at jury duty. During the selection process the judge made some joke about the colors. Now they have two kids." He made this sound like the greatest triumph.

Frances hoped Richard wouldn't arrive home with this subject still under discussion. She brought up the difficulty of making good bread products, and Adam said he was grateful that someone appreciated his wife's cooking. Just in the discussion stage of leaving, he observed Frances starting her fourth roll and hurried off to tell Alicia that her recent enrollment in the church culinary class was already a success.

Later Frances called information for Angie's number, then hung up after dialing it three times on different days until the husband answered on the fourth. She explained that she was an old friend of Angie's and was going to be in town.

"Oh, great. Well, why don't you talk to her, she's right here."

Did the woman never leave the house? Frances had hoped to save all conversation until it could take place in person.

"Hello?"

"Angie, this is Frances Dayle from Mariah. How are you?"

"I'm great. Wow, I haven't talked to you in so long—"

"I was telling Adam tonight that I was going to Atlanta. He mentioned you were there and asked if I would drop something by."

"Oh, that's so sweet of you. When are you coming?"

Frances told her it would be the following afternoon and when a baby started to cry, asked quickly for directions and a confirmation of the street address.

"I'm really looking forward to seeing you again," Angie said warmly. Then she giggled and delightedly commanded her husband to stop tickling.

After ending the call Frances sat staring at the wall with her sluggish thoughts until Richard came in asking about food.

Her elderly parents stayed with him the next day since she was planning to be gone overnight. They only lived a block away but seemed to prefer her house so much that she often wondered what they did there.

She felt very lonely as she drove off.

After Thad's first heart attack he told Richard to always listen to his mother. "She's never steered me wrong." Frances wanted to call an ambulance since both her husband's father and grandfather had died around the same age from heart problems, but Thad insisted he could drive there faster and cheaper. He suffered a final, fatal heart attack while getting into the car. Richard did CPR until the ambulance arrived, but Thad was pronounced dead in their front yard.

"Mom never steers us wrong, Mom never steers us wrong," Richard had chanted quietly now and then after that day. She pretended to ignore him but always felt defensive; she had suggested the ambulance in the first place. If that was even what he meant.

If he meant anything at all.

The house was easy to find, but Frances pulled up grinding her teeth with anxiety. She stretched out her mouth and felt her jaw crack. Although she usually woke up with her teeth jammed together, it didn't happen much during the day.

Angie was surprisingly fat, but maybe she had always been overweight; Frances couldn't remember. Her face was broad and flat, her eyes bulging out of dark, baggy sockets.

"You look the same, exactly the same," Angie said as she reached out the arm not holding the homely baby. "This is Justin and—Scott!" Another boy ran around the corner and charged his mother's legs. She grabbed him and swayed.

"I can't believe you're all grown up with two healthy boys."

"Yes, they're such good kids. Today they get a treat—a movie—so Mom and her friend can have some private time."

Frances followed Angie into the living room where the two boys turned into statues as their animated video began. Angie rambled on about its popularity a bit, but Frances was too nervous to focus on the alarming décor, much less a movie description.

"It's an unusual set-up, I know," Angie said as she followed Frances' gaze to the walls awhirl with bright orange and yellow flowers. "We read that kids' brains needed to be—uh, what's the word?"

"Stimulated?" Frances supplied, although she wanted to say, "Confused?" as she turned away from the bright colors and mismatched designs. Every object seemed to have come from a different nightmare.

"Yes, stimulated. I guess I've always liked colors too. My husband got his way with the dining room and our bedroom. They're neutral. The kids will be fine in here." Angie led the way into the refreshingly dull dining room.

She was chattering in a relaxed way, glad to have company, not visibly anxious. Frances remembered the gift she had brought to enforce her visit's pretense.

"Oh, I have the rocking horse Adam and Alicia sent in the car. Remind me to get it before I go." It had been quite expensive but besides that concern, Frances was worried that Angie might be the thank-you letter writing type.

"They are so wonderful. And thank *you* for bringing it. Would you like something to drink?"

"Water would be great."

"No coffee?"

"No thanks, but you have some. I stopped at a diner on my way in. I have a doctor's appointment tomorrow morning—just routine but I wanted a big clinic, not gossipy Dr. George." It was a bad lie since there was a brand new impersonal clinic in the town next door to Mariah, but Frances felt too forlorn to make up a joyful get-together with friends.

"Are you sure it's nothing serious?" Angie asked worriedly.

"Oh yes. I just prefer a female doctor."

"Me too."

Frances suspected she might have her own heart attack if she waited any longer, so quickly she began to say some of her carefully prepared words. As she spoke she knew this must have been how Angie felt, rattling out her message on the doorstep. "Since I have this chance to talk with you again, I wanted to bring up Richard. He—I—do you remember?"

Angie had sloshed some of Frances' water onto the front of her shirt, and she put the glass down. "I wondered if you would mention that. I never told anyone about it after you, except my husband. He didn't believe it was true; he doesn't think a child can do something like that on purpose."

Frances looked straight at her, into her brown eyes, around them at the forehead with only one timid line, the small freckled nose, the wide cheeks. "Tell me what you think happened."

"I know that Richard was rough with Scott and didn't seem to like him. I know that he was sitting on a pillow on Scott's face when I came back into the room after throwing the diaper away. I had heard Scott cry out a few moments before, and I yelled to Richard that I would be right back. Richard said something, but I didn't hear him; I think he was talking to Scott. I grabbed Richard by one arm and threw him as hard as I could across the room. I'm surprised nothing broke. Before I could talk to Richard the ambulance and parents had arrived. He moved at some point to the bed next to the crib and sat watching."

"Why did you leave Scott alone?"

"Alicia and Alex said I could for short times if he was in the crib. I could even take a shower when he napped. *Richard* wasn't in the crib when I left the room. I still feel guilty when I think about it. I don't know what Richard intended. He probably *was* just playing. I mean, of course he was."

Frances found herself telling Angie what had happened when she confronted Richard. It was frightening and wonderful to tell someone other than the therapists who never showed surprise or compassion.

"I put him in therapy right away. They thought he had done it on purpose, or at least the idea interested them. He raped a girl two years ago, but now they say he's totally better."

"He raped—?"

"Well, he was stopped in time. He was hospitalized but never arrested. The family didn't press charges. I think they blamed her because she was older and not a virgin."

"Oh."

"What else can I do?"

Angie didn't answer. She was leaning slumped against the counter. They couldn't look at each other.

"So if I overreacted and you took me too seriously . . ."

"It wouldn't be your fault."

"Oh my God."

"I just wanted to know. To make sure."

But there was nothing else either of them could say.

11

The room smells sweet from the cookies and muffins someone has brought. Tony watches for Ember, but even though it has only been a week since he was in her apartment, her eyes pass over him. Beyond her relationship to the crime novels and movies he devours, beyond even their shared grief, Tony believes he has a spiritual connection to her.

Irene is speaking today but doesn't seem nervous; she is joking with some of the others as they pile treats on their napkins. Almost everything she says causes smiles and giggling. She is the only person he knows that can induce laughter or tears whenever she feels like it. When she was healthy and happy her company must have been exhaustively entertaining. Tony wonders why she fussed until they had to flip a coin to see who would go first.

Up until today both he and Irene got by with giving only their names, but although Jill doesn't force anyone to share, she suggested last week that it was time.

"Irene?" Jill says when everyone is seated in the circle of twenty-two folding chairs.

"Hello, friends," she says in her forceful manner. Tony knows she is an experienced and captivating storyteller, and even now she makes visual contact around the room, her eyes clear and blue behind delicate-framed glasses. "I have really appreciated hearing your stories over the past few months. My husband died three years ago. He had cancer of the spinal chord, and it spread all over. We had a wonderful life together, but I feel that I'm done living now; I don't want to get over his death. I'm ready to move on. I've become ill a number of times but keep recovering. Nearly a year ago my eldest granddaughter somehow convinced me to come down and visit her in California—that was my first mistake." Everyone laughs.

"Once she got me here, I ended up in an apartment with a roommate. Not as nice as what I could afford in a retirement village in another state, but the company's younger and it's definitely warmer." More laughter. "I still don't know how it happened. I have four sons who pushed and prodded me to live with them, but this one, she's the only one as stubborn as I am—but with more energy." Tony sees relief in their faces that the smallest things can be funny.

Irene changes her tone and Tony, by her side, can see that her eyes are wet and she sniffles the tiniest bit during her next words.

"I dream all the time that Lou and I are doing something mundane together like cleaning the house. We clean the house and clean the house and it never gets clean, but it's fun for some reason."

The room is quiet.

Tony thinks of combing his oldest daughter's hair as she whined that he was hurting her, no matter how delicately he brushed, and how he would now gladly do that nonstop for eternity.

"More often I dream that Lou and I are driving somewhere—we used to travel all over the country together after we retired, for thirty years we spent winters in our motor home—and he tells me to get out of the car and we'll meet at such and such a place at such and such a time. But after I get out I get lost and can't find him. I wake up feeling so scared and then so sad because he's gone. I'm so alone, so very very lonely."

After a long silence Jill says softly, "Thank you."

Slowly everyone surrounds Irene, bending down to hug her in her chair. Tony feels guilty that he has sometimes thought she should be able to recover more quickly than others since she was given a lifetime with her husband.

"Let's have some more dessert," Irene says, standing up.

Tony watched her around the food earlier, and she never put anything in her mouth. She hardly eats at all, and he knows that as warm and wonderful as everyone thinks she is, she still wants to die.

12

Ember is going to Georgia, but only so she can spend time with Bridgett.

She's worried about Richard's mother. Is there going to be a shrine to her dead son or a wax sculpture to worship? Even more dreadful, will they look at picture albums and review genealogy charts? Does the woman blame Ember and plan to obtain some type of revenge?

This is not a good time for meeting new people. Often she feels overwhelmed imagining what each one is concealing and how the terrifying revelation might occur. Other times she is merely bored by the certainty that her companions have no worthwhile secrets at all.

Jill keeps trying to persuade her to become buddies with Tony and Irene. After hearing Irene speak in group Ember can't help feeling attracted to her, but the fascination with Richard is a barrier.

"They love mysteries and crime television," Jill says in their defense. "They're both lonely and bored and sad."

It's enough to have Jill, Jill, Jill filling her head with questions and comments and nosiness. It might help if the counselor weren't the only person she spoke to on any personal level. Last night Jill asked what Ember first thought when she heard her husband was dead. Ember excused herself and ended the phone call.

She can't even remember the comparative simplicity of having her most loved one dead from a heart attack. The recollection of identifying the too-perfect body and her tearful shrieking seems false. The police asked if they could talk to her just seconds after. Then there was a drink of water and assistance into the bathroom to wash her face and blow her nose.

At least two men spoke with her later, telling her how Richard was found. It took a while, but finally she began to focus on what they were saying. More clearly she remembers numbers on a wall poster. She started to memorize them even though she's not normally a number person. When she drove home the numbers were still in her head and they were the color of grape juice—the kind that looks dark, inky blue, almost black—but stains your lips and teeth purple.

With all the gore and mystery, she's sure no one wants to hear about the silly numbers that kept her calm until she could return to the privacy of her home.

13

"Tony is going to open our meeting today," Jill tells the group.

"Hello," he says nervously. He hated public speaking as a woman, but now as an imperfect man it makes him almost physically ill. He is convinced that Irene talked him down from vomiting earlier, which he hasn't done since his second pregnancy years ago. "Um, OK. I used to live as a woman named Sarah married to a man named Paul. We had two daughters. Shellie Ealia was four and Allison Catherine was six. We were on vacation in New Zealand two years ago visiting Paul's sister and her family. It was the middle of winter." He thinks he might already be repeating himself, and he is certainly already trying not to cry. He doesn't feel like a "he" any longer, but that mother of a million years ago.

Irene reaches over and holds his hand.

"I guess I'll start at the beginning.

"We were staying at a resort duplex cottage in Whakapapa Village. Paul's sister owns the place with her husband and teenage daughter, Melissa. They invited us up during the middle of the skiing season, saying our two little girls were old enough to learn.

"That afternoon I asked my oldest daughter to help me make the bed while her Dad bathed her sister.

"I walked into the bedroom and Allison followed, sounding puzzled, 'Why are we making the bed when it's almost bedtime?'

"I explained that it was because when we all took a nap together earlier we messed it up. And I didn't want Melissa to know what slobs we were. Allison started repeating the word slob and laughing.

"Then she asked me something, but although I've tried a lot I haven't been able to remember what it was. I didn't answer because she always had so many questions.

"We were all tanned and healthy, with all the bright sunlight on the snow, even during that unusually cold winter. I was sleeping more heavily every night than I had since having my first baby.

"Our niece Melissa had become chief babysitter and stayed with her young cousins even when the ski instructor was giving them lessons, so Paul and I enjoyed a week of freedom. That's what we called it.

"That day Shell hurt her arm in a little fall, so I was glad it was time to go home. She was upset and had wet her pants, so embarrassed too. I hoped her third bath, which her dad was giving her, would make her feel better.

"I felt bad for going out that night, but it was our last night there and we never used babysitters at home. We hadn't been able to find anyone we trusted like Melissa.

"I remember asking Allison while we made the bed if she knew that Mommy couldn't stand to have her feet under the covers.

"'You stick them out at the bottom?' she said in surprise. I said yes, and after thinking for a moment she said, 'I like to have my feet covered up always.'

"I wasn't listening closely, you know, and jokingly accused her of being a little copycat. She put her hands on her hips and breathed out loudly to show she was frustrated. 'No, it's not the same thing.'

"'OK. Then why do you like that?'

"'Because it's scary with my feet out. I'm afraid someone will grab them.'

"That made sense; Allison was very afraid of the dark. I told her, 'I put my feet out because I feel claustrophobic when I'm all covered up.'

"She nodded seriously. I wondered if she knew what 'claustrophobic' meant, but she wasn't often shy about requesting clarification if she didn't understand something. To show how much I trusted her, I brought up the slight worry I'd been keeping to myself and gave her some of the responsibility. 'Shell might walk in her sleep tonight. Will you keep an eye on her? If she gets up, don't let her out of your sight, OK?'

"'I won't.'

"'I'll tell Melissa too. And don't worry when you go to sleep, Melissa will stay up.'

"'Can I stay up late?' Allison asked slyly.

"'Maybe.'

"'Did Shell walk last night?' Allison threw pillows onto the bed randomly.

"'No.' I sat on the bed and chewed my fingernails. 'But she keeps going out the front door by herself—when she's awake.' At home we had a large porch where the girls kept most of their toys. 'And she got hurt today and sometimes when she's upset . . . She's been sleeping with Dad and I since we've been here but tonight we'll be gone late.'

"Shell often walked and even opened doors in her sleep. Once we found her between the open doors of our refrigerator. Her doctor said she would grow out of it.

"I found myself having second or third thoughts about the party. None of the bedroom doors had locks, not that I felt comfortable bolting the kids inside. Shell would probably just bump into a wall and wake up, but then she'd be terrified without us there.

"Denny and Carrie were so excited about it though, and their friends were hosting the party in my and Paul's honor. Even Melissa wanted us to go so she could be a big sister for one more night.

"'Don't worry,' Allison said confidently. 'I'll keep an eye on her.'

"I got up and scooped Allison into my arms in a twirling hug. 'You are the most wonderful big sister. Shell is so lucky to have you.'

"'You are the most wonderful mom,' Allison told me. 'Am I a good skier?'

"'Yes, you're very good. When it's winter again in Colorado we'll go skiing.'

"'Yay!' Allison scrambled out of my arms and hurried away to tell Shell. I noticed how her long yellow tangled curls seemed too heavy for her compact little body. She refused to let us cut them.

"I mentioned the possibility of sleepwalking to Melissa as we hurried out the door. She was a chubby, vibrant girl. Denny and Carrie were already waiting in the car. We were close to being late for our own party.

"Melissa was excited and said she'd stay in the living room and would be awake until we got home.

"'I love you,' Paul called to the kids as they shut the door. He kissed me quickly before we ran down the steps to the car."

Tony feels terrible and wonders if the others are bored. He can't force himself to look at anyone. "I wasn't present for this part of the story but Melissa—she wrote it out a few months later. She wasn't doing well for a while." Tony sighs and wishes the room were dark or that he was at a campfire telling a different horror story. Irene is still holding his hand, but Tony resents her for not getting over a husband who died when really old. "As soon as we were gone Shell started to cry, and Melissa lost her half-formed thought to lock the deadbolt as she picked her up. Allison was trying to get her attention by explaining what had made Shell sad that day.

"Melissa changed the subject. She was good with kids. Then she wrote about playing with them a bit, lifting Shell up a few inches, putting her down with a great exhalation of breath, saying how heavy she was. Shell laughed with tears dripping down her face and hopefully forgot about missing her mother. Allison wanted attention too and said she was heavier.

"Melissa put her hands on her hips and shook her head wildly. 'Yes, you are. I wouldn't even try to lift you. I'd break my arms.'

"Both girls dissolved into giggles and began to throw themselves against her legs, begging her to try and lift them. Instead she announced that they would have ice cream sundaes for a special treat. After the excitement of decorating their ice cream with sprinkles, whipped cream, chocolate syrup (and nuts for Allison), the girls barely had enough energy to eat them.

"Melissa half-carried, half-led them into the bathroom to wash their sticky faces and brush their teeth. She had been looking forward to telling them a story and was disappointed when they both closed their eyes immediately after being tucked in next to each other.

"Melissa loved having them with her and wished their last night hadn't ended so early. She was a motherly type of girl. She went to the couch in the living room where she could see and be seen if one of the girls had a problem or had to get up.

"Allison woke up some time later alone in the bed. It was dark and at first she must have thought Shell was sleeping with us in the other room. Then she would have remembered the whole party thing. The house might have felt cold and she might have wondered enviously if Melissa and Shell were having fun without her. The clock probably said 11:30 or so.

"Allison would have remembered Shell's sleepwalking and her heart probably began to pound loudly. Maybe she wanted to scream for help but knew her mom was counting on her to be responsible. So she jumps out of bed, the hardwood floor cold against her bare feet.

"'Shell?' she calls softly. She moves into the living room where Melissa is sound asleep on the couch, with a book opened across her chest."

Tony is telling the story from Allison's point of view, how he has imagined it, even though it might not be factual. "The front door is open and there's a stool next to it. Allison wonders what to do. She doesn't notice she has begun to shiver from the icy wind.

Shell couldn't be out there; the cold would have woken her up. Right? Allison shakes Melissa's shoulder and calls her name, but the older girl doesn't budge.

"Allison looks out the door and then steps onto the porch. She looks up the street and down the street and shudders when she sees a small, white figure illuminated by the only street lamp around. Shell is down the road in her nightgown. Or else it's a ghost, the white blur.

"'Melissa!' Allison yells, but Melissa continues to snore evenly, a half-smile on her face.

"Allison shuts the door behind her and feels physical pain at the cold on the porch, more terrified by the dark than the below-freezing temperatures. She hears her mom saying Shell is so lucky to have her for a sister and hops down the steps—Perhaps she didn't even try to wake Melissa, perhaps she wanted to be the hero, or maybe she considered it her responsibility.

"She cries a little at the pain of her bare feet in the snow. She promised Mom she would look after Shell and this is what happened—maybe it was guilt that propelled her outside on her own instead of getting help. She runs down the street calling, 'Shell!' The figure doesn't turn, but Allison remembers that Shell never responds when she's sleepwalking, she's like a zombie.

"Shell has turned a corner and Allison runs faster, finally catching up as Shell disappears behind some trees off the road where the pavement ended. There were no more houses around, but the night wasn't that dark with low, white clouds and fresh snow.

"Allison grabs Shell but the littler girl continues to walk as if unaffected by the temperature. The trees are more numerous now, and Allison can't see that well. She is certain there are bad guys behind some of them.

"Allison begins to shake Shell roughly and sob. 'Wake up, Shell, it's cold. Wake up, we have to go home!'

"Shell slowly focuses on her and then begins to wail. 'Mommy!'

"'It's OK, we're outside, let's go back in the house.'

"'Cold! I'm cold. I can't walk.'

"Allison can't see Shell's feet, which are purple, or her own, which have started to turn blue. She knows it will be fine as soon as they are home.

"'I'm cold too. Let's go home.' Allison is calmer now and she takes Shell's hand. It feels like ice and she can hardly hold onto it, her own fingers are so stiff. She can't feel her feet anymore, but at least they don't hurt.

"'I'm tired,' Shell says. She begins to cry more quietly and Allison yells out, hoping even a scary stranger might hear since she's lost her sense of direction.

"Shell falls down and grabs her feet moaning. Allison sits by her and puts her arms around her. She is so tired too. Surely someone will find them soon. You are supposed to stay where you are when you are lost anyway, and your parents will find you. Allison puts Shell's feet under her nightgown and against her stomach even though they are even colder than it is. They hold onto each other, their bottoms little slabs of ice without much feeling left. The snow is sort of like a bed. Shell stops crying and her eyes begin to close, freezing shut with the water around her lids. Mommy and Daddy are coming to get them, and they will have hot chocolate. Allison knows they will be proud of her for staying with Shell and keeping her safe. She is so tired now; she will just close her eyes for a minute. She uses all her strength to tighten her hold on Shell."

Tony pauses and a number of people take deep gulps of air.

"Tony," Jill says softly.

"That's how we found them a few hours later. A professional search party came when we called in the emergency. They were trained to look for lost skiers. I was with them when they turned—"

Tony feels a sharp pain in his chest, and he starts to breathe in shallow gasps. "They used this huge lamp."

People are crying, but after a few moments of silence they begin to gather their things and stand up. Tony desperately wants to put his jacket over his head. He knows they wish to say something to him, but he can't take any words now. From the corner of his eye he sees Irene gently nodding them away. He loves her and holds more tightly to her hand.

He is certain the meeting has gone far over its normal hour.

"Hey," Ember says softly. She was sitting near the door and has come all the way across the room. Now that she knows we have suffered she respects us, Tony tells Irene telepathically, but he doesn't think it transmits.

"Hello, how are you?" Irene responds to Ember too loudly after a delay.

"Both you guys talking . . . thank you. I could relate—I'm sorry that when you told me the same thing I was brusque with you. It was wrong and unkind."

"Brusque?" Tony doesn't mean to ask; he doesn't care.

"I'm going to Georgia for a week but maybe when—maybe we can plan to get together. I won't be here next meeting, but the one after. If you guys want."

Tony is distracted by a frightened feeling that this is a lost chance, that she'll never return.

14

When the rumors started after Richard's death, his hometown of Mariah insisted on his innocence. The residents bashed the infamous LAPD regularly, although it wasn't just the Los Angeles Police Department involved but many agencies across the country, coordinated by the FBI.

Frances expected the story about Scott to come out, but it never did. None of the professionals they had dealt with over the years appeared interested in involvement, despite the opportunities to profit from hungry news and tabloid shows. Years before, Adam and Alicia had moved away to live closer to their son Brett and his family in Atlanta.

The young police officer that informed her of Richard's death was unfamiliar, so she didn't invite him inside. She sat on a wicker porch chair without the slightest idea of what he might have to say.

"Ma'am, I have some really bad news. Your son Richard had a heart attack late last night. He died early this morning."

Her hands were on her knees and her back was very stiff in defiance of the boy's dreadful posture. It took a moment for her to comprehend what his words meant, and she felt her shoulders sag as the shock took her from grief to powerful relief in only seconds.

"Was it quick?" she asked in confusion.

"Um, I'm not sure, Mrs. Dayle. He was gardening last night and wasn't discovered until after he died this morning. Probably unconscious most of the time. We'll know more soon."

"Thank you," she said. "Thank you for coming to tell me. I think I'll go inside now."

"Uh, one moment, please." He spoke into his radio, and they both watched as a police van drove up to the house. "Some other officers are going to have to talk to you, if you feel OK?"

Men in regular clothes got out and loitered around the van, not looking toward the house but down the street. A black SUV with tinted windows seemed to be what they were waiting for. It pulled into the driveway and the young man next to her almost whispered, "The FBI."

"What?"

"That's the FBI, ma'am. They're taking over this case."

Frances thought of Victy and Bridgett and felt desires start up again. "Was anyone else hurt?"

"What do you mean?" he asked, abruptly urgent and suspicious.

"What's your name?"

"Officer Bill Greers."

"Bill, my son had an ex-wife and a daughter. Are they all right? Is that why the FBI is here?"

"I don't know. No one told me about them." An approaching man with thick gray hair distracted him.

"Hello, Mrs. Dayle. Special Agent David Chandrasekar, FBI. Thank you, Officer Greers," the new man said as he held out his badge. Bill stood up and jogged off to join the others at the bottom of the driveway. "I'm very sorry for your loss, ma'am. We have a search warrant for your house and yard." He handed her some papers, which she gripped tightly.

"Was my son murdered?" She hoped so, oh how she hoped so. Since he was dead anyway, and it didn't appear to have been a legally acceptable death . . . *So foul and fair a day.* "What happened?" *All happy families are alike, but unhappy ones, unhappy ones . . .* "This was my son."

"The medical examiner in Los Angeles just called and con—"

"His father died of a heart attack at the same age!" She hoped she didn't sound frenzied. But why hadn't he asked her if she was feeling all right, if she needed to sit down?

Then she realized she was sitting.

"Are my daughter-in-law and granddaughter safe?"

"I wasn't aware that your son and his wife had a child."

"No, that's his second wife. His first wife—oh no, maybe no one's told them."

"I'll have that taken care of in just a minute, Mrs. Dayle. Now I need to tell you something that will probably hit the news in California sooner than we wish. Your son was in the vicinity of two dead bodies when he was found. Early reports indicate he was in the process of burying two women whose identities have yet to be confirmed."

He paused and looked at her, and she willed herself to pass out so she could have a moment's peace and quiet. But she had never fainted before and even though she was holding her breath she doubted it would happen. She was too physically strong and mentally practical.

She stood up and immediately collapsed into a bright dizziness. The agent caught her, and she regained stability in seconds but was rewarded with permission to rest in her bed as her home was searched.

Afterward she was impressed by how tidy everything was, except for the destroyed backyard. Most of the damage out there was in the one corner that couldn't be seen from the house, as it had a wall of bushes carefully surrounding it.

Part Two

15

Vicky and Carl sit on the right side of the plane next to a window, with Ember and Bridgett on the left. There are four rows in-between. Ember was delighted with this arrangement at first. She thought it showed that Vicky was confident in her stepmotherly ability to deal with the child's intense fear of flying. Richard had the same problem, and they aren't sure if Bridgett's is genetic or learned. Unfortunately, her father also taught her a unique way—or so he surely thought—of dealing with this, which was to spend the whole flight rhyming every sentence. He said it required enough concentration that if done properly, it would conquer all stress.

Every sentence.

"Do you mind if I just close my eyes and rest for a bit?" Ember asks as calmly as possible. They have been in the air for twenty minutes of the predicted nonstop four-and-a-half-hour flight.

"Why quit? I mean, you really must admit, this isn't the safest place to sit."

"And if I'm sleeping that won't bother me."

"Ah, I see. But I need someone to listen with glee."

Usually such a self-reliant girl, Ember thinks sadly.

"Dad would always play, that's the only way. Otherwise I'll get sick, I feel it coming on quick."

"Lick, stick, pick, dick—oops."

"Better than poops. But you're not doing it right, it doesn't take concentration to fight."

"I'm not *fighting*." You little bitch.

"It's in the writing."

Jill has an opinion on Ember's recent introduction to swearing and irrational irritation.

"I'm not biting."

"Smooth denial, you're not on trial."

The counselor's theory is that she has misplaced anger.

"Can you stick to this the whole while?"

"You can start your own rhyme, Ember, that's part of the fun. I do it all the time, Ember, and feel like I've won."

"Don't you ever stumble, take a verbal tumble?"

Bridgett likes that one, and it causes her to pause for a moment to ponder an adequate response.

"Whenever I get lazy, I just say something crazy."

According to Jill, if Ember dealt with her emotions concerning Richard properly, she wouldn't be so quick to hate the grouchy old man blocking the aisle in the grocery store, the chubby baby screaming in the library, or the other innocent yet mildly annoying folks encountered daily. Jill doesn't think grief and regret are enough in Ember's case: there's a deep anger involved, and it's directed at everyone who is still alive, comparably innocent though they might be.

"Ember! We don't have till September."

"It feels like this flight is taking forever—" She can't think of anything. Her head is pounding in both the front and the back, and her neck aches. "If I don't take a nap I will die—and *you* will always wonder why."

"I'm going to have to go sit by Mom; you're turning into a bomb."

Ember leans her chair back a little and closes her eyes. She doesn't care if she never sees the girl again.

Sometime later, out of a doze, she finds Bridgett is sound asleep next to her, mouth hanging wide open.

In a singsong she whispers, "Now I love her, I do, as long as she sleeps the flight through."

16

"Perhaps there's a tentative relationship beginning," Irene tells Tony cautiously, "but we'll ruin it if we do something pushy."

"Ember's just . . . you know, a kindred spirit."

"Ah-ha! There—that *flaunts* your femininity."

"Oh, so now you're my gender coach?"

Although he enjoys goading her, he thinks she is finally beginning to accept the sex change she once pronounced "intriguingly gruesome in an unwholesome way."

Irene grumbles something.

"It's a great help," he adds hastily, "you telling me when I'm not passing. You're a great source with four—you know, masculine sons."

"I also had a husband for fifty-seven years. I suppose that has led to a certain expertise."

Tony is sitting on his bed, slouched against the wall. Their room has two twin-size mattresses on low wooden frames about three feet apart. A small desk is across from Irene's, and she uses its matching wooden chair to prop her swollen feet up.

"I promised myself weeks ago I would stop mourning your lost beauty aloud, but I can't help thinking that despite the therapy, you're making a tragic and irreversible mistake. I will stay quiet this time, but oh, how I hoped for daughters when I was young—at least one—and now even you, my belated chance, are turning into a son."

Tony has heard her say this a number of times but pauses to give it the appropriate respect before asking, "Do you think she'll really call us when she gets back?"

"I have no energy, but if it will distract you, let's go down to the Santa Monica Promenade. We can watch the men being manly."

People watching is Irene's favorite activity, but Tony thanks her.

She is trying to divert him from his mad trek-to-Georgia fantasy, and it's good to keep her occupied as well, with distractions from her health problems. Now that he has stopped nagging her to eat and started ignoring her starvation tactics, she forgets them at times and will often snack absentmindedly.

Their motto: An old woman at the end of her life and a young man just being born. Irene likes to talk about her death. Tony guesses it earned her a lot of outraged attention from her family.

As did the news that she was living in Los Angeles with a man. She seems to find their reaction the most fun she has experienced in years.

When they first met she told Tony that after her husband Lou died she floundered, selling the suddenly too-big house they had built together when their sons were young and moving nearby to a mobile home village for the elderly. When Irene was no longer able to eat, thanks to her undiagnosed lymphoma, she moved in with her youngest son. A year later, still not knowing what was wrong, her oldest son brought her to Arizona to stay with his family and try a new set of doctors. Her symptoms were finally identified and with treatment she became well enough to function on her own again.

From there she visited her granddaughter in California and was convinced to become Tony's roommate. They have lived together for nine months now, and Tony's greatest fear is that she will pass away and he will be alone. As a man, no one close to him has died.

Tony is getting dressed for the Promenade in baggy jeans and a large t-shirt, with a tight sports bra strapping his almost nonexistent breasts down.

"Do you think you would still want to be a man if you had a more developed chest?"

"Irene! I have the true runway model's body. Tiny breasts are part of the allure."

"For male supermodels? You aren't ready yet. You haven't told me one thing to convince me you're ready."

"Well thank all the gods I don't have to convince you."

This is their habitual argument, and it often becomes nasty.

"I'm ignoring your blasphemy this once. I understand you no longer want to be a mother," Irene continues loudly, "because your babies died in such a horrible way, and you blame yourself. And you no longer want to be a wife because Paul reminds you of the children and you probably blame him too. But can't you stay a woman with none of the typical responsibilities?"

"If you would just listen to me and believe me! I knew I was male ever since I was a *little* child—"

"Lots of girls want to be boys because boys seem to have more freedom and are allowed to do more things. Nowadays it doesn't have to be like that at all. You should see what my granddaughters are up to. Every one of them is going to college, three are already in graduate school, and one is a second-year medical student."

"But it wasn't just that I wanted to be a boy, I *was* one. I knew I was one. My gender was mistaken."

"God doesn't make mistakes."

"What about children born with horrible diseases?"

"There's a purpose—"

"Don't we cure the children whenever we possibly can?"

"Gender and disease are not anything close to the same."

"I am curing my disease, the disease of being a man in a woman's body."

"Can't you just have relations with women and enjoy your femininity and—"

"Irene!"

"Liora's been giving me books."

"My God."

"The Lord's name," Irene scolds as Tony says, "Withdrawn."

"You know the statistics, Tony. Women that change to men are never as successful as men that change to women. And it's irreversible—I know you don't care about that now, but you will have to have your breasts invasively removed. It's just—it's masochism to have a mastectomy without cancer. And you won't even get a full, functioning male organ. You won't be able to use it for anything."

Tony sighs. "I share things and then you use them against me."

"I found that out myself."

"Well you can't understand—this way I'm just half of nothing ... I want to remove the female from my appearance. It's fake, it's wrong, it's not anything you will ever be able to understand unless you've gone through it yourself."

"I just think you should try living as a homosexual before you go through all the surgeries or increase your hormones. They're changing your personality."

"You don't need to worry about this so much. It's going to be forever before they let me take the next step. But I do appreciate you not making rude comments about the so-called gay lifestyle any longer."

"You just seem too young—"

"Who doesn't, darling Irene?"

"I suppose I meant immature."

"Let's go, please."

17

Horace wakes up naked and sweating, his three-page manuscript making a tent with his hard-on. He was dreaming of the little thief from the day before—no, it was this morning—being nursed by Lilac like a baby. His sister's nipples were long and blue as if the oxygen had been sucked out of them.

His editing pen is still in his hand but point down in a big blue ink stain on the ivory couch cushion. "Fuck."

Yesterday he woke from his nap freezing even under the prickly afghan crocheted by his grandmother, but today must be ninety degrees. April is usually pleasant. He wonders if he is feverish—he never dreams about his sister except to rescue her from some horrific death.

He stayed awake just long enough to reread and edit the short story he has been working on for about four months, and then add two new sentences to bring it to almost three full pages—although with his large handwriting probably only until it's typed. He can at least say his first few paragraphs are almost perfect. They have been edited and fine-tuned up to a hundred times.

It happens quite consistently that whenever he finally forces himself to write (which reminds him why writing is his most enjoyable activity), he then begins to think that even if he finishes the story, even if it's great, he will never get it published. There is such a small market for short stories. It's difficult to know where to send any particular one and if the magazine doesn't want it, the response takes months and offers no explanation or advice.

So he falls asleep whenever he writes, and immediately after resting will grow weary again if further creative attempts are made.

Two lines are good for one day. He feels like a writer. Sometimes he goes weeks without a fresh sentence.

And now he has other things to do. Guests are arriving this evening: he needs to finish cleaning the rooms that Frances Dayle figured would be taken care of by his housekeeper.

He throws on the t-shirt and boxers peeled off earlier in a half-asleep overheated state and makes a shopping list of supplies. Everything has to be perfect in case Victy is still the sexy little sybarite she was before she married the serial killer. And if she longs for some comforting over the loss of her ex-husband—well, to a writer everything is material.

18

Ember is tempted to call Jill from the plane for reassurance that journalists will not be waiting as they disembark.

"What a cute little news story the mother meeting with the two ex-wives would be," an intoxicated Jill had said at the end of their most recent phone conversation.

"That would be cute," Ember replied, "since he was only divorced once."

Surely it wasn't a threat, although moments before Ember had turned down the suggestion that the grief group travel across the country to rendezvous with her in Georgia. The counselor's extreme Richard-based curiosity was possible to ignore before, but since meeting Vicky and Bridgett, Jill has stopped trying to disguise her desire to be involved. It upsets Ember, but she doubts Richard's kin are much of a story to anyone else any longer. None of them are talking, so the victims' families are the only useful sources for follow-ups. Her main concern is his mother blaming her if the press has been notified.

"I'm so excited to see Grandma," Bridgett says on waking up sticky-eyed but refreshed. "I hope she hasn't hurt her jaw."

"That was weak," Ember replies. "You're not at your peak."

"Well, I just woke up. I need to drink a cup."

"Put on your seatbelt, so the landing won't be felt."

"Lame, you're not into the game. Anyway, it's still on although I really need to pee—"

"It's too late the captain said—you see?"

"Aw gee."

They pack up their carry-on items in silence, and Bridgett doesn't flinch while discarding the thankfully clean airsickness bag she has clung to the entire trip.

Ember peers into her travel mirror and tries to enliven her face by desire alone before finally putting on a little makeup.

They don't speak again, not even after the plane lands and they are given permission to join the rule breakers already in the aisles. Vicky is yelling cheerfully at them from across the crowd, but Ember doesn't glance in her direction. They will all meet up soon enough.

"Jet lag, what a hag," she mutters.

"You can stop now," Bridgett says grouchily.

"I don't know if I can."

"Dad would have scoffed at our rhymes; they were lame. His always used to make sense."

"Your dad was very clever."

"I want to ask you something about him. I haven't seen Grandma since he died, and I don't know what everyone thinks."

"What has your mom said?" Ember stops trying to edge into the aisle and turns to face her.

"She first just told me that Dad died. I wanted to see you, and wondered about the funeral, but she wouldn't talk and had someone come take away our television. I got a dumb private tutor and wasn't even allowed to go back to school. Then we went to France and visited my other grandparents. She hasn't told me *anything*. I heard though, like about him—I don't know. Whenever I ask she says something stupid. And then if I yell and scream she starts to cry but *still* doesn't say anything."

"Hi, guys, how was the flight for you?"

Vicky and Carl nudge past a now-empty row of seats.

"Are you both planning to stay here all day?" Carl jokes.

Bridgett gives him a dirty look and sighs. "We were having a *private* conversation. And Ember is much better at rhyming than you, Mom. I see why Dad married her."

She stomps off ahead of them.

"Am I going to get this every time she talks to you?" Vicky asks, copying her daughter's angry walk and leaving Carl and Ember behind.

"Do you need help with anything?" Carl asks.

"No, thanks."

Bridgett is hugging her grandmother when Ember enters the baggage claim area. She slows until Carl is next to her.

"Vicky is probably with the luggage. She fears having her bags lost or stolen."

Frances hears Carl and waves. "You've guessed it!"

"This is Ember Oto, Frances. Ember, Frances Dayle."

They both mumble something, but Ember's lips feel frozen. She is surprised that Richard's mother is so tall although the dark gray hair in its high regal bun adds a few inches.

"Do you like this shirt I gave Grandma?" Bridgett asks her.

That explains the bright pink top with red velvet dancing fish.

"Yes, it's a lovely color."

Now when Frances and Ember look at each other there is some recognition present.

Ember follows Bridgett into the bathroom with the vain hope of finishing their interrupted exchange. More talkative around her grandmother, the teenager's chatter takes care of conversation through the final steps of the airport ordeal and drive. Frances tells them she rented a car they can share during their visit but borrowed a neighbor's larger van in order to fit all their luggage.

"I'm taking you to my home now, but you'll be sleeping at the only thing close to a hotel in the area. It was formerly a boarding house and is in a bit of disrepair, but I'm in the process of selling..."

"Where are you going to live?" Bridgett asks. "Move in with us!"

Ember doesn't have the strength to sustain open eyes, so she leans her head back against the seat cushion and closes them. She worries that her mouth will gape open and her neck will droop to Vicky's shoulder, and then she's asleep.

19

Frances didn't have the flight arrival time when she was making plans with Horace, so he won't expect them until later in the evening. She feels strangely reluctant to take her guests home, where they probably anticipate spending most of their visit. Vicky, Bridgett, and even Carl came by often before Richard died. Since then only her real estate agent and members of law enforcement have been inside.

It is unfortunate Richard stigmatized her as disliking Asians to excuse his lack of family connection.

He refused to see his mother for the last nine years of his life.

The long driveway looks guilty as she pulls into it. At least the lawn is decent again. A couple of months ago she hired a landscaping firm from Atlanta. The whole process was expensive, but she couldn't sell it the way it was, nor could she hire neighborhood children as she had been doing up until The Death.

That's what she calls it in her head, and it has become life before and life after The Death. A long time ago The Death was Scott's, now it is Richard's.

It was never her husband's.

She frequently has the feeling that someone or something can read her mind; despite the implausibility, she often silently explains her thoughts to the elusive listener, as if a recording is being made and these comments will lessen the embarrassment when she is eventually forced to hear it.

It started, or she became mindful of it, years ago, right before she turned sixty. A handsome man in Atlanta said she was stunning and asked her to dinner. Later that day at a grocery store a young security guard seemed to be staring at her with interest. After a moment she realized his attention was on a child leaning precariously over the side of a shopping cart. She laughed at herself, and to show how self-aware she was, gave any listeners into her thoughts a short, silent speech on the amusing nature of vanity.

Now she is once again explaining herself to this invisible audience while Bridgett chatters loudly, saying she can't believe they are already home. Frances nods and makes automatic responses. She uses her rearview mirror to check on the quiet adults and they are all sound asleep, Victy and Carl snuggled together, Ember with her head bouncing lightly against the window. It is probably the humidity, sometimes that knocks visitors out. Or maybe the novelty of being driven although Victy did mention years ago that Ember had a driver. That was a present from Richard. His second wife preferred to walk when she could but often needed transportation. Victy was still a bit jealous back then, thinking Richard treated the new wife better than he had ever treated her, but Frances thought it was a great gift, and it made her happy that her son was so protective of someone other than himself.

"Shall we let them sleep?" she asks Bridgett in a whisper, but they are already stirring as she turns the ignition off. "We can leave the suitcases here for now."

"I need to get a change of clothes out; I've got to shower immediately," Vicky says in a creaky voice.

Ember looks miserable.

"I have three bathrooms if you want to take one too, Ember," Frances says as she opens the van's sliding door. "There's plenty of hot water. Or cool water, if you prefer."

"Thank you."

"Bridgett, will you show Ember to the master bathroom?"

Frances holds Vicky's arm lightly as Ember and Bridgett disappear into the house. "Victy, we haven't had a chance to discuss what you decided to tell Bridgett."

"I've kept it all from her," Vicky admits. "And please don't call me Victy."

"I'm sorry, I always forget."

"Not that you still slip up and say Mrs. Dayle half the time, Vicky." Carl is cheerful and sticky with sweat, as usual.

"I know, she knows. I need a shower."

"We need to deal with the little princess, Vicky." Carl gives her a kiss on the head before she moves away. "She suspects something is going on."

"Well I suppose so since her father is dead." Vicky has unloaded two of her suitcases and is lugging them up the front steps. "I have to rinse my contacts off, my eyes are killing me," she yells back to them before going inside.

"I guess it's up to you and Ember," Carl tells Frances. "I think Vicky was hoping Ember would explain when Bridgett spent the night a few weeks ago. Perhaps we should talk to a child psychiatrist or grief counselor."

"No, that's not a good idea. At least not until we see how she reacts to the truth—or a sterilized version of the truth. How can she not have heard anything?"

"No television, no computer, no friends, no school. Then they were in France for a while, where they also avoided all media."

"Poor little girl." With such a suspicious delay, the details will make that much more of an impact. "We'll do it right now, all of us together. After the showers."

"Uh, I don't know about that."

"Her dad has been dead for almost nine months, and investigators are still uncovering new information. It's an ongoing case, and sooner or later Bridgett is going to hear about it."

"Wouldn't it be better to wait—what if she doesn't need to know?"

"The living room, twenty minutes." Frances motions Carl to walk with her into the house. She notices that he has lost a little weight and isn't as doughy. She has always thought he was pleasant looking in a large, soft way, with dark reddish hair and freckles all over his body—now with some of the padding gone he's close to handsome.

When Vicky first brought Carl home to meet her family, she also came by to introduce him to her ex-mother-in-law. Frances could only think of how different he was from Richard. In a slightly resentful way she was convinced that the relationship would be a transient one, as Vicky had always been interested in lean, intense men.

Ten years have passed since then, and Frances now wants nothing more than for them to be married. "Has the wedding been put off for an indefinite time?" she asks tentatively.

"Ah, I guess so. We haven't really talked about it."

"Grandma, are you still outside? I can't find the fish."

"I gave the whole tank away." Frances hesitates on the doorstep after Carl has gone in.

"You're letting all the cold air out," Bridgett says in exactly her mother's voice.

Before shutting the door Frances glances over her quiet street and wonders who is watching.

20

"Why did you get divorced?" Ember asked Richard before she married him. He had already told one story to a number of women he dated, but he was in love with Ember and decided she deserved a new one, created especially for her.

He sighed. He gazed around the restaurant where they were having dinner. He frowned. "Vicky has matured since it all happened . . . I would hate for you to hold this against her—we were too young when we married, neither of us knew what we wanted. We grew up together, you know." Ember hadn't. Richard rarely spoke of his childhood. "She was the most sought-after girl in our school. Adorable and bouncy, popular in all the trite ways. I suppose I liked her because everyone did. After Bridgett was born she changed. She became much less self-assured. There was a slight weight gain, but she looked great. She was a personal trainer before the pregnancy and during it she led a water aerobics class for other pregnant women. But after—I don't know, maybe it was postpartum depression. She began to have affairs with some of her male clients, then even her co-workers. She blamed me for the pregnancy in a way; she thought having a child had been my decision more than hers. Of course you wouldn't know it now." He focused on Ember and smiled. "She's the best mother in the world now.

"I decided to 'hire' her as my trainer so we could spend more time together, so I was often at the health club where she worked. I found out later that everyone else knew. She made a fool of herself and had an embarrassing reputation. I eventually saw some clues and confronted her. I should have gotten her help and tried to make things work, but I let my ego get in the way. I was humiliated, and she didn't seem to have any emotions left. Perhaps she was also using drugs during that time period."

"That's terrible. I'm surprised you didn't win custody."

"Oh, she straightened up before it got to that," he said abruptly. He was uneasy, dissatisfied with his story. Ember's eyes were moist, but he wanted her to weep. Vicky caused him all types of trouble. The truth wouldn't have made sense to Ember; she was too inexperienced. His tale should have been more successful in relating how he had felt. The basis for judging any story was by how well it transmitted emotion, not fact.

Ember was like bulletproof glass with the demeanor and carriage of a ballerina. Yet underneath there were so many layers; he doubted she would ever bore him. He had always enjoyed living with women, from his confused mother to tense Vicky. Even his daughter was charming when she stayed over.

"Let's not talk about this anymore."

"Of course." Ember began discussing their upcoming trip to Colorado to visit her family. Richard usually tried to listen carefully whenever she spoke since unlike Vicky she didn't chatter endlessly, but at that moment he was too overcome with fondness to concentrate.

The first time he saw her in Tanaka's classroom he felt an attraction. To some degree it was the knowledge that she was dating his friend, but sitting next to her he was still compelled to ask his favorite pick-up question.

"Why were you born?" He whispered into her ear.

Without curiosity she gave a succinct account of the reproduction process. He had heard that response before, but it was a sound one. Then he asked what the point of her life was. "It changes from moment to moment," she replied, knowing he was flirting with her. "Right now it's to impress you with my wit, in a second it will be to answer whatever question Tanaka-sensei asks without sounding stupid."

He lowered his voice until it was a caress, "I think you are a very good girl."

Goose bumps appeared down the arm he could see, and although she later denied him the pleasure of classifying her as a "girl" or even "good," at that moment he felt her arousal.

Tanaka observed their whispering and began to make fun of Richard in Japanese, which was clear to everyone, despite only one or two of the students knowing enough to recognize exactly what he was saying.

Once someone was branded a good girl she was good for life, no matter what her later actions revealed. Even cheating on Richard with a number of men didn't remove Vicky from that status. He knew she hadn't done so in *her* reality, but in Ember's? Well, that was another story. His story.

21

Frances pulls her granddaughter close on the living room couch and puts an arm around her warmth. She listens as adolescent chatter fills the room with words that jar her brain and make her head pound.

Ember enters with her hair smooth and shiny. She is wearing the same clothes, but they appear fresh. Her bone structure is delicate and she moves with grace, her chin tilted upward. Frances wonders if this is a defensive pose.

Vicky looks wet and harassed. She doesn't make eye contact with anyone. Ember sits next to Bridgett at her insistence, and Vicky rests halfway on Carl's lap in the large easy chair that Frances wishes were just a tad closer. It would be nice if they were all within touching distance.

"Bridgett, we need to tell you some things about your father."

The girl stares up at her grandmother's face with tears already forming in her wide-opened eyes.

"The reason you haven't been told before," Vicky says, "is because no one is sure of anything. Nothing has been proven."

"But we do have a few facts," Frances continues firmly. "Your father died of a heart attack while working in his garden in the middle of the night. There were two other dead people with him." She is silent for a moment. "The police think he killed them."

"I know," Bridgett says quietly.

"Where did you—who the—who told you that?" Vicky is trying to scramble off the chair, but Carl holds her back.

"She was bound to hear something." Frances glances at Ember, who is staring at the floor. "Is there anything else you want to ask about?"

"Dad didn't do it, did he?"

"Of course not," Vicky says in an intense whisper.

"The police think so. They suspect he killed other people as well."

Bridgett leans over and clutches her stomach. "I think I'm still airsick." Her voice is strained and she puts a hand over her mouth. She slides off the couch and begins to run out of the room hunched over, throwing up in the doorway.

At first it appears that she is hemorrhaging, then Ember reminds them of the entire bag of red licorice she ate before the flight.

"I'm sorry." Bridgett starts to cry.

"Oh, good job. Great idea, what a great idea," Vicky fumes as she follows her daughter.

"I'll clean it up," Carl says, and then pauses as if hoping someone will volunteer to help.

"The cleaning supplies are above the washer." Frances motions Ember to follow her through a doorway on the opposite side of the room. "When my husband Thad had part of this wall knocked out to create a second door I thought he was an imbecile. He always insisted on two exits per room. When we went to restaurants he would check the kitchen for an alley escape route before we were seated. It could be embarrassing."

Ember sits at the kitchen table and says "please" to Frances' offer of water. "So is this the first time one was useful?"

"Mm hm—Oh! No, it isn't. Once in Atlanta there was this holdup at a store and he ran out the back way, which he had noticed just moments before. According to him it was the greatest triumph. He retold that story all the time."

"Why was he so worried in the first place?"

"He was a volunteer firefighter. He took the job very seriously."

"Ah. Well, that's nice."

"Yes, of course. It's quite a noble position." Frances chuckles and tries to cover it up with a cough, but Ember is laughing too.

"What's going on?" Vicky asks suspiciously as she walks into the room. She looks prepared to scold and annoyed to find the two strangers—at least to each other—joyously giggling.

"She was laughing first," Ember accuses. "I couldn't help it."

"Ember always laughs when anyone else does," Bridgett says, coming in and taking her mom's hand. She is wearing one of her grandma's long white bathrobes.

"How are you feeling?" Frances asks Bridgett cheerfully. "You look much better."

"I'm fine. What were you guys talking about?"

"Your grandpa. He was a volunteer fireman."

"He helped save my house when I was a little girl," Vicky says. "One of my brothers was smoking in the basement."

"See, as I said, very noble." Frances and Ember start to laugh again.

"Well, it was. My brother would have died." Vicky's face flushes.

"Oh, Vicky—I'm sorry. It's not that. I've been so worried about this visit and anxious for it to happen . . . Thad and I built this house. I've lived here for over forty years. When I leave I'm not going to have much left to show for my life. I'll be someplace where hopefully no one will know me, but—Well." She sighs. "I won't see you two when you come home to visit your parents, or you three, I should say, since Carl's as much a part of my family. I never got to know Ember when Richard could have connected us . . . In the past ten years I've built up a very good life for myself—without Richard to worry about, I mean. But since he died I'm not welcome here."

When the silence starts to feel long Ember says, "It's the same for me. In my building no one takes the elevator when I do. They haven't wanted to see me since they found out about Richard, so they learned my schedule and now I don't dare waver from it. I'm like some sort of prisoner, and I can't defy them. We knew everyone; not many people live there, and we were constantly in and out of one another's places. These people don't even show the morbid interest of everyone else I've met since then. I wish they would. At least it would be something."

"They're scared," Frances says. "They were right next to evil and didn't recognize it."

"Dad wasn't evil," Bridgett says softly.

"Even if he murdered people?" Frances asks. She expects Vicky to explode with rage, but the room stays quiet. Mother and daughter are standing a couple of feet apart now, not touching. Both roll their shoes to the outside edge and jut their hips forward a little. Bridgett is bigger than her mom, Frances notices for the first time.

"I can't believe we're talking about this like it's nothing!" Bridgett says. "I've never known anyone who—I don't know why this is happening to me."

"Bridgett, would you like to take a walk around the block?" Carl is standing in the doorway smelling faintly of vomit.

"No. Thank you, Carl." Frances is firm. "This is why I needed everyone here. We're the only ones who can understand our part in this tragedy. There's no one else for us to talk to."

"Why don't you take a shower, sweetie. Thanks for cleaning."

"Thank you," Bridgett echoes, her eyes on the floor.

"No problem, I've had my share of upchucks."

"Car-al! That's gross!"

But the little girl laughs, so Carl leaves the room looking smug.

The talk begins to go around in circles, until it is mostly Bridgett on the endless track of how she doesn't have any friends because she has only been allowed around adults—and those all relatives, no less—and is going to die if she can't go back to school. Although Frances knows this is a serious problem for a teenager, it's tedious to hear about.

The doorbell rings and she remembers hinting to her real estate agent that this would be a good time to show the house. She was thinking all sorts of things at the time, like proving she had been telling the truth about selling it, so her insistence on the family bedding elsewhere was believable, and fear—maybe fear too. She had feared the family's authority. An imagined authority: it's now obvious they are a flimsy bunch.

"That might be someone to see the house." Frances gets up and is touched when everyone follows her to the door. Carl comes too, with wet hair and the appearance of someone who has been napping. Frances hopes he used one of the beds, but he's holding his head as though he fell asleep in a chair.

She looks through the peephole and says in surprise, "Oh. It *is* my realtor." This could be a good thing. The Mariah real-estate market has never done well. The young people will make the house friendlier and dispel whatever rumors might have been started about the place. "These are the first people he's brought, so I'd better let them in."

The realtor, Frank Wright, is staring adoringly at a young woman by his side and doesn't notice Frances opening the door. The girl is very small, much shorter than Vicky, which Frances thinks is probably part of the charm for Frank, who has never been comfortable with his height of six and a half feet. The stranger appears annoyingly familiar although it would seem difficult to forget having met someone with such unusual dark red curls.

Frances is fond of Frank, the son of her best friend. Pam and her husband divorced six months before she died of breast cancer. Frank, a year older than Richard, was four at the time. Years later his father married the woman who ran the real estate office, and it became a family business. As a child Frank planned to be successor to the great architect Frank Lloyd Wright.

"Come in, Frank."

"Frances, this is Alyssa. She would like to view your house."

"That's great, Frank. Come in."

He finally looks at Frances, and his neck and ears turn red.

"How's business in Mariah?" Carl asks curiously. Frances hopes Frank will lie.

"Well, our office isn't merely in Mariah. We—uh, officially Mariah is part of two separate towns. It doesn't have its own charter. We find it works better to present Mariah that way—as it is legally—since it lacks any commerce of its own."

"Frank!" He hears Vicky and blushes darker. A lot of boys had crushes on her in high school. They hug awkwardly, his hands patting her back.

"Can I meet everyone?" Alyssa asks a little shyly.

"I'm Frances Dayle, I own this house. This is Vicky, her daughter Bridgett, Carl, and Ember."

Everyone nods and smiles.

"Would you be living here by yourself?" Frances asks. Frank is standing there grinning. The door is still open and his hand is on the knob.

"Oh, the house would be for my parents. They want me to narrow down the choices so they have an easier time of it when they get here. This seems like a really nice place."

In a nervous motion Alyssa pulls her hair back from her face and then lets it fall again. Frances knows she has seen her somewhere. When Alyssa notices the puzzled stare she sighs.

"I can't believe you recognize me."

"Oh, yes. Horace's hotel. Willy-B's place. You work there?"

"No, no."

"If you're a journalist," she says to Alyssa, "pretending to be a prospective buyer, I will sue you and your employer." She is embarrassed even before she has finished saying it. Many journalists have tried to manipulate their way into her home, but she knows there isn't anything she can do about it beyond remaining wary.

Vicky and Carl are staring at Frances intently, as if to warn her to stop scaring this innocent person.

"I think I'll just come back later," Alyssa says.

"This is why we're not supposed to have the owners present." Frank seems upset, but he was always a high-strung boy. "I have to go, Mrs. Dayle, I drove her here."

Frances pats him on the back as he follows Alyssa outside.

Carl shuts the door. "What was that all about?"

Frances and Ember start talking at once. "You haven't—" "They've tried—"

"Sorry," Ember says, "Go ahead."

"Vicky, you hid from the journalists, which was a good thing, a smart motherly move, but what Ember and I went through after—after Richard died, it was horrendous."

The doorbell rings and they all jump, then laugh finding they are huddled together. Vicky leaves the room to search for a wandering Bridgett; they are treating the house as if it is haunted and shouldn't be explored alone.

"It's Frank and his client again." Frances says, opening the door.

"My name is Katherine Van Leden," the young lady says.

Ember and Frances look at each other.

"Not Alyssa," Carl says brightly.

"You don't know who I am?" she asks, and then yells something unintelligible. It is so unexpected it's almost funny, until she starts to cry. She doesn't cover her face, just stands and sobs. Her nose begins to run and her eyes swell up.

"Van Leden," she repeats timorously. "Alyssa Van Leden?"

"Is it Alyssa or Katherine?" Carl's voice is kind.

"Let her in," Ember says. "She's very upset about something."

They take the sobbing woman's arms and lead her to the living room. Ember gently pushes her onto the couch. The room smells very strongly of lemon detergent.

Frank carries a box of tissues from the bathroom, and Frances gives him an approving smile.

"What's going on?" Vicky asks. Bridgett is holding her mother's hand and eating a red Popsicle.

More red, Frances thinks.

"Katherine Van Leden," the girl repeats to Vicky. "Alyssa Van Leden?"

Vicky and Bridgett shake their heads.

"I can't—I can't." She has the hiccups. She blows her nose and drops wads of used tissue onto the floor. "My name is Katherine. My sister was Alyssa."

Frances looks at her encouragingly. "And?"

"I hate you all!" Katherine stands up and runs from the room, knocking into Bridgett, who drops her frozen treat on the light blue carpet and clings to Vicky.

Ember begins to speak very slowly, "Do any of you know her?"

Frank, bewildered but still polite, says, "I'd better go drive her back to the office. I'll see you later, Mrs. Dayle. Vicky. Bye, everyone."

Frances follows Frank to the door. "Please call me if you find out what's wrong."

She shuts the door behind him and leans against the antique washstand next to it, glancing absently at herself in its slightly blurry old mirror. The vase is gone. She moves away in puzzlement. It has collected dust in this same place since they moved in, an inexpensive article that Frances inherited from a great-grandmother. "Has anyone noticed my vase?" she asks loudly before turning to see that her guests are already forming a clog in the doorway of the living room.

They say no, and Ember asks quietly about the odd woman that was just there.

"Why would—?" Frances opens the front door but Frank's truck is gone. "How odd. As you just said. I guess I'll call him later. No one wandered off with it, did they? Well, you all look exhausted, should I call Horace and see if he's got your rooms ready?" She wonders about staying at the old boardinghouse herself. Sleeping hasn't been easy here. For the last few months she has had the sensation of someone spying on her. Of course if it's law enforcement it will follow her wherever she goes—and an impalpable force will be just as difficult to escape.

She will return the van to her neighbor and then follow the rental to Horace's in her own car. If he seems distracted or annoyed with having them stay, then maybe she can painlessly cancel the agreement and bring everyone back here again.

The hell with her decision making of late anyway.

22

Ember had no idea Richard grew up in such a lovely, large house, bigger by far than the one she was raised in with her four brothers and sisters. When he visited her childhood home he always commented on how lucky she was to have been surrounded by red cliffs and trees. This area might not have the colorful stone, but it has twice as many trees. The sunlight is filtered through green, and the hills are lovely.

Her impression of his childhood was that it was one of hardship after his father died: destitution with a mother of grave disabilities, perhaps alcoholism or insanity. A rotting trailer park and a sense of hopelessness. When she referred to a news story or memoir that focused on children and extreme suffering, he became sad and thoughtful. "Was that what your childhood was like?" she would ask with so much tender pity, as he turned away and said he didn't want to talk about the past.

"I imagined Richard's life differently than this," she tells Vicky as they wait outside for Carl and Frances to return from their errands.

"He wouldn't let Bridgett mention Frances in his presence—or rather in your presence since it started after he married you."

"What does that mean?"

They are standing near the end of the driveway looking up at the brick house with its brown shake roof. Ember feels an argument beginning, so she doesn't turn to the bitter little ex-wife. Richard once said that Vicky could put more poison into a pout than a bolt of lightening has electricity. Ember told him it was a ridiculous comparison, more than a little jealous at how complimentary he made it sound. He laughed and said that she was the poet; she should know better than he the foolishness of creative description. Insulted, she called his biographies more fanciful than factual, and that started an insult-fest.

"You are so pitiful," Vicky says now, sounding sad. "After all this time, when Richard has been proven to be a murderer—a murderer!—you can't accept that he lied to you about everything else too. Do you know why we got divorced? I came home from work early—in the middle of the day—and caught him in the kitchen with a woman. She was drunk and all over him. He just turned and glared at me, and I was more scared than I have ever been in my life. I should have been furious, but I was terrified. He *hated* me, that's what I could see. We planned our schedules out so one of us was always home with Bridgett, and she was in her crib in the living room. A one-year-old baby seeing her daddy do who knows what day after day."

"If that were true," Ember says, "then how would you have known I didn't know?"

"There is no way Richard was going to tell you that. Would you marry someone that did?"

"He said he caught *you* cheating on him. At work or something—you were sleeping with everyone."

"Of course," Vicky says. "I was a pedophile, is that what he said? Or was it with their mothers when they came to pick them up?"

"He didn't—"

"I was working at a daycare center for single mothers. Only women were employed there. He must have got a big kick out of that lie."

"What about personal training?"

"I didn't become a personal trainer until after the divorce. Richard was too jealous. I took the daycare job so I could take Bridgett to work with me if necessary, but Richard said it wouldn't be good for her to be around all those children. I thought he was being a concerned father."

She has no desire to distrust Vicky, but this new humiliation on top of the heavy heat makes her dizzy. A bee starts buzzing around her head.

"And this isn't one of those she said, he said things," Vicky continues. "I can prove I wasn't a personal trainer at that time. I can prove I worked at the other place."

"Yes," Ember agrees faintly. "How can I get this bee to leave me alone?"

"Just don't move and it will fly away eventually. There's Carl," Vicky says as a car pulls up along the street by the driveway. "Come on, the bee is gone."

Frances goes inside to find Bridgett, then the garage opens and a boxy old Mercedes with faded silver paint backs out. Ember is vaguely surprised, thinking a well-tended baby blue convertible Cadillac would be more appropriate.

"I was always so scared he was going to die," she tells Vicky, then wants to scream at herself for bringing Richard up again.

"Me too." Vicky sounds surprised.

"I was married to him for eight years."

"Me six. And we grew up together."

"He was never even arrested. As an adult, at least. As a child?"

"Of course not. You could never keep something like that a secret here."

"If it weren't for the bodies in this yard I would think he had found the ones in the Santa Monica garden, and that's what gave him the heart attack."

"No one really knows anything," Vicky says kindly.

"No, no they don't," Ember agrees, "except that I'm the biggest fool of the twenty-first century."

23

Anthea Martin showed up at his door on a Thursday afternoon. Bridgett was in her crib playing with a plastic train while he worked on his evening lecture.

The yard behind their small house in South Pasadena was fully blocked in by white alder trees. Richard had recently plowed up the lawn so he could redesign the area. Vicky didn't mind; she was happy as long as the front looked presentable. He hadn't been planning to use it for anything other than a relaxing garden until this woman arrived trying to sell cosmetics. Her lank hair and dull skin made for poor advertising. After inviting her into the kitchen, he noticed she was slightly drunk.

"I don't have the personality to sell anything," she said flirtatiously. "I need a drink or two so I can be more outgoing."

He pretended to be aroused by standing very close to her and staring at her tiny, brittle neck. He could see Bridgett in the living room, kneeling with her hands on the bars, watching him with interest. "Tell me about your life," he said to the woman, while peeking over her shoulder at his daughter.

"I just need to make some money so I can pay my rent," Anthea Martin answered too loudly. She closed her eyes and lifted her chin.

"You're a bit of a bad girl, aren't you?" He didn't need to strangle her; he could just break her neck. It might snap beautifully. He considered having his first audience, although not very seriously. Instead, he would take her for some conversation in the other room, then there was all that rich, churned dirt in the back. Bridgett would enjoy some time outside.

Suddenly the front door was open and there was Vicky, shocked and frightened. A second later and he would have had to kill her too. The horror of the attention that would bring to his life made his legs shake until he almost collapsed, but he calmed himself enough to accept that his marriage was over.

The greatest pain, almost physical, was that of letting the embarrassed Anthea Martin walk out the front door. He never saw her again, nor did he care to, but it was a loss nonetheless.

24

"Richard sent letters twice a year after he stopped speaking to me," Frances tells Ember. "There are eighteen."

Bridgett has already jumped out of the car and now stands on the doorstep waving for them to hurry.

"He said in between he jotted down notes of things to share."

"Why didn't you talk for so long?"

"I was surprised he didn't stop earlier. And after he got me out of his life everything went better. He met you, and according to Vicky became more of a father."

"He never would explain exactly what went wrong in your family," Ember says.

"He thought I took Vicky's side in the divorce. They were a terrible match in the first place. To her he was handsome and mysterious, and she'd tired of the other boys. She was the perfectly normal cliché of the girl-next-door head cheerleader type, although she wasn't on the squad. Bad ankles and knees and a klutz, but as adorable as they come. I think she played the flute."

"Wow. I see Vicky more as a tough businesswoman."

"We had a very high rate of pregnancy here, but luckily her family is French and was savvy to the world of birth control long before Mariah heard of Planned Parenthood. Vicky educated the boys well enough to bring us below the national average for the first time since they began to keep track.

"Well, we'd better join Bridgett. Remind me to show you those letters. Richard said you and I were exactly alike, which seemed odd since he loathed me."

Frances gets out and Ember follows slowly.

"The doorbell's playing a song," Bridgett says, leaning her head toward the house.

Ember is staring at the door when it swings open, and a man whose appearance consumes her stock of flattering adjectives stands in a long-sleeved untucked blue dress shirt and jeans. He's as tan as Richard, but his hair is brown and thick and wavy. His eyes are deep in dark sockets with eyebrows shaggy and low above them.

"Ember, this is Horace, he owns the place."

Horace? He smiles at her, then over her shoulder. She turns to see Vicky getting out of the other car, flipping her short hair away from her face.

"Victy," he says with a strange lilt.

"Oh, Horace. It's been so long. Have you met my daughter, Bridgett? And my boyfriend, Carl?"

"I'm really glad to have you here."

"Do you have an accent?" Ember asks to end the stare down between him and Carl.

"Me?" He seems flustered and looks at Frances.

"You are speaking rather oddly, Horace."

"I was going for exotic. It didn't come out quite right."

"I wondered if you were Italian. Maybe French?"

"No, he doesn't sound French," Vicky says.

"Come on in, y'all, I shut the windows and turned the air on. We'll see how it works."

"I like southern best." Bridgett is gazing at Horace a little too attentively.

"Hokey," Carl whispers.

"This is my collection of bowling paraphernalia," Horace announces as they all crowd into the entryway. "Obviously more valuable than it appears since someone tried to steal it yesterday."

"Did you catch them taking it?" Bridgett asks.

"Actually," Horace looks pointedly at Frances, "it was that person you assumed cleaned for me."

"She showed up at my house today." Frances explains to Ember, "That woman with Frank."

"She acted so strangely. And that vase."

"Yes, a vase is missing."

Horace leads them through a large kitchen to his living room, only a little cooler than outside. The raggedy furniture doesn't blend well with walls of stone and a deep, majestic fireplace, but the green chair Ember chooses is comfortable.

Horace sits cross-legged on the floor facing the rest of them in their semicircle of chairs. "I don't have a couch yet."

"These are just fine," Frances says before telling him all the details of Katherine and Frank's visit.

"Her name might be Alyssa though," Bridgett informs Horace loudly, leaning forward so she is almost on the floor beside him. "That's what she said at first."

Ember glances at Vicky, whose expression is stern as she watches her daughter.

"I should call Frank. If you'll excuse me." Frances takes a phone from her purse.

Ember finds herself staring out of exhaustion and turns her head. "This stone is gorgeous. It must be very old."

"Thank you. My grandpa wanted an authentic down-home boardinghouse. I live upstairs. It's now one huge room with a bathroom in each corner. You guys will sleep to the right of the bowling collection. I cleaned three of the rooms, and there's only one bathroom. Frances said that might be a problem, so I got one ready upstairs."

He is so eager to please and adorable. Ember is afraid of being as obvious as Bridgett.

Frances puts away her phone. "Frank said he's been planning to get in touch. He made Alyssa—as he still seems to think she's called—leave the vase with him."

"She just carries a vase right out of the house?" Carl asks. He's embarrassingly sweaty and obviously feeling unnerved by Horace, although Vicky hasn't given their host the slightest attention.

"Let's go find our room," Vicky says to him. "I really need to take a nap; I didn't sleep at all last night."

Horace begins to rise, then sits back down. "It's easy to tell which rooms are ready. They have beds."

"Thank you," Vicky says absently. She hasn't parted with her two suitcases since they entered, and Carl carries them out of the room.

"Mom is such a grouchy traveler," Bridgett says. "Whenever we go to France she has jetlag for days. I'm not tired though. What should we do?"

"Horace is just renting us rooms," Frances says. "He's not our entertainment too. Thank you for setting everything up. The flowers in the kitchen are lovely."

"They're from the garden, thank you. My sister helps me keep it up. She should be over later. She wanted to see Vicky—her old babysitter," he explains to Bridgett and Ember.

"Your sister babysat Vicky, or—"

"Vicky babysat my sister. Lilac is six years younger than me and Vicky is a few years older."

"Well, 'a few' is between three and five and Mom just turned thirty-eight, so you must be thirty-three, four, or five." Bridgett looks disappointed.

"I had a huge crush on your mom when I was about your age."

"Really? Did you date her?"

"No, I was too young for her. How old are you?"

"Fourteen."

"Would you date an eleven year old?"

"Ew."

"Yep. Poor me."

"It's too bad she's engaged to Carl," Bridgett taunts. "He's an amazing chef. He's thirty-eight too."

Frances stands abruptly and says good-bye. Ember follows her out.

"I feel silly about this whole thing," Frances frets when they reach her car.

Ember looks away from her to the house's vine-covered walls and wonders if it was because of her, the unknown element, that Frances arranged for them to stay here.

"You guys call me after you've rested up if you want to come over for dessert."

"What is wrong with that guy that he lives here all alone?" Ember asks to stall Frances before she shuts the car door.

Frances puts her key in the ignition but doesn't turn it. "Oh, he's a writer. You know. A bit antisocial, I suppose. His parents and sister live here in town. The rest of the family has since moved on. I hear his sister and her husband support him financially. Well," she smiles at her son's wife and takes a deep breath. "It was nice meeting you, Ember."

It sounds like she's leaving forever. "When Richard was a kid," Ember says almost frantically, "did he ever—"

A truck comes down the street and whips into the driveway behind the Mercedes, hitting the bumper.

"That's Frank's," Frances says as Katherine leans her red face out the window.

"He was going to kill her," Vicky says from the doorway. "Ember!" she yells. "Ember, he was going to kill her."

"Vicky." Ember looks at Frances, who is checking her car for damage.

Katherine passes them and walks toward the house. "Who?"

Vicky is focusing only on Ember. "The woman in the kitchen. I hadn't thought about it in so long, but telling you today—"

"Yes, of course. Let's—" Ember stops because she doesn't know what to suggest. Vicky's hair is ruffled from lying down and she might not be fully awake.

"Richard Earle Dayle was going to kill someone and you saw him?" Katherine asks. She twirls around to face Frances and

Ember. "Don't you say anything. I brought proof this time. I have a copy of the police file on my sister's death."

Katherine runs back to the truck and Ember whispers, "Let's go," to Frances, gripping her arm and pulling her to the house. The plan is to lock the door behind them and summon help. At least they can report the robberies.

But Katherine forces herself in after them, almost knocking Frances over.

"You lunatic, we're going to call the police if you don't leave immediately."

"Listen, Ember," she hisses, "my name is Katherine. Alyssa was my sister and Richard Earle Dayle murdered her."

No one moves for a moment until Katherine reaches up to brush Ember's face. "Sorry, I spit on you."

She has a folder thick with papers in her hand, which she holds up. "Open it!"

On the first page Ember sees a missing person report on sixteen-year-old Alyssa Van Leden, 5'1", ninety-eight pounds. The school photo stapled to the top right-hand corner shows a pretty redhead with green eyes.

The next page is covered with tiny, single-spaced typing and Ember turns to the third, which is a handwritten copy of a newspaper report on the search. Then eight or nine sheets are photocopies from different papers. Ember reads the headlines. Most are from Caldwell. Some of the fonts are cursive or script, which gives the articles an amateurish look. She grew up in a small town, and while she doesn't remember the local paper's format, she does recall all the grammatical errors her parents came across as they skimmed it.

Later in the file are the articles on Richard's childhood backyard containing skeletons. These are cut from the newspaper, but some of the words are smudged on the tired pages, signs of being held and folded many times. Last is a police report closing the case, stating that Alyssa's teeth were in good enough shape for her to be identified, as was a backpack buried with her containing personal items recognized by the family. Deceased Richard is listed confidently as the murderer. Ember wonders at the accuracy of such an assumption. What is with the local police, don't they need DNA, someone's DNA? They don't even state how she died.

Ember feels an expression of disgust on her face and alters it. "This is terrible," she says lamely. She holds the folder, not wanting to hand it back but wishing Katherine would take it.

"We didn't know what happened to her for fifteen years. She could have been kidnapped, anything. People said we were just being wishful, like she ran away or something. My family—oh, you don't care."

"I don't know what I can do, Katherine."

Katherine ages as her shoulders droop. "I don't know what I've been doing either. We were looking for my sister for so many years, then we found her, but there isn't any closure. A trial would be horrible, but it seems too easy, him dying first, without ever facing us. I imagine the things I could do to him if only he were alive.

"My mom is religious and she sees everything as being evened out after death. He will be punished, Alyssa will be given a chance to grow up . . . I wish that were likely."

"But what's the reason for your stealing?" Horace asks.

Ember turns around and looks for Bridgett, who for once isn't present.

"It's not important. I'm sorry."

"And were you following Frances around?" Ember asks.

"Oh, I—yes."

"I'm so sorry for your loss, Katherine," Frances says. "I apologize for Richard, and for not knowing what he had turned into."

Katherine nods, tears running down her face from closed eyes. She turns around and feels for the doorknob. Ember looks quickly at Frances and then Horace.

"Have some iced tea before you go," Horace offers.

"Yes, please stay until you feel better."

Vicky has taken the folder and is flipping through it. "I was married to Richard when Alyssa disappeared. How could this be? We were living in California."

Frances and Horace have moved to the kitchen with Katherine, so Ember whispers, "What if he didn't do it?"

"The police found her in his yard."

"But what about Frances?"

"What about the bodies in California?"

"Maybe they both did it. She started it and he copied. Suppose she always wanted a daughter and her desire became all corrupted. I don't know, I've read stranger motives. In detective stories."

"Yeah, right. Just be quiet and let me think. It was June fourth she disappeared. I was twenty-three. Bridgett wasn't born yet. Oh, wait. My sister got married that year. Here in town before she moved to Wisconsin with that loser husband of hers. Yes, we were here for at least a month because school was out."

"So you were here, and he killed this girl that summer."

"Oh, God. I don't know why, but I thought all his—I thought they were all older. Women in their twenties or thirties. Not that it would make it better, but—this makes it worse. Do you know what I mean? Why does it make it worse?"

"Didn't you hear about this missing girl?"

"Caldwell's an hour away, but I'm sure I heard something."

"He must have planned it; how could he have the time?"

"I was involved with my family a lot, and he was seeing old friends. We weren't together except at night. Doesn't it seem like Frances would have noticed something with all the burying?"

"Did she have a job?"

"Of course. They had the life insurance money from his dad, but she worked at some psychiatric hospital way before he died. She always took Richard with her."

"Where did she work? What town?"

"Oh." Vicky widens her eyes. "Caldwell. Is that what you're getting at?"

"I'm not getting at anything. Do we know where all the victims were from? Or even how many there were?"

They hear Frances speaking angrily in the kitchen, and Ember walks toward the noise.

She certainly didn't know the person that was a husband to Vicky and son to Frances. That person was a lunatic. A loony loon. She has always jokingly thrown those labels of insanity around. Richard didn't like it; he said an unusual mind was serious business.

Katherine has her forehead pressed against the kitchen table.

"You worked at a psychiatric hospital in Caldwell?" Ember asks Frances, who is standing over Katherine looking frustrated.

"Katherine was bugging Mrs. Dayle's phone," Horace says solemnly.

"What?" Ember laughs. "Richard bugged our living room."

Frances and Horace stare at her.

Katherine lifts her head. "I just wanted to know if anyone else was involved in Alyssa's murder. I'll remove it. I'll show you; it's very easy to remove." She sounds a little desperate now.

"You seem like a danger to me and my family," Frances says. "I'm worried about what you might do next."

"I won't do anything, I promise. I was obviously following a messed up idea. You don't know how it is for us. I thought everything would go back to normal if we found out what had happened to Alyssa. At least my father would come back. He went out looking for her and never came back. We haven't been able to find a trace of him. My mom throws things into our swimming pool. It's empty, and she throws anything breakable in there and watches it shatter. If there's nothing she breaks the windows with a bat. There was about a foot of broken glass in the pool until a few months ago when my husband cleaned it out. We steal things for her to break, my brother and I, because we can't afford to buy them.

"I married Alyssa's old boyfriend. Johnny was always around helping with my brother and everything after she died. And he was the only one who could understand. They checked him when she went missing, but he was in the school play that night. Alyssa was supposed to be watching, but no one saw her after she left work at the grocery store. No one saw her get in a car, or talk to a stranger, nothing. Please don't send me to jail."

Katherine is facing Frances, with her back to the rest of them. She puts her head back down on the table.

"Most of those bowling balls and pins are real. I don't think they would break even if dropped into a cement hole. The balls might chip, but then they would roll around a bit."

Katherine lifts her head so her wet eyes peer through shiny hair. "Would they make a tremendous noise?" she asks, sounding younger than Bridgett.

"Yes. The pins would probably just clatter or bounce around. Maybe crack. They're supposed to be mainly decorative, but . . ."

"What are you saying?" Katherine asks, sniffling. She tilts her head to look at him.

"We can put them in Frank's truck. I'm sure my mom won't mind me giving them up for a good cause."

"And then," Katherine says excitedly, turning around in her chair, "we can put only some out and hide the rest. They are all so different—"

"And the ones that don't break you can recycle for later use."

"She might kill someone with them," Ember says.

Katherine shrugs. "Her strength's not that great, just dropping them will take all her energy."

"I'll get Carl to help," Vicky says.

Ember wants to go along to Katherine's crazy house but ends up carrying loads of bowling junk, only to watch them drive off.

"Why are you outside?" Bridgett asks.

They have just finished explaining to Carl, and no one has the energy to answer.

"I was upstairs on Horace's computer," she says.

"Bridgett, you can't touch his things." Vicky has a headache in her voice.

"I didn't touch anything, the screen was up! It was all about—well, I think it was about sex. It was really gross."

Frances gently pushes the girl into the house, and they go to Bridgett's room. Ember follows to the only bed left and is grateful for the ceiling fan that whispers around in circles. She locks the door and curls up on her side, pushing her hair above her head. It's nice to be alone now. She would be far too hot with someone wrapped around her.

25

"You'd better drive. I don't have a license."

He accepts the keys greedily, prompting Katherine to ask if he owns a car.

"No, just a fucked up motorcycle my brother-in-law gave me. I'll bet Frank has something brand new."

Katherine points to the red Toyota Tacoma jammed up against Frances' Mercedes.

"Is it a stick?"

"Nope."

Horace bends over to look at the touching bumpers. "I wonder if we should go by the Dayle's first so you can get rid of that bug. She was pretty upset."

"O-K," she says with emphasis, before getting in and slamming the door.

"Do you not need me to take you home?" He puts on his seatbelt and sits for a moment, but she knows he craves the driving opportunity too much to make conciliation necessary. After inserting the key he turns it almost reverently, causing Katherine to wonder suddenly what he's like in bed.

"I'm curious about this wiretap deal. I might use something like it in a story sometime."

"I didn't do what pros would call a wiretap. I used walkie-talkies. Some kids I babysit had real nice ones they never even played with," Katherine says grouchily as Horace swings onto Frances' street. "There are much better ways to do it if you have the equipment." She jumps out before the car is fully parked.

Entering this backyard for the first time had made her nervous. Not about getting caught, but because of its history. The signs of the excavation were terrifying enough after two nightmares that her sister would be strewn about in recognizable pieces. A few old trees were the only life, but even they seemed uneasy surrounded by holes and piles of dirt.

"Walkie-talkies?" he asks as he follows her across the front lawn and through the gate. "I thought you would use some kind of transmitter or radio—something more high tech."

"I would have loved to." She stops walking. "Oh wow."

"What?"

"When I was back here last there was no lawn left or anything. It was completely torn up." Now it's a perfectly ordinary expanse of green grass, which gives her the creeps.

"By the cops?"

His eyes keep wandering to her breasts, and he doesn't think she can tell. Typical loser assuming he's subtle. She has observed that white guys never figure you notice. Hispanics want to insult you with their eyes, black guys tell you what they're enjoying, and she's never met an Asian, but they probably have their own deal. Men are so fucking stupid. And what is the accent he keeps slipping in and out of? He sounds like her brother when he was a teenager. Poor Alex has an excuse though.

She walks around the house and is annoyed by how closely he follows.

"Did you tap the phone or bug it? Is there a difference?"

The phone box is a couple of feet away from the gas meter on the back of the house. It is still held shut with one loose screw. She jerks the cover off and the screw goes flying.

"Damn. Find that, will you?"

Everything looks the same as when she saw it last. Horace dangles the screw in her face.

"Hold it," she snaps.

"What did you do?"

"This is one of my walkie-talkies," she says. "I detached the wires to the speaker and microphone and hooked the mic leads to these two screws." She points and then takes the mic leads off and pulls the walkie-talkie out. "It's on voice activation so whenever someone spoke over the phone line it was transmitted to my receiver."

"What's your receiver?"

"The other walkie-talkie in the set. I had to disable the microphone on that one to make sure the person on the phone couldn't hear anything from my end."

"So where's the back?" Horace asks, holding the half-destroyed object cautiously.

"Took it off so I could get to the mic and speaker."

"What if it hadn't worked?"

She shrugs.

"Did you record stuff?"

"Yeah, I set up a tape recorder next to it, but it didn't work that well. It was hard to find a quiet place. I still have the tapes, but the lady didn't talk on the phone much. There are only four for five months—well, I wasn't recording all the time, and after I found out when her family would be visiting it wasn't really necessary."

Horace replaces the lid and twists the screw in far enough with his fingers that it stays on.

"How did you figure all this out?"

"Home ec."

"What?"

"Let's go, this place is spooky," she says.

"Home economics in high school?"

"Yeah."

"They still have that?"

"They didn't when you were in school?"

"I don't remember."

"It was on the way out when I graduated, but I'm not as young as I look. I was eighteen when Alyssa disappeared. I don't count birthdays anymore, but it's been fifteen years since then. How old did you think I was?"

Horace won't answer. She laughs and slams the gate shut. In the truck she puts her feet up on the dashboard.

"Did you really learn about walkie-talkie bugs in home ec. class?" Horace asks as he backs the car out of the driveway.

He probably talks to himself when he's alone.

"Not exactly."

"Come on."

"Our home ec. teacher was divorced and very proud of it. Her husband cheated on her, and her dad helped her catch him on video so she could get the house and car. She wanted us all to be prepared to defend ourselves, so she taught us about phones. We could take one apart and put it back together at the end of that class. She took us to her house and showed us the phone box. I could tap one in at least seven different ways if I had the equipment. That was way before everyone had cell phones. Instead of saving up for a wedding dress, or household stuff, she said before marriage we should each own a surveillance camera. She was 'let go' the year after I graduated. Now she's the head administrator of a correspondence school on the Internet."

Katherine's house is almost fifty minutes from Mariah, and Horace is quiet for most of that time, but as they enter Caldwell he starts to annoy her with his endless quest for details.

"I can't believe those toys would work this far away."

"I know. Spoiled brats."

"I've never heard of walkie-talkies that worked over—I don't know, maybe five miles."

"OK. God. I didn't keep it at my house. Stop harassing me. You're really a nuisance."

"I was just curious."

"Stop looking at me, you're going to wreck."

"Well, put on your seatbelt."

"It's at Lucy's, that teacher I told you about. She lives in Mariah now."

"Your seatbelt?" Horace teases.

They drive down the main business street in silence, even though Katherine has stories about a lot of the people that own the shops they pass. At Main Street she says, "Left," at the next light "left" again. "It's a ways, then there will be a sign that says 'Washington' without the 'A.' Turn left."

Horace laughs when he sees the sign, even though she warned him. "Do you have a retarded sign maker?"

"Yes. My brother."

"Oh, fuck. I'm sorry."

"It's OK. He's pretty slow. And hey, if you can't make fun of the stupid people, then what's the point of being smart?" From the corner of her eye she watches Horace whip his head sideways. "His name is Alex. It doesn't show in his features except he's really tall, which in my family would have to be a genetic mishap because hereditarily we're as short as can be. Is that a word? Hereditarily?"

"I know what you mean."

"You remind me of him a little. He's a year younger than Alyssa, and before she disappeared he wanted to be a supermodel. He thought from sitcoms they were tall and stupid, just like him. He tried to imitate the accent so many of them have, Scandinavian or something. The same accent you've been doing off and on. Anyway, Mom would always tease Alex, before Alyssa was gone, that model scouts would come take him away. It was all fun until Alyssa went missing; then he was scared it might come true no matter what we said, so he gained a lot of weight."

As always on coming home, she feels jittery. The place is a disaster: suddenly the trees vanish, and it is flat, sad land. Alex chopped everything down, and he cuts the grass with a riding mower he found years ago. The house is an untended white with one boarded-over window. Driving up the hill to reach it they first pass the full-length, empty lap pool. There's no driveway, just dirt.

Horace is struggling to make her listen to something he's saying, but she's distracted by Alex running out to see the truck (with Johnny behind him).

"Hi, guys," she says, getting out. "I brought a surprise. Where's Mom?"

"Sister Helen picked her up for choir practice. Then they're going to Bible study with a potluck dinner."

"Good. What do you think about this?"

They inspect the truck's bed as Katherine introduces Horace.

She looks at them, Alex, tall and fat with sun-bleached blond hair, and Johnny, dark and thin with the same shoulder-length untended hairstyle as her brother. Horace has longish hair too, but it's different on him. He probably has it styled once a week.

"Bowling balls."

"For Mom?" Johnny asks.

"Yep. Horace gave them to us. We should hide them. Where do you think? We brought pins too. They're very pretty, aren't they?"

"Yes, thank you," Alex says. He lifts the yellow ball out. "Do you think she'll like it if it doesn't break?"

"I hope so."

Katherine wonders if Johnny will be jealous that she brought such a good-looking guy home.

"We have a freezer," Alex tells Horace. "It's in our shed. No one uses it; it's not even plugged in. Would it be OK if we kept them there?"

"That's a great idea," Katherine says.

"It's fine with me. Does your mom use it?"

"No, it's Dad's for hunting and stuff. He doesn't hunt now. I can carry two if I hold them like I'm bowling. Do it this way, Johnny." Then back to Horace: "Dad hasn't been around for many years. Katherine's been finding him for us, ever since she found Alyssa."

"That's good," Horace says with some embarrassment. He grasps the heads of three bowling pins in one hand and pulls out a bowling ball with three fingers of the other.

"Are you sure you don't want to keep one for a souvenir?" Johnny asks.

"Well, maybe," Horace admits. "I was just thinking that. Maybe that blue one with my name in calligraphy? My mom painted the name herself, and she was pretty excited about it."

"It looks very nice," Alex says.

Katherine is proud of her boys. They don't get out much, but they are so kind—it makes her eyes sting a little.

26

Richard had sex with one of his students the same year he married Ember. He did it in a calculated manner, not expecting his future wife to find out.

The lingering animosity of Dr. Tanaka wasn't considered.

Like Vicky before adult life, the student was an undeniably attractive little thing named Jenny. It was only once, in his office. She left, rumpled, at approximately the hour his colleagues were known to take off for their weekly drink together.

Another girl made this necessary—one that showed up at his office far too often the year before, a very bad girl, who had the audacity to vanish and never be heard from again. He joined the search energetically, assisted in the questioning eagerly, but still felt people were looking at him suspiciously.

"Unfair certainly, since the first two adverbs should have eliminated the third," he muttered aloud to himself with increasing agitation.

He had hoped in vain that Jenny would be a noisy sort of girl, but things worked well enough, with his male coworkers slowly becoming friendlier. Before, he'd had the reputation of a cold, distant perfectionist; after, he was certain they considered him just another guy.

Fourteen days following the afternoon with Jenny, he was summoned to the history department's weekly drinking session for the first time.

Later he acknowledged that he had once again misjudged his colleagues; the lack of invitations had been due to his inaccurate label as a homophobe. They had apparently never related the missing girl to him at all, nor had the Jenny liaison been what eventually led to his acceptance.

A group of his freshmen were researching rumors that the fifteenth United States' president and his running mate, as well as the thirteenth vice president, were homosexuals. This was a topic created by the students themselves for their independent project, but he had approved it.

He had no personal feelings about men having sex with each other. When a boy on his soccer team was accused of being gay and Richard told his mom about it, she said calmly, "Well, I guess that leaves more girls for the rest of you," and that's how he had thought of it ever since.

At the same time that he was anxiously plotting to soothe his coworkers' imaginary suspicions, he was also dating Ember. Three weeks after Jenny, he went to pick her up and found a note taped to the cheap gold doorknob. It explained that she never wanted to see him again and continued, "I know what you did with one of your students and I know you don't really love me. No matter what you say I will never be able to trust you again." There was no signature.

His initial plan was to talk his way out of it. No one could have given her the definitive truth. At first he tried to explain the situation through her thin door. He knew she was sitting in her apartment with tears on her face and her heart beating noisily, desperate to be convinced he was a good man.

"I love you so much," he said loudly, hoping no one could hear him in the apartments on either side.

"Tanaka talked to the girl. Jenny Miller."

He hadn't remembered her last name but did recall that she received an A- in his class. He had failed to regard her after that day, which hadn't been wise.

"She's lying." He could stick to his own lie for years but quickly decided a confession might make them closer and add protection from any incriminating details solicited by Tanaka.

"No, I'm lying," he said.

"What?"

"I'm lying. I slept with that awful girl. It was my revenge, and I would rather kill myself than admit it. I was so angry at you—"

"At me?" She sounded shocked. He could picture her fingers tentatively touching the knob on her side.

"Because you're just using me. You don't want to get married and I do, and I was trying to prove to myself that I didn't care."

The door opened, and Ember stared at him with a serious expression.

"How can you say that? You've never asked me."

"I've hinted about it many times, but you always changed the subject."

"I wasn't sure you were hinting. I didn't want to pressure you."

"I don't think Vicky was ready to get married, I thought—"

"Are you saying—?"

"And I mentioned a brother or sister for Bridgett, but . . ."

"I don't—"

"Ember." Richard bent dramatically to one knee. "Will you forgive me and marry me?"

It was the flurry of tears and hugging that he had expected. He was soon off the hard ground in an embrace, but he knew that when things quieted down her doubts would flourish again, stronger than ever. "I'm afraid though—afraid that you'll never be able to trust me, like you said. What can I do to prove myself to you?"

"Don't shut the door when you're with a student, for one. I don't know what else. I'll think of it."

And she did, and he suffered, but it was worth it—he loved his good girl.

27

Alex declares loudly, "The loot is unloaded," and then Johnny motions everyone into the house.

Horace finds them less pathetic than at first, although the boys behaved like children playing pirates, calling him "matey" and saying "land ahoy" each time they sighted the freezer; he was uncomfortable with Katherine's explanation that they always acted like this around stolen stuff.

The house is as bare as the property, and he can't imagine it was otherwise before Alyssa disappeared. The only decoration is a wooden plaque with at least twenty nails holding it to the white wall above the fireplace. He moves up close to see the engraving since he can't think of anything to say.

"'Anger is a brief madness,'" he reads aloud. "Horace, *Epistles*. Sixty-five to eight B.C." Alex is reciting the words with him. In tiny writing below the name it says, "Roman lyrical poet and satirist."

He steps back and then up close again. Due to Alex's unexpected chorus, he can't remember what he just read. "'Anger is a brief madness.'"

"I'm named after this fellow," he says finally. "I'm not familiar with the quote, but I'm named after him. My parents studied Horace in school."

"So did ours," says Alex.

"Well."

"Our dad made that sign before he left. Before Alyssa disappeared." Katherine looks at Johnny for confirmation. "I can't remember it not being there. It's because of Mom. So we can forgive her and she can forgive herself." She sits on the only chair in the room, which is in front of the computer at the wall opposite the plaque.

"That's a lamp-place, not a fireplace," Alex informs him. "All the comfort of a fire without the mess or danger."

If Alex were a typical thirty-something year old, Horace would laugh.

"Mom gets very mad sometimes and she breaks things. We run away when it happens because she might accidentally hurt us. It's not her fault; madness is no one's fault." Alex sounds a little strange, the way he moves his mouth sloppily, but Horace wouldn't have known if he hadn't been told. He might have thought the guy was a jokester, a clown.

"A good person to be named after," Johnny says.

"When the name is Horace it doesn't matter who's the namesake. I never tell anyone anyway."

"I would. I'm named after my drunk dad who's named after his drunk dad who's named after his drunk dad, and on and on and on and on and on."

"Stop!" Alex says.

"If I ever have a son I'm not naming him Johnny."

"Or John or Jack. Those are his brothers." Katherine rolls her eyes. "You did turn out to be a writer, didn't you?" she asks Horace.

"I guess so. But my sister's named after a flower, and she didn't turn out to be one of those."

This is his standard response, although sometimes people reply that she *is* a flower, which is just annoying. He might not mind any of it so much if he were published.

Horace suspects the ancient Roman was warning against anger—or at least against taking action during it. He wonders if that wasn't really what their father had been trying to say to his wife.

28

"Remember Bridgett's fifth birthday party?" Ember asks Vicky.

"Of course. It was the last one where parents were invited."

This morning Frances suggested Bridgett visit her Andres grandparents for the day, so Ember is trying to start the conversation about Richard's psyche that she imagines Frances desires.

"This is the easiest bread in the world to make," Frances says from the counter, where she is stirring the ingredients for oatmeal and molasses loaves. "No kneading, just mix everything up and wait for it to rise."

"It's delicious. Bridgett calls it Grandma's bread."

"Anyway, Bridgett's party is where I met you—"

"No, it was before that at Richard's apartment when I dropped Bridgett off."

"Oh yeah, but—"

"He introduced you as his fiancé at the party."

"Well, that's when I almost broke it off with him permanently. It's the closest I ever came to thinking he was possibly psychotic."

"Really? What happened?"

Frances has placed a clean hand towel over the bread dough and is finally paying attention.

"He cheated on me. Earlier that year. I found out he'd had sex with one of his students. I'm embarrassed to talk about it—he convinced me it was my fault because I didn't want a commitment. We ended up formally engaged, blah blah blah.

"I wouldn't fall for that now, but I was in love and stupid. He was very penitent and did everything I requested, but it makes me ill with humiliation when I think of the details.

"Bridgett's party was a few months later. Richard worried that Carl wanted to adopt her and cut him out."

"Richard hated Carl. He said my tastes had declined dramatically from when I'd married him, the lean scholar—"

"He didn't say that!" Ember protests, laughing.

"And that he'd made a mistake thinking I was valuable in the first place. The small town special, he said. Also that his mom had wanted him to get more world experience before marriage. Even though he'd already been to school in California."

"I wasn't warning him not to marry you personally; I just didn't think he was ready."

Frances has been holding her hands under running water, and the sound is starting to bother Ember, who says loudly, "Yes, he caused you lots of problems, Vicky, but your ancient animosity is not the point. These things you're getting mad about are the same things you've been fuming over for years."

"What *is* the point?"

Ember looks at Frances for help. The latter finally turns the water off and grabs the towel that was covering the rising dough. "Oops." She places the damp cloth on the table. "We need to get Richard out of our systems."

"Ember still can't admit that she's not the only one he hurt."

"One of the fathers at the party was an FBI agent," Ember continues. "He was a polygrapher and interviewed new recruits."

"Oh, Luke Rastree. His daughter was in Bridgett's dance class. The family moved that summer."

"I don't know if you were in the room when this happened, Vicky, but the kids were all playing elsewhere. The agent kept watching Richard, and when another guest asked him to give an example of a hiring interview, the agent remembered Richard's name—they had just met—and used him as a pretend applicant. The agent was telling us questions the FBI asked. One was if they had stolen more than five dollars a day from past jobs. I guess everyone's done that to some degree—taken pens and whatnot—and the question is just to throw people off, unbalance them.

Anyway, he asked Richard on a scale of one to ten, how ethical did he consider himself. Richard said seven. I was shocked so I said, 'Are you sure you're a *seven*?' He nodded confidently and everyone laughed like I'd been joking, but I felt paralyzed."

Frances and Vicky are still looking at her intently. "Because of the whole student sex thing. He still thought he was a seven. After *that*. He had—I asked him in private, and he said he really was a seven. 'I'm not perfect,' he said, 'but I see myself as basically a good person.'"

"Not to mention that he cheated on me in front of—"

"I didn't know about that. Obviously it means nothing when we think of the murders. But this had been a huge thing between us. I was more hurt than I described, despite the engagement. I would cry all the time; he knew how terrible it was for me. He admitted over and over how wrong he had been. I was paranoid for the first time about what he might be doing at any moment. He was a proven liar! Then he says he's a seven and believes it."

"I can imagine how you felt," Frances says slowly. She sits down across the table from Ember, next to Vicky.

"Because of that one thing I thought he might not have a conscience. He didn't defend himself; we just stayed away from each other for a week, and then I excused it all and ended up apologizing myself for being crazy."

"Why?" Frances asks.

"I decided that he meant he had *become* a seven because he had repented and would never do such a thing again. Right after it happened, he would have considered himself a one or a two or a negative number."

"Did you tell him this?"

"Yes."

"What did he say?"

"That he had hurt me worse than he'd thought, but my assumption was true."

"Yuck," Vicky mutters.

"I wonder if I should be as angry as Vicky is, if it wouldn't be healthier." She tells them about Jill and the grief group.

"Should we find something like that for Bridgett?"

"I can ask Jill." It has been less than two days, but Ember feels as if she left home months ago.

"I don't want to hear about everything I've already done wrong."

"Vicky, you didn't do anything wrong. You're in an unusual situation." Frances puts a hand on her arm.

Vicky makes a growling noise in the back of her throat.

"Maybe *you* should call Jill," Ember tells Vicky.

"I'd just as soon get advice from that transvestite."

"She's a grief counselor, for Pete's sake. Someone Ember knows and trusts."

Ember is relieved that Jill answers the phone quickly and provides the information without asking any questions. "That was abrupt," she tells Francis, "but she gave me some ideas. There are teen grief groups in Southern California, but it's a little different for Bridgett than most kids that have lost someone. Where's Vicky?"

"Horace's sister showed up. They're all in the yard. We can discuss this together later when Carl's here. Maybe Horace will distract Bridgett. Although we do need to be careful not to bother him."

"Do we have to stand around in a garden?"

"I don't much care for them myself."

29

When he was thirteen and living at the hospital for three months, a doctor named Leslie Burton introduced him to gardening.

"What you do, Richard, is you dig a hole, place something in it, then cover it up. With everything you bury, you put one problem or feeling that makes you angry or tense in the hole with it. Then you'll be worry free and something beautiful will grow. Vegetables are a favorite of mine, but you can grow flowers if you like. There are bushes, trees, whatever. Your mom told me you have a big backyard and that if you want to start gardening when you get out, you can have free reign of the whole space."

Dr. Burton never talked about the rape, which Richard's mother told him he should have gone to jail for. The parents of the girl were as mad at her as they were at him. The guys thought he was cool, but he hadn't done anything. He got a boner when she kissed him, but then when he pulled her skirt up and ripped her panties and she was scared and crying he lost it and didn't even want to shove it in her anymore, which had been his greatest fantasy up to that point. Instead he wanted to smash her head against the stony dirt until she was quiet, but they were outside on the hospital grounds and people heard her making noise and stopped him.

He now understood that some girls were for sex and others were to stay away from because they made you want to kill them. He had thought this one was for sex because other boys claimed to have done it with her, but listening to them had been a mistake.

He needed to figure it out on his own. The yelling and hysterical faces were too much to deal with.

"How do you know what to do with a girl?" Richard asked Dr. Burton.

"You ask them. You ask them what they want. They'll tell you. It's hard these days. Kids are confused, getting mixed signals from the media and their friends. I figured that's what happened with you and that girl. She's a bad seed."

"How can you tell if they're good or bad?"

"I'd suggest you keep to yourself for a while, young man. But when you're ready, you'll know who's good and who's bad. You're not going to want to mess around with the bad ones, or you'll end up in the kind of trouble you narrowly escaped this time. Prison with all men, televisions blaring, terrible food."

Richard already knew he didn't want to live in a cage being watched nonstop all day and all night. No hiding.

"Just bury the things you want to get rid of. We bury seeds because they're useless aboveground, but look what they become."

"What about if we bury garbage?"

Dr. Burton was moving his lower jaw back and forth the way he did when annoyed. He didn't like being asked the wrong questions.

He wasn't a psychologist but a general practice physician that checked up on the basic health needs of all in-house patients once a week. "I'm the only one who does anything useful around here" was one of his favorite claims. In Richard's opinion, since the doctor volunteered his services, and the Grangage Pediatric Psychiatric Hospital existed on reasonable fees, research grants, and state-funded assistance, no one minded what he said, as long as he protected the patients' physical well-being.

When Richard "graduated" at fifteen, he was their longest running weekday patient, even though he slept at home for all but three months of the ten years. Only the really messed up ones lived there the whole time.

30

"Lilac has actually started to work with flowers," Horace says dryly, after introducing her to Ember. Then he tells them about his experience with his namesake at Katherine's house.

Ember doesn't think Lilac is nearly as attractive as her brother although their features are similar. She has the same hair, which she wears shorter, and the same squarish face, but the dark recessed eyes with her pinkish skin make her appear ill.

"'Anger is a brief madness,'" Frances repeats. "When I was in high school we studied a biography written by the governor, or some relative of his, and it was all about Horace. It was used in every twelfth grade in the state for four or five years. We had to write all our papers for the class on it, and those that did the best won a prize. Probably a trip to the governor's mansion.

"It was interesting, except the teachers acted like they were pressured to have someone from their class write the best essay."

"Did Richard study that?" Ember asks Frances. "In school, did he study Horace?"

"Probably not that same book, but he was surely familiar with the writer."

"It's the title for this paper he's been working on forever. He'll never—I mean—" Her face is already flushed, and now she can feel the heat pushing into her eye sockets. "Never mind."

"Please tell me."

"Of course he used the expression 'a brief madness' to describe a lot of things, including the existence of humans. It's just that all the time he was writing his books and other papers, in spare moments he was working on this never-to-be-finished essay. It's over three hundred pages long, and he was continually saying it was his most important work. It's called, *A Brief Madness: Lapses* in *Justice from the Beginning of Man*. Everything else he wrote is so easy to read, but this is incomprehensible. He started it way back in grad school."

"Why the excitement?" Lilac whispers loudly.

"I have to show you something in back," Ember hears Horace say as she explains to Frances, "He starts with definitions and the history of related words, like *justice*, but without dates."

"He always hated dates," Frances says. "He hated having to memorize them. I was surprised he decided to major in history."

"He would tell his students on the first day of every term that 'without dates the history of man is a brief madness,' but he never made them learn any."

"And he never used them in his books."

"You've read them. No, he never did, which was the focus of his toughest criticism. Many historians never got past that."

"Of course I've read them. I have a signed copy of each."

"It's so odd you two have never met," Lilac says, edging back toward them.

"I'll tell you what's madness," Horace says, "and this will probably be brief as well—Lilac is growing flowers and giving them away. It's her current hobby. Why don't you sell them? I'll gladly spend the income."

"But it's such a pleasure to give stuff away. People love flowers and they're so expensive. We have no flower shop in Mariah," she tells Ember. "We have very few stores. They've almost all shut down. Legally we aren't really a town although we elect our own unpaid mayor. The capitol split us up a few years ago, so now we're petitioning to at least have the entire Mariah together. We don't expect independence, but come on. Towns need enterprise, movement—"

"And flowers, Lilac. If you sold them that would be an enterprise."

"I don't need the money."

"Trese sells his carvings." Horace tells Ember, "Her husband carves for a living."

"More like a hobby. I inherited money from my paternal grandparents. They left everything to me because our mom was rich from her father, and Horace was supposed to inherit from him too. He got this boardinghouse."

"She supports me though," he admits.

"Just until he writes that bestseller." Lilac touches Frances' arm. "Horace was telling me about that girl—"

"Oh, I forgot. Mrs. Dayle, we went by your house last night and Katherine removed the bug. It was just some toy radio deal, I doubt it worked."

"That's a relief. I was furious at first, but I've felt that someone—I almost thought it was supernatural, this creepy feeling I've had for months. It's nice to know it was only her I was sensing. She seems to be in a difficult situation."

"Things are very strange at that house. And I don't think she was exaggerating because I looked at the bottom of their pool. She says her brother is retarded, and her husband acts like she's his mother or something. I wonder if their dad is still alive."

Ember imagines the man endlessly searching for his lost daughter. Or married again with a whole new family. Probably he is dead or addicted to something that relaxes his mind. While it would be possible to never return, no one with a conscience could truly forget.

31

Bridgett wonders why no one ever tells her anything. Her mother is impossible and her grandparents do whatever her mom says. None of them noticed she was eavesdropping on Katherine, but they didn't think to share the story with her later.

Everything is terrible. No guys will ever want to date her since she's taller than all of them, and she just wants to die. Carl used to say that murderers should be put to death. What if Dad couldn't help killing people, and she takes after him? And why would he kill someone as young as Katherine's sister anyway? Why couldn't he have been murdering criminals instead? At least then he would be sort of heroic.

Carl is talking to her grandparents because she won't. She's mad at them and will wait in the basement with the stored food and paperback books for as long as it takes until it's time to leave. She's not even interested in what they are saying up there. None of these people know anything important.

"I don't see why Victy insists on remaining close to that Dayle woman," Grandma Andres said right in front of Bridgett when they got here. This grandma used to like Frances, but now she can't admit Bridgett is as much related to the Dayles as she is to the Andres.

It's a relief she didn't try to phone Myesha from Frances' house. The calls might have ended up on tape. When they were in France she called her best friend in Glendale briefly once a month since those grandparents watched their bills. She knows they never said anything to her mom because Mom would have been furious that she was talking to anyone outside the family.

Myesha gives her reports on Jason, the guy Bridgett was going out with. He doesn't have a new girlfriend, but he also hasn't grown at all in the last eight months. Myesha says Jason is hoping Bridgett will be back in time to start high school with them. High school!

Everyone still talks about her dad, and some people say she is dead too since she disappeared. If only her mom weren't such an idiot. An idiotic bitch. A *stupid* idiotic bitch. Insulting her mother makes the time go by faster, and soon Carl is calling her from the top of the stairs.

She doesn't answer him and he comes down, sounding more and more annoyed. "I know you're unhappy, but you don't have to be mean to *me*."

"It's not that," she says without knowing why, "it's just that I don't want to be called Bridgett anymore. I won't answer to it. I want to be called Venezuela."

Carl sighs, and she knows he is going to say that she's acting like a baby. "OK, Venezuela. And I want to be called China."

"That's a girl's name."

"Africa."

"Still. It can't end with an 'a.'"

"How about Brazil."

"OK. But really, you have to use it, I'm not just kidding."

"I know, Miss Venezuela."

"No, then I sound like a beauty pageant."

"A whole pageant, huh? All right, Venezuela. Let's go."

"OK, Brazil. But we must avoid the traitors at all cost. I don't want to say good-bye to them. And you can't stop playing even when Mom gets mad and says it's stupid. Promise you won't."

"I will play until you command me to stop, my royal dictatorship."

32

It bothered Richard that he couldn't remember the names of the women he had killed. There was no list or cache of newspaper clippings. He avoided reports of the crimes, but it would have relieved his mind immeasurably to have everything written down in an organized fashion.

In some ways he wanted their deaths to have meaning, to be part of a ceremony, but he didn't feel that he followed any system. All he knew was that some women were bad. If he told them his secrets, he killed them. If something prevented this exchange of information, it was easy for him to let them go.

Well, easy enough.

He preferred using his hands in strangulation, or breaking their necks. He didn't want to deal with blood. He didn't want to have sex with them before or after their deaths. He just wanted to bury them three to four feet under the ground. The burial was the main purpose, but even that involved nothing more than digging a hole and then covering it up.

After analyzing this, wondering if he shouldn't try it with an animal to see if he found the same satisfaction, he accepted that the limited ability of other creatures to comprehend human discourse would result in an unproductive experience.

He had extensive insight into the typical serial killer's inspiration: the compulsion was to repeatedly destroy a memory or emotion. It wasn't that way with him. He wanted to believe he didn't fit any of the usual molds, but years of studying up on the subject had taught him that there was no definitive profile. It was impossible to avoid patterns the experts didn't know existed.

The likelihood of capture seemed insignificant, but he feared posthumous exposure. He had willed the garden plot to Ember, asking her to leave it to Bridgett; by the time they were both gone, nothing should be traceable.

Richard was the Secret Garden's first customer; later most plots were leased rather than sold. He was disconcerted by the name, which the presumed property owner said was based on a granddaughter's favorite book. Walter Altman claimed to have come up with the brilliant idea to rent out garden plots to condo dwellers that missed the land, and he was upset when Richard informed him that others were already doing the same thing.

"Is it any less creative to invent an idea on your own if someone has thought of it before?" Walter asked, his eyes watering.

So far the place was empty, which was why Richard had been able to convince him to permit the purchase of two portions in the dark jungly area (Walter's description), on the left side of the fence, and one in the middle of the hill on the right that looked out over a busy road.

"I wasn't going to do anything with that weedy place," Walter said slowly, going back to Richard's proposition, which had already been signed and paid for.

"Just rent out the hill first like you planned," Richard said. "It will be nice for me to have some privacy."

By the time Richard died both sides of the road were fully cultivated with mostly twelve-by-twelve-foot garden patches. His central hill area followed those general terms, and he owned a space of thirty-by-ten feet to the left. It was on the smaller plot that he had his fatal heart attack—in sight of a bend in the road although somewhat protected from view by the 50-mile-an-hour speed limit.

Richard was still mulling over having disappointed the moody entrepreneur by pedantically informing him of his lack of originality. He hoped the man wouldn't rip up the hastily written contract.

"I wonder when my granddaughter's going to bring my beer and newspaper," Walter muttered. "I'm thirsty."

"Yes, a drink would be nice. So. This was all your idea," Richard said admiringly. They were sitting under a large umbrella in the rocky area where the broad hill flattened out. It would later become a parking lot for the gardeners.

"Yes, I gave my granddaughter *The Secret Garden*. She loved it. Or maybe her mother gave it to her. But I came up with the name for this town. My wife's name was Deborah, but sometimes I called her Monica. A true saint."

The granddaughter arrived and introduced herself as Patty, the owner of the place. To Richard's relief she approved his contract. His payment added up to about ten years' worth of rent, but it was much cheaper than buying property.

He didn't think he could stand to live on the ground again after being in a condo for so long, and it was also imperative to keep Ember separate from the garden.

"We can really use this money," Patty said. "Grandpa's easy, but everyone else! Hopefully this place will succeed cause I can work another job while the tenants take care of themselves. There won't be nearly as much trouble as renting a residence."

"I have a huge loan out on this land, so it's got to pay off."

"Well, good luck," Richard said, saluting Walter and shaking hands with Patty.

"You take good care of that jacket, young man. Patty's husband went to jail for a jacket like that. He's the best consumer spy the industry ever saw."

Patty rolled her eyes so hard her head moved in a half circle as well, then winked at Richard, who nodded politely and walked to his car, glancing over his shoulder and waving a couple of times before he got there. He never saw Walter again; he never forgot him either, which was more than he could say for the women he had buried.

33

Horace has written an entire paragraph since his sister left. Having all these people in the house seems to be giving him energy. The problem is that he's tired of his four-month-old pages about a woman who wants to reproduce with her brother's sperm. His character thinks she and her sibling have the perfect DNA to create the next Les Paul-like inventor and guitarist. According to her, the taboo against inbreeding is merely for genetic diversity, and Horace has her currently trying to obtain a copy of her brother's DNA readout. He has reached page three.

One of his worries is that Les Paul might not be widely enough known, although he doesn't want to resort to a stock genius like Einstein or Mozart. More importantly, he can't decide whether to make the story sensual instead of focusing entirely on logic.

He isn't interested in writing about the people downstairs, but their presence is giving him fresh ideas. A new character has entered his mind, a man who is growing marijuana and has the reoccurring desire to do cartwheels. He might be a tornado chaser or a former teen idol, but all that will come out later. In the background a struggling small town diner is starting to take shape, lots of grease and a pretty waitress who deserves something better . . .

Thinking about these characters is enough for now. For authors, he has read, the mulling process is as important as the actual writing.

He decides to go downstairs and subtly grill the women for their life stories. Hopefully Carl and the little kid aren't back yet.

He finds Victy and Ember at the table looking lethargic with drooping shoulders and half-closed eyes.

"Hey, Victy, Ember. I'm taking a break."

"Vi-key."

Ember sits up straighter. "Are you writing a book?"

"Well, I'm working on a short story at the moment, but who knows what it might turn into."

"What's it about?" Vicky asks wearily.

"Fiction writers hate that question," Ember says.

"I suppose you would know, being married to Richard." Vicky makes a snorting noise.

"Richard wrote biographies," Ember tells Horace, "but they delved into the unknowable, so he gave the readers options as to what might have happened in certain situations."

"She's still quoting him," Vicky tells the air.

"They weren't fictional biographies or historical fiction. He created a new genre."

"When I knew him," Vicky said, "he loved to be asked what he was writing about. He would tell you even if you didn't ask. He would go on and on and on."

"I was speaking from my own experience with poetry."

"Poetry, that's great," Horace says. Then he asks the question he most dreads: "Have you been published?"

"A couple of times in college, but since then I've kept it to myself. I'm not very good, I just like arranging words—um, have you?"

"Not yet."

There's an awkward silence. Frances comes into the kitchen and greets them with a vague smile. "I hope we're not bothering you, Horace?"

"Oh no."

"Sit down, I'll fetch you a slice of bread."

The whole guest thing is less nerve wracking than it would have been if Frances hadn't paid for five days up front. He trusts her, but it's nice to have the money. On the first of May when Lilac or Trese brings his monthly allowance by, he won't be waiting and feeling desperate. It's much, much worse with Trese, who draws the encounter out, pretends he has forgotten the purpose for the visit, and makes endless inane small talk.

"I'm glad to have you here," he says suddenly. He feels his face flush as the women turn to him.

"It's nice to be here, to have everyone around. I find it easier to talk away from my house. You don't do any journalism, Horace?"

"No, and I would never repeat anything."

"Your parents would kill you," Vicky says.

"Is everyone getting over it?" Frances asks Horace abruptly.

"They blame you less since you put your house up for sale, and everyone agrees you should stay here. My mom thinks people are ready to treat you like someone who suffered a regular death in the family, but no one is sure how to begin."

"We're home," Bridgett yells. She comes into the kitchen looking defiant.

"What's going on?" Carl asks, entering behind her.

"We're just sitting around. How was the visit?"

"They were rude," Bridgett says. "They don't want us here. They want us at *their* house."

"Bridgett hid in the basement."

"Car-al!"

"Sorry, Venezuela hid in the basement."

"Don't say *anything*, Mom. Anything about anything. I'm off to change my clothes from these stupid ones your parents gave me, which don't fit right anyway."

Bridgett leaves and Vicky makes a face.

"I'm sorry—" Frances begins.

"What's this Venezuela thing?"

"She wants to be called that."

"She's acting like a baby. Fourteen is too old for name games."

Carl puts his hands on Vicky's shoulders as she starts to get up and begins to massage them. "It's no use fighting over this. I think we should let her act a little immature if that's what she needs. She's going through a lot, Vicky, we've got to be easier on her."

"Oh, Jill. I called Jill, Vicky. She gave me a list of ideas to tell you. About the grieving thing." Ember leans back to pull a folded piece of paper out of her pants' pocket, and Horace notices her smooth, pale skin and flat belly button before her shirt covers it again. "She mentioned a grief group for teens but said it might be complicated in Bridgett's situation. Mainly we should let her say whatever she wants on the subject without disapproval or shock. Ask her what she needs. Get a picture of the person—of Richard, and ask her to talk about him, share her memories, etcetera. Ask about her experience with his death, dreams she's had, and—oh, this one's good—she can write a letter to the deceased saying good-bye." Ember finishes in a rush and looks up from the sheet.

Horace assumes she's wondering if Vicky can do those things without throwing a fit. They all jump as the doorbell starts its merry song, and he gets up to answer it.

"Hi," says Katherine.

"Come in, we're all in the kitchen. How are the bowling balls working?"

"Thank you so much. We left the yellow one out, and my mom thought it was very cheerful. She went on and on about how she used to love to bowl when she was a kid."

"How'd you get here?" They are in the kitchen entryway and Katherine waves at the tired room. The doorbell finally stops.

"In our van—we share it with some neighbors. I left it at Frank's yesterday. He and his dad acted really strange when they brought it back. I wish they hadn't seen the place."

"Hey, Bridgett," Horace says.

"Hi, Horace. Hi, Katherine."

"How do you—" Vicky begins.

"I heard you all talking yesterday. I heard the whole story."

Horace motions them to the chairs and runs upstairs to find another one. He puts it at the head of the oval table so he is across from Frances. This feels official. Ember passes him his half-eaten piece of bread on a paper towel.

"I just felt lonely for someone to talk to," Katherine is saying. "I'm sick of discussing it endlessly with my family. They're just not—I guess they'd rather not hear about it anymore."

"Is there a grief group nearby?" Ember asks.

"I doubt it."

"We should start our own," Bridgett says.

Horace looks at Vicky, who is now having her head massaged with her eyes closed. He is the misfit here; if he stays he might regret it when everyone becomes weepy and depressed.

"That's a nice idea," Katherine says.

"I don't know about this," Vicky mutters.

Carl whispers something to her.

"Well, should we do it?"

"Go ahead, Ember," Frances says.

"OK." Ember takes an audible breath and lets it out. "I was always afraid my husband would die young because heart problems run in his family. He refused to go to the doctor for a checkup. I'm sure he wanted me to worry. Before I met him I didn't think about death much, but after I would often imagine all the horrible things that could happen to him. Mainly heart attacks and car wrecks. He was so amazing, and he loved me so much. It seemed perfect." She shakes her head.

Bridgett tells her, "I'm afraid that I might be like my dad, and that's why I was hidden away. Maybe I'm a murderer too and everyone knows but me."

"You're not a murderer," Ember says.

Vicky is biting the joint in her index finger.

"Dad didn't kill people until he was older. Maybe his dad did the same thing."

"No, his dad didn't kill anyone. But yours—"

"We're all just saying whatever we want," Vicky interrupts in a high voice. "I tried so hard to protect Bridgett from these horrible things. Don't you worry about her sanity?"

"It might help Bridgett to know that when Richard was five he was involved in the death of a little boy who was badly crippled."

"Yes, I'm sure that will help a lot."

"The babysitter said Richard was sitting on a pillow on his face when she came into the room. Scott never could walk; he was in a crib at the time. After talking to Richard about it, I believed her. He admitted it was on purpose and he had a reason, but who can know if he really understood. He went into counseling at Grangrage until he was fifteen. I got the receptionist job I still have at the facility to help pay for everything, and we pretended Richard went to a school nearby for convenience. He had a tutor but didn't receive much regular education until his sophomore year of high school although he was still at the top of the class at graduation.

"I don't know if the counseling made him what he became, or if it just didn't stop it. I wondered that before, when he had problems with a girl at thirteen. He lived at the hospital for months then."

Bridgett stares at the table and a couple of tears slide down her cheeks. "I didn't know five year olds..." After a silence she says, "When Dad died no one would tell me anything, and I lost all my friends and my school too. It was like everything disappeared at once. It was like we were criminals because we left the whole country and people connect us to what happened."

"To what happened?" Katherine says indignantly. "What happened was that my sister was killed. It's completely worse for people that love the victims than for people that loved the bad guy. Dad was supposed to give her a ride to the school play, which her boyfriend was in, but he forgot. We looked for her everywhere, everyone did. We both worked as clerks at Artie's Groceries, and I was staying for another shift so she could leave early.

"She and I slept in bunk beds in the same room, and every week we would change the sheets and switch who had top or bottom. Singing was her favorite thing to do. She and Johnny wanted to go to New York and be Broadway stars.

"We would watch the news and be afraid that every terrible thing they mentioned was being done to her. We worried about rape and torture. That she'd been kidnapped and sold into slavery—we couldn't think of anything good because good things never happen to people her age that disappear. When we found out she was dead—I guess we already knew she was dead because nothing else was possible. Her neck was broken. That just seems like it would hurt, no matter how fast it happened."

Vicky is gnawing on her knuckle now, and Carl, still standing, is holding her other hand.

Horace realizes his hand is at his neck and quickly lowers it.

"I felt scared for my own life after Richard died," Vicky says, "It was senseless and selfish, but I kept—I *keep* getting chills up and down my body, and I wonder why he didn't kill me. It turns out he was doing it the whole time we were married. When he would call me a 'good girl,' his dumb pet name, he would rub my neck. He loved thin necks, and I teased him about having a fetish. Since hearing about the two women who were strangled—"

Bridgett makes a choking noise.

"—I keep wondering, we never got along that well, why did he kill them and not me?"

"Oh my God. We knew him, we knew that guy." Katherine looks around with unfocused eyes. "The police couldn't find anyone that fit his description. He was in disguise, of course, we knew that from the first. He said he was a famous singer hiding out from his fans and the media. Alyssa was really excited and would ask him all sorts of questions about getting a recording contract. He wore big, dark sunglasses, and he had a goatee and long mustache."

Vicky catches Ember's eye and shakes her head, then repeats the movement to Horace when she sees him staring.

Katherine continues, "I described him for the police. He came into the store, that's how we met him." She hunches her shoulders down. "He was very friendly. He would tell Alyssa she could be famous. Stupid bastard. We just thought it was a joke—mild flirting. He always paid cash and he'd tip us." Her tone becomes intense: "I guess she might have gotten in a car with him.

"I know the last two were strangled, but they can't tell about my sister. Besides her broken neck, they can't tell what else he might've done to her. They can't tell how long he had her first."

Horace wonders about this discussion idea. Family of victim with family of perpetrator might not be such a brilliant combination.

"I wish he were here so we could ask him things," Bridgett says fretfully. "It's terrible not knowing what happened or what he thought."

"Then you might have to watch him be punished," Katherine tells her. "Of course, that's why *I* wish he was here."

"Would you want him to be in jail his whole life or get the death penalty?" Horace asks. "Because then he would be dead anyway."

"At least he would have to suffer. He would know what he did was wrong."

"So you don't believe in some system of punishment or reward after death? Millions of people do. It helps them deal with the unfairness of life."

"Do you?" Katherine asks him.

"No, but I don't need to . . . yet. At least not as much as people that have suffered like ya'll."

"It's something that comforts most of my grief group. They're always saying it was God's decision someone was taken."

"Then why do they go to a grief group?" Bridgett asks.

"Bridgett, if you would like to go to church—any church you want—that would be fine with me."

"You told me that before, Mom. And I've been to churches. A Baptist one here with your parents, and a Catholic one in Britain with your grandparents." She explains politely to the rest of them, "Mom's grandparents used to live in Britain. They retired to France because the health care was better."

"You told me that they lived in a town called Condom," Horace says.

"It's true. Right, Mom?"

"There's really a town called Condom? Condom City, we wear them right," Katherine teases Bridgett. "Did they invent them there?"

"No one knows," Vicky says. "A condom is actually a *preservatif* in French, so . . ."

"I need to go upstairs for a minute," Horace says, standing. He just might have an idea for a new story.

34

Ember feels trapped, repeatedly peeking down the hall to see if it's her turn for the bathroom. Vicky is always in there. At least when she shared with three siblings she was able to yell at them and bang on the door.

At home she felt that the loneliness was gnawing at her sanity, but being with people makes her wish for her private space where she doesn't need to worry about her clothes or look in a mirror.

There she has her job five days a week as a manager at a marketing firm for the major movie studios. Before Richard's death she planned to quit since her more fulfilling position as director at a women's shelter was about to be extended to full time. It was clear why the Board of Directors for the shelter withdrew that offer when the crimes were publicized, asking her not to return even on a volunteer basis, but a chance to resign would have been preferable. There was no time for her to take any action: their formal letter arrived before she had fully accepted his guilt.

One of the tenants in her building is a doctor, and years ago Ember convinced her to volunteer at the shelter one night a week. Now she wonders if the woman still goes there; she thinks about surreptitiously watching the shelter's entrance on Wednesday evenings to see. It would be nice to know that even one thing she arranged back when she was an enthusiastic member of the management team is still functional.

She is the sole beneficiary of Richard's life insurance policy, for which she opened a special savings account. Although so far she has only used the money for donations to various causes, she is constantly tempted to withdraw it all and bury it in the garden plot, which she also inherited (with instructions to keep but never visit). She has yet to respond to the owner's offer to buy the plot back.

If only he had been caught before he died, then everyone could have asked for an explanation.

Frances taps on her partially open door, and Ember straightens her shoulders out of their deep slouch.

"Are you still waiting for the bathroom?"

"Yes."

"I'm afraid you missed your moment. Bridgett just traded places with her mom. I'm worried about her. Horace said someone was on his computer and has gone through his drawers."

"What day is it?"

"Friday. The computer incident took place earlier in the week; his hunting knife went missing today."

"It must be Katherine. She's been around constantly."

"Maybe." Frances sits next to her on the bed. "I can't believe you're all going home so soon."

They both sigh deeply.

"Vicky's mother called me. In one breath she said she had been unfair and then invited me to her younger daughter's baby shower.

"I don't think we've even mentioned Richard in the last couple of days, but talking about it all did help, didn't it?"

Ember nods. "What about his letters?" She has asked Frances this daily and is tempted to enlist Katherine in a little thievery.

"Oh, of course. Let's plan on that tomorrow."

This is the usual response, but Ember assumes she will see them eventually. They sit in companionable silence until Vicky starts calling for Bridgett.

35

When Bridgett borrowed Frances' mobile phone to call Myesha today, she was told that Jason had been seen holding hands with an unknown girl at the mall. A girl that looked a lot like Bridgett but was his same height with a tiny, tiny waist, breasts, and long hair. Myesha sounded a little too admiring, and she got off the phone a little too quickly when someone arrived to pick her up.

Now when she goes back to school Bridgett will be the only one without a waist, breasts, long hair, a boyfriend, or a best friend. And almost worst of all, she will be the only one *with* a father that would have gone to prison for life if he still had a life.

She will have to eat lunch all alone. Maybe people will throw food and bits of paper at her, like they did to that one girl.

Sitting on the toilet lid, ignoring her awful mother (who was in here way longer anyway), she is trying to cry quietly so everyone won't be all over her. Mom will say there are lots of boys, and she can make new friends, and the others will think she's sad because of the stupid dad who she doesn't even care about any longer.

Ember might have understood before, but now she seems tired of Bridgett. Only Katherine is really nice, and Bridgett's excited to tell her how she took Horace's knife. It's long and curved with a fancy sheath. When she touched the blade to her hand earlier it made an almost painless little stinging cut.

She pulls the knife out of the front of her pants and removes it from the sheath, then runs it lightly across her wrist. A sudden string of blood pops out. She knows you have to cut in the other direction to slit your wrists, but she's still careful. It hurts a little and eases her worries over Jason.

She makes some more lines across her left wrist, and then marks up the right to match. Drawing it lightly against the base of her throat doesn't do anything except tingle, so she presses a little harder. In the mirror she sees a tiny trickle of blood. Her dad didn't like the sight of blood; maybe that's why he killed people with his hands. Katherine says he probably had a neck fixation.

She swipes a couple more times at her neck. The collar of her yellow shirt is getting drips on it, and they probably won't come out. Maybe she'll throw it away so she doesn't have to listen to the Mighty Bitch go on about it for ten years.

That's enough cutting, but she won't clean the knife off; it will scare Horace when he looks at it again. She giggles aloud.

"Bridgett?" It's Ember. "Can I come in and brush my teeth? Frances is leaving for the night, and she wants to say good-bye."

Bridgett holds her breathe and can hear her heart banging. She sticks the knife in its sheath and puts it in the front of her pants again. There's a dark blue towel hanging over the shower curtain. She holds it up against her neck with her palms facing inward, covering the knife too. In the mirror she can't see any blood, but she almost drops the towel when unlocking and opening the door.

"You can have the bathroom." She forces her voice to sound cheerful, but Ember stops her before she leaves.

"What's wrong with you?"

Ember pulls at one of Bridgett's arms, and the towel falls.

"Oh Bridgett, what were you doing?"

The knife is a hard shape under her shirt, and Ember finds it before Bridgett can stop her.

"Have you been cutting yourself?"

"Shut up." Bridgett tries to move around her, but Frances is coming down the hall.

"What's wrong? Bridgett, what happened?"

"I think she's been cutting herself."

Her mom adds her voice to the noise.

"Be quiet!" Bridgett shrieks. "If you don't stop yelling at me I'll kill you all!"

They freeze.

Carl pushes by them and pulls Bridgett back onto the toilet seat. He wets one corner of the towel and gently brushes off the mostly dried blood. "Let's go find the ointment in your mom's bathroom bag."

He leads her past the women to his room and shuts the door behind them.

"I don't think you'll have scars."

"I don't care," she mutters.

"What are you upset about?"

"Jason." She's going to cry. Carl hands her a tissue and rubs ointment on her sores.

"Did you talk to Jason?"

"No, I haven't talked to him since we left, but Myesha told me he was holding hands with another girl."

"That bastard!" Carl says, and Bridgett has to laugh at how mad he sounds. Carl never says words like bastard. "It's a good thing we're going home soon; I've been needing to practice my Kung Fu."

"You don't know Kung Fu."

"Yes, I do."

"Mom's going to freak out."

"She'll be afraid you were trying to hurt yourself."

"It barely hurt. I was just seeing what it was like."

"Why did you take the knife?"

"I was going to put it back."

"Lie down in here so I can intercept your mother and explain that you weren't trying to kill yourself."

"I wasn't."

Carl watches her take her shoes off and then tucks her fully dressed under the covers. She feels him kiss her forehead and hears him leave with a warm, heavy feeling as she falls asleep.

36

Since Richard employed a reputable chauffeuring service for Ember, he was furious to learn that one of the drivers had taken her to his apartment and become verbally abusive when she refused to enter. It was then she admitted that for some time the young man had been making increasingly inappropriate personal comments.

Although the driver resigned the same day, Richard was still uneasy. Unlike parenthood, loving Ember had provided him with a life to worry over as obsessively as he did his own. Bridgett was a pleasure; he never imagined alarming things happening to her, but he was constantly worried over Ember's health and well-being. In bad moments late at night his mind fixated on tragedies, and he then spent considerable sums of money making sure they never transpired. The condo was safe; the marketing office where she later worked evening shifts was satisfactory. The women's clinic was more stressful even though she was there during daylight hours. It was in a bad area with a single guard for security. Richard only hinted that he would like her to drop her shelter work; she had shown herself to be very stubborn on that topic.

Before their marriage Richard was fascinated by Ember and wildly attracted to her, but he wasn't in love. He didn't know this until he was suddenly experiencing the wonderful and terrifying emotion for the first time. Thinking back he could never remember exactly when it happened, or started to happen, or when he first acknowledged it, but it was very soon after their wedding.

Prior to legalized partnership they lived together for a couple of weeks. Minor things relieved him, such as her fairly even temperament and ability to prepare quickly for an outing. He liked how she could sit still for long periods of time, either while reading, watching movies, or staring off into space over one of her poems.

With love came a sense of headiness that lasted for about three months. She appeared perfect to him, and then he learned to treasure her for her limitations. As the first delicious emotions wore off, the worrying began.

He later wished he could have protected her without causing alarm, but his fear was so unexpected that he didn't think his response through in advance. After he decided he had done all he could, he forced himself to stop before destroying their relationship. And even though he pressed his hand against the left side of his chest when he wished for more frequent phone calls, he was careful not to overuse the trick.

Years passed, and he didn't appreciate his wife as deeply every day, but when reminded by another woman's death, he was relieved and grateful that his loved one was still alive. This wasn't something he was going to forfeit to a burgeoning psychopath, despite any hazard his actions might cause for himself.

He obtained the address from the chauffeuring company and visited at three the next morning. The boy opened his door absently, half-asleep but unconcerned. "I'm Ember Oto's husband," Richard said, pushing into the small entryway. "Let's shut the door and converse for a moment." He spoke calmly, and his eyes looked directly into the young man's. "Your behavior was repulsive. If you interact with my wife again, you will have accepted an invitation to spend the final month of your life alone with me."

Even after his point had been made and the boy's terror was apparent, Richard continued, this time in a hiss, "Killing's easy. I have suffocated and strangled, and torture won't upset me," leaving his wife's former driver entirely convinced of the type of man his beloved had married.

37

"I've let you decide everything since Richard died," Carl tells Vicky as he leaves the bedroom, "but now you need to listen to me. We're going home to California and putting Bridgett back in school. Her old school or a new school, whichever she prefers. We'll take her to talk to Jill, or someone Jill recommends. And we are going to let her say whatever she wants about her dad."

"How can—you aren't—"

"Her real father?" he asks.

Frances cringes. Vicky collapses crying onto the floor, and Carl scoops her up.

"I'm going to be her father. You said you'd marry me—let's do it as soon as we can get the license. If Bridgett will let me, I'll legally adopt her. She needs as much order as possible. I believe she wasn't trying to kill herself; she was just depressed because her boyfriend was seen with another girl."

Carl is rocking Vicky and seems to be feeling her weight. "Let's sleep in Bridgett's room tonight. I don't want to disturb her."

"But we have to watch," is what Frances thinks Vicky mumbles.

"I'll stay with her," she says quickly.

Carl carries Vicky into the bedroom.

"I'll give this knife to Horace tomorrow," Ember tells Francis after Carl shuts the door.

"He must be out somewhere or he'd have come down."

"But what about Bridgett?"

"I don't know. Did you do anything like that when you were a teenager?"

"I wasn't as careful as my parents wanted me to be."

"Sometimes teenagers don't think they're ever going to die. That's different than trying to make it happen."

"I was jealous when Carl was holding Vicky," Ember admits, looking at the ground. She adds quickly, "Not for Carl—"

"Does it seem like you never had a real relationship with Richard?" Francis asks gently. "Now that you know, I mean?"

"He was wonderful to me after we were married." Ember laughs. "He was egotistical sometimes and controlling other times, but wonderful in between. I just can't—" She sighs. "Maybe he had a problem he couldn't help? I've been thinking about what you said, when he was a little kid—wouldn't that mean . . . I don't know."

"Let's go sit down near Bridgett. We can talk quietly and make sure she doesn't wake up and cause any more trouble."

"I'll tell you all the good deeds Richard did." She sighs again. "Do you still love him?"

Frances doesn't want to answer casually, but she isn't sure how to describe her feelings. "You love your children unconditionally."

"Do you?"

"I don't know, Ember. I still love him in some manner."

"Perhaps if we don't hate him then we're depreciating all those lives he stole."

"Come on now," Frances puts her hand around Ember's wrist. "We'll only speak of the cheerful things."

Part Three

38

Ember feels the world shudder when Bridgett is arrested. After listening to Vicky's frantic phone message, she spends the next few hours in a panic.

Vicky finally calls again that night and insists on coming over with a very subdued husband and daughter. Full of nervous energy, she tells Ember how the mother of Montgomery Lloyd, Bridgett's boyfriend, wanted fifteen-year-old Bridgett charged with attempted murder. This turned against her son of eighteen when he vehemently insisted it had been a sex game gone awry.

Ember doesn't dare minimize the situation by asking whether Bridgett was truly arrested, as the rushed message had claimed.

"But it wasn't a sex game or attempted murder," Vicky says triumphantly.

Neither Bridgett nor Carl stops staring at the floor. Ember hasn't seen Bridgett much this past year. In the summer months after they returned from Georgia, Vicky let Bridgett stay over for five or six days at a time. Then after high school started, the teenager lost all interest in adults.

Nearly a hundred percent of Bridgett's conversations during the summer had consisted of how terrible school was going to be and how no one would like her. She whined and cried and moaned, and Ember reassured her endlessly, taking every approach possible to show Bridgett how she could survive any situation. It was quite tedious, and when Bridgett started school Ember felt at first unburdened, then annoyed, as the girl kept breaking plans without notice to do this or that with her new friends.

"This is a horrible thing to say, Vicky," Ember risked announcing over the phone two months into the school year. Bridgett had contacted her mother and informed her that the dinner theatre plans she had begged Ember for had lost out to a "last-minute" football game. "Well, you might think it is. I feel quite good about it at the moment. Since I had to listen to that weeping and wailing and gnashing of teeth all summer, I just wish one of those worries had come true. Then all my forced sympathy and headache medication wouldn't have been entirely wasted."

Vicky laughed hard and immediately repeated what Ember had said to Carl. "How did you put it, about the sympathy?"

Then Vicky asked, "And did you catch that it was a *last minute* football game?"

"I missed that. Well, do you like dinner theatre? I have an extra ticket."

Vicky accompanied her, and they both agreed it was more fun without Bridgett.

Bridgett's first year of high school has now officially ended. Her grades were all boring Bs, but Vicky has heard rumors that the child is trading in on her dead father's reputation to gain respect. Refusing to be called a "freshman" was her other triumph, and the replacement, "hottwoman," became popular among the girls.

Carl is still losing weight. Ember has seen him a few times at the restaurant where he is the executive chef. The place has become low-cal gourmet and popular enough with the semi-famous for paparazzi to swarm at times. She wishes she had gone in the past before everyone else discovered it.

"Darcy—that's the boy's mother—and I made a deal that we would both keep quiet about our child's part as long as they didn't see each other again. Thank God she has as much stake in it as I do. If he were seventeen we would be in a lot of trouble."

Ember assumes she means with the media.

"Bridgett wouldn't talk to us about it unless we came here. Not that she deserves any privileges—"

"I wanted a reasonable person present," Bridgett says.

"I'm not reasonable?" Carl's voice is low.

Ember asks her what is going on, thinking that Carl's demeanor would shame anyone not in her teens.

"It's hard to explain," Bridgett begins rather proudly. "Gummy—"

"Gummy!" Vicky says incredulously.

"Mom, you *know* that's what people call him."

"It's just that Montgomery is such a *nice* name."

"Gummy is really different. He plays lead guitar in a band called Selppin. And he sings. The name has a hidden message if you can get it." She gloats a little, not seeing her mom's look of contempt. "He's the only person who I can tell *everything*, and he really understands me. We're really just friends too—he has a girlfriend who goes to UC Berkley. I told him about Richard. I told him about when I cut myself and you all freaked out, but he said it made sense. I was manifesting my internal pain on my external being. I told him how I was afraid I might be a killer because I want to murder people all the time. He said everyone feels like committing homicide—"

"We've told you that," Vicky says.

"—and that hardly anyone ever does it. He said I could start to kill him to see if I liked it. If I didn't, then I would know I was OK. If I did, he said I should get help. So I was going to strangle—to pretend to strangle him with a noose-like thing but I wasn't strong enough. Then we tried a bread knife, but it was way too dull and didn't do anything but create white lines on his stomach. He said it hurt like hell—I mean, bad. His mom came in when I was trying to hit him over the head with a pan. I guess she saw him get it from the kitchen and was being nosey. He says she's a—a nosey person. It was a really heavy old frying pan, and I had just sort of dropped it from a few feet above. On his head. He was sitting on the floor, and I was on the bed. Anyway, he was a little dazed when his mom came in, so he couldn't explain until she had already run away screaming and called the police. She's crazy.

"Anyway, it was just a game. I like him, so I wouldn't want him dead. He's my best friend in the world.

"This has nothing to do with Richard dying. I don't even care about that. I'm glad he did. Carl is my real dad."

Carl doesn't look grateful, but when he gives the first strict speech of his parenting career, they all listen: "You have to quit your job at the video store, and you can't get your learner's permit unless you meet with a counselor once a week all summer. I don't care if you won't be able to get your license when you're sixteen. I do not recommend arguing with me about this."

Carl has always taken the easy-going, friendly approach with Bridgett, and she never appreciated it. Ember thinks it must be a relief for Vicky not to have to be the mean one for once.

"You can see your friends at home, or at Ember's, if she doesn't mind, but never without one of the three of us present. If you break these rules, we will put you in summer school, and if that doesn't work, a boarding school in another state with bars on the windows."

Bridgett is staring ahead sullenly, but she doesn't say anything.

Carl continues, "If you have any ideas about what might help you, please suggest them to us, and we'll see what we can do."

Ember thinks Bridgett might obey him—at least until the shock of his new role wears off. She wonders if the girl is a danger they need to prevent, and if success in this case will compensate for their failure to stop Richard. Then she jiggles her head in annoyance at the nonsensical drama residing there and glances up to see her three guests watching with very odd expressions on their faces.

39

Jill stares peacefully over Bridgett's shoulder during their second session together as the girl repeats "Fuck, fuck, fuck, fuck" in a dull monotone. Jill isn't shocked or dismayed. Nor is she frightened that this little wretch is festering murderous tendencies. Although people often replicate their parents' behavior, socially unacceptable though it may be, she doesn't think Bridgett is going to kill anyone. However, she will keep getting into senseless trouble if her anger and angst aren't given a more salubrious focus. In Jill's opinion humans are all dangerous and highly unlikable at this age, and Bridgett, with her traumatic example of a father, is in a whole new category.

When Jill was preparing to see Bridgett for the first time, almost a year ago, she decided to approach the girl as she would someone who had been sexually abused by a parent—or at least to think of her that way. In her opinion Bridgett has been comparatively lucky.

Jill wishes she were sitting behind her desk instead of companionably face-to-face with her patient. The "fuck" is still continuing, and she has an urgent itch a little too close to her crotch area. The shaving of her pubic hair is causing it—or not that so much as the decision to grow it back. She hadn't meant to clear everything away in the first place; she was trying to make a daisy shape while sloppily drunk. She woke up lying on her back with her mouth full of water. The shower was on and the drain open. She likes to joke to her friends that overcoming alcoholism has made her unable to hold her liquor.

From the changing tone of voice, it's clear that Bridgett is starting to feel humiliated by her repetition. If she isn't provided with a way to stop she will begin to cry, loathing Jill even more than she does already.

"I meditate too," Jill interrupts, "but my mantra is 'Episcopalian.' Lovely word, huh? Always makes me crave scalloped pasta noodles. Then I end up ordering Italian food, which is far more relaxing than meditation anyway. Of course it keeps me plump."

"You're not plump, you're voluptuous," Bridgett says with polite relief.

"Hmm. I'm not sure about that, but it sounds good."

"Carl tells Mom she is when she thinks she's getting fat. He's a cook, but lately he's been losing weight and she hasn't."

"I've been to his restaurant—I hear it's been ruined in the name of health. Your mom must like to work out."

"You mean because of the Clean Cut?"

"Yes, it's supposed to be a great health club. All women though, which is why I don't belong."

"Where do you go?"

"I hike in the foothills now and then. And get massages. Does that count?"

Bridgett nods. "That's very healthy."

"Are you close to Ember?"

Bridgett nods again.

Jill has received Ember's approval at being a topic of discussion, so she continues: "I'm worried about her. She's been going to my grief group for almost two years now, but I'm not sure it's helping. Do you have any ideas?"

"She was very in love with Richard."

"That's true."

They are quiet for a few moments.

"Maybe she feels bad because she didn't know a lot of things about him. I mean, he kept secrets almost no one else ever has before."

"Doesn't everyone have secrets?"

Bridgett thinks about this. "People might have their privacy, or not have told everything about themselves, but his kind of secret is different."

"How was it different?"

"First of all he was breaking one of the most important laws."

"What makes some laws more important than others?"

"I don't know. The punishments, maybe. I guess there's nothing worse than killing someone who doesn't want to die and wouldn't hurt anyone if they stayed alive. Even war is just murder, and the people that are in charge should be punished . . . if everything is fair in the end."

"Do you mean after death?"

"I mean whenever."

"Do you believe everything will even out in the end?"

"I don't know. No."

"Then what happens?"

"I guess we just try to do better—so everyone can have better lives. If we all improve then less pointless deaths occur. I guess that's modern evolution or something. Really it would be easier if there were the whole God and judgment day thing. That's why people like it, I suppose. We can't understand how it will all be measured and figured out, but if we say that someone better and smarter than us will deal with it, we can relax and not worry so much about the point of—of whatever, of suffering. Laws are just the best we can do. Like some people believe in karma. My parents sometimes mention it, and Ember once said that she liked people that believed in karma. I think karma is a state of mind for people that believe it. It doesn't work on the people that don't, which sort of denies the whole point right? Because I look at really awful people that are so successful and everything goes well for them and sometimes things keep getting better and better. And I know we could say that we never know what's going on inside of them, like maybe they're miserable or whatever, but I think that's just envy. Or wishful thinking."

Jill can hear a lot of different influences in Bridgett's words: Vicky and Carl, certainly Ember, and maybe the boyfriend as well.

"My dad—or Richard, I mean, thought that people lived through what they did in their lives. Like his writing and teaching. Of course it's a joke now with everything else. Maybe he meant that too. Probably something was wrong with his brain. He was—I can't explain it. But he was this whole person besides that. I don't think criminals can be whole people to strangers."

"You're probably right. We want our bad guys to be bad all the way through, not to have qualities like our own."

"Someday someone might want to write a book about him."

"I'm sure."

"I'll tell you my biggest secret."

"OK."

"You can't tell anyone until I say. No one else knows yet."

"I won't tell anyone. You have doctor-client privilege."

"OK. My dad told me the other day, after I got arrested, that I could think of anything that might help me deal with the situation—I guess with my dad and everything."

Jill is a little confused with Bridgett calling both Carl and Richard dad. "Which dad did what?"

"My dad—Richard—wrote biographies and I want to write his. He said it was the greatest compliment someone could be given, and he didn't mean—he didn't mean a—a—"

"A true crime novel?"

"Yes, I want to talk about all his good stuff, but the bad stuff too, so it's as honest as possible. The thing I think everyone might freak about is that I want to talk to all the families of the people he killed and put little pieces of their stories in the book."

"I think the book is a great idea, but I don't know about talking to the families of the victims. They might not want to meet you. Anyway, wouldn't you prefer writing about *his* life? Their lives aren't part of his life."

"Yes, they are! That's the problem. Don't you see? I want to use my experiences, and Ember's, and Mom's, and Grandma

Frances', and we all knew him, but also his friends and students—the students are really important because I think he was a great teacher—"

"His friends and students might have distorted memories because of everything that they've heard since."

"I know it's not going to be perfect. I think if his daughter is there it might help them—"

"Some people—the families—might be cruel to you. They might mistakenly—"

"That's good. Then we can give them something to focus on, and we can put it in the book, to show that what he did had a negative impact as well as positive—I don't mean the murdering, I mean the teaching and stuff."

"You've thought this through."

"I was planning to write his biography forever since I was a little kid and he would let me research his books with him. He would say how it was the greatest honor to the deceased, and I would think that when he died in a million years I would do the same thing for him. I never told him, but it helped me worry less about him dying. He was always talking, considering his own death, and at first it made me sad that I had no control over it, but then I had this plan. When he really died it was a shock, and I didn't think of the book for a long time. Then I kept getting little details about things he might have done, what people were saying, and without planning to, I would think how I could write the book if those things were or weren't true. I think I was always writing it whenever I was with him, in my head. That was how I'd think about him. I can't explain it."

"Give it a try—can you think of an example?"

"I don't know. Like when I was ten, I think, and I went to one of his lectures. I was describing it in my head as I watched, like I was narrating it. I would do it all third person, but now I think I will write the book first person. I don't know how it will be; it's just that it's different now. I can't just write the story of someone's life, he's not *famous*, he's that other word—"

"Infamous?"

"Yes. And I'm his relative, which is what I have to tell everyone I interview. It's the only possible way. In other circumstances I would have pretended to be a disconnected scholar. My last name is different, so only people that cared would have known. Also, I thought I would be old by the time I wrote it."

"I don't know what your mom is going to say about this." Bridgett's expression tells her she has chosen the wrong words. "I guess you want me to help with that, don't you? Is Ember going to be the person that goes with you on your adventures?"

"They aren't adventures; this is a serious thing I'm talking about. The book doesn't have to be published or read, it just has to be written. But I bet it will be published and read because I have the edge on everyone else who wants to write about him. No one in our family is going to talk to them."

"If they even talk to you. Sorry. I *am* taking you seriously. You seemed like such an awful brat, and now suddenly you have a decent idea that could really help. Help you."

"Thank you," Bridgett says primly. "I think I do need a project. It will focus all my confused emotions and restless energy."

"Isn't that what I'm supposed to say?" Jill asks with amusement. "Or does Montgomery read philosophy?"

"Gummy could teach you a thing or two."

"Try to avoid clichés in your book. And platitudes. Now. Are you sexually active?"

"No. I'm not going to have sex until I'm over the death of my biological father."

"I bet *that* didn't come from Gummy."

Bridgett sticks out her tongue automatically, and then blushes. "Also, my mother was very promiscuous when she was young, and I don't want that kind of reputation."

Jill leans forward in her chair. "Why don't you tell me more about that?"

"Isn't our time up?"

Jill laughs loudly. "Just one thing, what are you reading right now?"

"I'm rereading *Anne of Green Gables*—"

"That's just the type of thing I was going to recommend."

"—and I have a poetry book my dad gave me that I read out of sometimes, by Swinburne, I can't remember his whole name, and a book about Horace that Grandma Frances sent me. She studied it in school and the quote was in this—well, it's a long story."

"Ember told me about the 'Anger is a brief madness' quote. And about Katherine Van Leden. Are you still friends with her?"

"You can't tell anyone that either. I'm not supposed to be. But about the quote, I thought I could use the same thing for the title of his biography. It's not about Horace or anger—my title, I mean. Dad never seemed angry to me. It's more because Ember showed me his unfinished essay called *A Brief Madness: Lapses in Justice from the Beginning of Man.* Like his life was a lapse in justice?"

"Lapse in judgment, you mean?"

"No, like when he killed people? More like life is a brief madness, if there's no definite form of justice during or afterward. He hated dates—like the month, the year, and those are what give everything form. I don't think it is justice that Richard died then because he would most likely have died around that time even if he'd never killed anyone."

"But if he'd been inside, I mean, if an ambulance had come—there's so much they can do nowadays."

"I guess that's one way to think of it. And he did die slowly knowing he would be found out and what it would do to all of us. It could have taken hours and hours. He couldn't move to bury those women—He must have tried and tried."

"Bridgett, where do you get these ideas?"

They had stood to end the session while Bridgett was listing her current reading, but now both sit back down again.

"Someone got the coroner's statement, you know?"

"Autopsy report?"

"Yes, and they put it on the Internet."

"Bridgett, you can't believe—"

"I know that! I'm just saying, if it happened that way, then there was some form of justice, wasn't there?"

Jill takes the box of tissues and sets them on the girl's lap as she begins to cry.

40

It has always seemed to Frances that Mariah contains more people per capita who have never left the state of their birth than any other place in the country. While they all talk incessantly of Atlanta, few have traveled further.

This group included her until yesterday, when she flew into Los Angeles and was escorted by a guide to the Pasadena shuttle. Frank arranged the travel itinerary for her; he feels at fault over the removal of her home from the market. The least she can do is pay him for keeping an eye on it while she's gone, whether he expects her to or not.

Her trip is excessively interesting to the rest of Mariah, with the normal intrigue of the West Coast amplified by Lilac Greene-Jean bankrolling the book-writing process on behalf of her brother Horace. He has been incorporated into the project; Ember insisted she was terrible with prose and wouldn't mind having a workhorse to do the hard part.

"It's not the same if I'm just *arranging* the biography," Bridgett complained at first, as she had planned to do all the writing herself. Horace convinced her through phone calls that he would only assist in the editing and that sort of thing.

Frances isn't sure why he wants to be involved at all. Although he did tell her that his writing output, stimulated by her family's visit, died off again after they left. He is apparently still working on the story their visit inspired. Lilac has provided a grant to cover much more than Vicky could, and Horace says he will accept any excuse for a trip.

They both agree that after visiting two or three of the victims' families the process will prove unbearable, and the book will simply become the memories of Bridgett. The plan is to research backward, from his death to his birth, despite Richard's belief that a subject's childhood vitalized the biography.

Sleeping in the family room in Ember's condo turned out to be very comfortable, despite the temporary hospital in the sitting room next to it. Ember called it a sudden and unexpected thing, just days before Frances' arrival, that a sick old woman and her transsexual roommate were evicted from their apartment. But that can't be the entire story.

"Maybe you should stay with us instead," Vicky says now. She and Carl have one spare room that stores both weights and office equipment, where they are planning on placing Horace. "We can figure something out."

"Everything is just fine here," Frances answers loudly, in case Ember's two friends have overheard Vicky's tone of disgust. "This condo is bigger than your house; there's plenty of room."

"Where is Ember?" Vicky is tapping her fingers on the kitchen counter and looking around anxiously. "We need to get organized. Where did Bridgett go?"

"She went down the hall. They're both in the sitting room with—uh, with Ember's friends. I think someone else showed up before you too; I was on the balcony."

"Have you met them? Have you met her friends?"

"Vicky, we're fine here. Just go straighten things out at work."

"I wanted you to tour the Clean Cut."

"OK," Frances says brightly, reminding herself that this is what visiting people is all about. She hasn't seen any of them in more than a year though and wishes they could just sit around and talk.

The family has already made it clear that she is expected to go places and express a great deal of enthusiasm over the marvel that is California. She would prefer to dwell on the adventure that was her first plane ride. In Mariah she was told endless horror stories, which made her feel accepted again. She felt no fear, deciding it would be indecent to be scared for her own life doing something her grandchild did all the time.

Frances knocks on the wall next to the sitting room before peering in. There is no door, nor is there one in the entryway to the family room, but both have a pair of tall, dark Chinese screens.

"Come in," someone says.

She pushes the screen open and sees the elderly woman, just a couple of years younger than her own mother would have been if she were still alive, lying on the couch with one of her hands being held palm up by a plump stranger.

"Hello again, Frances," Irene says weakly, and the rest of them turn to her. "This is my nurse Deirdre. I don't think you met her yesterday."

Deirdre nods at Frances and looks back at the arm.

"Tony and Ember are learning to clean the pick line," Bridgett says in a reverent tone.

Tony is sitting on the edge of the couch at Irene's waist. "What if we accidentally use too much?"

"Then I'll die a painful death," Irene says dramatically.

"No, no." The nurse shakes her head. "Heparin isn't dangerous."

"Have you ever heard of a shunt before, dear? That's what the doctors drilled into my arm," Irene explains to Frances, trying to see her around the nurse. Frances moves closer. "This pick line makes it so they can stick needles in without having to find a vein every time. It was such a trial for the poor nurses at the hospital to find my veins. They had to poke me four or five times before they could get the needle in. One sweetheart was almost crying, she felt so terrible. She kept apologizing. These darlings are learning how to keep it clean for me. You have the most brilliant granddaughter; she's soaking everything up. Although I think I have plenty of helpers if you want to go do something else, Bridgett."

"I'm gonna learn just in case."

"It's pretty simple," Ember says. "We just inject a little of the Heparin in once a day and that flushes the pick line out. We need to keep it in the fridge—"

"So nobody drink any," Bridgett says.

Irene laughs. "Heparin chicken. It might be just the thing."

Frances had the chance to ask Ember yesterday who was paying for the medical treatment and was relieved to find out that Irene had Medicare and was in the Hospice system. This includes a daily nurse for baths and a less frequent one for physical therapy.

"Her son in Utah is taking care of the paperwork," Ember had explained. "He wants her to move up there as soon as possible, so we've been trying to arrange it. He found a doctor that specializes in this and is willing to work with her current treatment plan. The only problem is Tony. He doesn't want her to leave, and obviously he can't go with her. Two of her sons really want her and have made all the preparations. She can switch from one to the other after a while if she gets bored. I'm afraid even the idea bores her though. After Tony."

"But why are they with you?"

"I met them in grief group. Their stories—well, Tony's is horrible, truly horrible. We've become friends. They were obsessed about Richard at first, but now—I found Tony a part-time job where I work. I guess their apartment manager raised the rent, and there were other problems."

"It seems like a wild lifestyle for a dying woman," Frances said. Then Tony called Ember, and Frances went to bed exhausted before they had another chance to talk. Or went "to couch," as she heard Irene enjoys saying. The couch is marvelous. Something must be missing in Frances' mattress at home if daytime furniture can beat it so easily.

"I'm going to run to the gym with your mother," Frances tells Bridgett. "Do you want to come?"

"Don't go there. It's so boring," Bridgett says.

"I've never seen it though."

"Go ahead, Bridgett, we'll be doing this again tomorrow," Ember says.

"Why don't you come too?"

"No, I—"

"Go dear, we're fine here. Go have some fun. Tony, you too."

"No, I'm OK."

"Bridgett, will you get me some sandals, please?" Ember asks. "My black ones are behind my bed."

Bridgett runs out of the room.

"OK, guys, we'll be back soon," Ember says.

They hurry when they hear Vicky's voice raised in frustration.

She drives them in Carl's new Toyota Prius, which he says he bought to help cut down on the pollution problem. Frances noticed the yellowish thickness in the sky on her ride from LA yesterday and hopes it works.

"What is it Irene has?" Frances asks, turning from the front seat to see Ember.

"Lymphoma—cancer of the blood cells. It's a very aggressive type, but she has this marker in her blood that will allow them to try a fairly new treatment. They're going to give her an antibody. It's supposed to strengthen her immune system. Some people have bad side effects, but it seems to mostly help. They've used it on a lot of older people."

"What about chemotherapy?"

"The doctor thinks that would be too tough on her. If this doesn't work she probably won't be around much longer. Luckily her granddaughter lives nearby; she's coming over today."

"Are you sure her family wants her?"

"Oh yes, I've talked to two of her sons—I told you, didn't I?"

"I thought they came to you at the last minute," Vicky says.

"They weren't really evicted—it was just creepy. There were some problems that no one was fixing, and the rent was going up in a month. I don't think Irene will leave until she's sure Tony has a safe situation. Liora said he could stay with her for a few days. I think she has a tiny place though."

"Who's Liora?" Bridgett asks.

"Oh, that's Irene's granddaughter. She's about twenty-five. She works at a theater in Hollywood and wants to be an actress. Not a movie theater, one for plays."

The health club in Glendale is the first one Vicky opened. The outside is white brick, and Frances wonders if she should comment on how clean and cut it looks but decides that will sound too flippant. "It appears to be a lovely place to exercise," she says as they step inside.

"The building used to be a dance school," Vicky says. She holds the glass door open while they walk in.

"How do you keep everything so white?" Frances asks next.

"I have a special cleaning crew just to do laundry. We also lend out white towels and washcloths to people that want them. If anything is stained beyond repair, the staff takes it home."

"If you use our bathroom you'll see," Bridgett says, rolling her eyes. "We have a million hand-me-down towels. And they don't stay that white the way *we* wash them."

A thin, dark-haired girl is smiling and standing alertly behind the receptionist desk.

"Good afternoon, Ms. Andres," she says as soon as they pause.

"Hello, Merry. How are you? There are my friends, Frances and Ember, and you remember my daughter?"

"I almost didn't recognize her."

"Frances was my only initial investor, so I'm going to give her the royal tour. Just think, without her none of us would be here."

Vicky has always been overly grateful for what turned out to be a very small favor, but the public praise is so unexpected that Frances feels the need to protest. Instead she forces herself to smile and mutter something about Vicky's success.

Although Frances did hand over most of her retirement savings when Vicky needed a down payment for the building, after only five years she was paid back every cent of it (relieved that her sincere refusal of interest was accepted). This was after the divorce, and Frances had planned to give Vicky some financial assistance but wasn't sure how to make the offer. She was ashamed of her son's behavior and wanted to separate herself from it. Vicky got by with her daycare center job and child support from Richard until she became certified as a personal trainer. By the time she had drawn up the plans for her business, she seemed determined and mature enough to make it work.

"Let's go into the free weights room."

"Do you ever work out?" Frances asks Ember.

"I like to walk."

Ember is thin but soft, in the way of people who come by it naturally. Frances has a weight set in her basement that she uses regularly according to a plan Vicky designed for her. She also power walks and jumps on a miniature trampoline. For a while she bounced up and down without any fancy tricks, so she wouldn't fall off and break a hip. But just in case, there was a phone on the floor. When she asked a doctor a couple of months ago about the safety of a woman in her sixties on a trampoline, he started laughing and never answered. Throughout the rest of the exam he would glance at her, shake his head, and chuckle. He pronounced her in fabulous health and snickered as he left the room.

At home she looked in the mirror and wondered what the hell was so funny. There wasn't much on her to bounce around raucously, nor did she appear feeble. Maybe it was her long hair in a bun, when the style was the very short, fluffy coiffure. Of course the doctor had been under thirty, so perhaps he found all older women ridiculous. It was impossible to tell, but it didn't ruin jumping for her; if anything, it made her more adventuresome. She began to perform twists and hop from side-to-side.

She also changed to a more mature, female doctor.

"I do aerobics at Mom's club that's closer to our house," Bridgett says. "Only eighteen year olds and over are allowed to join normally, so all my friends are really jealous."

All the weight equipment is white, but the mats are dark blue. The floor is a soft and spongy black. Every wall is covered with mirrors. It's bright and cold.

"Oh no," Bridgett says softly. She ducks behind Frances and then pulls her into a dressing room. "That's Amy Frier. Don't let her see me."

"Montgomery's girlfriend?" Vicky asks.

"Yes. Oh no, what if she knows."

"He won't have told her," Vicky says. "Go through the front and up the stairs. I'm going to show them the pool, then we'll meet you there."

The women look at Amy curiously as they walk through the room. "She seems too ordinary," Ember whispers as they enter the pool area, "to be the one cheating on the great Gummy."

"Thank God the great Gummy is scared to death of being seen anywhere near Bridgett. He won't even return her calls."

"I thought she wasn't supposed to have anything to do with him either," Ember says.

"We've been bad parents, eavesdropping on her phone conversations and interrogating his friends. Gummy already has a new girlfriend, besides Amy. Someone with the reputation as a major slut—and I'm just quoting what the kids said. Bridgett thinks she was in love with him and can't understand why he stopped caring about her. She'll get over it."

"Just don't tell her that," Ember jokes.

The poolroom has white walls and rough white tile that Vicky tells them to feel with their hands. It's to prevent slippage.

Frances nods and tries to think of something to say. "Is this a—a lap pool?"

"Two laps each way. We have water aerobics and all types of swimming classes. You can take whatever you like while you're here. You too, Ember, you can have a free membership."

"Oh, are you sure? Thank you," Ember says. "I loved to swim when I was a kid. I would do laps with my mom at the community pool. It was adult-time only, so I was really proud when she convinced them I could behave maturely enough."

"How is your family, Ember?" Frances asks.

"I don't know. I think they're still upset that I didn't move back there after Richard died. I almost did, actually. We're from a tiny town by the Four Corners, and no one would have blamed me for getting caught up in a scandal near the evil Los Angeles."

"I should have asked you how the news of Richard affected them. I didn't even think of it," Frances says soberly.

"They're fine now."

"How did you end up here?" Vicky asks as she ushers them into the stairwell.

"My best friend since kindergarten wanted to be an actor, so after we graduated from college we moved here together." Her voice echoes around the metal of the steps and rails. This is one area of the gym that isn't solid and clean. The stairs are rusty and unpainted, rattling with every step they take.

"We have an elevator too, but I never use it."

"Does your friend still live here?" Frances asks.

"Oh no. No, she caught—" Ember makes a face. "She was infected with syphilis pretty soon after we got here and went back home. I already had a job and couldn't bear the thought of that stagnant town. After high school I never lived there again."

Ember is slightly out of breath at the top of the stairs and Vicky gives her a triumphant look. Frances feels a little winded too but gains control of it quietly.

"Richard was always telling me I needed more exercise. It annoyed me to be compared unfavorably to you."

"Oh," Vicky says, apparently surprised by this confession. "Oh no, he never loved me as much as he did you."

Ember shrugs. "Maybe not, but he still admired a lot about you."

"Where were you guys?" Bridgett asks, opening the stairwell door. "I've been waiting forever. What if Amy comes up here?"

Frances wishes she could do something to preserve this flash of affection between her daughters-in-law, but at the same time she wonders why they still seek proof of Richard's admiration. It makes her worry even more about Bridgett, writing what she thinks is the book he always wanted written about him . . . and all the rest of them helping to create this grotesque family memorial.

Richard never thought of doing anything like that for Thad. Neither did she. But maybe peaceful lives result in peaceful deaths, with no need for digging and reshaping.

41

Vicky called Ember after picking Horace up at the airport and asked if he could visit for the evening. She and Carl were having "difficulties" with Bridgett.

Horace might end up sleeping where he sits, on the floor in the family room, since Ember doubts his hosts will get around to guest preparations tonight. Jill is half reclining on the couch above him, rubbing her bunions together and making purring noises.

"I wonder if childhood is being extended into the thirties now," Tony says idly, sitting upright in the recliner. "That would explain why none of you are married with kids."

A few weeks ago Ember asked Jill why Tony never seemed to mind discussing children, and the answer was that he separated his old self from his new one. To Ember's "that sounds unhealthy," Jill had impatiently replied, "Having his little girls die was unhealthy." Ember decided she was developing the same curiosity over Tony that had been so frustrating when directed at her. She still couldn't resist asking how he could admit to once being a woman, to which Jill responded, "He didn't lose his memory."

"I *was* married," Ember tells him now. "So was Jill."

"And I *did* have a son," Frances adds.

"I guess it's just me that's immature then," Horace says. "Besides you." He doesn't know about Tony, who has trained himself to speak more deeply and is cautiously masculine. Since Tony has decided not to surgically alter his body yet, this is an important test of his ability to pass.

"Well, my ex used to say that he—" Tony stops, embarrassed, and only then does Ember catch the slip. They glance at Horace, then start to laugh. "I have bigger pecs than you," Tony jokes suddenly.

"Did I miss something?" Horace asks. He looks nervously at Jill, who is staring back.

Ember thinks Horace has great muscles, even if he's not as big as Tony, who has been training with a professional body builder the last few months. The bulk toughens Tony's appearance but also enhances the slenderness of his face and neck.

"Do you eat meat?" Tony asks.

"A little too heavy on the macho recovery," Ember whispers.

"Not on my own; too expensive. I buy protein mixes in bulk but they taste like shit. Or—excuse me Mrs. Dayle—crap."

"I wonder who decides what makes one word profanity and another harmless slang?" Ember asks helpfully.

"You can try some of mine," Tony continues to Horace.

"It's too bad Vicky's not here," Frances says. "She knows everything there is to know on the subject."

"But I wouldn't be talking if she was around," Tony says. "She dislikes me."

"And me," Jill adds.

"Bridgett said she had her parents come to your office to tell them about the book idea," Ember says. "What happened?"

"They thought it was a wonderful plan until Bridgett said she was going to interview *everyone* connected to his life. Then both were upset and it went on and on. I billed them for the whole time because they wouldn't leave."

"Ah," Horace says. "That explains why she doesn't like you."

"Then after the book thing seemed semi-settled, we got on the subject of justice, which is big with Bridgett. I teased them that it was their fault for being liberal, the other side never cares about that sort of thing. They didn't think I was funny. How are the book plans going anyway? You've got finances and a professional writer." She winks at Horace. "When do you start?"

"We-ell." Ember scrunches up her face. "Bridgett wrote letters to all of Richard's old friends and coworkers in the area, but no one responded. Then she followed up with calls, but those she got a hold of were less than enthusiastic."

"So no one agreed to be interviewed?" Horace asks in surprise. "Can we afford to pay them something?"

"I got one of his old friends to agree. He said he thought Bridgett was a prankster or reporter. I don't know about the payment idea. Frances is in charge of your sister's donation."

"Grant."

"And she—your sister, I mean, is paying you a separate salary?"

"Three hundred bucks a week plus travel. That's three times what she gives me at home."

"Gives you at home?" Jill asks.

Ember has been wondering about that as well.

Horace smirks. "My family has a reputation to keep up in the non-town of Mariah. I said all I wanted to do was write, and I guess they felt bad I was the only one that ended up without a substantial inheritance. My job until that point had been mostly in Atlanta, but somehow they found out about it and didn't approve."

"Male stripper?"

"Well, he certainly wasn't a female stripper, Ember." Tony laughs, and she grins back.

"I don't think there's anything wrong with *male* strippers," Jill says. "I'd love to see you in action."

"I wasn't a stripper. I was a clown for children's parties."

There's a short silence and then Jill says, "Well, that's funny too" and stretches her legs out on the couch in the direction of Horace's head. She's wearing tight, taupe slacks that make her look unnecessarily bulgy.

"And your parents disapproved, so now you don't have to work at all," Tony says mournfully. "Although I would insist on a bit more cash for controlling my life that way."

"It's a long story. Will someone call Vicky for me and see what I'm supposed to do for the night?"

Frances gets up, and he follows her into the kitchen where the phone is.

"I'd better get to sleep too," Tony says. "Irene wakes up so early. Are you working tomorrow, Ember?"

"Yes, last shift before vacation."

"How long do you have off?"

"Six days. I really don't think we'll still be writing the book after that. Bridgett just needs to get it out of her system."

"I wonder if Frances will want to go to sleep soon."

"Don't be so humble, Tony, you're an equal guest."

"Well I did invite myself. I'm not related or dying."

"I feel like a hospice. No healthy folks allowed."

"Did you grow up in Colorado like Ember, Tony?" Jill asks.

"No, Paul and I moved there from Idaho when offered a partnership in a hardware store, which we eventually bought."

Horace comes back in the room, his hands deep in his pockets.

"Are you staying here?" Ember asks him.

"If it's OK with you. Carl sounded frustrated."

"I'm planning to move Frances into my office tomorrow, so if they still aren't ready you can take the family room then. Someone will have to go grocery shopping while I'm at work. I'll call here on my break and arrange it with my driver. There aren't any stores close enough to walk to."

"You have a driver?" Horace asks.

"I'd better go home," Jill says. "When is Irene getting her first Ritoxin treatment?"

"Friday morning. Ember and I are going too. It will take about five hours, but we're bringing a lot of the books she likes."

"Are you planning to stay the whole time?"

"Probably. She'll be conscious. We'll just see what happens."

Ember says good-bye to Jill at the door while Frances gets extra bedding from the laundry room for Horace. Before going to the bathroom Tony whispers to Ember, "Tell him, will you? I'm glad I passed, but I'd rather he find out before we spend the night in the same house."

"If you're sure? You're doing so great."

"Thanks, but I feel good about letting him know now in case it comes out later."

Ember finds Horace in the kitchen, and says, "About Tony. He's a transsexual. He was a woman once, and now he's a man. He's becoming a man."

Horace stares at her. "Are you kidding?"

"Nope." Ember isn't energetic enough to discuss it further. "Good night, see you tomorrow."

He doesn't respond.

She goes down the hall to her room. She will move the contents of her office into Richard's in the morning before work. Then she will lock the door, as she has been doing since her first guests arrived. She can imagine any of them feeling curiosity although she has no idea which ones might act on it. The indoor pin tumbler locks only have two keys each. One is in the safe with the listening device and the other she carries.

Before Frances arrived, Ember's old paranoia about his mother wanting to claim him resurfaced, and she hid the silly metal urn with Richard's ashes in her closet. It was a relief when Tony called with his desperate request, as she thought three housemates might distract one another. She supposes it was a little like the way Frances had them stay at the boarding house when they visited her last year: nerves and mistrust all mixed together.

42

Horace feels humiliated caught lounging on his pile of blankets next to the table when Ember gets home from work. He did get around to showering earlier in the day, but the disdainful glance she slides over him discounts that.

Everyone else is covered in the long, cold stare, but they aren't lying in bed in comfortable clothes that could pass as pajamas. Vicky and Bridgett are sitting at the table arguing. Frances and Carl are in the kitchen trying to cook and whining about the absence of supplies. And Ember had an unimaginably long day. He woke up briefly when she made herself toast over fourteen hours ago.

Somehow looking more put-together than the rest of them, Ember snaps, "Who left the balcony door open? And the screen? Did you know there are monstrous cockroaches out there?" She walks briskly out of the room.

"Am I staying here again?" Horace asks quietly.

"Maybe just one more night." Vicky sounds apologetic. "We aren't quite organized."

Horace gathers up the pile of blankets and pillows and carries them past the room where Irene is sleeping. Tony has gone to a therapy group. That guy is one buff woman. A female shouldn't be allowed hormones that make her bigger than a man. He would like to know what she does for a dick. Maybe an animal transplant.

The tile is hard under his bare feet, but he admires how expensive it looks. His place is without flooring of any kind, the result of a deserted remodeling project. It seems absurd to him that a guy who could earn the money to buy a pad like this was a killer on the side. The energy of some people. And possibly Ember made even more. Tony said she used to have four jobs: shelter director, marketing manager, researcher, and most interesting of all, hand model.

Despite women seeming to believe otherwise, Horace doesn't notice fingernails, but he's eager to glimpse the hands that make as much in an hour as Ember's reportedly do.

He piles everything on the floor behind a couch in the family room. The mood in the place is rocky, but he already knows that motels in the area are way out of his price range. Still, he would prefer not to be sharing a bathroom with two old women and a switcher. That makes him queasy.

Ember is standing with her arms crossed in the hall outside the kitchen when he returns.

"Did you have a bad day?" he asks. It's too hot in here, but no one was sure if they should turn the air on.

She shrugs, sighing through her nose. "What's wrong?" she asks Vicky sharply. Then, "Bridgett?"

"I found someone with a link to the families."

"*Someone* is Katherine. She's flying over here."

"She has a website," Bridgett says, "for people who want to make sure their missing person isn't one of the dead. She posted about the book and lots are willing to talk to us. She's checking up to make sure they're the real thing, with police reports and all that."

Horace heads back to the family room during this explanation; he already heard Bridgett and Vicky go through it once before, and it wasn't pleasant.

He's interested in seeing Katherine again, despite her married state. The Lilac fund is paying for her flight. His sister is such a goose. It took him forever to convince her to support the book (although hopefully everyone believes otherwise), and now she is praising the project as humanitarian all over town. She's a born marketer until she loses interest. Luckily Ember has the bulk of the money in a bank account. If Lilac is still intrigued when they run out she'll give them more, unless her husband decides to change her mind.

43

Ember watches Horace's muscles move in his shorts as he walks away. She used to be attractive to men; when she gazes in the mirror she appears the same, yet it's often hard to focus on her reflection: sometimes too familiar, other times she looks like a person she has walked by often but doesn't really know.

From the moment she understood about Richard, there was this empty thud in her chest, and ever since then it has vibrated through her body from her heart to her abdomen. She is certain only a strict routine has prevented her from becoming slovenly.

Forcing herself to concentrate on Vicky's hatred of Katherine, she wants to say that the help will be useful; she's terrified of contacting any of the families herself. At least this way Katherine can examine their attitudes beforehand.

Bridgett starts to talk before Ember can think of a response beyond a sympathetic frown. "Sometimes I think I—I think I'm not ready to write Dad's book yet. Like first I need to experience something like what these other people experienced. I mean having someone they love brutally murdered."

"You're trying to get your way by scaring us again," Ember scolds.

"I never scared you."

"You never scared us," Vicky says, moving her face close to her daughter's. "What about the boyfriend and the cutting?"

"I didn't—"

"Bridgett," Carl says sternly, and she glares at him.

"If you want to get into your dad's mind, maybe it would be easiest to start with his childhood, in Mariah," Ember suggests.

"Katherine is coming, and Bridgett has insisted she consider our house her hotel. That is the point of this discussion."

Ember says, "I suppose she can stay here..."

Tony shuffles wearily toward her. Even with the nurses, Irene is a fulltime job. And Ember just hired him to work nights at the marketing center. Soon he will be glad Irene has loving relatives.

"Ember," Tony says. "Tomorrow's the big day. Irene's latest plan is to move to Utah after her third treatment. Her family's looking into assisted living. She's not happy about it, but she refuses to live with them, and she's in no shape to be on her own."

"Why won't she live with her family?" Vicky asks irritably.

"Because they're oppressive," Bridgett says. "She needs her freedom or she will suffocate along with all her other problems. Who wants to live with their awful kids?"

All of them, except Vicky, laugh at that. Bridgett does without meaning to, and then her eyes fill with angry tears.

"What are you guys making?" Ember asks the cooks.

"Sausage and pasta," Carl says. "But without real meat."

"It smells like real meat."

"It tastes like it too," Carl says. "I promise. Do you think Irene would like something to eat?"

"Oh, Bridgett and I brought her some fast food earlier," Tony says. "She's been craving grease lately, and we're glad to oblige. This is the first she's really eaten in a long time. Her husband used to cook elaborate meals, and I guess they were both quite plump for a while, but since then..."

"Is that why she stopped eating?" Carl asks. "Did food remind her too much of him?"

"That's what everyone thought," Tony says, "but now the doctors say that depression and lack of appetite are some of the early symptoms of her type of lymphoma. It's just extremely hard to diagnose." He laughs. "At Change—my trans group, I mean, they complain that all I talk about is Irene's health."

"Trans as in transsexual? It's very strange that you and she are together," Vicky says. "Isn't it selfish of you to keep her from her family? It would be one thing if they didn't want her—"

"Yes, it is selfish. She has a lot of choices. But you know, before the diagnosis I was good for her. I was the only one who interested her enough to keep her living long enough to get help. Despite everything she was feeling, her desire to straighten me out is what kept her going. And she *has* been seeing her oldest granddaughter every week."

"Irene's so interesting," Bridgett says. "Did you know she's writing a book called *Twiddle Your Thumbs*? It's about this old woman who's close to death, and her family is sitting around waiting for it to happen—but it's funny. The family loves her and they don't *want* her to die, but it seems inevitable. So they give away all her stuff, and then she gets better. It's about when that happened to her, when the doctors didn't know what she had and were convinced she was dying. Her sons are supposed to write their parts, but they haven't. She says they are too embarrassed since they donated most of her things. She jokes about having all garage sale clothes and needing to buy silverware again."

"The cover of the book is going to be an old woman in a casket with one eye open," Tony says. "She's finished writing most of it."

"She's lucky really," Frances says thoughtfully.

"You need a living trust, so all your requirements are listed carefully. Paul and I had one of those in case we died while the kids were still young. The guardians lived in New Zealand, so we didn't want them to have to go through the long probate thing or worry about all the taxes."

"Wasn't Melissa from New Zealand?" Bridgett asks.

"Yes. Paul called last week about buying out my half of the hardware store. He also mentioned that Melissa tried to commit suicide on her seventeenth birthday."

"Who is Melissa?" Vicky asks.

"She's my niece. Just got her GED; I assumed she was fine."

"I wanna do that. I can't stand high school."

"No one can stand high school," Vicky says sharply.

"You don't want her life, Bridgett. She's very unhappy. She doesn't date or have any friends. I guess she gained a lot of weight and sits at the computer talking in chat rooms."

"Why don't you try to help her?" Bridgett asks.

"Dinner's ready," Carl says.

"What can I do? I'm sure her parents would rather she not have my influence in her life."

"That's true," Vicky agrees without malice. "Bridgett, you were supposed to set the table."

"I was too busy listening."

"I'll serve," Carl says. "You have to get the sauce just right."

"I'm worried about Katherine. I think she's out to get us."

"Mo-om. You don't even know her. Anyway, I was trying to tell you about that earlier. I asked Lilac—"

"Are you talking about my crazy sister?" Horace says, appearing suddenly and putting his hands on Bridgett's shoulders. "I hear sounds and smells of dinner."

"You hear smells?" Bridgett teases.

"These kinds of smells you can hear."

"Don't tell him it's not real meat," Tony whispers loudly.

"I ain't no redneck, but I smell me some red meat."

There aren't enough chairs at the table, so Horace and Bridgett sit on the floor.

"Throw us scraps." Bridgett moves close to Horace and smiles.

"But what about Katherine?" Vicky asks. "What are we going to do about Katherine?"

44

Katherine stands on Ember's balcony with her cigarette, exhaling away Vicky's shock that anyone still possesses such a deplorable habit. Nowadays smokers are expected to come with a warning reek and yellow teeth, perhaps even a tattoo of a blackened lung.

Ember joins her, sliding the glass door shut. She sits in an uncomfortable plastic chair, putting her feet up on the four-foot-high rail. "I never come out here anymore."

"If you had a hammock it would be the perfect place to sleep."

"Bugs. You can if you want though."

"What's the deal with those people that annoy Vicky?"

"You mean besides you?" Ember grins, and Katherine likes her despite her ownership of a whole house in the sky.

"Have you traveled outside Georgia before?" Ember asks, adding quickly, "Frances was telling me—"

"No, I haven't. I told my brothers—I mean, my brother and Johnny—that I was going to LA to look for our dad. I've searched but there's no Gregory Van Leden anywhere."

"It sounds unusual. German?"

"I don't know. Of course my dad *could* be here. When I got off the plane—God, the airport! It was so huge and jam-packed."

Frances knocks on the door and opens it when Ember motions.

"You know, it's lucky we found you, Katherine. You told Bridgett the time, but not the flight number."

"I know. It was stupid. I didn't think about it, figured I'd just walk out and see you guys."

Using the arrival time, Horace and Ember pinpointed the only two flights Katherine could possibly have been on, then separated to check them out. Ember waited outside the baggage claim; Horace stood instead next to the closest exit from the building, and that's where he found her. Katherine had been so confused that her eyes filled with tears when she saw someone familiar. She felt like a much different person here, a smaller, weaker one. Even her hair wasn't as red.

"Then Vicky drove us here in complete silence," Katherine tells Frances.

"Vicky's under a lot of pressure," Frances says. "Besides Bridgett, there's some workers' comp thing going on at one of her health clubs."

"That's why I would never want my own business," Ember says idly. "It's too hot. Everyone is crabby. Professor Tanaka is coming over for our first interview in about an hour. I was thinking of doing it in my office. Just Bridgett and me since I know him. We don't want to be overwhelming." She yawns.

"I can call the victim's sister that agreed to meet with you and set up a time. She seems pretty safe."

"What about the liability of publishing interviews?" Frances asks.

"I was supposed to look into that." Ember sighs. "I meant to. I guess it can't hurt to have something for them to sign. We want to ask if we can use a tape recorder too."

"Bridgett's already written down her memories of her father," Frances says wistfully. "They're really nice. She's been writing every day." After a pause she adds, "They do need work if people besides her family are going to read them."

Katherine has been using the rail for an ashtray, but with an audience she isn't going to risk dropping the butt. "I need to put this in the garbage," she says. "Are you guys coming in?"

"Soon," Ember replies.

Frances nods that she will stay outside for now too. Katherine has the not-unpleasant feeling that they are going to discuss her after she leaves.

45

Ember's new office is only big enough for one person, with Richard's huge oak desk against the wall under the window and two tall wooden file cabinets, one in front of the other. She will move his cabinet into the other office eventually, when it's no longer Frances' guest room. She hasn't gone through all of Richard's things, and this way she can jealously guard them from his mother.

She wonders what she would be doing if he were in prison.

Both of their desktop computers sit next to each other, with his laptop on the chair. Hers is in the bedroom, so she can stare at the blank screen every night before falling asleep. She is supposed to be writing her memories of Richard for Bridgett's book, but she doesn't know where to start or what she wants to share.

For Tanaka she wears a straight, knee-length skirt and a blouse with a scoop neck. She hasn't had her hair cut for too long, and it has grown past her shoulders. Since it's straight and thin, it looks best short, just below her chin. With it long she seems younger but plainer too, less sophisticated. Richard used to say her hair felt like silk and that she should grow it out, but at this length it's duller and wilted. She puts it up in a chignon and feels tidy.

Her dry, patchy skin is another problem. She rubs in moisturizer and smiles until tiny lines form around her eyes. Lovely.

The intercom buzzes, and she joins Bridgett at the door a few minutes later.

"Hello, Tanaka-sensei. How are you?"

He gazes at Ember as if analyzing the changes in her appearance. She is uncomfortable being judged by someone who once found her attractive, and he has aged much more than her. His hair is thin and his face bloated. She remembers comparing him unfavorably to Richard once when they were standing together.

He puts both hands out and calls her "Akiko-san." She places her palms on his and then removes them. "Come sit down." In the office she says, "We don't have to record you—"

"I don't mind."

Bridgett sits in the desk chair, which is the most comfortable. Ember wishes she had left it for Tanaka since he walks with a shuffle, as if something hurts. He ends up facing Ember.

"How have you been?" he asks her, and Bridgett pushes the record button. She puts the tape player between her legs and holds her clipboard and pen.

"Fine," Ember says. "And you?"

"I'm still teaching. We've gotten a lot more people interested in the Kanji Proficiency Test."

"That's good." She failed him in that area too. She learned just enough Kanji to pass the first level. The Japanese alphabets of *Katakana* and *Hiragana*, however, she still uses to write private notes to herself. "You and Richard were roommates together at Stanford as undergrads, right?"

"Yes we were. Our freshman year. Then Richard got an apartment of his own, and I moved in with my brother. If I had known he would steal the woman I loved years later—"

"How did you both end up at Pasadena City College?" Ember asks quickly.

"Richard was hired there after he earned his doctorate from UCLA. He asked around in the Japanese department when I wrote him that I didn't like teaching high school."

"Did you both date the same person?" Bridgett asks.

"Your stepmother here."

"My step—Oooh."

"Yes, I met your dad in Tanaka-sensei's class."

"I didn't know teachers could date their students."

Tanaka stares at Ember again without responding. Does he hope she remembers what Richard did with his own student?

Tanaka draws out the details of the boring jokes he and Richard played on their dorm mates, tells stories about girls they dated, and insists he could never finish reading any of Richard's books. He says nothing about missing women or Richard coming home bloody and disheveled.

"What did you first think when you heard that Richard was suspected of murder?" Bridgett asks professionally.

He leans forward in his chair with his hands on his knees. "The students in my ten o'clock class told me that a longtime instructor at PCC had died, but we didn't know who until later that day. After Richard's name came up, I assumed he'd been in a fight—some kind of self-defense situation. Later I found out the details. He was committing these crimes when we lived to together, it seems, although I'm still friends with a woman he dated seriously, and she says he was the most normal of her boyfriends.

"He was certainly successful at separating his two lives," he muses to Bridgett, who doesn't look up from her writing. "Have you figured out what was wrong with him? Did something happen when he was a kid?"

"His mom is here if you'd like to meet her," Ember says.

"I only have a few more minutes. My wife and I," he pauses, "are going out to dinner. Do you have any other questions?"

"I don't think so," Bridgett says hesitantly, chewing on her pen. "Oh, wait—did anyone go missing when you were in school with him?"

Tanaka looks at her thoughtfully. "I just remembered this last night and haven't had a chance to contact the police yet. I will, of course, since the possibility of giving a family closure . . ."

"What?" Bridgett asks, leaning forward.

"On a dare of sorts, Richard dated a stripper at a club we would go to on the weekends. I don't know why we thought the whole thing was so hilarious. I never got to know her well, but she had a daughter who was about fifteen. The rumor was that she dumped Rich because he couldn't keep his hands off her kid. As odd as it seems, I always thought he started it. The rumor, I mean. He did that sometimes—start rumors about himself—and it wasn't like we were going to check out his story."

"Gossip is not what we're looking for," Ember says.

"Well, another stripper who worked there disappeared a few weeks later. Her body was found in the sand dunes above Glamis. Strangled. And even if he didn't kill her, the situation with his girlfriend's daughter fits with his pre-marriage incident, wouldn't you say? Never mind, I'm sure you think molesting an underage girl is quite a bit different than having consensual sex with a barely-legal adult. But is it consensual when one is a professor in a position of power—"

"If you don't have anything else to tell us, you'd better go."

He looks so smug Ember wants to punch him. She doesn't care if her knuckle breaks into pieces afterward. "I don't feel well," she says when he's finally gone. "Being raised to be nonviolent has its drawbacks."

Bridgett follows her to the bedroom, almost stepping on her heels. The room has two windows on opposite walls, so it stays cooler than the rest of the place. She rolls onto her bed, hugging one pillow to her chest and relaxing her head on another. Frances washed her bedspread yesterday, and it smells fresh.

She feels Bridgett sit down. "Did we get anything good?" the girl asks anxiously.

"Mm-hm."

"What?"

"Freshman year of college stuff." Speech is exhausting. "Him helping . . . his old roommate get a job . . ."

"Do you feel bad because of him?"

"No."

"Are we going to forget that last rumor part?"

"Yes."

"And are you going to tell me about the student? Wait, I don't want to know. It's not connected, right? I didn't like that guy, Mr. Tanaka-sensan or whatever you called him.

"You always lie around now. Dad used to say you *never* got sick."

"I'm not really sick; I just feel that way."

Bridgett lies down next to her. "Katherine is going to invite a sister of one of the dead people to come over tonight. Do you think she and Horace like each other?"

"She's married."

"Probably everyone likes Horace. Except Mom, who wouldn't date him in high school. She dated everyone else."

"Where did you hear that?"

"The parents of kids I used to play with when we'd visit down there. They thought I was deaf or something."

"They were just jealous. Forget that, no one is just jealous. They are also bitter, vindictive, nasty, and evil. Let's take a nap."

"Are you anorexic?"

"Of course not. Why would you ask that?"

"Because you're so thin and food always makes you sick. Maybe you have lymphoma."

"Oh, Irene. I haven't talked to her or Tony all day."

"Let's get up. I'm not tired."

"Then go away."

"Maybe we'll be asleep when my mom comes, and then I can stay overnight."

Ember doesn't want to sleep, just to lie in silence with her eyes closed. Bridgett fidgets around and then takes a book off the nightstand. Ember doesn't know which one it is but hopes it's something appropriate. Or that if it isn't, the girl doesn't mention it to her mother.

46

Frances moves Horace's bedding to the washing machine while he rearranges the couches in the family room. The blankets give off the scent of masculine sweat, and she finds herself squeamishly hoping Katherine chooses another place to sleep. These two will need more than a tent for protection from each other.

Her month of paid vacation from the institution where her son's name is never mentioned has been long and crowded so far. Thad was never clear on why his wife and son spent so much time at the hospital—or he pretended not to be. Even now the memory of his capacity for denial irritates her.

He worked for the electric company in a skilled and slightly dangerous position, dealing with problems both in the office and outside with the electric lines. Once a week, usually on Wednesday, and every weekend on either Saturday or Sunday, they copulated at around two in the morning, after Thad woke up to urinate. Sometimes she wanted more, and at a time when she wasn't half asleep, but not necessarily with him.

Far too late she understood that he was just shy—powerfully, unhappily shy.

After Thad died Richard was always watching her, until he turned eighteen and moved away. Then she found herself having nonsexual, not-quite affairs with married men in the town. They were unsatisfactory and stopped when she became aware of the rumors and began to lose respect for herself.

Frances wonders about Ember's life outside work; does she have any hobbies beyond her grief group? Of course someone could wonder that about herself, but there are always books, movies, and errands, along with endless household to-dos. She volunteers a lot, mainly involving cooking.

The best times are when she's in her lightheaded, forgetful state, where everything seems likely and fantastic, but those are occurring less since the family visited. Bridgett's problems have been keeping her centered. It was lovely right after Richard died, even with all the people in town avoiding her and the turmoil of the investigations. As soon as she knew his family was safe, she felt released from years of waiting.

Bridgett, carrying a plastic shopping bag, is the first to join Frances. She sits next to her on the couch and removes a clipboard and tape recorder, then stares straight ahead, sometimes mumbling to herself. She stops when they hear voices in the hall.

"I don't mind a big group," Ana Kritov says, following Ember into the room. Ana is around Ember's age and height but much sturdier, with wide hips and broad shoulders. She's wearing jeans and a long-sleeved white silk shirt. Her hair is long, frizzy, and mostly white, a lovely fluffy-looking white mixed with dark blond. With her thick, interesting features, Frances doesn't imagine she is ever mistaken for anyone else.

Katherine pushes Horace through the doorway and tells Ana, "It's wonderful to finally meet you." They hug briskly, with Katherine reaching up on her toes. "Thank you for coming. Take a seat."

Ember makes the rest of the introductions while Ana decides to sit next to Katherine and across from Bridgett.

"Is it OK—do you mind being recorded?"

"It's quite all right. How old are you?"

"Fifteen."

"Is the tape recorder on?" Frances whispers.

"Oh. Woops." Bridgett pushes the button with a trembling finger.

"Don't worry, I was just going to tell you my age since I was rude enough to ask yours. I'm thirty-six."

Bridgett lets her breath out.

"I'm eighty-two," Irene says from the doorway, slowly pushing her wheelchair into the room. "What do I win?"

Bridgett smiles. "Aren't you supposed to be *in* that thing?"

"I'm getting around just fine."

"We need to see about a walker," Ember says. "Come join us. Park your wheelchair across from Horace."

Tony stands shyly in the doorway.

"You're in trouble if you can't keep up," Irene tells him, bending down next to her chair.

"I'll get that." Tony hurries over and flips the break into place before he helps her climb on.

"This is Ana Kritov," Ember tells them. "Bridgett is about to do an interview."

"Oh, we interrupted," Irene says.

"No, it's OK, but my recorder's on, so I'd better get started. Will you tell us—um, please tell us about the website."

"Katherine has a website for the family members of the victims of Dayle. My sister was one of the two women found with your father at the Secret Gardens. Her name was Cynthia Marks, and she had two little boys, James and Logan. They are now seven and nine and living with me. She made me their guardian after her divorce." Ana is speaking slowly for the sake of Bridgett's frantic scribbling.

"Where—what about the rest of your family?"

"My parents live in Orange County. We were their only children. They are very sad, of course. Please don't contact them—they're angry about your—about Richard not being caught earlier. My father used to be in law enforcement, so not being able to take action makes him feel useless, like his whole life was useless. It's even harder for him than for my mom, I think. No one can figure out if Cynthia knew the other woman or Dayle. She had a date that night, but over near Hollywood, not in Santa Monica. She told him she was taking a taxi home."

"I went to bed at midnight that night, so he must have left after that." Frances can't believe it when Ember begins speaking.

"I don't remember him saying he was going to the garden, but usually he just left a note in case I woke up while he was gone. I never found a note. He might have just had—well, I assumed he had insomnia," she finishes apologetically.

Ana sighs and reaches over to touch Ember's leg. "It must be as hard for you as everyone else. I'm glad my memories of my sister are intact. And my feelings for her. I don't think anyone cared to find out where he met the girls since they already had enough evidence to be sure of the facts—or enough facts. But if somehow you guys figure it out, I would appreciate knowing."

Bridgett and Ember nod.

"Where were her kids?" Bridgett asks.

"They were with a babysitter."

"I don't know what else to ask you. I just want to show the bad as well as—well, the bad effects of his actions. So it's honest. Because that's what he said a biography should be."

"I almost read one of his books out of bitterness and curiosity. But then I heard they became bestsellers after he died. I'm sure they wouldn't answer any of my questions anyway."

Just yesterday Ember told Frances that Richard's will donated the proceeds of his biographies to the American Historical Association, but it was organized so she could redirect the money if she ever needed to.

"I hate life without my sister. She was my closest friend. I wish I hadn't loved her so much. But the love isn't the worst part; it's the *like* that I miss the most. I could tell her everything, from bad gynecological appointments—that comes to mind because I just had one—to boyfriend gossip. No one else will ever understand me like that. I trusted her, and I don't easily trust people." She folds her arms across her chest.

"There are so many reasons for humans to kill, but murderers like Dayle are the most frightening. Especially since he was successful at life. Who was that famous one—Ted Bundy, of course. With the apparently nice family, which Dayle also had, I think. You're all here . . ." She sighs.

"The only thing that makes me feel better is that one hundred years from now, no one will care about our stories. I don't know what changes the world will have experienced, but if someone were to read about us all, perhaps in your book, we will just be a story from history. Hopefully their present will be better, and such things won't happen." She pauses and the tape clicks off. "But I doubt that very much."

"Life is a brief madness," Horace says, and then they wait as Bridgett replaces the tape. Frances plans to copy them for backup. She has glanced at Bridgett's illegible notes.

When the recorder is restarted Ana begins to speak again. "I imagine lives untouched by murder. They might be cursed with cancer or a multitude of other diseases, fatal accidents, betrayals, debt. Wrinkles, fat, divorce, embarrassment—enough to fill up any life. But no murder. Your book will be about murder; that's what readers will be hoping for."

"It's not true crime, it's a biography."

"You know, I've read novels entirely focused on the tiniest thing, like a mother's feelings about her child leaving home to go to college. And perhaps if that's all that has happened . . . Death changes everything, and murder is worse than death. The natural deaths I've known have been peaceful and described as timely, although there are natural deaths that are horrific and make as little sense as murder. But they are unavoidable.

"By the way, Katherine said you were trying to establish a pattern?"

"If possible," Ember says. "Of what compelled him, why he killed some people and not others." Frances winces. "He and Bridgett's mom had a rough divorce, but he never even threatened her. Of course it's difficult to kill a relative and not be caught. That shows us it had nothing to do with bouts of insanity—"

"Madness," Horace says.

"Still seems like insanity to me," Irene says. She was asleep a few seconds ago. "You are a very handsome woman," she tells Ana. "I think it's raining."

"No," Tony says, but they all look out the window and the evening sky, which should be light for two more hours, is dark. "You have amazing hearing."

"I can smell it. Tony, will you please push me out onto the balcony? I want to see the little hills these Californians call mountains. Come say good-bye before you leave, dear."

"I might have another question," Bridgett says. "No, never mind."

"You can always contact me later. Here are the pictures. These are copies, so you can keep them. This one with her boys is from a studio and the most recent, and this other one is her alone—it's not great, but it's all I have."

Frances takes the studio portrait and sees a laughing woman, a younger, more delicate version of Ana, with the same hair. The two boys are laughing too, and they are all leaning in different directions.

"It was Cynthia's favorite because the photographer made some kind of strange noise, and the boys thought it was hilarious."

"Thank you," Ember says faintly.

"Will you sign a paper saying your words can be used in our book?" Bridgett asks, pulling a contract out from under the stack on her clipboard. "We'll let you read your part beforehand if you want. Just sign this second one, and we'll call when we're done."

"I would like to read what you write rather than risk hopeless anger after it's published. Hopeless anger is so tedious." Suddenly sarcastic she adds, "Please let me know if you come up with a plan to stop random murders like Cynthia's."

"You should join one of the groups I mention on the site, Ana. Then you can talk to people in the same situation."

"Did you join one?"

"I told you, there aren't any where I live."

"I'd better get going. The boys are at a party that's supposed to be a sleepover, but something usually goes wrong when fifteen boys under ten are in one house together. Last time Tyler, my younger nephew, started throwing up."

Ember leads the way out of the room. Frances is last and realizes that Ana didn't put her purse down, nor did anyone offer her anything to eat or drink.

"We're so rude," she says after Ana has left. "I can't believe—I have that whole tray of snacks in the fridge. Whatever will she think?"

"She'll understand," Katherine says.

"Turn the recorder off," Ember reminds Bridgett.

"I'm going to put these tapes away somewhere safe. I'm glad she wasn't mad at us."

"No one should be mad at you, Bridgett," Frances says.

"That doesn't mean they won't be. I know that's why Mom is so freaked out. And that last guy was creepy."

"How are we going to fit everyone's opinions of life and death and everything in a book about your dad?" Horace asks.

"Listen," Bridgett says impatiently, putting her journalism tools on the kitchen counter. "I told you ten times, we're just going to use their feelings about their loss and what they think murder does to people. That has a lot to do with his life. And I think we should call him Dayle from now on—at least in front of other people. He's not a friend to them; it will be nicer that way."

"Can I get some of those plastic boxes for files? I need to keep all this stuff organized."

"I'll call my car and we'll go to an office supply store. Anyone else have errands to do?"

"We do need some groceries," Frances says. "Get a hold of your mom, Bridgett, and tell her we'll drop you off later."

"I'd better go too. I have to take these damn contacts out soon, and I need a replacement screw for my glasses." Katherine rubs her eyes carefully.

"My mom probably has one," Bridgett tells her.

"I'm going to ask them if they need anything," Horace says, pointing to Tony and Irene, who are still on the balcony although there is lightning flashing in the distance. Frances has already opened the glass door, and she holds it for Horace.

The four of them stand silently for a moment, until Irene begins to count "one lightening, two lightening" after the next electric flash. The other three join in, getting to five before they hear thunder.

47

Jill invites Katherine to a Wednesday grief session with the provision that she not discuss how her sister died. Tony and Ember aren't regular participants any longer, but since Bridgett wants to be where Katherine is, they attend as well.

The meeting is on a dark, dusty-smelling stage in a high school auditorium. Beyond the small space cleared for the circle of sixteen chairs are piles of cardboard boxes, costumes, and props. Katherine thinks the place is creepy and can't help glancing repeatedly into the dark corners as she tells about her father's disappearance.

"We filed a missing person's report with the police a few years later, even though Mom didn't want to. So I doubt he's been arrested or anything because I've checked back in every year and nothing has shown up."

"Christy, do you know—?" Jill asks the police officer, fairly new to the group and the reason Katherine is here.

Christy, tall and eight months pregnant, is holding hands with her husband, who also has the physique of someone very close to giving birth.

"If a person is reported missing the information is recorded with the National Crime Information Center. Then if they're arrested anywhere in the country, this will show up when their information is entered into the system. Now if your dad just got a traffic ticket or something, it's unlikely anyone would check to see if he was wanted by law enforcement."

"What if he died?" Jill prompts.

"Unless he was never correctly identified, someone would probably have found his family. Do you know which state he might be in?" she asks Katherine.

"I don't know anything."

"It's possible to do a driver's license search, but because of his missing person status, an alert would have shown up if he tried to replace or renew it. Since you have a report on file, you can also have a social security check done. If there's been no use of the social security number over a long period of time it's likely that person has died, unless they've taken another identity."

Katherine nods and looks away, glancing at Bridgett, who is squirming around and trying not to stare at the others in the circle. The girl's skin has started to break out recently and large patches of it are covered with swollen, painful-looking sores.

After group Jill talks to Christy until the officer agrees to help. Katherine doesn't dare think of how much she hopes this will work.

She has been sleeping in Ember's family room in a tent, and after arriving home she goes directly there, takes off all her clothes, and rolls some flowery perfume on the back of her neck and under her breasts. It's not what she would normally choose, but she borrowed it from Ember's bathroom while pretending to need tampons.

She waits for Horace, who is probably close to exploding with lust since there is no privacy to jack-off or whatever he normally does. He can't have that active a sex life back in Mariah, without a car to get around.

Unless they come to him.

One lamp is on in the room, and the light is dampened and eerie through the blue nylon of the tent.

There will be no sleeping tonight. She wonders what Johnny and Alex are doing at home. She knows they lie next to each other when she's not around, which is most nights, but it's not clear how far it goes. They seem to wrestle in slow motion more than is normal for thirty year olds. But this line of thought is not appealing.

Where is that boy?

This is why she agreed on the tent, as the room has no door, just those stupid screens.

Someone, please God be Horace, comes in and carefully closes the dividers; she can hear them knock against the wall.

Her tent opening faces the opposite side of the room, and abruptly she wonders if she imagined his pent up desire. He's probably impotent, and after this they will have to live together in awkward closeness for weeks to come.

"Katherine?" he says softly.

"I'm here." Her voice is too loud.

"OK, I was just going to turn out the light and go to sleep, unless you need it on?"

"No, but come here a minute first, I want to ask you something."

Damn, she should have done it the other way around, waited to approach him when he was almost asleep.

He is suddenly looking down at her and undoing his belt buckle. She can hear his breathing quicken and feels a little letdown. This must have happened to him before.

"Nothing like this has ever happened to me before," he says reverently, stepping out of his pants. He is wearing light blue briefs, tight against his bulging penis. This guy is way bigger than her last one, and whoever says size doesn't matter should do it with Johnny.

Horace pulls his shirt off and kneels down to crawl in the tent. "You're gorgeous."

So is he. She points to the condom by her head on the pillow, as much as she wants to grip his bare dick and stick it in her mouth. He fumbles with it predictably and isn't smooth enough to caress her while he does. She sits up and pulls his underwear down, watching his member pop out. He gets the condom on, and she lies back. There's not enough room for anything complicated.

He is lucky she has been stroking herself because he pushes straight in, skipping foreplay. She's afraid he will be way too fast, which he isn't, although they start and finish with him on top.

She rolls the used condom off, wraps it in paper towels, and puts it in the garbage can by the screen. Then she leans in the tent where he's resting and gets another one from her bag. She turns off the lamp and moves to the couch.

"Where are you?" he asks in a whisper. She hears him get up and fumble around. "Katherine, are you all right?"

"I'm here," she says, standing up and finding him. "Look what I have."

They try to be quiet, but one time she sees someone move in the hall, lit by a distant gleam from the kitchen.

She sleeps partially underneath Horace, waking now and then sweaty but too content to disturb him. When the sky starts to lighten through the window she gets up to use the bathroom, creeping naked down the hall. She covers Horace and throws away the second condom, which has spilled onto the floor.

She gets in the tent and focuses on her dad until people start moving around. Then she takes a shower and gets dressed, pleased to see that Horace is still sound asleep. She doesn't want to talk to him now, not with the phone call to think about.

No one looks at her oddly when she goes in the kitchen for whatever Frances is making today. Her stomach growls despite her fear.

When Tony sits at the counter next to her he winks, and she flicks her tongue at the spying pervert.

Instead of eating, Katherine goes out to the hallway in front of the elevator. She sits against the wall away from the door and pulls her knees up to her chest. Her stomach is queasy.

"Please just don't let him be dead," she says over and over as a mantra blocking out other thoughts, until the door opens and Tony solemnly hands her the phone. She waits while he goes back inside before saying hello.

"Katherine, this is Christy Hernandez. Your father's Georgia driver's license hasn't been renewed in twenty-one years. Nor has another been taken out in that name. Without his social security number, I'm afraid that's all I'll be able to do for you. Good luck," and she hangs up.

Katherine feels as if her ribs are collapsing and wonders why the woman had to be such a bitch about something as simple as looking up a name. If only she had her father's social security number, but none of his things are left in the house. With the help of the boys Katherine has repeatedly searched everywhere. Her mom refuses to discuss him; she must have been so upset when he left that she threw away all his papers. Sometimes she is irrational like that.

Katherine's back is against the cold wall, and she holds the phone to her chest. She starts to make a plan to convince Bridgett that finding Gregory Van Leden is vital to the book project.

48

"I'm so happy to be away from my prison guards for four days," Bridgett says, jumping around the kitchen.

"Katherine's not the cold schemer you think, Ember," Tony insists. "She waltzed into the apartment quivering with excitement, then sat on a stool and immediately started to cry."

"She cries when she wants something," Ember protests, leaning against the counter with her arms crossed. "She wanted to go look for her father."

"Katherine?" Bridgett asks. "That's not true. She used to cry all the time in Mariah. Because she was sad."

"She and Horace were together last night," Tony says.

"What do you mean?" Bridgett asks.

"They were having sex on the couch."

Ember suspected something like that when Horace was so eager to go to Nevada. Not that any guy from the backwoods wouldn't be, but if he'd been interested in—well, it's too stupid to think about now.

"I *thought* she liked him," Bridgett says angrily. "What about her being married?"

"You put two animals in a cage together..." Ember says, and Tony laughs softly.

"I'm glad my mom never did it with him. You didn't like him did you, Ember?"

"Oh no. Well, he is handsome. And a writer. OK, I admit it, I'm jealous!"

"No, you're not." Bridgett hugs her.

"You didn't throw yourself at him," Tony says.

"Any guy would be excited if Katherine threw herself at him."

"I suppose I'd be flattered, not that I could satisfy her."

"Do you like women, Tony?" Bridgett asks.

"I do, and I'll tell you who I like the most."

"Who?"

"Jill."

"Jill?" Ember repeats.

"She's the first woman whose known the truth and flirted with me. I can't just go around and date any girl. I don't even have a *dys*functional—you know."

"Will it be a relief when Irene leaves? She's what's holding you back from going all the way, isn't she?"

Tony sighs. "I guess so. I'm glad she stopped me from having my breasts surgically removed though—I'm in enough debt and pain already. With the hormones and the working out they aren't that much of an issue anyway. I've seen guys whose nipples stick out more than mine, but I'll get them reduced eventually. The rest—I haven't decided about the skin grafting surgery. I keep hoping someone will come up with something better."

"Why do you want to be a man?" Bridgett asks, her eyes wide with the things she shouldn't be hearing.

"It's a long story," Tony says. "I forgot Irene. She sent me in here for potato chips. I tried to convince her she'd eaten them all."

"Are you going to tell me?"

"It's not that exciting. I told you before how I always knew I was a boy, right? Then I found out I was all wrong physically. It was easier for me than for the men I've met who are really women. If a girl is masculine she's a 'tomboy,' and it's considered cute. That's how it was with me. But it's socially unacceptable for a boy to want to be a girl. No matter how young they are their parents are embarrassed, or worse."

"So you think some people are accidentally the wrong—uh, wrong sex?"

"Gender," Ember supplies.

"Yes, I do. Changing's not fun. It's hard work and very expensive. That part is easier for men though. They can pretty much become replicas of women on the outside, from head to foot. The female-to-male transformation is less perfect. If you're curious, you can come to a meeting with me."

"Is my mom afraid I'll decide I'm a boy or something? Because I can tell she sort of doesn't like you."

Tony shrugs as he opens another cupboard door. "People think we're creepy. They can't imagine wanting to change their own gender, so they decide we're all slime balls."

Bridgett laughs. "My mom said people are mean to homosexuals because they fear their lifestyle, but I've heard they are secretly scared they're gay too."

"Maybe," Tony says. "But we all just need some type of person different than us to feel superior to. For me it's drag queens." He makes an evil cackling noise.

"I never thought about whether I felt like a girl or not," Bridgett says.

"That's because you don't need to. You're all right; you're perfect. And lucky."

"It's weird that even though it would be way worse to be in the wrong body like you are," Bridgett says, "it doesn't make me feel better about my life that I'm not. Do you know what I mean? Like that story where one person has the flu and is throwing up and someone says, well at least both your legs aren't broken, like that guy over there. It doesn't make the flu guy feel any better."

"I think it's a guy with one broken leg compared to a guy with two broken legs," Ember says. "That gives the story more symmetry."

"Thank you, Ember," Tony says snidely. "I knew what she meant."

"She's right though," Bridgett says with mock horror. "The flu could kill you. Although," she continues, "do you think it's worse to have a dad who killed people or to be a transsexual?"

"What if you had a father that killed *and* you were a transsexual and in a country being invaded by a conquering army. Even worse than the worst."

"I don't know about that, Ember. If there was a war on in her country, one more murderer wouldn't stand out, and there'd be no time to worry about her gender at all."

"But if both my legs were broken I couldn't escape."

Someone knocks on the door. There was no call from downstairs, but Sammy might be off duty; Jill, who talks to various residents in the elevator, says the other guard is about to be fired for slacking off.

Ember stopped taking the elevator after finding herself breathless in Vicky's gym. She now runs speedily up and down the stairs, saying a polite hello to the blurs she passes. Although it's squinting that blurs her vision, rather than her sprinting. Escape from her post-death elevator schedule is worth even eye wrinkles.

"Check the peephole first," Bridgett reminds her.

Ember was leaving the door unlocked for a while, with everyone coming and going, until Vicky (appropriately for once) "chewed her head off," as Irene described it.

"Grandma!" Liora yells as she steps into the room. "You're up and walking!"

"Stay there, darling, I'm coming." Irene is slowly pushing her wheelchair along the hall.

"Look at Grandma go," Liora teases. "Thank you so much for everything you've done. You guys are great. Guess what, my martyr uncle called in a panic today. His mother changed her mind again! He thinks she's angry because he had to postpone the trip by a few days for a work emergency."

"I thought you were planning on moving to Utah," Ember says to Irene, who has almost reached them.

"I like my doctor here. I've looked over my financial papers, and I can afford to pay you a good solid Utah rate of rent."

"Rent?" Ember asks.

"I was never going to live *with* the family. It was assisted living until I proved my independence, then a duplex. All my expenses are paid from my—and Lou's—investments and social security. I would like to stay here."

"That's fine with me," Ember says, hoping it's the truth. She never thought of the woman dying here. "But if you end up needing some sort of assisted living it will be much more expensive in California. And what if the Rituxin treatments don't work?"

"Medical marijuana," she says with a grin. "Liora can probably hook me up."

Liora rolls her eyes. "A friend of mine offered her a joint and she's telling *everyone* about it. But what about this change of plans?"

Irene is breathing hard and has paled as if she might pass out, or even away, at any moment.

"We'll see you all later," Liora says. "My husband's in the car since there was no parking nearby. We're not only going to dinner on this fun outing, but I have also promised to try and talk some sense into Grandma."

Tony attempts to guide Irene into the wheelchair, but he finally gives up and lifts her high above his head before setting her lightly on the seat.

49

It is such total bullshit, Katherine thinks, lying across the backseat of Vicky's Volvo station wagon. This trip is to look for her father, but everyone is focused on Las Vegas. They insist on escorting her to Ely, yet grumble enormously at the terrible traffic crossing the border: "Even at noon on a Thursday," Frances said like someone who knew.

They talk about the I-15 as if they're truckers, Horace and Frances taking turns driving, sitting in the front and checking on her fondly now and then, thinking she's asleep.

Carl and Vicky are in his car, either in front or behind. Why those two couldn't just head to Las Vegas she doesn't know. And to top it all, the first stop in Ely will be at what is apparently the town's only gym.

In the light everything was brown and orange and burnt, now endless headlamps flash by them at amazing speeds. Both Horace, who is driving now, and Frances have become very quiet the last few hours, and Katherine imagines that like her they are scared of the big trucks rushing by in the dark, their bulk creating a current of air that shakes the car.

Unless her father has become a derelict gambler, there's no reason he would still be in this stale, parched state. The gambling thing would be so pathetic, so clichéd, so perfectly forgivable. They could lead him, weak and quaking, away from his tormenting debtors and nurse him to moral health in Ember's apartment until they have raised the money to return home.

Frances' new cell phone rings.

"It's Carl, wanting to know if we need a stop. He says we're less than an hour from Ely, but if you want to switch out?"

"Not unless they need to," Horace says tersely.

Katherine sits up and shakes her head. She's had enough of stopping with Vicky, who insists they run around and stretch while she wipes the dust off her white vehicle. She has it cleaned and waxed every single week. The seats are white leather, but for this trip she covered them with stained white towels.

"You missed the Extraterrestrial Highway," Frances says. "There was nothing to see or we would have woken you up. Maybe on the way to Vegas we'll look for tourist stops."

Katherine hates the way they say "Vegas" so casually. They're from Hicksville, Georgia, for God's sake. It's like her father hating people born after the Vietnam War calling it "Nam." He wasn't in the war either, but at least he was born then. Here they are just trying to be hip, which is especially sickening in a sixty year old.

Now that everything seems possible, she's starting to think of reasons it might not be a good idea to bring her dad back home. Her mom is so content with her progressive Protestant religious group, and Dad was an extremely conservative Baptist. Mom even gets angry less often—or at least she channels it differently. After injuring her right arm twice while trying to toss bowling balls into the pool, she joined the churchwomen's aerobics class and has talked about getting a punching bag for stressful moments. And the boys—well, she isn't sure what they are up to, but her father would definitely be more alert than Mom in ferreting out the meaning behind their games which always end in tickling.

"I think I'm going to throw up," Katherine says.

"What?"

She lies back down and holds her knees up against her chest. If she stays in California and gets a job, she will never have to deal with any of them again. All their problems, all their faith in her to solve them, never recognizing that she can't, she doesn't want to, she doesn't even know who the hell they are.

50

Bridgett is sitting between Tony and Ember in the backseat of the Lincoln Town car. It's always the same type of black car with darkly tinted windows, but Bridgett feels affronted when the interior and exterior aren't expressly clean. Ember is usually distracted by paperwork and doesn't notice if it smells musty or of someone else.

Tony is chattering to Bridgett although she knows he really wants Ember's attention. "People are too obsessed with their parents," he says. "Seriously, look at you and Katherine."

"They have unusual situations," Ember responds.

"You're not obsessed with your parents," Tony tells her. "They're there, you're here. You hardly think about them, right? You had a lovely childhood."

Ember nods, but her pen continues to move across the form she's viewing, then she opens her laptop and peers at it with her forehead creased.

"Does Ember ever talk to her drivers?" Tony whispers.

"I don't think so. One got a crush on her a long time ago and would take her places without asking permission. Dad told the company only women drivers."

"I think it would be easier to just get in your car and go."

He leans forward and knocks on the solid partition blocking the driver from view. It slowly slides down until they see long brown hair.

"You're a woman!" Tony says. "Sorry, I expected—"

"Weren't you listening to me?" Bridgett asks.

"I'm Lisa." The driver turns her head briefly and smiles, showing large teeth that seem far too white. "Ms. Oto always has a female driver. Only three women work for the company, and we all want her call because—well, I was going to say there are never any guys to deal with." She chuckles.

"Oh, I'm not a guy," Tony says, and then blushes. Lisa laughs and seems to think he's flirting; Bridgett accepts worriedly that he probably is. This can't turn out happily for either of them. "Does this service work like a—like a, uh, taxi?"

"Not usually. Our regulars tend to have scheduled times then pay extra for extra, which is how Ms. Oto does it now. Mr. Dayle had it set up differently."

Tony asks too many questions, Bridgett thinks. He is always so eager and lonely; it's sort of embarrassing. Of course it would be horrible to have to tell everyone you dated that you didn't have a penis. Gummy showed her his once when they were smoking pot. It was clearly important to him. She touched it when he asked—more like a poke really.

Ember's hair is hanging over the side of her face. It looks sort of raggedy. She used to have the sleekest hair; even Mom admired how it was like glossy silk.

Lisa flashes Tony another smile when they hit a stoplight, then gestures toward Ember and rolls up the window. Tony talks about this and that a little too loudly and with a lot of bravado, reminding Bridgett of the boys at school. She is pretty sure Lisa wouldn't hear through that glass even if he screamed. Ember doesn't seem aware of Tony's silliness. She's not paying attention, and Bridgett, stuck between them, is bored.

"I wonder if Irene's family was impressed that she's being treated in Beverly Hills," Tony says when they pull in front of the medical building. The driver's window remains up.

Poor Tony, Bridgett thinks.

The office for Irene's doctor is on the second floor. The door is huge and heavy against the thick carpet, opening to the soothing sounds of water from a fountain against one wall. They know Sharon, who sits to the right of the reception desk, and she smiles and waves her hand with long French-tipped nails as they enter.

"Go right in."

"They want to keep Irene entertained at all costs," Tony whispers as they walk past the nurses' station.

Irene is the only patient in the room today, and she's eating fried chicken out of a box with napkins carefully covering her chest. Liora sits on an empty bed, and Irene's son Bradley has a stool in the middle of the room.

"No problems this time, I guess," Tony says.

Last week Irene was given a blood transfusion and some tests to prepare for her trip to Utah, which she had agreed to again. It was delayed when one of Bradley's sons developed appendicitis.

"She's had a bottle of V-8 juice and is planning on two candy bars for dessert," Bradley says with awe. Irene weighed seventy-five pounds when she started her treatment for lymphoma, and now she has made it back up to ninety-nine.

"It was scary when she stopped liking chocolate," Liora says. "That's how I *knew* something was wrong."

"I wasn't hungry for anything." Irene is holding a bone.

Bridgett hears her own stomach growl, and she hates fried fast food.

"Remember, Bradley, when you or Grandpa would make peach ice cream and Grandma would make soft fudge and say, 'Have a little ice cream with your fudge.'"

"When do you know if the lymphoma is gone?" Bridgett asks. She wishes they would test Irene early, just to get an idea.

"Four more Rituxin treatments and then they'll scan her bone marrow."

"Please hand me a candy bar." Irene gives her son the empty box stuffed with her spotless napkin bib.

"You have perfect manners, even when eating with your hands," he says. "But you still need a sound spanking. Aren't your kids allowed to control your life now that you're old? You think you're still in charge here?" In a pretty good imitation of a ten year old he whines, "All my friends get to tell their parents what to do."

"Speaking of spankings, you didn't get enough. I remember your dad spanked your oldest brother a few times, but it was so much more of a punishment for himself. He would go in the bedroom and cry afterward, when your brother had forgotten the whole thing. By the time the rest of you came along he'd given up entirely."

Bridgett wonders why bringing her husband up always makes Irene look sad; she enjoys it when anyone else talks about him.

"Ember," Bradley says. "I wanted to ask if you have to pay extra when we use your car service."

"The book fund can pay for some of it," Bridgett says.

"That fund seems to be paying for a lot when we've only done two interviews."

"We have one tonight."

"When my nurse, you know Nancy, found out I was writing a book," Irene says, "she talked to her author son and his advice was to pay attention to my five senses at all times. Do you do that?

"Of course I don't have much hope of ever finishing my book since my sons aren't doing their parts. Bradley's the only one who might come through."

"I'll write my segment. I have some funny stories about when you were delirious."

Tony excuses himself to use the bathroom, and Bradley hands his mom the second candy bar. He motions for Ember and Liora to follow him outside. Bridgett stands next to the doorway with her back to them so she can hear.

"I guess I'm going to have to leave Mom until she changes her mind," he says out in the hall. "She seems proud of how she takes care of that transvestite—"

"Transsexual," Liora says.

"Maybe she wants to save him from his perversion, but whatever it is, at least he seems like a nice guy. And he's given her a new lease on life. Even I have to admit that. She hasn't said she would rather be dead lately. If we forced her to go home she would enjoy having us nearby, but we wouldn't need her like he does—or like she thinks he does.

"Mom—your grandma," he tells Liora, "doesn't have as much money as she assumes. We'll have to talk more with Ember about expenses. I can't believe how much Mom eats now!"

"Did you get the results of the labs from last week?" Bridgett asks Irene when they come back into the room.

"Excellent vital signs," Irene says. "Strong and steady heart rate, clear lungs. Hemoglobin is 8.1, whatever that means, and my platelets are a whopping 103,000. Up from 44,000."

"Bradley couldn't interpret Rosa's accent, so Irene repeated everything after her slowly and clearly," Liora says. "It was quite embarrassing."

"And Rosa's the nicest nurse too."

"I told her my son is from Canada and she understood."

"Why Canada?"

"Because people around here haven't heard of Utah."

"Everyone's heard of Utah, Mom."

"We should go," Ember says. "We have some victims coming—I sound like a vampire. Interviewees. It was nice to see you again, Liora, Bradley."

"Did I ever tell you that Bradley used to look just like Clark Gable? Oh yes, the women would swoon. Not so much since he shaved his mustache off though," Irene says fondly. "I don't know why you did that."

"I haven't had a mustache for over fifteen years."

"And when he still had hair in front," Liora adds, jumping out of the way as he pretends to swat her.

On the way back Tony somehow maneuvers to sit by the driver, but Bridgett is glad because she has enough room to take a nap. They were up until three in the morning playing charades.

She feels heavy when Ember wakes her but slowly follows them out of the car. Tony is extra hyper and starts to race Ember up the stairs, a ridiculous activity that the nice lethargic Ember of a few weeks ago wouldn't have participated in. Another one snared by her mother's exercise propaganda.

Bridgett can hear their pounding feet until they open the stairwell door and call to see if she's coming.

"I'm fine, I'll be there in a few minutes," she yells back.

It becomes totally quiet. She wants to be alone now and sits down where she is, on a stair between the third and fourth floor.

She remembers she's supposed to be aware of her senses, so she sniffs for the faint mixture of cigarette smoke, paint, and cologne. Then she wonders if it's all her imagination because she knows Katherine has smoked here even though it's against the rules, she saw someone touching up the walls yesterday, and she herself spilled cologne from a free sample bottle. Another sniff and she can't recognize anything. Imaginary senses might be fine for an artist of fiction, but not of biography.

She bores herself describing the flat but clean gray carpet and the cottage cheese textured off-white walls. She hears someone coming down and listens to the footsteps combining with the beat of her heart, which has become more apparent and ruins the description she is creating by getting louder. She doesn't look up as the person comes closer and is soon staring at two slick brown slippers with hairy legs poking out of them. The legs also have disgusting moles. They are very white and thin, and the hair is very black and curly.

"I'm Randall Murphy. We met in the elevator last week. You know, your dad owed me ten bucks when he died. We'd play monopoly using real money, and one game could go on for weeks."

Bridgett slips her tiny wallet from the front pocket of her shorts. She knows she has two ten-dollar bills, and she takes one out and holds it above her head.

Randall Murphy doesn't do anything for a few moments, and then he pulls it from her fingers. "Well," he says and then clears his throat. "Debt paid." He continues on down the stairs. Bridgett keeps staring at the floor until she is sure that he's gone far enough that he won't be able to see her. She doesn't know why she just gave away half of all the money she has.

Randall Murphy lives in the penthouse above Ember and is very wealthy. He was also mean after her dad died, arranging for everyone to sign a letter asking Ember to move.

And she knows that just now he hadn't wanted the money back; he was trying to be friendly and maybe funny. It doesn't seem right that people never apologize though; they just expect everything to go back to normal as soon as they feel ready. Like they were the sufferers and have good-naturedly let their animosity go. It's becoming clear to her that only one or two people in the world are aware of their own thoughts and actions.

That Murphy guy might be coming right back after he checks his mail, so she stands and trudges up the stairs, going extremely slowly until her thighs ache. She doesn't remember what he looks like from the elevator and is glad she didn't glimpse more than his calves this time, so if she passes him again she won't know it.

The rich old jerk is probably buying ten dollars worth of breakfast and feeling a warm glow over his excellent fortune.

51

Horace stares blearily at Vicky, who has already been up for an hour and has a handful of brochures and a list of things to do in Ely. She mentions murals, trains, and hiking before asking why Katherine hasn't joined them at the diner.

The light coming in the windows is very yellow and relaxes him despite a rough night and the lingering grittiness of traveling. They rented two rooms at Hotel Tokoro (just to tell Ember) in the middle of town, after driving by the health club that was predictably dark at one in the morning. In the first room Frances and Katherine slept in the twin beds and Horace used a cot on the floor, while Vicky and Carl shared the second.

"Katherine was throwing up all night." Horace drinks coffee and tries to avoid looking at the syrup and leftover bites of soggy pancake on Carl's plate. "She's too sick to leave her bed."

In a commanding voice Vicky spews out a list of instructions and suggestions, all of which Horace and Frances discussed earlier between patchy moments of sleep.

"I'm going to visit the place her dad used to live."

"Do you want to meet back at the hotel at a certain time?"

Old Carl looks pretty happy, Horace thinks with bitterness. They probably had a great vacation fuck while he and Frances were cleaning up vomit. Then he remembers wearily that the couple barely knows Katherine, and Vicky did lend them her new car for the trip.

"Don't worry about it," he says. "I bet we'll stay overnight again anyway. We'll leave you a message at the front desk."

"We packed our luggage back into the car this morning, so if we have to move it's fine." Vicky kisses Carl on the cheek and they go off to find Frances, who is paying her bill.

Horace glares at the table. He almost puked watching and smelling Katherine throwing up. After the first time all over the covers she made it to the toilet, until Frances got her the ice bucket.

He felt fond of her even during this and was quite aroused when he saw her take off her soggy tank top. She had nothing underneath and Frances instinctively shielded her, but he already had a hard-on.

Maybe he is in love.

"Are you ready to go?" Frances asks. She takes a deep, appreciative breath of the air outside the café.

"I've got the map—should we go check on Katherine first?"

"Maybe we should ask her what she wants us to do. I don't know if she should be left alone."

"No way you're deserting me. What if he's there? I don't want to be the one to scare him off. And we can't wait." Mockingly he whispers, "He might hear we're in town."

"Let's hurry then, it would be dreadful if we brought her father to see her moments after she chokes to death on her own vomit."

"That's not funny."

"I'm sorry. It's being around that rotten Carl."

They climb in the car, and Frances drives while Horace navigates. Yesterday he found that unless she's behind the wheel, she tends to fall deep into thought and forget to watch the map.

"This is a big city compared to Mariah," Horace notes wryly. "Go right at Wyatt Boulevard. Good old Wyatt Earp. Hey, Ember was saying our town song is in a movie?"

"Yes, *Paint Your Wagon*. But we adopted the song before that; it was written in the 50s by the Kingston Trio."

"I always thought our founding father wrote it for his lost lover."

"No, it's about the *desert* wind. Haven't you ever listened to the words?"

"Here, sorry, turn left—the street we just passed. It's a tiny sign, almost didn't see it. Then the next major intersection should be Wild Bill Cody Ave. On the right-hand corner. I think—Here it is."

They pull up at a small, pale yellow building with dry, patchy grass. A startlingly white, knee-high vinyl fence surrounds it, but the space between each two-inch slat is more than a foot wide.

Horace is disappointed in the place. He imagined a ramshackle boarding house, dark and spacious, where fallen men and women gathered to pool their resources. He pictured them not talking much but growing their own food and chopping their own wood.

He sighs. "Let's go."

They walk through the open gate to the front door, and he pushes the doorbell. There's no sound, so he waits a moment and then knocks loudly with his knuckles. They both move back a little and stand silently.

"I guess no one's home," he says after a moment.

Frances knocks again and pushes the doorbell long and hard.

"Who are you?" a female voice asks.

"We're looking for a man named Gregory Van Leden," Frances says firmly.

After a silence they hear a deadlock being flipped. The door opens onto an empty hall, and Horace is about to step in when Frances pulls his arm. A woman peeks around the door and then shows her entire self. She is taller than Horace and appears to easily carry around three hundred pounds, with hair more gloriously red even than Katherine's.

"Gregory Van Leden? I haven't thought of him for a while," she says, moving down the hall.

Horace follows Frances in and shuts the door.

"I was sketching and I generally don't bother with visitors, but things weren't going well, so I thought, what the hell."

"An artist?" Horace asks.

She laughs. "Just to decrease my anxiety. It's the seventh or eighth thing I've tried, but I'm afraid it's not been successful so far. I give them each a month, which my doctor says isn't enough. Never marry your doctor."

They end up in a room with couches and a television but no easel. "Sit down, please. I won't be showing off my husband's portrait today. He will think it's grand and hang it in his office, then repeat compliments from anxious patients and lament over me quitting when I had such great talent. It was the same with piano and belly dancing.

"So who are you?"

They give her their names and relationship to the Van Ledens, and she introduces herself as Claude.

Horace sits next to Frances on a green couch, then Claude chooses a chair off to the right, so they both have to turn sideways to see her.

"Gregory Van Leden lived in our garage and worked for my father. He was like a brother to me. Why are you looking for him?"

"The police were told he might have moved to Las Vegas, but we decided to try here first."

"I can't imagine who would have told them that. I guess this means he's still missing? His daughter has been calling us more than a dozen times a year. She wanted to come out here before, wasn't convinced we didn't have him hiding in the basement. Her dad chose us for their godparents although we never met the kids. We send presents on their birthdays and at Christmas. He was born over there, but his family was no good. I couldn't believe it when he decided to move back permanently. He found this place when he was hitchhiking and fell asleep in the back of a truck. He meant to go to Las Vegas but didn't know the slightest thing about how to get there. I'm surprised he landed in the right state. Well, I was an only child and as glad to have a brother as my parents were to have a son."

"When was this?" Frances asks.

"I don't know what year it was. We were the same age and I'm—well, none of your business—"

"We know her dad is fifty-seven," Horace says slyly.

"Well then, there you go, smart ass. Just hearing those digits is a shock. Since we were the same age we'd pretend we were twins— You must not have met him, or you'd be laughing hysterically."

"I don't think I ever saw him," Frances says, and Horace shakes his head. "We aren't from Caldwell."

"Well, he was small and wiry, while I was always large boned. He left Ely at eighteen. Eight years after he showed up."

"My goodness."

"Yeah, he was a brave little bugger. Planned to go to Las Vegas at ten years old and get rich. His dad died after he turned eighteen and he got some property, that's why he returned. Said he would sell it and come back, but he never did. There was something he was afraid of here, I can't remember what it was... Gregory—I mean George—might remember. Now I'm going to be mixing their names up all day. George and Gregory were never friends, but they hung with the same crowd. I'm going to call him." She stands and hurries through the doorway.

Horace settles back, worrying about Katherine. They left the number to the cell phone, but who knows if she is delirious with fever by now.

"George is coming home after his next patient, an ear infection," Claude yells, following her voice back into the room.

"Maybe we should come back later," Frances suggests. "We left our friend, Gregory's daughter, at the hotel. She has the flu."

"You can bring her here," Claude says. "The building we call the garage is really quite a nice little apartment. When my parents were alive they took boarders, with the condition they vacate immediately should George—Gregory come back. And we've had our flu shots."

"Could we rent the garage for one night, or is it too small?"

"It's big enough. There's one room and a loft. We'll just have to get out the sleeping bags."

After more discussion Frances returns to the hotel to fetch Katherine and leave a message for the others. Horace isn't sure why he is staying behind. Is Frances worried Katherine won't be modestly attired?

"Are you hot?" Claude asks.

Horace nods. "A little." There's a layer of wet over his face. It feels like the house is closed up.

"This is cool for me. Let me change out of my painting smock slash pajamas into something warmer, then I'll turn the air on."

Horace has always thought that large people had more body heat, but maybe not. She appears to be mostly muscle and great big bones. He smiles imagining her husband being thrown about during sex, but when the doctor shows up thirty minutes later he is a wide wall of muscle at least six and a half feet tall.

Claude enters as soon as they have introduced themselves and is wearing a low-cut, emerald muumuu, which makes her look like a stretched out Katherine. Horace doesn't stand; he's not used to being the smallest person in a room.

"Beautiful," George tells her, then murmurs something in her ear.

Horace stares at the floor.

"What do you think?" George asks him.

"You look a lot like Gregory's daughter," Horace tells Claude. "Not in height or anything—"

"The enlarged version?" Claude asks helpfully. "I can't wait to meet her!"

"He probably married someone who looked just like you. Gregory was always in love with Claude."

"It was nothing more than brotherly affection, you jealous old fool. Come help me get some refreshments for our guests."

After what seems like an hour, Horace gets up and walks around to wake his right foot from its numbness. He sits back down quickly with it in the prickly stage when the doorbell rings. It rings four long times before he decides to answer it himself.

"I'm sorry, I kept thinking they would let you in," he tells Frances, who is practically carrying Katherine. He supports one limp arm, and they lead her inside. "Do you feel any better?"

"Yes," she says, her eyes glazed with exhaustion.

"She fought me about coming here. Said it was something she planned to do alone and I was ruining everything. She was really upset until she collapsed. I guess she had some energy earlier because she changed rooms so they could clean the other one," Frances says as they both help her to the couch. "They were so nice I paid for an extra night, so we can go back if we need to. I left a message for Carl and Vicky at the front desk. No need to call and interrupt their day. Let's ask Claude for a pan."

"You're here!" Claude says. Her face is very red and George's clothes are a bit rumpled, but Horace can't be sure they weren't just mixing the iced tea, a drink he loathes.

George is carrying a low table, which he puts in front of the couch for Claude to place the tray on. Then he removes a red plastic mixing bowl and sets it next to Katherine.

"I'm so glad to meet you," Claude says, handing her a mug. "This tea will make you feel better immediately. Be careful, it's hot. After you drink it, I want you to take this little pellet and let it dissolve on your tongue. In fifteen minutes you'll be ready for some chicken noodle soup, which is easy enough on the stomach. If you keep that down—well, I shouldn't get ahead of myself."

"I'm a doctor married to a homeopath—similar to psychopath," George says. "When my patients aren't happy with what I tell them, they come to my wife for the real deal."

Horace looks at Frances, a little nervous about the stranger's pellet, but Katherine gulped the hot tea and is already putting the capsule on her tongue. Claude takes the mug for a refill, and Frances asks about the ingredients.

"A mixture of herbs good for the flu. Let's see, elderberry, ginseng, coriander, cinnamon, ginger, rosehips..."

Frances is forced from politeness to rise and follow Claude out of the room as she continues to answer the question.

After Katherine has her soup, she blows her nose like a little girl and sits up straight.

"Well," Claude says when she returns, "I remembered why Gregory wanted to leave, besides his inheritance. There was a man in town he used to help out to make extra money. Kip Smith. They would repair porches, haul away tree branches, that sort of thing. Kip was arrested for sexually abusing a number of children, and the police and prosecution lawyers kept trying to get Gregory to say something had happened to him. He insisted nothing had, but they wouldn't stop bothering him."

"And the other teenagers didn't help. We teased him about being gay and other stupid things. I was jealous of the way he followed Claude around like a desperate puppy—"

"I'm sorry, Katherine, George and Gregory never got along."

"That's OK," Katherine says. "I like to see how things were when he was a kid. I know Dad liked you because he used to say Mom looked the same. I don't see the resemblance now. My mom did have red hair, but it faded and now she gets it done blond. She looks older too; she's all wrinkled."

"Well, she's had a hard life. What does she think about you coming here?"

"She doesn't know."

"Was I drugged too?" Horace asks. "Because I'm confused. You told us that the police listed this as your dad's last address."

"No, that's not what I said. You misunderstood."

But Horace is sure he didn't. Katherine said the police scanned the driver's license database and found her father's name listed with this address in Ely, Nevada, and after contacting the address heard he had left for Las Vegas. So they drove here to find some clues for where to look in the big city and to make sure he hadn't returned.

"It doesn't make any sense that they gave you this address," Horace says.

George stands up and stretches his arms out in front of him, palms up. "Sometimes by the grace of God things just work out."

"No they don't," Katherine says furiously, and then slouches over as if in pain. "Oh, I forgot. Where's the bowl?" She throws up into it and then carries it out of the room.

"She would have been fine if we hadn't let her get so excited," Claude says. "Oh, dear."

Katherine comes back, clean but pale. "Don't worry about the details. This is my investigation. Why don't you guys just go back to the hotel, and I'll get a ride over there tonight. Where are Vicky and Carl?"

"They're sightseeing."

"You can go sightsee too."

"Katherine," Horace says, feeling a little slow. "You already knew this address. Claude said you've always known about them. Why would you need the police?"

Katherine groans loudly. "Listen, the police found nothing. His old Georgia license wasn't renewed, and they're too fucking stupid to check for anything else. I had to come here because I thought he might have come back, or they might have some of his personal papers with a social security number or something. My mom got rid of everything we had—It's all gone."

"We still have boxes of my parents' things in the shed behind the garage. We could check them."

"We're spending the night here," Frances tells Katherine.

Horace is annoyed that Katherine is getting away with this. She could at least have told him. Her plans must have been to visit

Claude on her own and never have anyone find out the truth. He sees her watching him with her eyes wide and her mouth turned down so her chin is all dimpled up.

He sighs. It's impossible to stay mad. If it were his parent he would probably do the same.

52

Ember tries not to dwell on how annoyed Richard would feel over so many people staying in their home. It helps that thoughts of him lately have seemed impersonal, like reflections on a natural disaster. Even the habit of reminding herself to share Bridgett's cute sayings has decreased. Still, she wonders if he would find it amusing that his daughter wants a write-up on their sex life for his biography. Besides being steadfastly private in that area, she doesn't plan to dredge up the memories. Making love is personal, but so is taking a life. She can't believe she slept comfortably next to every woman's worst nightmare.

And as they sit down to interview another family for the biography, she wonders what she would be feeling now, almost two years later, if he had died at home and never been caught.

"Ready?" Bridgett asks her.

Ember nods and considers Mrs. Thompson, with sleek frosted hair and skin that seems to have been tanned and creased and struggled with and then re-stretched over fine bones. Her husband is large in a fit way, with the healthy complexion of someone who plays nonstrenuous outdoor sports. Their son doesn't resemble either: too tall, with almost-shaved dark hair, serious acne, and a twitchiness that emphasizes the contrast between himself and his parents.

"First of all, is there anything you would *like* to talk about?" Bridgett asks. Frances and Vicky vetoed this question, thinking it left too much room for abuse.

"You're brave to do this," the son tells them. "But I'm worried that the book will honor the man that killed my sister, and even though I wouldn't blame you for that, I don't want our names connected to it. Then it would be like—"

"We've forgiven him, Brad," his mother chides gently. "It's not up to us to judge."

Bridgett says, "I plan to show the devastation of Dayle's negative acts and the impact of his positive ones. I want to try and understand what made him the way he was, and how he could be so good to some people yet—just, *destroy* others. I would like your story, the story of your daughter. I want to show the people who died and their loved ones."

Brad nods. "I've thought about what I want to tell you. I just wanted you to understand. As you know, my sister was named Ann, but everyone called her Summer. She was a very blond baby. I wasn't born until she was five, and she always bossed me around." His eyes roll up toward the ceiling and he smiles. "I'm sure she's telling everyone what to do in heaven.

"She'd been anorexic and bulimic in high school and college but was recovering. Had recovered. She spoke to other teenage girls at church about self-image. Three months before she died she got engaged to Heath Gardener. We don't know how she met Mr. Dayle because she never went to bars and didn't drink alcohol. We don't think she knew the woman found with her either."

Bridgett and Ember look at each other. Katherine hadn't told them this was the family of one of the last two victims.

"She was in Santa Monica helping some teenagers prepare for a beauty pageant," her mom says. "She arrived before it started, but no one saw her afterward, when she would normally have still been around. Summer used to compete herself—she got a scholarship to college."

"That covered half," Mr. Thompson says. "The other half was paid by basketball."

"Her talent during pageants was piano."

"And she could sing better than anything," her brother says. "She wanted to have six kids—and to teach music and coach b-ball. She was the best on her college team."

"As you will be," his father tells him firmly.

"Me?" Bridgett asks, looking up in surprise. "Oh, sorry." She blushes.

Ember almost laughs imagining Bridgett's next plan is to take up the victims' lives where they left off.

"She was careful," Mr. Thompson says. "She never took any stupid chances."

"But she never believed anything bad would happen to her," Brad says. "I wish she'd been majorly paranoid like Mom."

"I'm not paranoid," Mrs. Thompson denies half-heartedly, and then no one speaks for a while.

Richard was paranoid, but that was probably connected to his criminal activities. This is another aspect of his posthumously revealed self that disappoints Ember. The paranoia was sometimes frustrating, but it was part of him and could be amusing and endearing and many other "-ings." At times, she had been convinced that the eavesdropping device merely showed his interest in human behavior, along with giving him a chance for a little harmless revenge on his detractors.

"We tried to get Heath to come with us," Mrs. Thompson says suddenly. "He needs to talk to someone. His family is telling him to start dating again, that it's been almost two years and he needs to get married, but he doesn't want to be sealed to anyone else. We're LDS, and when members get married in our Temple, we're married to that person for all eternity."

There's another long moment of silence.

"What if you loved the second one more?" Bridgett finally asks with dismay, and Ember isn't sure why until the girl glances at her. Is she thinking of Ember being attached to Richard forever? Although under those rules it would have been Vicky in that position. Unless divorce undoes the eternity clause.

"We have to trust in our Lord to work everything out," Mr. Thompson says.

"Maybe Heath should be creating a family," his wife adds uncertainly, "but he can't be forced to marry before he's ready."

"He could marry someone who has been through the same thing?" Bridgett suggests as a question.

"Good idea," Brad says, smiling at her and flushing.

"Although he'd still have to be in love," she adds.

"Not in the same way," Brad replies.

Mrs. Thompson sighs long and deeply. "He's an accountant now, and he volunteers nights and weekends at the Crisis Call Center, making him more and more depressed. Apparently a lot of people call who aren't getting along with their spouses, and he has no empathy. He's been told twice not to say they should be grateful their true love wasn't brutally murdered. He and Summer grew up together, and even though they didn't start dating until they were both at BYU, I think he had a crush on her since they were tiny."

The conversation moves to a news story about the bodies of two unidentified little girls that were found recently. The Thompsons leave soon after, and Ember thinks they look disappointed.

"Maybe it doesn't matter if someone is killed," Bridgett says sadly.

"Why do you say that?" Ember asks, sitting back down, this time across from her.

"Think about Heath. Everyone already wants him to get married. Who knows if he won't fall in love with this new person as much as Summer and not even care that she died anymore. It's unfair. If someone gets remarried that means they didn't really love the first one. I mean, a general person, not *you*."

"Why not me?" Ember asks.

"I don't know. Would you still have loved Dad if you knew what he did?"

"That's the question." Ember sighs. "I wouldn't have if I really *knew*, but if he had lived I would probably have believed in his innocence for a long time, despite everything, unless he admitted guilt. After he was caught, I mean. Some wives of killers might be able to look back with all the evidence and say, 'Oh yeah, I was just in denial' or 'So that's what that was all about,' but besides him leaving in the middle of the night to garden and having dirt on the knees of his pants, nothing has jumped out at me. After I believed he did it I would have divorced him. The memories I have of your father are so tainted I wish I could just forget the whole relationship."

"I wouldn't care if you got married again. Or just fell in love," Bridgett murmurs as Ember continues, "I do sometimes wonder if he would have had a good enough explanation—I know there isn't one. It's just one of the irrational things I think about sometimes. I don't feel it's about me, what he did. Still, I don't want to love someone who murdered people. I'm definitely not planning on a devoted widowhood. But think of this—if I ever want to get serious with someone again, I'm going to have to go through the whole story first. Unless I fall for a reporter."

Bridgett laughs.

"Which would only be excusable," Ember adds, "if I didn't know he was a reporter until after his death."

53

George and Claude are both asleep, one snoring softly and the other giggling and muttering. Katherine continues to search the Internet on their only computer in the bedroom. Frances and Horace are finally too tired to stare at the static screen in the dark, so they pat her on the back and head to the guesthouse.

Frances thinks the little cottage they call the garage is much prettier than the house. The door, large enough for a car to enter, has been sealed down with a smaller one cut out of the center. There's a thin rectangular window above it and between the two openings it's quite drafty. The walls are painted a rose color, and the entire floor is thickly carpeted in the same shade, including the stairs and the loft. In the middle of the room is an enormous gray couch in front of a gas fireplace. Earlier George set them up with a heap of only slightly musty blankets and pillows from the closet next to the bathroom.

"I wonder if Claude's parents lived here themselves after she and George were married?" Frances muses.

"It looks like someone did."

"I'm going to sleep right next to the fire," she says. "I can't believe how cold I am all of a sudden."

"You don't have Katherine's flu, do you?"

"Please, no. You'll have to shoot me."

"I'll wake Claude up to feed you pellets."

Vicky and Carl opted to stay at the hotel, which is fine with Frances since they sounded so relaxed—she only spoke with Vicky, but she knows that if Vicky is happy then Carl is too. She chides herself for thinking of him simplistically. If something were wrong at his restaurant—well, of course then Vicky would also be worried. Although . . .

"Darn," Frances mutters, rubbing her forehead.

"What?"

"My mind—I keep thinking in circles."

"Are you thinking about Katherine lying to us?"

They are sitting on either end of the couch.

"I guess it's the only way she thought she could get here." Frances wasn't surprised by the trick. "As far as her search, coming here makes a lot of sense. Besides Caldwell, this was his only home, right?"

"But she can't really believe we're going to find him in Las Vegas using information from people who haven't seen him in thirty years?"

"Well, she's never been there. Maybe to her it's manageable. Remember the airport? Surely you've wanted something so badly it skewed your judgment."

Horace thinks for a minute. "No, I don't think I have. I've failed jobs I didn't even apply for. I was wondering, wouldn't her dad's social security number be listed somewhere on his missing person's report?"

"I don't know. Do you think he's still alive?"

"He must be, or someone would have informed the family."

All afternoon and most of the night they had stared at pictures of the unidentified dead. At least four websites were organized for that purpose, and it was ghastly seeing all the distorted faces. Most were bloated and bruised, but even the open-casket worthy looked deceased. Frances was sure it would make Katherine throw up again, but she just scrolled through page after page, pausing on any likely man and reading all his information.

"Do you think she's done that search before?" Horace asks. "She seemed to know right where to go."

"Probably," Frances says morosely. "The poor girl is never going to get over this without some closure. Even if we could find out that he was dead . . ."

"I'm not sure about that."

"Well, she can't spend her whole life looking for him. It's too bad there was nothing in those boxes."

"She's thinking he had a false identity, but why would he? Did he think Richard was after him?"

"What about fingerprints?" Frances asks. "Katherine doesn't think he was ever printed, but maybe we should call the police station back home. They take prints for all sorts of reasons now. Children are sometimes fingerprinted for safety purposes. Not so much when *he* was little, but you never know. We can ask about the social security number at the same time. And if *that* doesn't work, she can convince her mother to try some government agencies."

Horace isn't listening; he's heading up the stairs to the loft with an intent expression. Frances is afraid the idea of Richard having killed Gregory Van Leden is playing around in his lovesick mind, about to cause her family more havoc.

54

Bridgett is ready to burn her entire book project after the interviews with Samantha Frank and Casper Sentinnel.

But she made such a big deal about wanting to hear what people really felt, and they will all use it against her forever if she quits now, so all she says is, "I feel like today has lasted for years."

"Because your parents are still gone?" Ember asks with some surprise.

"No. Not because of *them*. Never mind."

Samantha Frank's daughter was killed. She yelled at Bridgett about white men and racism and the exploitation of women of color. The shouting didn't bother her little boy; he just looked around with curious, wide eyes.

Bridgett was truly worried because her family, on her dad's side, has a terrible secret, and for a few minutes it seemed Samantha had discovered it. People that find her mysterious because of the murders would avoid her if they knew that her ancestors once owned a slave. At least she expects they would.

Years before she knew her family's history she cried through *Roots*, then fell in love with *Uncle Tom's Cabin*, so finding out her relatives had a part in slavery was horrible.

Even her mom and Carl don't know about the slave; her dad told her one day when she asked why he hadn't written his family history. Sometimes she hopes he was lying since he had been trying to get her to leave him alone. When she got upset he immediately became very interested in telling her all sorts of details.

The slave, Mary, was given to the rather poor family as payment for a debt. Although they were against slavery on principle, they were unwilling to let go of the opportunity to have someone work for them for free. It was fourteen years before she was given her life, and by then she had two sons. Their father was a slave elsewhere and his wife and boys had to head North without him. No one in the family knew what happened afterward.

"Finally someone who wasn't falsely calm and pleasant," Ember said when the Franks left. "This is important stuff to put in the book. This is the reaction we expected, isn't it? You know the only reason I'm doing this is to make you happy."

"I didn't expect anyone to hate us because of our race."

"Whatever ethnicity you are, there are people that will hate you for it. I'm surprised you haven't experienced that before."

"Is it right to be bitter about slavery, even though it was a long time ago?"

"Well, for something you might be able to relate to more, look at the treatment of women all over the world and from as far back as the written records go. It's hard to get over that just because a few things improve. There's a realistic dread of the past being repeated and equality never being reached. It sometimes seems that to make women equal we have to tear men down. It happens now, and it's at the same time sad and glorious. Only when I think about the injustices my gender has faced can I even begin to imagine how other minorities feel. And it's not just white men; it's all of them. In a country that allowed the slavery of Africans, with the excuse they weren't really human, black men still voted before *any* women."

Bridgett isn't interested in this feminism stuff, but she and her friends at school talk about race and skin color all the time in a joking way. Her black friends joke about being black, and her white friends make fun of themselves for being white, but no one gets mad or anything. People do fight about other things, and then they might bring up racial stuff in their insults. There's a lot of jealousy toward the students of Asian decent since everyone thinks they always earn the best grades. The others are lumped together as Mexican, even her ex-boyfriend Jason, who is Puerto Rican.

During elementary school her classmates were sometimes rude about French people, but no one knew why they were supposed to hate them. It didn't stop her friends from being jealous that she went to Europe often.

Then after Samantha made her feel all confused about racism, Casper showed up. His first wife died almost ten years ago. He was the last family member in California that Katherine was able to trace. Even his appearance was horrible, with his face red and swollen, but then he threatened to sue them for the time he spent in prison wrongly accused of his wife's murder.

"I paid legal fees and wasted two years of my life in intolerable conditions," he said, " as you and a jury can imagine." His entire face seemed to swell, and the puffiness of his eyelids made him squint.

Ember gave an impressive defense, saying it would look bad to sue Dayle's innocent daughter and widow. The best was when she threatened to uncover that he really had murdered his wife, but then he started screaming at them. After Ember lifted the phone to call the police he left.

"He *couldn't* sue us, could he?" Bridgett asked.

"Anyone can sue anyone, but he might just be a prankster. We shouldn't have left all the checking to Katherine."

Bridgett imagines her mom's business and their house being taken away. It's so unfair that their whole lives could be ruined all over again.

55

Ember is waiting for Tony to finish the phone call with her ex-husband. Or should it be *his* ex-husband? (Only in connection to his history does she still confuse possessive adjectives and pronouns.)

For the last two hours she has been trying to forget the awful man's threat, but her mind keeps trudging through the possibilities. At the very least they would have to hire an attorney, followed by media attention—she's sure Casper What's-his-name desires publicity.

"Paul's coming here," Tony says.

"Paul?"

"My ex-husband. He's bringing his niece, Melissa. The babysitter."

"Oh," Ember says.

"Another thing: he's sold the hardware store. He didn't buy me out, so I'll be getting half of whatever he ends up with."

"That will help a lot. And how was lunch with Bradley?"

"It was good. He doesn't seem as upset about his mom staying. She behaves better around me. With him she tries to cause trouble. He admitted I give her a project to live for."

"So what's it like being a project?"

"Oh, very inspirational. But listen, I can't see Paul. He'll—I'm going to have a heart attack. Melissa tried to commit suicide again. They must be pretty worried to resort to me for help."

"Can—have—can you help her, Tony?"

"I don't know. I think I've stopped blaming her, thanks to Irene and Jill and all the rest of you. But I haven't forgiven myself, so why should I forgive her?"

"You know, I have to call Jill anyway. I'll see if she can come by."

"Paul and Melissa are flying down on the nineteenth. When is that—Tuesday? What are they going to do when they see me?"

"I hope you've told them."

"I've tried to tell Paul, but I don't think he really comprehends. I mean, my whole family *knows*, but I can't tell if they get it. I look different."

"You do look different, and you need to shave your little mustache. You're more masculine without it."

"Fine then. OK, you call Jill. I'm going to go tell Bridgett about Melissa. How old is she again?"

"Bridgett? Fifteen. She's in Frances' room transcribing today's wonderful interviews."

"Melissa's seventeen. That's close."

Jill says she's gooey with excitement but has a date, promising them her undivided attention the next day. "I must meet the man who did the man," she adds. Ember ignores that as Jill graciously agrees to assist with her connections if Casper's lawsuit ever becomes reality.

Ember goes to her room after telling Tony about the call. He and Bridgett say they will stay up until Irene gets home; it's already past her normal bedtime. Ember thinks about writing in her old journal, deserted under the bed among her library books.

Horace told her that the only things of value in his house were library books, and if the place were on fire that's what he would try to save, or he'd owe at least a thousand dollars. And even worse, he wouldn't be able to borrow any more until he paid.

Lilac Greene-Jean called this morning so early that it seems like a dream. Ember didn't wake up fully until the end of the conversation. Lilac wasn't happy that Horace was off in Nevada, and she suddenly asked if Ember would insist on staying in California if she married again. Blearily Ember said no, and Lilac talked of sending more money for the project. Someone in the background scolded her over the time difference in California—it was around four, and Lilac ended the call with hasty apologies.

Now Ember suspects Lilac wants her to marry Horace. The grant is probably meant to bring them together. That is, if the call truly took place. She tends to have very realistic dreams.

She decides not to find the journal. Its purpose was to talk about her life with Richard. She started it two years before he died, and it's full of lovely memories: how they met, gifts they gave each other, fun things they did. A lot of the pages are about sex; she ought to shred it to prevent posthumous publication (by Bridgett). The main reason for writing was so whichever of them survived the other would have something to refer back to, something more satisfying than a photo album.

Now she will probably never be able to read it. Although she can picture herself at seventy, a regal white-haired woman, a little like Frances, but more brittle if she doesn't start taking those calcium supplements again—the women in her family tend toward osteoporosis. What was she thinking? Oh yes, she will still be in this same bed, and she will put on the gold-rimmed spectacles dangling from a chain around her neck. Reaching down she will pull out the forgotten journal and begin to read about the only relationship she ever had. Maybe by then she will be able to recall their happy little lives and appreciate them, rather than wonder if the night of the day they had sex standing up in the forest in Colorado (or the night of the day they ate brownies on Santa Monica beach during a lightning storm) was also one of the times he later left to kill someone. Although he never went out on those exceptionally good days—did he? Nor necessarily on the gloomy ones. And sometimes he must have actually gardened.

Have all the victims been found? Some families of missing women with connections to places Richard lived are still searching for answers (and blaming him for the questions).

It's bad enough that not every body already discovered has been identified, at least according to Katherine.

The alarm on her electronic planner goes off, and the readout says "manicure." She glances at her hands and decides to make another laser resurfacing appointment for them as well. Her finger joints look a little rough.

This evening she has a dish soap shoot—normally not the type she accepts. Jewelry, lotion, and nail care are the products she prefers to advertise. Better for the hands, and she is almost always allowed to sit down for the bulk of the shoot.

Right after Richard's death she couldn't stand to think of hands and tried for foot work, not wanting to give up her industry connections entirely. Her feet are too long, narrow, and bony to be ideal though.

Finally the local jewelry store that first started her in the business (when she went in with Richard to try on engagement rings) begged her to photograph their new ruby line. She agreed since she enjoyed it too much to quit. A new benefit was the simplicity. Only her hands were given any attention, and they were arranged for her. It provided human interaction without any annoying questions or commitment. All she had to do was sit still and make small adjustments.

Now she thinks about Richard's hands and how, when he couldn't open jars easily, he claimed to have a progressively debilitating disease.

Ember never experienced the hands that could destroy, but sometimes she can't help picturing them around the neck of the talented young Thompson woman or the cheerful mother with the two boys. Thank goodness she didn't get to know all the others.

56

Katherine wakes Horace by flipping the light switch down and then up and then down over and over between light and dark until he is alert and protesting.

"There you are, rise and shine. Where's Frances?" The whites of Katherine's eyes are lined with red veins. She looks older and crazed.

"Probably under a blanket, hiding from you. What time is it?"

"I don't know. Why were you asleep with the light on? I've been at it all night, and I haven't found my dad. I'm sure he must be dead—even George and Claude have heard of my sister's body being discovered."

"You told them," Horace says, sitting up in the loft. "They said you called—"

"I never told them."

"What's wrong?" Frances asks dazedly. She is peering over the back of the couch, her face furrowed and gray.

"You don't even feel guilty anymore, do you?" Katherine says to her. "You killed my father. He committed suicide because we expected too much of him. He probably burned off his fingertips so he wouldn't be found until his body deteriorated. Or drowned himself. That's how I would do it."

"Katherine, you're being ridiculous. You haven't slept. We've been through all of this before."

"You won't be able to convince me now. I've done everything I can to find him." She collapses onto the floor, sobbing loudly.

Horace looks at Frances, who appears more wary than sympathetic.

"I'm going to the hotel," she says. "You can take care of her tonight. Did you get your suitcase out?"

He shakes his head and goes down the stairs in his briefs and t-shirt. He drags Katherine to the couch where he lifts her over the back and onto the cushions. She is surprisingly heavy, as if soaked with tears.

"I'll be right back," he tells her. "I'm going to get our things."

Frances is waiting by the door with the keys in her hand. They walk silently around the house to the driveway and she opens the trunk.

"Good luck," she says. "Call in the morning."

He nods and carries the two small bags to the guesthouse. Katherine is at the table wearing only a lacy yellow bra and worn green panties. Her skin is bluish.

"Don't you think they killed my dad? Even if not literally?"

"Richard maybe, but not the rest of them. Mainly he killed your sister; your dad made his own decisions. At least by leaving. We might never know what happened to him after that."

"I have to know, Horace. I really have to know. I can't live if I don't know."

"You're sure he killed himself?"

"Yes. Or was in an accident. He could have been burnt up or any number of things. Perhaps he was killed because he questioned the wrong person." She puts her hand over her mouth. "Oh my God. What if he figured out it was Richard and confronted him?"

"How could he have figured it out when no one else did?"

"Maybe everyone that did was killed."

He can't reason with her if she refuses to think logically. "Katherine, you know Richard's family isn't to blame any more than yours is to blame that Alyssa was abducted and murdered."

"But whether we're to blame or not, *we're* the only ones suffering. My dad died for it, and I've spent my life trying to find him. My brother is probably gay. My mom became a religious freak with a violent temper. I think we've all been punished enough. But look at them—Frances has a huge, fancy house, and she was just saying that everyone in town has accepted her again—just two years after they found out about her fucked up parenting. Ember has that huge, fancy apartment and thinks she's perfect. Bridgett gets everything, three parents, two places to live. Sure her dad is dead, but she'll probably become rich and famous by writing a book about him—not to mention all the other ways she can profit off his evil life. None of them have been destroyed the way I have."

"You're wrong about that. Just because they're private—"

"What does that mean? You think they're more sophisticated because they have college degrees and lots of money? They know how to mourn silently?"

She stands up and pushes the table angrily, but it only shakes a little, so she lifts and drops her chair, then kicks it over.

Horace puts his arms around her and holds tightly while she struggles. She stops abruptly and leans heavily against him. There's something calculated in the way they end up kissing and having sex lying half-on the table, but he doesn't mind—he's sure now that he is in love, and he'll do everything he can to help her fix her life.

57

Vicky and Carl return with Frances on Sunday night after showing her Las Vegas. They decide that Bridgett can continue to stay with Ember during Melissa's visit. Frances is sleeping in Bridgett's bedroom for a few days to prove she doesn't favor Ember's place.

"Paul must stay in a hotel," Ember says. "I don't want them to have to share a bathroom. Imagine how traumatic it's going to be for him—seeing the woman who was once his wife shaving her face?" She puts her hand over her mouth, remembering that Tony can hear every word.

"He might make sarcastic jokes," Bridgett says. "That's what Carl would do. Oh, I didn't tell you that Jill called earlier! She had an emergency."

Bridgett and Ember have been designated to greet-and-warn as Tony waits nervously, listening on the headphones. The decision to let another person in on the eavesdropping secret involved a long, passionate discussion, and in the end Irene was informed as well. She played with it all Monday, but today Tony is alone.

"Any news?" Irene asks now, coming slowly down the hall behind her wheelchair. A nurse has given her a bath and helped her dress. "I'm taking a walk to warm up before my exercises. Rita said I could take a break and see what's going on. I think she wants to meet Tony's husband."

"I do not," Rita yells from the doorway, where they can only see her folded arms. "I'm a medical professional without the curiosity of you lower beings."

"She has amazing hearing," Irene says with a grin, slowly turning herself around and heading back.

Finally Sammy calls, and Ember stands at the peephole. Bridgett sits near the microphone that Tony is listening to.

"Here they are," Ember says before the door is all the way open. "Hello, come in. I'm Ember Oto and this is Bridgett Andres, my step-daughter."

"Nice to meet you, I'm Paul Lloyd," the man says. Trying to hide behind him is a very fat woman who looks far too old to be Melissa. "This is my niece Melissa Muollo."

Bridgett gives her a small wave and smile. Melissa is huge all over, but it must be her enormous drooping breasts that make her seem ancient. Tony will be as surprised to see his niece as she is to see him.

"We wanted to talk to you for a minute first," Ember begins hesitantly. The three of them are still standing, which makes the situation more awkward. "Tony's been living here for a while, with an older friend who is ill. I don't know how much you know about him . . ." She pauses, her hands clasped against her chest.

Paul's face hasn't changed from the sad expression he had when he first came in. "She told me she changed her name to Tony." His voice is calm and level, but suddenly he barks out a short laugh. "I'm sorry, I'm sorry. You're calling Sarah a 'him.'"

"He looks like you." Bridgett feels her neck flush. But it's true, she thinks defiantly, although Paul is perhaps taller, with slightly darker honey-colored hair. His face is also masculine yet fine-boned, and his muscles aren't nearly as big. He's thin, and Bridgett can see definition in his arms, so he probably works out. Her mom could tell exactly what exercises he does. Bridgett feels a very unexpected thrill of pride.

"Oh, don't be embarrassed," Melissa says, "people always thought they were brother and sister."

Ember gestures toward the hall and raises her eyebrows to give Paul a chance to guess the challenge Tony is giving him, in case the latter's absence alone isn't enough. Although this is against Tony's instructions, Bridgett thinks it is a good idea. The former couple is unlikely to have much of a psychic bond.

"It's been hard for me to accept Sarah as a man, but I've started to deal with my own problems—ones I never shared with her. We were still good for each other and good parents. I'm not angry with Tony, I want to be—his friend again."

Bridgett can't see down the hall but she's not surprised when Ember glances behind her in the direction of the bedroom and then moves away, toward the kitchen.

Paul and Melissa stand waiting, and when Tony appears they watch him with frozen grimaces that are probably supposed to be smiles. Bridgett feels like crying, and she forces herself not to make any noise as tears start dripping from her eyes.

"Sarah Tony," Paul says, and they hug for a long time. Ember hands Bridgett a paper towel as Tony moves toward Melissa, who is also crying.

Paul watches them hug and his eyes are dry, but his face looks sadder than ever. He should be a soap opera star, Bridgett thinks, he's so permanently tragic. It would be interesting to know what he kept from his wife. She will never marry someone she has to have secrets from.

What would she have thought if her father had been suggested as someone who murdered people, back when he was alive and no one had any evidence? If she had read about the child of a murderer in a book, and the character had been a gardener or a history professor—or anything else that might have made her think of Richard—would she have been amused by the idea? Probably. It's unlikely she would have been worried or made any connection.

"I don't like it when you say step-daughter," Bridgett tells Ember quietly.

"I don't like it either, but it wasn't the time to explain in detail, and I can't claim you as my daughter..."

"Why not? I've had two dads."

"It's not fair to your mom. I don't want to call you my friend either because then you'll get mad if I ever need to be parental."

"Unless I can do the same to you."

"Nope. I deserve something for having lived this long."

Tony and his guests are listening rather than talking to one another. "Do you guys want to go down and meet Irene?" Ember asks. "She's probably waiting impatiently."

Bridgett feels uncomfortable having them all following behind her. In the family room Rita and Irene are sitting suspiciously still on the couch, not even pretending to be busy. Rita leaves after introductions, whispering to Bridgett that she wants full details on Thursday.

"Well, you do look alike," Irene tells Paul. "You're Tony's twin brother, right?" Her expression is that of bland sweetness.

Paul offers a weak, "Thank you," before Tony and Bridgett start laughing.

"He wasn't about to tell you your longtime roommate was really a girl in her past life," Tony says.

"You might look like a boy," Paul imitates the teasing tone of voice, "but tell me more about the new, high-society manners you claimed on the phone."

"That was thanks to Irene," Tony says, bowing slightly toward his instructor. "You would probably like me better now, wouldn't you? I was Paul's act of rebellion," he tells the rest of them, "because both of his parents were teachers at our high school. One did Science and the other Writing Comp. I was a disinterested student that always caused trouble—not any teacher's favorite. Our friends set us up because neither one of us had ever dated anyone—outside a group date, at least. And Paul wanted to live dangerously."

Bridgett grabs Melissa's big, doughy hand to pull her down beside Irene on the couch. "What happened next?" she asks, always hungry for every detail of how Tony became who he is.

"Well, the reason *I* didn't date was because I was confused about myself and didn't feel like I fit in as a girl. Paul—" he hesitates, "Well, Paul was extremely shy, but everyone liked him. They thought I was shy too, or at least that I lacked self-confidence. I always hated the way I looked."

"Which none of her friends could believe. I was so excited to go out with her and relieved that she wasn't pushy like the other girls. The meaner boys had called me a fag, among other things, but this ended the torment. As soon as Tony and I started together life was much easier. For once my parents didn't approve of something I did. I played basketball and actually became popular. We were even nominated for prom king and queen two years later."

"Who won?" Tony asks.

"I don't remember. I do remember that we didn't vote for ourselves. You were not excited about being nominated."

"I couldn't imagine dancing under a spotlight."

"Were you gay—sorry, homosexual?" Bridgett asks. "I mean, are you like Tony, you just couldn't admit it until later?"

"Bridgett," Ember says sharply.

Paul laughs. "No, I'm not homosexual. Are you?" he asks Tony.

"No, I like women now. I can't say I did before the hormones though. I wasn't really attracted to anyone that way. I loved you though, Paul. I still do."

Paul has a strange expression on his face, but he nods.

"You can be like brothers," Bridgett suggests quietly, glancing at Ember.

"Thank you, Dr. Andres," is all she says.

"Maybe Jill can use a good assistant, Bridgett, you have talent," Irene adds, then yawns loudly before she is able to move her hand up to cover her mouth.

"Time for bed," Tony says tenderly.

Bridgett sees Paul quickly wipe his eyes, and she imagines he's thinking of his dead kids. He seems so nice. She wonders if he deserves to have his kids alive more than her father, who, although wonderful in some ways, could never have been described as nice. Of course a switch would mean she had died young. She's almost willing to trade her life, at least in her imagination, so this lovely man won't be sad.

58

Paul and Melissa left for the hotel in their rental car an hour ago. Tony was still unsettled, despite agreeing that the visit went unexpectedly well, so he and Irene decided to tell one of their stories until they fell asleep. This has been their main form of entertainment since Tony destroyed the television in their old apartment, and Bridgett usually loves to listen. Ember assumes that's where she is until her upstairs neighbor's longtime lover knocks on the door.

"What's wrong?" Ember asks Boxer, a man whose identity seems to revolve around having played professional football. His partner, Randall Murphy, was a good friend when Richard was alive but later wrote the petition for her eviction.

"Bridgett's fine, but she had a little accident on the stairs. The paramedics came and she has a mild concussion. She's at Murphy's."

"Why didn't you bring her here?" Ember asks, grabbing her keys and wondering what she's going to tell Vicky. "The paramedics came?"

"Yes. With the police."

"The police?"

"I'm not supposed to be telling you this. Bridgett is writing it out for her book while she's still inspired. That's what she said. She doesn't want you to come up yet."

"Of course I'm going up. I can't believe the police didn't want to see me."

"Randall will explain about that."

He opens the stairwell door and walks closely behind her until she reaches the top, then he jumps in front to grab the knob first.

"I have to call her parents, Boxer, they are going to be seriously angry with me, no matter what happened."

He opens the condominium door. The entryway is heavily furnished, and Bridgett sits on a leather recliner with her feet up, scribbling in a notebook. Without pausing she says, "I knew you'd insist on coming!"

"Bridgett, I have to call your mom. She's never going to let you near me again when she finds out there was a delay. What is going on here?"

"I am *writing* what happened for the book, and if I tell you first, it will ruin it. Mom will *force* me to tell. How about you call Carl and get him not to tell her, then it will be all his fault."

"Are you OK?" Ember asks. She can see Randall out of the corner of her eye.

"Yes, I have a bump on the back of my head. There's an ice pack but it keeps slipping."

"Don't glare at me," Ember replies to Bridgett's pouty look. "I'm not going to hold it in place."

"I'll call Carl," Randall says. As a retired defense attorney he should be good at manipulating information, so Embers tells him the phone number and they all watch as he dials.

"You have to go in the other room," Bridgett whispers urgently.

He walks out while Ember considers having Boxer spank her.

"You can sit down if you want," Boxer says.

Ember shakes her head. "How long has she been at this?"

"She started as soon—about half an hour ago."

Randall comes back after a few minutes and says Vicky's in a meeting, and although she will be mad, Carl will tell her that since Bridgett was fine he decided not to interrupt. He is on his way over now with Frances.

Bridgett doesn't seem to hear him. She has her lips compressed tightly together, and she's squinting as she turns the page and continues on a new one. They all stand around not looking at her until she finally drops her pen triumphantly.

"I'm done! I haven't had time to read it over yet, except the beginning, that's why it's so crossed out." She arranges the notebook so the first page is on top and hands it to Ember, who sits down and reads while the men take Bridgett to the kitchen for a drink. The forgotten ice pack lies melting on the leather seat.

There was finally a day when the impact of my father's desparate actions hit me in a physical rather than purely emotional ~~way~~ *manner,* she writes after many scribbled out lines. *The dashing Katherine Van Leden, whose sister Alyssa's tragic story has been told earlier, has become a dear friend, and helped me arrange the interviews to make this book possible. Katherine returned unexpectedly from Las Vegas, arriving at the condo complex and calling me to come talk to her. I was just starting down the stairs when Katherine came running up and immediately began telling me that her father had killed himself because of her sister's death, so now she had no sister or dad. Then she said* ~~my dad~~ *Dayle might have literally killed her father too. I told her I was sorry and that there was nothing I could do and asked her to please stop yelling. "I've never liked you," she screamed, "I've just been waiting for a chance to destroy you." We were standing on the landing on the floor below Ember's. I asked her how she even knew her dad was dead. I was sort of mad because I was the one who arranged for her to come to LA, and then to go to Nevada. I have been trying to help her ever since I met her and no one else in my family even liked her that much especially my mom who really hated her and will now probably feel really justified to rub it in. "He might have a new family somewhere and not want to come back," I told her. Her face was red and feirce and her feiry red hair was all over and she pushed me down the stairs. It was very fast and luckily the man that lives upstairs, Randall Murphy, saw her do it and called the police on his cell phone. Then he made sure I was all right. Oh, when I fell I went to the next landing, which wasn't that far, but Randall said I went down backwards and slammed the back of my head into the wall. He was afraid for a minute that my neck was broken. Katherine looked shocked, he told me, since she was probably thinking the same thing, and she ran down the stairs right past me, but she didn't hide well because the police caught her before they came to talk to us. Now she will go to jail and might have a trial and everything, although I wasn't that hurt, so maybe not. This is a tragic example of how grief can lead people to do terrible things, and also of how one person's crimes (example: Richard Earle Dayle's), can lead to the death of someone who is killed by the family member of someone they killed (even though I didn't die I could have, and that might have been her intention.)*

"What do you think?" Bridgett comes back in and asks before Ember has a chance to throw it off the balcony and invent a giant bird with a taste for notebooks.

"I'm so glad you're OK. It must have been painful."

"Aren't you glad I didn't just tell you?" She hops from foot to foot.

Ember nods, hoping the concussion is more major than they thought because for heaven's sake, not losing sight of what's really important here—that a maniac who stayed in her house tried to kill her almost-daughter—Katherine comes across as both the dashing hero and the passionate heroine of a romance novel.

"Thank you for your help," Ember tells Boxer. "We'd better go."

"Maybe I should go with you," Boxer says. "I'm an expert on concussions. I had so many the doctors predicted brain damage."

"But will *one*—" Bridgett begins worriedly.

"No, of course not. Not even three or four . . ." He shrugs.

"Thank you, but we'll be all right. I'll call you if there are any odd signs."

"Just give her Tylenol if she needs something. No other drugs."

"Oh, I forgot the part about Russell asking me questions. Did I say he thinks I passed out? He asked me all sorts of stuff. One funny one was how much money did your father owe me? I already paid it back though. Then the paramedics asked the same sorts of things, but not about the money. They were impressed that I had forgotten nothing that happened right before or right after although I can't remember the actual falling part, but they said that's normal."

Ember finally looks at Randall with her face stern. He shrugs and reaches into his pocket, but she turns away to leave.

Bridgett interrupts Tony and Irene, who are almost asleep, and tells them her story in the dark. Ember is glad they are not made to read it. She goes to her office and puts the notebook in a drawer. She is sure it's perfectly fine writing for a fifteen year old although she doubts it contains anything that will appease Vicky.

Sammy shows up at the door with Carl. "I'm so sorry I let the red-headed girl up," he tells Ember. "It's just that she used to be around all the time, and I heard her call Bridgett to come down. Then she asked me if she could meet her, and I opened the door."

"It's fine, Sammy. *I* let her sleep here for goodness' sake."

Sammy grabs her shoulders and kisses her on both cheeks. Then he does the same to Carl and says he is supposed to be on guard duty downstairs.

"She's with Tony and Irene," Ember tells Carl. "I don't think I can bear to hear the story again. I don't know what we're going to do about Katherine. Do you think we can have her transferred back to Georgia?"

Carl laughs and shakes his head. "We'll let Vicky loose on her. At the most she'll probably be given a fine or something. I'd better take Bridgett to the emergency room to be safe. Is Horace with Katherine, by the way?"

"I don't know. He might not know she was arrested."

"Well, they haven't returned the car yet, so I hope she didn't push it over a cliff with him in it."

"Then Vicky really will kill her."

59

Horace is waiting in the car, parked illegally by a red curb to the side of Ember's building, when two police vehicles and an ambulance pull up. He gets out and peeks through the gate, keeping the corner of one eye on the road to watch for a parking enforcer. He sees Katherine come out of the building and is about to yell to her to hurry up when an officer stops her. After a few minutes she walks with the woman to a police car in front of the building. Katherine gets in the back seat.

He follows them to the police station. After parking in the visitor's lot he goes inside and tries to find out what is going on, but the employee at the front desk seems indifferent to his concerns.

"Will you just look up her name? I want to know if she's all right or if she needs any help."

"This isn't a hospital," she says. "What was she arrested for?"

"I don't think she was arrested. They didn't put handcuffs on her, but she went with them."

"Well then, you'd better keep your phone handy in case she tries to call you."

Horace goes back to the car and hopes Katherine will appear. He has been driving all day, and he closes his eyes until a nearby vehicle alarm wakes him with his neck bent torturously to the side and drool wetting his shoulder. It's dark and the dashboard clock tells him two hours have passed since he kissed Katherine temporarily good-bye.

He drives to Ember's building, getting lost one and a half times on the way. A few blocks down, in front of Green Street Flower Shop, he finds a metered parking space with ten minutes left. As he walks he sees the street is named the same thing as the shop, which reminds him that he has a headache. It's very confusing that an ambulance arrived and now Katherine is at the police station. Maybe she witnessed an accident and is already back at Ember's apartment, worried about him.

He and Katherine have spent days calling morgues and investigating online pictures of the unidentified. There aren't as many as he imagined; they ended up looking at a lot of them more than once to make absolutely sure. All the time Katherine was fuming over Bridgett and Frances and Ember, but mainly Bridgett.

The ambulance is gone. He buzzes at the black gate under a gazebo-like awning and gives the attendant Ember's name. Then he walks down a long flat stone path to the second identical awning, this one attached to the building and guarded by a woman reading a magazine with a flashlight.

"Hi, I'm Horace Jean-Greene, and I'm here to see Ember Oto on the fifth floor."

She watches him as she pushes a button on the intercom. No one answers.

Horace was hoping to stay, but he leaves, feeling ridiculous and a little bit desperate.

He stops at the first hotel he sees although it looks historic and touristy. He hopes he has enough cash for the night because his one credit card is close to full, and he hasn't called the bank in too long to be confident of what is left in his account. Even with the extra money he has been getting from his sister, and all the free food, the trip to Ely sucked him back into poverty.

Pulling out his wallet in the dim light of the streetlamps, he sees there is no cash left at all. No credit or bank card. He has only his driver's license and his library card.

He wonders if there is anywhere in this city he can sleep in the car without being arrested or murdered.

60

Frances and Ember sit on the bed after Carl leaves for the emergency room with Bridgett.

"Your neighbor was out of bounds. I won't blame Vicky if she decides to take some sort of legal action against him."

"That's what he's like, Frances. He's a terror. It was amusing when we were friends, but I told you how he tried to get me kicked out for associating with criminals and endangering lives."

"He's the petition writer too?"

"Not to stand up for him, but Bridgett is very manipulative."

"She's fifteen. I wonder at parents trusting their daughters with men just because they have been labeled homosexual."

"You're right." Ember feels totally defeated. The intercom buzzes and she waves it off. "I'm not getting it."

"We'd better see who it is," Frances says, leaving the room.

Thinking that the adult in charge is always to blame, Ember wants to shut the bedroom door and put her pillow over her head.

"I suppose it was Horace, but he'd already left," Frances says when she returns. "I wonder where he's staying tonight. Do you think he even knows what happened?"

"Hmmm" is all Ember can force out.

"He's very fond of Katherine. When she was sick with the flu he took care of her all night. She was distraught over the dead end in Ely. Let's contact the police station in Caldwell tomorrow and see if they can find out what's going on." She pats Ember's shoulder. "Now stop thinking and get to sleep."

61

Frances sets her travel alarm for five and wakes up a few minutes early. She showers, noticing that the bathroom needs cleaning. This will be a good task for Tony; he can put his muscles to use.

She fills a glass with orange juice. No need for caffeine this morning: it will be pleasant to take a little nap later. At home she avoided resting in the daytime, uneasy over what it represented, but even Ember and Tony take a siesta now and then.

First she calls Margaret Heller, whose son is a police officer. "I haven't left California," she confirms, after answering a few questions about movie stars, Beverly Hills, Bel Air (which she has yet to visit), Venice Beach, gangs, and drive-by shootings. "I have an important question about police procedure, and I was hoping your son could help me out."

"Oh of course, he's just finishing his breakfast. Tim, for you."

Frances has never liked this young man who can't tolerate a quiet or contemplative moment, but as a result of that quality she expects him to be familiar with the surrounding towns.

"I need to talk to someone at the Caldwell police station, and I'm not sure who would be best."

"Why over there?" he asks. "I'm sure we can help you with whatever the LAPD can't." He snorts.

"It's about one of their citizens."

"Ah. Ralph's a good guy. Ralph McCoy. He's an old gossip, and he knows everything about everyone over there."

Tim only has McCoy's extension, so she calls information for the station number and hears Ralph's voicemail two times in a row. On her third try he answers.

"Yeah, Timmy said you'd be calling. He just rang, invited me out for a drink tonight. Guess he's curious, huh?"

Frances has never met this guy, but he sounds much older than Tim, and his voice is loud.

"Are you familiar with Katherine Van Leden and her family?"

"Yes, I am, but let me pull up her file. Just a minute. OK, the darn thing's slow today. I'll go get the hard copy. One sec."

Frances hopes he doesn't connect her name with her son's.

"As usual, as soon as I walk across the room and get it the system kicks in. The Van Leden case is still in our active file section because that child is a nag. We keep track of everything but don't really listen to her anymore, you know? Now what do you need?"

"I'm in Pasadena, California, right now, visiting some family, and Katherine is here too. She befriended my granddaughter then tried to injure her last night—well, she might have.

"I wasn't present when it happened, and my granddaughter is fine. We think Katherine was arrested, or taken in for questioning by the police, and she hasn't been heard from since. I was wondering if someone could call up and explain about her history—"

"Are you on her side?" he asks. "Because I wouldn't mind calling up, but her history probably isn't going to help. Having just cause the first time won't stop them from looking at her all the more carefully now."

Frances pauses. If there has been some other trouble in Katherine's life that she is unaware of, she doesn't want to find out. "OK, I guess you can't tell them a portion instead of the whole, can you? She's understandably bitter toward our family because—do you know about—?"

"Yes, I know of your unfortunate situation. There was some activity over on our side also."

She wonders if he means murders or publicity.

"However, I don't think that's an excuse for Kathy's behavior. If anything she should be more sensitive toward your granddaughter. I imagine that's why you befriended her in the first place. I'm afraid I can't be of assistance, Mrs. Dayle—even if Kathy deserves your forgiveness, I don't feel right bringing her past into this."

"But I think her past will help. It will give her a motive that's reasonable at least."

"I'm afraid I don't agree with you there. Just because her own daddy was a murderer, doesn't give her any excuse to try and do the same thing."

"Bridgett—are you talking about Bridgett?"

Ralph clears his throat. "I thought we were talking about Kathy."

"Katherine's father was a murderer?"

"Yes, ma'am. She killed him."

Frances looks up and sees Tony and Ember.

"What?" Ember mouths, but Frances waves them away. They sit across the table, leaning toward her and staring.

"Katherine killed her father?" Frances asks, wishing she didn't have to say it straight out.

"I thought you knew her. Listen, the case is officially closed, and I don't—"

"She told us her sister and father—I mean, that my son murdered her sister Alyssa. And her dad had disappeared when searching. That's why she wanted—"

"Wait a minute, wait just a minute. I see, I see." He raises his voice, "Lizette, pick up and hit line five." Then he repeats what Frances just said. "Lizette talked to Kathy the last few times she came in. She was on the initial case too. Go ahead, Liz, tell her about the Van Ledens. From the beginning."

"The beginning? Wow. OK...Well, there were always rumors about Gregory Van Leden messing with his kids, but no one was able to do anything about it. They were often bruised, and a school nurse reported that all three had signs of sexual activity—this was in elementary school, but they swore it was with their friends. They never wavered and no one tried hard enough to get the real story. I'm ashamed to say it, but people that live on that hill are sort of ignored. Or they were back then."

"She doesn't need their whole history, honey."

"This is just the background, Dad, and you said from the beginning."

"Well, I have to go, can you handle this?"

"Thank you, Mr. McCoy."

"I'm glad to help. Call again if you need anything else."

"Lizette? I'm sorry, I don't know your surname."

"I'm still here. I was just waiting for him to leave. I'm forty years old, but my dad still tells me what to do. He's retiring at the end of this year—if he doesn't change his mind again."

"I hope he isn't bothered that—"

"It's fine. Anyway, I'll tell you what our guys reported. I wasn't called to the scene initially, but everyone ended up there in a matter of hours. We got a call from the retarded boy, that's Alex, the Van Leden boy. He wasn't making sense, but he led them to the shack out back where the fifteen year old was found dead. Apparently the father had been in the act of sexually molesting her when Katherine showed up and beat him to death with a shovel. Alyssa had been suffocated with a plastic bag that Katherine removed to perform CPR. That's what she was doing when they found her, who knows how much later. We assumed the bag was a sexual thing, or a punishment—the other kids wouldn't say if anything similar was ever done to them. Katherine wasn't arrested; no one had the heart. She was trying to save her sister, even though the girl was probably dead when she got there."

"My word." Frances looks up, but Tony and Ember are gone.

"We got it all cleaned up, had the funerals, and kept everything out of our newspaper except the sad story of two accidental deaths. Of course most people in town know the truth, but no one wants to admit it. I think a lot of us felt guilty for not doing something to prevent the situation, but now it's nothing more than solidarity. We even got a police psychologist from Atlanta to come down and talk to the kids. She stayed in town a few weeks and then told us children adapt quickly and they were both doing well."

"I think I remember something about a father and daughter dying. It seems like it was reported as a murder suicide. Could that have been the same thing?"

"I'm not sure what you're thinking of, but we've never had a murder suicide."

"Go on, sorry I interrupted."

"OK. Well. A couple of months later Katherine comes in to the station and says she needs to file a missing person's report for her sister. She's told that her sister is dead and buried, but she won't listen and keeps coming back. Now she was a very beautiful little vixen even at sixteen—or I should say even now that she's in her thirties; when she was sixteen she was hard for men to resist. Finally she convinced a rookie, Charlie Langston I think it was the first time, to fill out a missing person's report, although he never did anything official with it. He gave her a copy, which was another mistake. We didn't know if she was going off guilt or denial or just plain insanity. Then we hear she's using her missing person's report to pester the newspapers to publicize Alyssa's disappearance.

"Her future husband was working at the newspaper then—she married the boy Alyssa was always with. He begged to be allowed to type and print some stories in his spare time. Katherine made copies and taped them up all over town. It was very awkward since we had tried so hard to cover up all the details.

"They have a pool on their property but they couldn't afford to keep it up—the town had a fundraiser for the family after the tragedy, but they'd never had much in the first place. Anyway, the pool was empty—Is someone else on your line? I thought I heard something. Well, in the last few years we've heard that Katherine has been breaking everything they have in the house by throwing it in the pool. Her brother and husband go along with all of it. I don't know what they believe, but they've certainly learned to humor her. The mom spends a lot of time at church. Katherine has also been suspected of stealing.

"Where was I? When she was seventeen or eighteen—I have it here, eighteen, she tried to report her father missing, and when we wouldn't do it, she made her own report, copying the format of the one for her sister. She gave it to us and asked us to put him in our system. She said he left and came back before, but this time he'd been gone longer than ever. The truth is, before he died, he never went out of town for a single night after marrying.

"Ever since then she's checked back a few times a year to see if we've heard anything. When Dayle's—well, when that all came to light, she pestered us to look for her sister there, and eventually brought us an autopsy report she had made. It declared her sister's death officially solved, said she was a victim of Dayle, and it even said her backpack had been found with her skeleton. Then the sheriff warned everyone at the station to stop humoring her. We tried to remind her of the facts, but she just asked politely that the backpack be returned as soon as our case was concluded. I have to admit we were all relieved she was finally finished looking."

"She must be completely mad."

"By a number of definitions."

"Shouldn't she be getting help in some locked institution?"

"There isn't the room or the money for everyone needing that kind of care. Think of all the homeless in the big cities, quite a few of them are mentally ill. Most haven't been violent though. I don't know how our town's going to come out if we have to defend our actions. I'm afraid they'll see us as pretty backwards."

"Will you at least call and see if you can establish a history of psychological problems?" Then Frances remembers that Lizette doesn't know all the details, so she tells her of Katherine's current predicament.

"I'm not an expert in that area, but I'll certainly be glad to try. What time is it there now?"

"It can't be later than six."

"OK, three hours."

"Thank you for talking to me, Lizette. Katherine is in the Pasadena City Jail as far as I know. Listen," she says tentatively, "Timmy Heller thinks your dad's—"

Lizette laughs. "Oh, we know not to tell Timmy the truth."

"Thank you for your help." Frances hangs up and waits for Ember and Tony to appear looking sheepish. "You almost ruined everything," she says when their expressions don't reflect the proper amount of guilt.

"I can't believe it," Tony says. "Has she been scamming us or what? Maybe Horace is in on it."

"I don't think so," Frances says. "He was pretty upset when we found out she'd invented the police lead." Which she hadn't told them about, so she explains it until the intercom announces Horace, and Ember allows him to be buzzed up.

"Let's wait to hear what he has to say," Ember says.

Horace has a faint beard, and he is holding his head at an odd angle. He smells sweaty. "Can I please use the bathroom? You can't pee outside anywhere around here."

"Did he sleep in the car?" Tony asks.

"Yes, I did," Horace tells them a minute later when he returns. "My wallet was empty. So what happened yesterday? Everybody all right?"

"Katherine pushed Bridgett down the stairs," Tony says.

"She's fine though," Frances adds quickly.

"Oh hell. Bridgett's all right? What happened? Is she here?"

"No, Carl took her to the ER to make sure. We don't know what Vicky's going to do, but no one else wants to press charges."

"Well, that's not up to us," Frances says. "That's why I called her hometown to try and get her some help. We'll probably be able to influence the decision, if anyone talks to us. Of course it will be difficult making a case against her anyway since Bridgett got a stranger to pretend he was her parent with the paramedics."

"OK," Horace says, slumping back in a hard wooden chair across the table from Frances. "So Bridgett is fine, and we'll all help Katherine, right?"

"Right," Frances says. "Now I need to tell you what I found out when I called Caldwell Police Department this morning."

62

Katherine can still see Bridgett lying with her head propped against the wall, looking like her neck is broken. The push didn't seem to have anything to do with the fall. Bridgett's body was hoisted backward into the air and against the wall, where it slid into a heap. She didn't roll, she flew.

The staircase is divided into landings and turns, making it impossible to tumble from the top to the bottom. She and Bridgett were standing somewhere in the middle of one section, so the height was only around four stairs.

She ran away at first, then once out of sight slowed down. While hoping for a sound from Bridgett, she could only hear the man on the phone.

When she steps outside the police station for the first time since last night, the sun is too bright and she feels frazzled, reaching for her glasses and adjusting them. She must have bent the frame a little by sleeping on her side. She feels a small whiny ache in the back where her head—no, no, it was Bridgett's head that hit the wall.

She stands at the top of another set of stairs. These are wide and flat and concrete. The doors behind her are glass, and although she would like to sit down to think things through, she's afraid that if someone catches her hesitating they will call her back.

She almost passes Horace before she notices him sitting on a lower step, leaning against one of the thin, metal posts holding up the handrail. His head is down against his chest.

"Horace!" she says with relief and delight.

His head jerks back and then he stands, disheveled but smiling widely. They both start talking at once and then he's lifting her to kiss although their mouths are dirty and they both smell of sweat.

"Where did you stay?" she asks, overriding his questions. "I took your credit card and money. I'm sorry, but I didn't know we'd be separated. It was just a joke."

"Whew, I almost canceled them, but I thought you might have had a reason—I slept in the car on the street until people started moving about, then I drove around for a few hours. I went to Ember's to see if they knew anything. We're out of gas. I hope we can make it to a station. Now tell me about you—are you free?"

"No, I escaped, we'd better get moving."

"Wha—Oh, I can't take a joke now, I'm too hungry."

"Oh, dear. I was just fed. Let's go to a gas station and you can run in and get something while I fill up."

They hold onto each other for the short walk to the car, which is parked illegally in front of the police station.

It's lucky she was wearing a sweatshirt and jeans yesterday because it was chilly in there, but outside today her clothes are already plastered to her, not helping the unwashed state. Her top is red and white and form fitting with a hood; it matches her tennis shoes. A non-wrinkle outfit, perfect for driving from Nevada or spending a night in jail. She has her glasses on because of the car trip too, and isn't wearing make-up.

The holding cell surprised her when they first brought her in, being very clean with metal bunk beds painted white like the walls. The mattresses on the beds were thin and hard, and she was given a gray blanket and gray pillow without a case. They both smelled nice and had more dignity than Vicky's blemished white towels.

She first sat on a bottom bunk but decided that if a heavier person arrived later she might be ousted so climbed up top. Three beds out of eight were empty when she arrived, and two more by the time she woke this morning. She slept very well, getting up to use the bathroom twice and finding it all clean, cold metal with a door that didn't lock but shut firmly.

"I've been dismissed like a naughty little girl. They said Bridgett's fine. I guess some character witness or something from Georgia called."

"We need to return the car and figure things out. We don't have enough for a hotel or motel or dive."

"We'll call from the gas station," Katherine says, wishing she had a license because Horace doesn't look capable of driving.

She fastens her seatbelt and then unfastens it to lean over and give him a hug. "Thank you for coming to get me," she says.

He turns to her eagerly. "I love you," he says, and she feels a surge of love for him too, but he kisses her long and hard before she can respond.

63

Paul waits for Melissa to knock on his hotel room door. He knows it takes her a long time to become clean, but she said she was getting up at seven and it's ten already. While not wanting to embarrass her, he's worried that she might have hurt herself again.

He tries to think about Tony and the day ahead, not allowing any what-ifs to creep in. He and his sister Carrie had their own little what-if party a few weeks ago: What if he hadn't visited New Zealand? What if they hadn't taught Shellie to ski (which led to the scary fall which might have led to her sleepwalking)? What if they hadn't gone to that horrible party or let Melissa babysit? What if they had made sure the doors were bolted, what if they had stayed home—at either home, what if they had never married and had kids, what if Sarah hadn't told Allison to watch her sister, what if someone had found them in time . . . Their mother led them through a childhood of what-iffing, and they can't stop now.

There is a knock on the door and it's Melissa, in a blue dress. He wonders how much she weighs now. At the hospital it was nearly three hundred pounds, and she has widened in the months since then.

"Sarah didn't seem surprised by how fat I am," Melissa says as they walk down the single flight of stairs. Not using the elevator was her idea, but she's panting and with each step he's sure she will lose her balance.

"It's Tony, remember."

She doesn't answer until fifteen long minutes later when they are in the car. Paul wonders if she notices the people in the lobby and on the sidewalk looking at her. He hopes not; it will do nothing to help her change. For her, hurt leads to depression, and depression leads to self-destructive behavior. She gained about fifteen pounds in two weeks under the care of a therapist who tried to spur her on through criticism.

He hopes Tony will support Melissa, even if becoming a man was all the assistance he himself needed. The new person is much more confident and playful among adults than before, although as a mother she was wonderful with their daughters and any other children that happened to be around. The fact that Sarah makes an attractive man after being a striking woman seems unfair to people like poor Melissa, who is still panting too much for conversation.

"I don't think I'll have any trouble remembering to call her Tony when I can see her," she says finally. "She isn't really the same at all, is she?"

He shakes his head, thinking of what his sister told him of Melissa in her dark bedroom on the computer. At first not eating until they suspected she was anorexic, and then giving in to their pleas and eating whatever they asked, followed by eating whatever was in the kitchen, then using her money—eventually everything she had carefully saved from years of babysitting—and ordering pizza and take-out from any restaurant that would deliver. She would wash herself carefully most days, but her room was full of food containers that stank and grew moldy. Finally she stopped bathing entirely, and they couldn't make her leave the house.

After months of this, and the arrival of insects, she tried to kill herself with the contents of the medicine cabinet: her mom's birth control pills (two month's worth), who knows how many hundreds of Ibuprofen capsules, four or five Sudafed, and a bottle of cough syrup—after which she started throwing up.

A year later she slit one wrist very successfully and then passed out with an enormous crash, hitting the shaky shelf above the toilet and knocking bottles all over the tile floor and into the tub.

This was when her parents decided to move to Colorado, to be near Paul and Sarah. Paul didn't know they were coming, so he couldn't warn them that Sarah had left and was changing her identity. They sold their house in New Zealand, but not the lodge or the cabins; they hired a manager to take care of those and bought a house a few blocks from Paul without ever viewing it.

The plane ride to the United States was described as "insanely bad." Paul still isn't sure what happened—if Melissa did something or if it was just uncomfortable (although her parents were empathetic enough to reserve two seats for her in first class).

Paul was working at his store one day and suddenly Carrie was there, saying her family was in a rented van out front and they needed his help. They hadn't brought enough possessions, or the right ones, and were always having friends in New Zealand go into their storage unit and send this or that.

Paul was unable to fix Melissa, whose weight kept increasing, but she would leave her computer to sit with him, which her parents saw as an improvement.

His sister and her husband still don't know about Sarah's sex change; they assume it is grief that drove her away—which he has to admit is what he believed for a long time too. Melissa was informed a few months ago in secret, supplying her with something new to research on the Internet.

Recently there was an incident that's still blurry to him, where his sister insisted Melissa tried to commit suicide again, and Melissa insisted she didn't. Both were hysterical in defense of their point of view, until Paul bought plane tickets to California. He bought two, and Carrie's husband added two more. These were in coach, but with the row to herself Melissa said she was fine. She told him she didn't use the bathroom on either plane from New Zealand, but waited for the one airport stop in Los Angeles.

Melissa makes her weight sound like a somewhat surprising, mischievous pet that attached itself to her unexpectedly. "That's why walking is really frustrating," she says now, "but I want to try more."

Despite this goal, Paul groans when repeated turns reveal only one distant parking spot, this time at a meter that will have to be fed by the hour.

After the slow walk to the building they take the elevator up, and one woman crosses herself on the way. She gets off at the second floor saying, "Thank you, Lord." Paul would love to think of a lighthearted joke to make the moment less hurtful.

"Bridgett told me her mom owns health clubs," Melissa says. "She wants me to come with her to the water aerobics class."

"Would you like that?"

"I'm afraid her mom won't want me to. I might repulse her skinny clients," Melissa says. She never holds anyone other than herself to blame for the woes of the world. His sister told him that when she checked her daughter's Internet search history all the pages were on human-made catastrophes. She asked Melissa why she spent all her time reading about such depressing things, and instead of getting mad at the violation of privacy, Melissa told her she felt it was the least she could do.

"That's why she's in there crying all the time," Carrie told him. "I thought she was sad about herself, but she's looking at these awful wars and murders and crying because she can't do anything to fix them."

Paul understands though; he is often awed by the horror that is humanity.

Ember's door is open, and he knocks lightly before entering. Melissa shuts and locks it after them, turning the deadlock firmly, then facing him, their eyes meeting and her expression filled with such hate that he finds himself taking a step backward.

He wants to ask her if she despises him, but then intuits the tears halted by violent blinking and sniffling and decides that if she does, it is probably beyond her control.

"I know what you're thinking," she says in a tight voice, still trying to keep her face dry.

Paul sees someone out of the corner of his eye, but he doesn't turn away from Melissa.

"I was thinking that you hated me," he admits.

She pokes a fist against one eye socket. "I hate myself, whenever I think of the lock that would have saved everyone."

"No," Paul insists. "That hadn't even crossed my mind. I was just waiting for you."

"Well, I do. I hate myself whenever I think of that lock."

Tony says, "I hate myself whenever I think of how I knew Shell was going to sleepwalk, and I let Allison take responsibility."

Melissa doesn't look at him. "You gave me the responsibility. You just let her think she had it so she would feel grown up. I was told to lock the deadbolt and to stay awake and watch for her—"

"I was the mother, and I went to a party."

"All parents use babysitters, and they're never blamed if something bad happens to their kids. And don't say you don't blame me because I know you do."

"What I said then—I was in shock, I was horrified, miserable. I'm not going to apologize for how I behaved. I'm not holy."

"It was an accident," Paul says. "No one is to blame. We don't even know exactly what happened. Who would have thought Shellie would unlock the door, even without the deadlock? It was a terrible thing, but people forgive themselves for a lot worse."

"I can't bring them back. I truly would if I could, and if it seems fair to you, I will kill myself. Please just tell me what I should do."

Don't be melodramatic, Paul wants to say, your death would not improve anything.

They stand in silence until Bridgett wanders in and hugs Melissa. Her arms just span the larger girl's shoulders.

"Tony is a scum bag," Bridgett says, "you shouldn't care what he thinks. He was never even a real woman. If his kids were alive he would still be suffering in his wrong body—wrong gender."

Tony steps forward and Paul lunges in front of him, feeling silly afterward, but he thought Bridgett was going to be smacked. Tony has turned away and is walking down the hall. Paul looks at the girls and then follows his ex-wife.

"Where's your friend?" he asks, as they enter the empty room.

"She's with her granddaughter. They went to lunch and a matinee. They're going to work on Irene's novel later. It's about her illness; a satire from the viewpoint of a woman near death."

"Only the elderly can be satirical about death."

"Maybe you could help her, Mr. Mastered in English and then—what did you do then? Oh yeah, you got a job at a hardware store."

"Putting me down has always cheered you up."

"At least you're good for something."

"Predictable."

"I'm out of practice."

"Do you care for Melissa?"

Tony drops his long, muscular body onto the couch. Paul is relieved he's not attracted to this new person; he wasn't that physically comfortable with the old—which was his own problem, not Sarah's.

"I still blame her, Paul."

"Would you have become a man if they were alive?"

"Eventually. Probably not until they went to college. I was perfectly content to have no identity other than parent at the time. That's the only thing I've ever done that's made me feel right. Being with Allison and Shellie, I mean. But I was still impatient with them at times; I really took them for granted. How can we do that with our most precious things?"

"Being human . . . makes us tired."

"That helps, Paul."

"Sorry, but even with scares—like in college when Carrie's appendix burst and she almost died—I—she was my closest relative. I was so worried that I was sure I would call her every day, give her all the money I made that I didn't absolutely need, devote my life to protecting her. She got better and we had arguments again, we would be too busy to talk for weeks. That's the way people are. Never mind—I don't know why I'm trying to boost you up." He motions for Tony to sit so they can share the couch. "I have to admit that despite everything you've said, I sometimes think you're changing your sex as a way to never again incur such pain on yourself by bringing life into the world."

"Surely there are easier methods."

"Grief can do terrible things to people."

"Don't worry, I'm in lots of therapeutic groups all designed to make sure I don't do anything for the wrong reasons. I just wish someone were really able to empathize with what's been going on in my mind since I was a child. I mean it. I'll probably never have a sexual relationship. Or never again, if you can call having sex as a male in a female's body normal. This isn't something I chose. I'm not a woman; I'll never be fully physically a man."

"I'm sorry. Tony."

"As Tony I don't think of our girls every day. Or maybe I do, they're so ingrained in my brain—no, in my soul—that they're always there even if it's not in a way I can describe. But it is easier. As for you, well that was unfair. I married you on false pretenses. I did love you though, just in a weirder way than a wife generally loves a husband."

"Well, there are some strange relationships out there."

"What do you feel? About us, I mean."

"You leaving made everything worse. I was alone. I guess it made it easier too, if that's possible—both everything worse and some things easier. I could be miserable by myself, and with you I felt the extra weight of your pain. I wanted to help you, while you never thought of me. I'm not blaming you, but that's how it was."

"Well, you aren't alone anymore."

"No, Carrie's family is right there. Melissa and I spend a lot of time in each other's company."

"How are Carrie and Denny?"

"They've aged. Much more than you."

"Paul, I have to tell you. I am happy a lot of the time. As Paul. I mean—wow, that's a Freudian slip."

They both laugh for a long time.

"I'm glad you're happy," Paul says finally, after swallowing his laughter too well, so its absence is a letdown. "You look really good for a man."

"It's not fair, is it?" Tony sounds delighted though. "And Melissa is so huge. She's obese. Even if she lost the weight, she would need to have skin removed and her legs might be bowed, and her heart—"

"Please, Tony."

"I don't feel like blaming her at this moment, it's just when I think of it in detail, of all the things that went wrong... Have you seen a counselor?"

"I have, and that's something I want to talk to you about, but with complete privacy. Somewhere with doors, at least."

Tony makes a Sarah expression: his mouth set to whistle, eyes wide. "There's a room down the hall."

"I haven't met Ember's husband yet. I feel like I'm taking advantage of their home—but you live here, right?"

"Her husband—I'll tell you about him later. I met her at my grief group, which is also where I met Irene. I guess I still expect you to know exactly what's going on in my life."

"I wanted..." Paul has doubts about telling Tony. This person doesn't have a connection to his life the way the old one did.

In the much smaller room Tony locks the door and they sit on the only piece of furniture, a small mattress on the floor. Paul takes the offered pillow and leans against the wall with it behind his back. Tony faces him with crossed legs, his broad shoulders slumped down.

Paul needs to picture Sarah now, and he does, squinting his eyes and looking off to the side a little, until Tony loses focus.

"I went to a counselor about Allison and Shellie, and your sex change. A friend gave me the idea. Well, you know Leslie."

"She always had a thing for you."

"We've dated a couple of times, but then she decided I needed to be fixed so she made me an appointment with a grief expert. It sounded to me like skillful torture. I didn't end up going to her expert, who I found out specialized in helping people contact their loved ones—their dead loved ones."

"Leslie is such an airhead."

"I asked that neighbor, the urologist, for a recommendation."

"Do his patients often need therapists?"

"Anyway, this therapist helped me. Just someone to talk to who wasn't connected, I suppose. Did your grief group do the same thing?"

Tony looks at him briefly and then begins to describe Jill and their weekly sessions. Paul is disappointed, even though Tony has always been this way, even as Sarah. If you are hesitant to talk about something that's really important to you, that's fine with him or her, he or she has plenty to say about himself or herself. Of course that wouldn't change with the gender. Paul gets up in the middle of Tony's sentence. "You need to talk to Melissa."

"Hey, was there something else? Since we came in here?"

"No, not now." *No, you silly stupid little child. Just the reason I didn't like sex, and probably the reason I even married you and put up with your cowardly ridiculous self-obsession. It's unbelievable you had the strength to both know you wanted a sex change and keep quiet about it—the little-known valiantly long-suffering Tony? You must have felt truly ashamed to let anything get in the way of your satisfaction.*

He's seething until he sees Melissa's worried face at the end of the hall.

"These are squats," Bridgett explains, giggling as he registers them holding onto the counter and bending their knees. "But not real ones until Melissa gets in shape. I'm going to be her personal trainer, and we need to know how long you guys are staying here."

"At least a week," Paul says. "We'll see how it goes."

"Mo-om," Bridgett calls out. She tells Paul, "They are having a serious discussion in the other room. I was attacked yesterday and no one took me to the hospital, including the paramedics."

"What happened?" Paul asks, and Bridgett and Tony start to talk rapidly at the same time, with Melissa joining in now and then to show that she has already heard the story.

The loud buzz of the intercom draws Ember. "Oh hi, Paul. Melissa. It's nice to see you guys again. I'm sorry I've been hiding, but Bridgett's parents arrived right before you. I'm sure you've been told of our little excitement." Her hair is rolled up on top of her head, with strands sticking out.

"Grandma," Bridgett says to an attractive woman coming down the hall. She introduces them, and the room is suddenly loud with a jumble of voices.

"It's nice to meet you, Frances, you look just like your daughter," Paul says as they shake hands.

"I'm not her daughter," Bridgett says.

"I meant Ember."

Bridgett and Frances both grow quiet and stare at Ember, who seems to be arguing with the intercom.

"My goodness, you do look alike," Bridgett says.

"I've thought the same thing! At least since Ember started wearing her hair that way," Tony says.

"It's not just the hair, they have different hair; it's their body types. The way they walk," Melissa adds without her usual shyness.

"What's wrong?" Ember asks when she turns and everyone is watching her.

"Paul thought Frances was your mom," Bridgett says.

Ember smiles blankly. "Guess who? Horace and Katherine. Sammy would never have allowed *her* up here again, even if I asked him to, but there's a temp downstairs today. Sometimes they're kind enough to warn us *after* they've let someone in."

Paul is introduced to two more people before there's a knock at the door, and he thinks he has a few of the details of Bridgett's injury straight, along with some shocking and muddled facts about a father being murdered.

"I know you're all upset," says a pretty redhead in the doorway. There's a tall, longhaired guy behind her. Ember stands still, holding the door open. "You have the right to be mad and never let me in here again, but I wanted to apologize in person. I'm really confused right now. Horace said—"

"I told her what you told me, Frances. Someone from Caldwell called the Pasadena police station."

"Horace and I are going to contact his sister to get plane tickets home."

"It ruins the whole book," Bridgett says. "Yours was the best story. And you're the one who created the website and became friends with all the families—"

"I know, Bridgett, but I have to go back home and find out what really happened."

"You know what happened. I don't believe you don't know," Bridgett says. "Now you're not even connected to us through my dad. It was worth it to get pushed down the stairs if it would have helped the book, but this makes it just a huge pain in the back of my head." Bridgett starts crying. "I had to go to the stupid ER for five hours and then Mom would only let me sleep for one hour at a time the rest of the night, even though that's not what the doctors said. And I've already written up the part about you pushing me."

"You can still put it in the book," Katherine says helplessly.

"That would be stupid." Bridgett's anger is increasing, and she starts to gesture wildly with her hands. "You have absolutely nothing to do with any of us except because you pushed your stupid self in and caused all sorts of problems."

"Bridgett," Katherine says, "it's still relevant because if your dad wasn't a murderer, I wouldn't ever have thought of him as having killed her."

"We've done nothing to you, and you've done everything to us. I want you to take back every negative word you said. Every one. You're the murderer; you're the one who killed your father, who you've been tormenting everyone about forever."

"We'll give you the money to get home out of the book fund. I doubt Lilac will want to support the project now that Horace is leaving," Ember says. "Why don't you guys come in. I'll go get the laptop from my office so you can search for plane tickets."

Paul follows her; he doesn't know why. She notices him before she enters the last room at the end of the long hall.

"Need help finding the bathroom?" she asks.

"No, I'm sorry," he says.

"I'll bet you're confused." She looks past him down the hall and then grabs his wrist, "Come in and I'll explain while I delete my most recent searches. I don't want them to know what I view."

"What do you view?" he asks, a thrill tracing around his groin and up through his abdomen.

"Nothing terrible, I just want to stay private. Especially with Katherine, who I don't trust."

"Are you divorced?" he asks.

"You don't know? My husband was Richard Earle Dayle."

He thinks she's making some kind of joke. "Tony never—"

"Yes. Vicky was his first wife and Bridgett his daughter. Katherine claimed Richard abducted and murdered her sister, and that her father went missing while searching years later. Today we found out that her dad was abusing his kids and murdered his own daughter, then was killed by Katherine. Richard wrote biographies, as you might know, and Bridgett is writing one in his honor, but also to show the bad things he did—it's something to help her make sense of having him for a father. Horace is a writer and his rich sister was funding the project so he would have a job and also, I found out recently, in hopes that he would carry me back to Georgia as his bride."

"Now I'm caught up," Paul says faintly, wanting to touch her softly, just on the shoulder—no, the cheek. "So why did Katherine make up that story?"

"Who knows. Her story—well, I don't know why she would unless she really believed it. Some kind of memory defense mechanism." Ember becomes nervous and begins to fiddle with the laptop on her bed. "I would never let them near Richard's computers, imagine that. At first we thought Katherine was a journalist, and maybe she is. If she could make up that mess because she's unbalanced she could certainly do it for a story."

"She must have been traumatized."

"I'll feel very sorry for her if it turns out to be true. Maybe she never even went to the police station. Perhaps she and Horace are out there robbing and killing the rest of them as we dawdle."

Paul opens the door and puts his head out for a moment. "Nope," he says, shutting it again. "Who is Frances?"

"Oh, she's Richard's mom. My mother-in-law. I like the way she looks, but I think I'll get my hair cut again. Defying vanity has gone on long enough."

He knows this is the time to compliment her, but such a move seems too predictable, too banal, so he lets the moment pass.

"Just now is the first time Bridgett has cried about the whole incident, being pushed down the stairs and everything. Her frustration makes sense, but she's an odd little girl, isn't she? Wow, I have to call my friend Jill. She'll never get over how much she's missing. Please take this to the dining room, OK?"

Paul delivers the computer to Horace and sees the pretty blond lady, probably Bridgett's mom, talking seriously to Melissa. They look funny together, one compact and curvy with energy vibrating even from her hair, and the other huge and old, with her head covered in tufts from the frequent hackings she gives herself in place of professional hair styling. He rarely focuses on how bad it is anymore, and most people don't see anything but her size.

"Oh, Paul," Melissa says. Now she's crying.

"What's wrong?"

"No, it's good, Paul. Vicky's going to let me use her gym while we're here. Bridgett can help me along with a real trainer, one who used to be fat herself."

"We need to get your heart checked out before you start anything though. Have you had a doctor's appointment lately?"

"I can't," Melissa says.

"Sure you can. I know a doctor that's been recommending patients to the Clean Cut for years. Why don't we try and see if we can set up a meeting today."

Melissa looks pleadingly at Paul. He can only imagine how little she wants to wear a paper gown.

"Maybe a female physician would be better?"

"Why do you assume mine is a man? My friend specializes in women with weight problems. She's as comfortable as Santa Claus and I'll be there the whole time, if necessary. Bridgett, we're going in a minute, want to come?"

Paul motions for Vicky to follow him into the hall where he says quietly, "I can't thank you enough for taking her on as your project, but her eating was caused by emotional problems."

"We're not going to mess with her eating. I have some great nutritionists on staff, but the best thing I know of for depression is movement. If she needs counseling you'll have to arrange that. This will be good for Bridgett too, help her get out of herself, away from people who are doomed, like Irene and Tony. At least Melissa has a chance." Vicky pats Paul's arm and goes back to the girls. "We'll take my Volvo if Horace will be kind enough to give us the keys. Carl."

"I heard," he says, getting up from the stool he was straddling.

"I'm going to take these two to the airport, and then I'll come home." They kiss, pull apart, then hug and kiss again. He whispers something in her ear and goes back to his stool.

Paul feels anxious separating from Melissa. He squeezes her shoulder and tells her he's proud of her. "Why didn't you ever want to do this at home?" he asks quietly.

"I don't know," Melissa whispers back. Then in a normal voice she adds, "It's like I got really lucky, meeting the perfect people to help me. It's not as scary this way, and I think Vicky is nice although I would hesitate to disagree with her."

"Well, you'll have Bridgett on your side. Where did she go?"

"I don't know. She's pretty mad at Katherine for messing up her book."

"Was my mom calling me?" Bridgett asks irritably, appearing from behind Melissa.

"She invited me to go to the doctor and then the gym," Melissa says uncertainly.

"OK. Maybe we can do water aerobics if there's a class, or just play in the pool. You can wear shorts and a t-shirt and I will too."

Paul would be surprised if Melissa has any shorts. "Will you need to stop at the hotel?" he asks.

"If I do, the key card is at the front desk."

"That's right. You're set then. I might meet you back there. Just make sure you call both places if you need me."

"Oh no, the car!" Melissa says.

"Damn!" Paul takes off out of the apartment, running down the stairs and past the doorman. He hears someone jogging behind him when he gets to the sidewalk and turns to see Vicky, not even breathing heavily.

"I'm parked in a two-hour free spot," she says. "Let's switch."

He doesn't have a ticket although the meter has expired, and he drives Vicky to her car a block further down, where he pulls into her space as she vacates it.

"Just remember it's only safe for two hours," Vicky says as she takes him back to the condominium. "And after five you can't park there at all."

He thanks her and passes Bridgett and Melissa leaving the building.

"Have fun," he says, thinking of Carrie entrusting her damaged baby to him.

"We will," Bridgett replies. "Don't freak out."

He watches them walk away, tall and thin and blond, and not-as-tall and fat and almost bald. They are achingly young, their arms around each other, laughing at how adults worry way too much.

64

Katherine doesn't want to go back. Once again she feels like abandoning her family and hiding in Los Angeles. There must be something for her in that mysterious configuration of energy and self-hate. But perhaps she's giving her own mood to a city that can handle it, unlike the calmer Pasadena, so civilized and sane.

"We can be back in our beds by midnight if we leave at three," Horace says.

For Katherine, home sweet home is stark and unbelievable.

He mutters, "Let me choose a closer airport . . ."

She has always sensed an embarrassed sympathy toward her family in Caldwell. They are the pathetic Van Leden kids, the way their closest neighbors are the awful Ellwangers; the rumor is that when the father gets angry, he lets his chickens live in the house with him and makes his wife and two sons sleep in the barn.

"I'll call my dad and ask if he can pick us up at ten-thirty tonight, our time," Horace announces. "No, wait, I'll see if we can get tickets first. I'm sure someone will be willing to make the trip. These are five-ninety each, but if we wait . . ."

Now that all these people think they know what really happened to her dad, they expect to be told every detail, as if remembering is so simple. Step one leads to step two leads to step three—well, unlike those with innocent little lives, she knows that's not always the case. Sometimes step one leads you backwards into disastrous memories you should have been allowed to forget.

65

"There's a rumor going around that you're married," says a woman with blond hair hanging below her large, lumpy buttocks. Tony doesn't know her well—he normally works nights and is only early today for the twenty percent incentive on a rush job. He's pretty sure her name starts with a *p*, and very sure she laughs too often, a grating sound that doesn't make him merry, especially at six in the morning.

"I've been married," he says casually. He doesn't have time to chat, being at a disadvantage here, as fast reading and writing are skills he lacks. Ember hired him, so he needs to do well.

"Listen," she says, leaning toward him but not lowering her voice perceptively, "Amiel's embarrassed she told everyone she was interested and you haven't responded. You got a girlfriend?"

"Yes," Tony says. He wouldn't mind going on a date with a non-transsexual for once, but he can't explain his situation to Amiel without everyone at work finding out.

"Is it because she's Indian?"

"I have a girlfriend."

"Everyone wants to date Amiel."

It's true and mainly because, according to whispered conversations (the sexual harassment rules are strict), Amiel has very large breasts, rumored to be implants. In Tony's opinion they're too heavy looking to be anything but natural: the kind women have reduced for causing back pain and indentations in their shoulders. Tony's friend in high school, Danielle, could hardly stand up straight until her parents took her for the surgery that lowered her to a manageable size B. Tony, an A at the time, listened curiously to the other girls say they thought she should have at least left them at C, or even a small D, but Danielle was delighted.

Tony isn't sure how he feels about breasts himself. After hating his own for so many years, he can't imagine what it would be like to stroke someone else's—although he has tried. From the interesting thought of Jill's it is easy to drift to Amiel's. She has a delicate attractiveness that is hardly flashy or noticeable at first; that's where her chest comes in. He could possibly go on a date with her, put a sock in his underwear in case there was groping.

"Don't worry about Penny," Doug says.

Tony glances at him and grins. They sit at scarred black tables of four, compiling the data from surveys in order to give movie studios information on how to best advertise to different segments of the population. It's complicated but not brain taxing once you master it, which Tony is finally starting to do.

"I hear Pen wants you too, but even she's not dumb enough to think you'd look twice."

"Sometimes women have no idea what they're getting into," Tony says with a headshake and Doug, scrawny and old and many times divorced, laughs and winks.

"Thank God for that, or none of us'd get laid."

"I hear Pen is interested in Amiel herself."

"Oh oh oh, don't let me be hearin' that."

Tony likes it here, despite the incessant tests, which are intimidating. They call what they do in his department "coding," and the rules are very detailed although it's rumored that enough repetition makes it automatic.

"When's Ember coming back?" Gil next to him asks, as he does every day.

"I don't know; her schedule's been strange. Family stuff."

"She's not quitting, is she? We need someone with class in this dump."

Yet they still talk about her like she's a sex toy half the time.

They're on the west side of the twenty-eighth floor of a building on the outskirts of Hollywood, and the view is fantastic, with a sliver of ocean visible on clear days. Other than that, working conditions are a little uncomfortable. No air filtration makes a lot of people stuffy and causes rashes, and the floor is only mopped once a year. The main problem is the intense heat; on the other side of the building, in the phone survey department, the air conditioner works too well, and employees are always shivering in their sweaters.

"You *don't* have a girlfriend," Doug remembers. "Not serious."

"I'm not into the work dating thing," Tony says.

"If I were a dozen years younger," Doug says, glancing across the room where Amiel is writing with a large mechanical pencil.

"If I were a dozen years less married," Gil says with a smirk.

You couldn't be any more lecherous, Tony thinks, then wishes he hadn't. He wants to be comfortably lecherous himself, with a hard-ass cock in his pants at all times.

Oh, then he'd date Amiel all right, and Poppy or whatever her name is, and Jill and Katherine, and that girl he sees in the elevator every Tuesday. Fuck it, he will ask Amiel out. It will be his first gender-correct date.

He's had sex twice with a male-to-female who still has a penis. It sort of works in an odd way. Tony looks like a guy, and the man looks like a gal although his implants are still bandaged up. Since their equipment is opposite, it feels fine. Soon the man is having his final and most dramatic surgery, and Tony will be in the waiting room for all the good it will do him.

"One of you tell Amiel I want to talk to her," Tony says.

"All right." Gil pounds a fist on the table.

It's funny they want to live vicariously through him, when if they knew a little more they would be kicking at the windows in their rush to get as far away as possible.

Maybe he exaggerates, people are pretty accepting around here: they would probably escort him calmly to the elevators. Love of the trans-anything isn't quite up there with love of the gays.

66

Frances sits in Ember's office, which is crowded with Richard's things. She's not going to snoop around; it's clear from the constant use of keys that Ember needs to have control and privacy. At first she told herself it was all done for the strangers, the non-relatives that is, but now she's sure that she is high on the list of people who will never be allowed free range of drawers and cupboards. There are probably embarrassingly intimate pictures and letters anyway.

It's difficult to relate to the son that was married to Ember. She never knew him as a person that could have the type of relationship they seemed to. She wants to understand more about it, to burrow deep in its seams, making it possible to imagine that if he hadn't died he might have stopped doing evil. This allows her a tentative respect for him. She can't go as far as to suppose he would have turned himself in, or provided the families with closure, but she has never been good at maternal deception.

Curious to peek in some of the books but afraid even that might appear undignified, she picks up one of the gray squeeze balls on the desk. She wonders if it was Richard or Ember that used them to relieve stress.

There is no reason for her not to return home—what is she doing here, getting involved with these people in this manner? Time is almost up if she wants to keep her job. Ember has been suggesting she leave it, saying it's not worthwhile to go daily to that slowly failing place with its unhappy memories, where she is not appreciated . . .

Frances ponders over whether they are good for each other, she and Ember, or if they will wither aesthetically away with no clear ties to the world, becoming more alike each year—the family is already saying they look similar, and sometimes it's hard to remember that Ember is so much younger.

At home she will have endless stories to entertain the neighbors with. It will be a change from the constant chatter over what famous person was possibly seen at Mariah Restaurant.

Then there are all the meetings and fundraisers she cooks for. Cooking generally makes her feel safe. She has always had the idea that most people will come to the food; if she makes it, she can keep an eye on them.

It didn't start with teenage Richard's neighborhood gardening parties but earlier, when her parents, who ran the one-room schoolhouse in Mariah, began to have students over for tutoring. That was when she learned the power of food. "Go to bed now, Franny," they would tell her when she was four. To stay near the warm, bright room off the open kitchen, she said she was hungry for cookies that they didn't have. "I'll make them," she insisted stubbornly, and was surprised when they let her.

She can't remember what her first batch tasted like, but everyone praised them. After a few years her parents taught her what they knew how to bake, and her stalling technique developed into a skill.

The schoolhouse is still there although not many children are left in town, and some of those are bussed to the bigger school in Caldwell. It is probably the fault of Vicky's birth control teaching, which gave that generation a chance to grow up properly and leave the stagnant town before becoming laden down with parental responsibilities.

But she keeps forgetting: she's not going to cook for others any longer. She decided in Las Vegas while eating at a restaurant with a glass-encased kitchen, where the staff was entertainment for the patrons. The activity behind the window involved a lot of movement since it was so long and narrow. Vicky said, "You could work at a place like this, Frances. You never drop anything."

Carl could tell the comment pained her; his expression seemed to say that yes, the appreciation of good food was ephemeral.

Frances places the stress ball back on the desk and notices Richard's name near the top of a page sticking out from under a book. She moves it a little. There is only one complete sentence, and it has been partially crossed out: *No one knew that this was what frightened Richard the most, ~~although it wasn't as if he would have been giving anything away to tell.~~ and if they had figured it out it's not as if it would have had meaning to anyone. He asked himself if he should take this chance.*

The handwriting isn't recognizable, and this isn't the format they are using for Bridgett's book project. Surely Richard didn't write it himself?

She was correct that looking around the office wouldn't be a good idea—not when something this insignificant disturbs her so deeply.

67

When Paul enters the condo, Katherine stands up and makes the strangled scream of a nightmare, then collapses to the floor a little too dramatically to convince Ember.

"No one will believe me now because I've been so confused about the past," Katherine says plaintively, seeing Ember's expression after she opens her eyes. Horace is holding one arm, and he looks at her with tenderness. Paul, with the other arm, appears bewildered and apologizes for the second time.

"You're the first person I've ever met who faints," Ember says with soft sympathy.

"She spent the night in jail," Horace explains.

"I've always been delicate."

Ember suggests she lie down.

"No, I'm fine now. I was dreaming; I must have fallen asleep."

"If you're OK then we'd better get going," Carl says.

They check for things they might have missed when they packed for Nevada.

"Horace will be back to work on the book again," Katherine promises. "He'll know the rest of the story by then."

Horace bumps Paul on the shoulder with his fist, presents a smile to Ember, and then she's alone with Tony's ex-husband.

"Despite that performance, I'm certain Katherine saw you earlier. They're going to insist Carl turn around and come back if they figure out who you are. But Vicky wants Katherine far, far away, and now there's ammunition. Tony should be home soon. He went in early this morning."

"Unless he's avoiding me—and Melissa."

"I think he's a little scared of family relationships right now. It is quiet here today, isn't it? Irene stayed with her granddaughter last night, to help her adjust to her husband's graveyard shift. Liora calls his job 'lifting things.'"

Paul doesn't know these people, but he grins. "I guess I'll go walk around the town a little. I brought a book on the history and architecture . . . See you later."

He smiles, not moving, his eyes staring directly at her chin. She feels a flurry of feathers brushing the bones of her pelvis and hips, like the sensation on her tongue when she eats something very sweet and rich. Or when Richard kissed her so lightly that his lips barely brushed the fine hairs on her cheek.

"Have fun," she says.

As soon as he is gone she can no longer remember what his face looked like, but Richard's is clear and focused. Paul is fair, with light hair and pale skin, while Horace has dark coloring—Richard was a combination. Horace is the most strikingly good-looking of the three; few people could disagree with that. Richard was handsome in an interesting way, with deeply damaged skin hard against his bones and that unusual white hair. Paul is just attractive. His light brown hair is mostly gray, and he is thin. Very blue eyes. Richard's appeared black, but she sometimes saw flecks of color in them, and at moments they appeared purple. Horace's—she can't remember Horace's.

She used to think it was the mind that interested her: brains and depth and poetry of the soul. But it's harder to be fooled by the external. Men aren't good at disguising their physical flaws.

There is a knock at the door, and she opens it to Paul.

"I'm sure you're busy, but—what direction should I take?"

She thinks it's an invitation.

"Let me get my shoes. I'll come along."

They walk down the stairs, and outside the gate he remembers his car.

"Let's take it back to the hotel and walk from there. Where are you staying?"

"We're on Los Robles Ave."

"Up by the freeway?"

She tries to make conversation as they drive to his hotel but keeps seeing words fluttering in front of her, then losing them before she can tell what they mean. She hasn't written a poem since Richard's death—that cathartic experience for which she imagines romantic artists subconsciously yearn. One that while painful leaves behind sudden depth, character, and marketability.

The only thing she *has* written terrifies her with its analytic dispassion: it is her attempt to enter into Richard's mind, to interpret his actions. She has succeeded in creating a character that's called Richard and that is recognizable as a combination of the man she was married to and the one she has learned about since, but it frightens more than it soothes. And if anyone else saw it they would be certain she was unhinged, or perhaps even complicit.

As they walk from Paul's hotel to the library, the wind blows his hair and he squints even though the sun is covered with clouds that appear pale blue through her tinted sunglasses—the ones Bridgett told her were sexy. She and Paul are both wearing taupe pants, but hers are form fitting. She wishes her shirt were more flattering and feminine; she doesn't want to remind him of his wife. First ex-wife. No, ex-first wife sounds better.

"Shall we go in?" he asks.

They walk across the street and up the steps through the gates. She sits down on a bench while he admires the little courtyard with its plants and fountain.

"So Tony was saying you got him a job at the firm you manage. Movie marketing?"

"Yes. I'm just one of many managers."

"It sounds interesting."

"Not really." She laughs. "Well, if you mention some movies I can probably tell you how the clips used in the trailers and commercials were manipulated to attract teenagers. Luckily we rarely have to watch the actual films."

"Tony said you used to work at a women's shelter." Ember nods. "He claims he's interested in Jill, but he sure talks about you a lot."

"Jill doesn't have the serial killer connection going on. I'm sure he told you that's the reason I was fired—why did you bring it up?"

"I'm sorry; that's not why I mentioned it. I worked at a place for alcoholics and drug addicts in Denver when I was in college. It was part of a volunteer credit program, and I wanted to bring *that* up." Paul laughs, a deep, amused sound. "How did they excuse themselves?—when they fired you, I mean."

"I spent all my time making that place welcoming and effective, but the board, my coworkers . . . The media made it look as if I'd known all along. Still though, why was that believed?" She sighs. "There, you know more than Tony now."

"That's the kind of work you really want to do?" Paul asks.

"I did. Now I just want revenge—not on the shelter."

"The media?" Paul asks soothingly, his fingers tracing down her thigh.

"Not on the media." She watches his hand touch her and wants to lift hers to stroke it, but she can't. There's not going to be any honest and pure mistake-obliterating romantic movie magic with the second single man that has been thrust into her life since she became a social pariah.

"Not on the media," she repeats. "On a dead man."

68

"You should be inspired to write after all we've been through," Katherine tells Horace, as she lounges on his bare mattress. He is staring at his computer screen. The damn thing is still the old piece of shit it was when he left, and even after its long vacation he can tell it's getting ready to freeze its ass up again.

Now he's swearing like a bitter old bastard in his head because he can't vent out loud with someone here. He feels crazier this way. The fucking house is cramped with someone who feels she has a right to all his space. He is going to have to talk to her about that, but not today.

Finally the story he was working on when he left appears. He is hoping it will be better than he remembers, inspiring him to write blindly through the night, not noticing the time or stopping to eat. He has imagined such a thing, sometimes for hours, but so far it hasn't happened.

He reads the first few lines, and they are hopelessly self-conscious. No, worse than that: they are humiliating. Still, he won't delete anything; there might be a phrase he can use someday.

"Write about my life. I give you permission. Then change whatever you want as you go along."

He glances over at her and tries to remember how strange she seemed that first day, but now she just looks pretty, adorably ticklably pretty. If only he could read her mind. That is the one thing he really wants.

Instead he leaves the computer and tickles her until she stops laughing and yells at him to get away.

"I can't fictionalize real life unless I know what happened."

"Why? It's just a starting point."

"I'm too preoccupied with what really might have happened."

"Well, you talked to the Caldwell police, didn't they tell you what really happened? You have my permission to interrogate my family. *I'm* not ever going out there again."

"Maybe we can get them to come here," Horace says.

"Are you even any good as a writer?" Katherine asks. "You haven't let me read anything."

"I'm good at the basics. I know all the rules. I need magic."

"Go sit at the computer and write me a silly story."

"Uh-uh, you'll judge my whole career on whether you like it or not. You'll leave me for a banker."

"Go sit at the computer," she commands when he grabs at her breasts and kisses her neck.

He sits down, and she says she will dictate the first line to him.

"There was once a handsome prince who was trapped in a big empty boarding house until a beautiful redheaded charmer broke in to steal his world class collection of bowling crap."

69

After Melissa's third full day of exercise, Paul asks her when she will be ready to go home. They have open-ended return tickets that need to be booked for a weekday forty-eight hours in advance. Today is Sunday, and he's hoping they can leave Wednesday.

"I'm so tired," she says. She showered at the gym and is in bed with a book Bridgett lent her, even though it's not yet dark outside. "But I never have time to think bad thoughts anymore. Even when I'm in pain from moving and I'm so hungry and just want to sleep forever, it's still so much different than being depressed and wanting to die."

Seeing Melissa's state the first couple of days, Paul worried that Vicky was torturing her, but he watched part of her workout this morning and was amazed by how very little his niece was able to do. She weighed in at four-seventy and the doctor called her heart sound, but the bones in her legs have been slightly damaged from lifting the abnormal burden. "Her legs are going to be bowed," Vicky told him, "but the doctor said she'd seen a lot worse."

Most of Melissa's workout is done either from a sitting position or while in the water, and although Bridgett grew bored after the first day, the trainer made up for it.

"What about going home?" Paul asks.

"When do you need to get back, Paul?"

Immediately, he wants to say. He misses his house, where he can picture his daughters running around and playing peek-a-boo from behind furniture. And since he sold the hardware store, he needs a new career. It wasn't any fun working there without Sarah; they used to share every detail of the business, and he hated being solely in charge. Of course the house makes him miss her too. Over the years they remodeled it all with the help of their employees from the store. They added a deck, a gazebo, a small pool (which they drained and filled with dirt after Allison was born), and a tree house for whichever one of them needed some peace and quiet.

Seeing Tony is ruining these memories. Tony seems to have all the bad qualities of Sarah magnified and none of the good ones. Sarah was never boisterous. Is that so terrible, never being boisterous? No one wants the company of a relentlessly energetic person.

Paul tells Melissa good night and goes to his room to call his sister.

"We'll move there," she says after he describes Melissa's routine. "Why didn't you call us sooner?"

"Well, your daughter doesn't want to go home. Vicky is having a trainer work with her, but she must be paying the woman herself. I don't think they're salaried."

"My God, Paul, we'll pay for it."

"You couldn't get a decent house in LA for four times what you'll sell for there."

"We'll live in an apartment. How's Sarah? God, why haven't you called before now? We haven't heard from you since you left that message. Give me your hotel information, damn it. I'm so excited."

Paul finally gets her off the phone. He calls Vicky to say Melissa's parents might move to California but warns her not to mention it to anyone yet.

"I would love to see this project to the end. You know if Melissa tries to quit we'll hunt her down."

"I was talking to her mom about paying the trainer..."

"When they get here we'll sort that out. The trainers get a regular salary besides what they earn for each paying client, and I typically assign them tasks to cover their extra hours. Anyway, we all like Melissa. She knows every detail of more manmade disasters than I ever imagined. Her trainer loves that kind of stuff."

"That's what she talks about?"

"We try to keep clients chatting to distract them from the pain."

That reminds him of his therapist. Smiling, he picks up the remote control and turns on the television. The local news is talking about a pair of celebrities getting married, so he flips to a tabloid show discussing something similar and mutes it, watching the semi-familiar faces come and go.

He thought the purpose of therapy was to burden someone with his grief, but she pried into his childhood and quickly referred him to Matthew Bowhart, an expert in his older problem. Paul was amazed by how quickly he told the first one the secret he had hidden so carefully; it was harder to tell it a second time to the huge furry man that was Matt, all long gray hair and beard.

His mom's older sister was going through a difficult divorce when he was five, and cousin Lucy came to live with them for a while. Lucy was fourteen and big and mean. She pinched and pulled hair. She came in his room when he was in bed, took off her underwear, pulled up her nightgown and put his hand against her where it was all gross and gooey. Then she made him lick it off until he threw up. She wiped his face off with his sheet and fixed her clothes, telling him not to move until she got back. He didn't. She returned with a big kitchen knife and told him to follow her into his sister's room. The door was open and Carrie was snoring quietly. Lucy went over to the bed and held the knife pointed down. "If you tell, I'll stab her to death," she whispered.

They went back into his bedroom, and she told him to go to sleep and tell his mom in the morning that he had been sick. He doesn't remember if he slept or not, but he refused to stay home the next day, despite being ill, because Lucy would be there. She wasn't enrolled at a local junior high yet.

The visits took place a couple of nights a week and continued even when he pushed his little desk against the door. He begged his parents for a bedroom lock, but when they asked why, he only said, "I'm interested in how they work." They gave him a book on the subject instead.

Sometime in January, not quite a year after she arrived, Lucy went into his sister's room. Paul heard a piercing scream, and he got there right as his parents did. His dad must have flown because he had been in the basement.

Carrie was standing on her bed yelling, "She showed me her privates! She told me to touch her private area!"

Lucy was gone the next day. His parents asked him over and over if she had ever done anything like that to him, but he never admitted it. How could he when his four-year-old sister had ended the problem on her own in exactly the way they had been taught?

The knife threat seemed like a stupid excuse after Lucy was gone. He was a big wimp. How could she have hurt his sister if he had screamed too?

Now he is supposed to relieve himself of years of feeling disgusting and pathetic by talking to Matt. He has also gone to group meetings for guys who have been abused by women. They talk about how society says males are expected to desire sexual attention from older women, no matter how young they are.

He doesn't feel that the abuse made him dislike women, as Matt seems to imply, although the only one he has ever slept with is Sarah. His therapist insists that his ex-wife's gender identity has nothing to do with him or his sexuality, and that his daughters' deaths and his childhood abuse are the first subjects he needs to focus on.

But Matt also says there's nothing like talking about vaginas with other men. Therapy sure makes him feel messed up. Paul is attracted to women; he just doesn't want anything to do with their genitalia. He needs porn where the panties stay on.

He doesn't like the person that allowed Lucy to make him do things, and he is also uncomfortable with the one who talks about it out loud. Still, he has chosen to believe that Matt's "brain archeology" and "excavation of pain" will eventually yield results.

He wonders if either he or Tony would have straightened out their messes if their daughters hadn't died. He wouldn't mind being a miserable garbage dump of unresolved issues forever if it would bring them back to life. And more, so much more.

Thinking of this leads him to imagine how their physical bodies must look now, so he flips through the television channels violently to empty his mind out. That's what television is supposed to do, isn't it? Stop all brain activity?

He wishes they had chosen cremation. Previously he and Sarah believed in it as a way to save space, but they were unable to burn their daughters' bodies.

During the burial, lines from that poem about Sam McGee, the guy who froze to death but was revived when stuck in an oven, kept running through his mind. He couldn't remember the exact words, but his exhausted brain made up for that by replacing them with rhyming requests from his daughters that he not bury them in a chilly grave.

Part Four

70

It is Tony's second dinner out with Jill. The first was over two months ago, at the beginning of July. Jill left a few days later for a weeklong trip to Scotland with her three graduate school roommates, all divorced. Tony waited another six weeks until she called.

Jill pours wine into her glass, watching carelessly until Tony is sure it's going to spill over and drip off the table. But she stops just in time, then leans down and sucks the top layer off. She smiles up in greeting as a waiter clears away two cans of beer. Tony sits down. It's a moody place with stern, gliding waiters—certainly not aluminum can decor. "I know the owner," Jill answers Tony's raised eyebrows. "Sit." He shifts in his seat. "Are you still a strict shoot-it-up guy, no alcohol?" He joked to her once that drinking interfered with his hormone shots.

"I ordered for you," she says.

He wonders if she knows how wickedly deep and smooth her voice can be. "Where have you been?"

"You know about Scotland, right? It was lovely, a marvelous country. While I was gone my mother died. I didn't leave my destination with anyone, so I found out three days after. I went down there to get all the boxes of my childhood that Mom had kept."

"What did she die of?"

"Everyone asks that."

A waiter, a wonderful waiter, brings a dessert tray to the table. Tony is grateful for the mistake, a subject changer.

"Oh, silly Marta remembered I like dessert first. Just get us a basket of her little shortbread cookies. We'll have them for an appetizer. Marta owns this place as well as a tiny bakery, if you ever want dessert to go. How has everyone been? Did your cute hubby go back home?"

For a moment Tony thinks she's talking to the waiter. "Oh. Yes. He and his sister are getting their houses ready to sell. I don't know what Paul's going to do, but Melissa's parents are coming here. I have an apartment all lined up for them. Melissa's still staying with Vicky—she's lost something like fifty-four pounds, an average of six a week. That girl works very hard. I hope she doesn't get discouraged. She got her GED in Colorado at sixteen with an age waiver, and Bridgett wants to do the same, so strife abounds." Jill is staring at him intently, but it might be with what she has described to him as her psychobabble mask.

"And your relationship?"

"It's good. Weird but good. Melissa and me studied together and took the personal trainer certification exam. I'm already making some extra money at my gym, but even if Melissa passes Vicky said she won't hire her until she's down to one-fifty. Her goal is something a little less."

"That's great. What about you?"

Definitely the mask.

"I'm going to train full time when I get my certification, maybe quit the movie job. I've been helping Ember for fun and she's really toned now. I can't work at Vicky's all-woman place—" Jill snorts. "And where I work out is free-weights with mostly boxers and stuff, so I've found another little health club."

"Not the Bona Marx?"

"If I pass I'm hired."

"You're going to be training the hottest of the gays in Gaytown. Will you give me a discount?"

"If you don't tell anyone about my humble beginnings."

"I bought the most expensive five-year membership to that place with three still to go. They take a monthly chunk of my bank account, and I can't get out of it unless I die or move to Antarctica."

"I remember you telling me that."

"Then I realized I not only hate to exercise, but I would be left entirely alone as all the pretty, pretty boys paw at each other and roll their eyes at the chubby old lady marring the landscape."

"Homos have no kind of taste in women."

"Are you still dating that girl from your work?"

"That's another reason I want to quit. She's always looking at me and laughing."

"Oh, poor little Tony is being teased. What happened? Did you tell her?"

"Uh-uh. I had to claim I didn't want to have sex with anyone outside a committed relationship." Eating the crumbly cookies in handfuls has made a mess all over the lacy tablecloth. "Oops."

"Very manly," Jill says. "Here, just brush it all into the basket."

"That's why I love you," Tony says, then thinks, "Oh wait, wait, wait. Fuck, make it into a joke" because she looks alarmed. "Ah, salad. More croutons than lettuce—I bet Marty made this just for you, didn't she?"

"Marta. When will you start your surgeries?"

"I can't yet, I haven't been on the hormones long enough. That's the rule unless I go to some shady surgeon. Sometimes I feel crazy wanting it, other times I know it won't be enough."

"Medicine and technology are ever improving."

At her house he sits on the couch in front of the blank television, feeling anti-climatic. Dinner is a convoluted memory, as if he were drinking too. The odd Marta showed herself, and they received plates of raw salmon heads which were quickly removed, thick, thick coffee oozing sickening sweetness, and a huge chocolate thing that Jill ate on her own. He can't remember a real main course and on the bill with zero dollars and zero cents Jill wrote a hundred percent tip. He plans to go back with Irene or Ember and try the food without Jill and Marta's irritatingly private games.

Jill will come out with drinks; they will sit around awkwardly for a time, and then go into the bedroom for lesbian slithering. He wants it, he does. He is attracted to her, not comfortable with her; as a matter of fact he feels like throwing up, puking out the fish heads he didn't eat. It's just that he is fucking tired of not having hetero sex.

"I was thinking of you," Jill says. He turns but can't see her in the hall. "I was thinking of you when I went to this conference. There was this woman there who wrote a paper a few years ago on the transgendered. I didn't read it then, but this time I asked her for a copy. It was ludicrous. Female-to-male was based on a mother's depression and the daughter's desire to have a penis in order to be a father figure—making the child theoretically her own grandfather. Well, that's the bulk of it. She found or made up a single perfect case story on which she built her entire theory. She told me proudly her research was still up to date. I told her she was a dumb bitch." She giggles. "Not in those words, but she got the point. It's still an area where not much has been figured out.

"Anyway, I bought you something then I wasn't going to show it to you. It's a little freaky, something I've never tried before. I have a vibrator but—my imagination is limited."

Tony wishes the lights weren't so bright.

"OK, I'm not going to come out there and present this to you. Wait a minute then come to my bedroom. You'll find it; there are only two possibilities. OK, now."

One door is open, and Tony sees a candle's flame in the dark. He walks in slowly, timidly, and waits for his eyes to adjust. There's Jill on her bed, still wearing the same clothes, no slinky negligee or defiant nudity.

"I didn't need to take so long, I was just thinking. Deciding. You don't have to use it if you don't want."

He is glad it is dark but wishes he could see her face, to help him come up with some idea of how to react, what to expect.

"This is not a seduction set-up, it's just—*We* won't use it, that's for sure."

She reaches under the pile of pillows behind her and pulls out a large cloth bag.

"This feels wrong, doesn't it? I don't want the mood to be so awkward, but that's my fault. As a friend I want to help you."

Tony pictures his own long, ungainly silhouette and wonders what to do with his arms, which don't seem to be hanging properly. Finally the thing is shoved at him, and he pulls it out of the box.

"It's a strap-on dildo deal. Have you heard of them? I'm sure at your transgendered group—"

"Whoa-o-o," Tony says, deciding quickly that amusement is the best reaction. "Huh, I knew things like this existed—At least I think I did."

Jill starts speaking incredibly fast, "It's a leather harness. The legs and waist are adjustable. It comes with a rubber dong but you can get a million types, vibrating ones, whatever. Ones that look and feel realistic, skin color even. There's another slot where you can insert a smaller dildo-deal, a double—so it's inside you. You know what I mean? The pressure imitates—well, more than otherwise—what you might feel if you were actually—if you had a penis."

"Have you tried this?"

"Oooh, God no. No, no. I'm not—No."

"Thanks for—This is great. The weirdest present I ever got."

"Good, I'm glad you like it. Whew. Now go on home so I can sleep this whole experience away."

"There are only three other female-to-males in my group, but you should come speak to us. You're a medical professional; you could give a little informative talk. It would also be useful because I think two of the people are in love, and the guy's already had all his surgeries."

"I'll arrange a presentation if you'll help. I find the whole sex toy universe rather upsetting. I always thought I was sexually open, but even though I've had my lonely moments, some stuff... At first I assumed a lot of women must be completely replacing men with all these vibrators of every size and shape, but then I saw little vaginas too. Lips so guys could give themselves blowjobs.

"Oh, and the blow-up dolls! One of the pictures looked like a seductively arranged female corpse from one of those misogynistic mysteries. Who are all these people alone in their rooms, in love with plastic women with huge breasts and removable vaginas!"

"You're exaggerating."

"Not a bit, my dear. There's a whole 'nother world out there."

"What would Irene think—not that I'd tell her."

"With AIDS and all, I suppose some of that stuff makes sense. If only they could make a victim doll so rapists would stay away from real women—terror in her eyes and a voice that screams for them to stop. Men are horrible. And I have a very early morning. I've got to get to sleep."

"Well good-night," Tony says. He is still standing in the doorway.

Jill has forgotten that she picked him up, so now he and his dildo belt have to go find a taxi.

71

Bridgett calls Frances before Irene's good-bye party and asks her if Mariah is close to Charleston, South Carolina. "I think it's about a five-hour drive. What's wrong, sweetie?"

Bridgett pauses for a moment, afraid she has called the wrong grandma. Frances never uses endearments, while Vicky's mother throws one into every sentence. "Irene's leaving. She's going to live there."

"Well, at least she's not moving to Alaska. You'll be down here at Christmas, and we'll work out a way to visit. How is she doing?"

"OK, I guess."

"Come on, future doctor, you can do better than that."

Bridgett takes a deep breath. "Her last CT scan showed that the lymphoma was *not* progressing."

"That's wonderful."

"The cysts are still there, they just haven't grown. She might die before Christmas."

"Have you been spending a lot of time with her lately?"

"No, thanks to school. You know Melissa doesn't have to go, right?" Bridgett was horrified to find that with California laws it would be impossible for her to escape for at least two more years.

"You might be able to graduate early," Frances says absently, adding quickly, "But only if you are a really superb, fantastic student. Advanced placement classes, summer school. And you'd have to be older than fifteen."

"I'd be a loser if I did that. Of course Melissa says that high school socializing is nonessential to real life. She's seeing a counselor like everyone else around here. Were people this messed up in the olden days?"

"Oh no, we were perfect. How is Melissa?"

"She's lost forty-eight pounds. Mom suggested four a week but she's up to six. We're all obsessed with her weight. She eats exactly what we eat for meals and is supposed to tell us and complain openly when she feels hungry to limit sneaking around. It's very obnoxious. She's hungry every minute it seems like."

"How's that working with your mom?"

"Mom's never impatient with *her*. If I were fat or training for the Olympics she would probably let me quit school right now. Anyway, Melissa gets to eat whenever she wants. If she's craving something she gets it."

"It's just the exercise that's helping her then?"

"No, like if she really wants chocolate cake, we make it ourselves and we can snitch and stuff, and then we each get one or two pieces, and we give the rest to the neighbors right away so it's not sitting around. I'd never even met some of the neighbors we're friends with now. We tell them we're dieting and can't have it in the house even though we use applesauce or yogurt instead of oil and shortening."

"Tell your mom I finally tried that, just to make her happy, in a cake for a school fundraiser. No one could tell. I think it was even fluffier than usual. It works for most brownies too, but not cookies."

"When was the fundraiser?" Bridgett asks suspiciously.

"Oh, a couple of weeks ago."

"I thought you were never going to cook again. Your big resolution."

"I shouldn't have told you, smart aleck. Anyway, I missed the good smells. If only someone would invent a scented spray that could measure up."

"Grandma, I've got to go. The party's starting."

They are gathering in Irene's room since she has amassed an entire entertainment center; she occupied the last two months by watching endless movies and listening to recorded books and music. Tony bought all the equipment out of guilt after he began spending more time with his lovers and transgendered friends. He hasn't told Bridgett anything about the former. She only knows what she has overheard. Including the fact that two weeks ago he was going on and on to everyone about having dinner with Jill, but afterward he didn't say a thing. He hasn't gone out with anyone since Irene decided to leave.

Bridgett looks at Liora, already on the couch drinking lemonade, to see if her belly is showing yet.

Her husband is home packing, and both Tony and Ember have agreed to go back with her after the party to help load the moving truck. Irene was supposed to take a plane, but she used to drive all over the country with her husband and says she prefers to travel that way. They had to rent a truck with a bigger cab and backseat, which Tony paid for because Liora has no money.

"We're going to come see you at Christmas," Bridgett tells Irene, who is sitting on the old leather recliner that has been her throne for months.

"Why, that's wonderful. I'm going to have an extra room for guests."

Bridgett peers at Liora, who shrugs. Liora's parents live in Charleston, and when Liora found out she was accidentally pregnant, they convinced her to move there, where she can afford a house instead of a one-bedroom apartment. The only reason she was living in California was for her acting career. She's good too. Bridgett saw her in a little film she did with friends, and her character cried and everything.

"It's so sad," Bridgett told her when she first found out. "You would probably have been really famous." Liora thanked her, but her eyes got all red and watery. She explained that she was always planning to have a baby eventually, and it would be an excuse for her failure to get into the Screen Actors Guild. "Why can't you stay here and do pregnancy parts?" Liora said they couldn't afford it here because health insurance cost more, and food cost more, and the smog was maybe dangerous, and she couldn't stand to live with a third person in a tiny one-bedroom apartment.

Bridgett decided not to ask her anything else, but she wonders what Liora will think if this baby has birth defects or is mean or ugly. Will she wish she hadn't ruined her life for it? It seems like a lot of pressure for the poor kid. Mademoiselle Vicky would probably say that when a child is born the mother loves it no matter what, but that's not true for all mothers. Melissa has told her about all sorts of child abuse and child murder cases committed by the mother. Vicky and Carl don't let Melissa use the Internet. When she lived with her own parents she got away with everything.

Not that it turned out that well.

Melissa arrives with Carl, which is a relief. Last night the family was in the kitchen eating bananas, and Vicky said she and Carl should go away for a weekend while Melissa was living with them. Without thinking he joked, "I don't know about that, look what happened last time Melissa babysat." Of course he regretted it right after, but they were all there frozen for a long time. Then Melissa started crying. Things would have been worse if Bridgett had said it, but Vicky never gets mad at Dad.

Her parents haven't noticed that since Melissa moved in with them Bridgett stopped bringing friends home. Melissa would be way too hard to explain, and even if she told her schoolmates not to be mean, they would still stare.

Not that Bridgett cares about standing up for losers. The way she sees it, if everyone loved everyone else then there would be nothing special about being loved.

72

Paul left seven weeks ago. He first called Ember a few days later, apologizing for the bother and complaining that no one ever answered at Vicky's. She updated him on his niece, and he described preparing both houses to sell. He planned to rent an apartment and help the new owner of his former hardware store settle in.

They talk every day now, sometimes more than once. Their discussions aren't sexy, but if it's late at night she occasionally locks her door and takes off her clothes. Mainly she looks at herself in the mirrors that line the wall to the left of the bed. These are the only times she has analyzed her body since Richard died. At first it surprised her how young she still was.

She started to visit her hair stylist again, which she hopes no reporter will note. It seems hopelessly vain for someone in her situation. She had a few gray hairs, in what her well-paid expert called the "pull out by the roots" stage; then the hairdresser recommended zinc supplements, and only black has grown in since. She tells Paul all this, finding out about his interest in vitamins and herbs.

He is eager to learn Japanese, and when she says her grandmother came from Japan, he asks if it would endear her parents to him if he pressured her to study the language.

This is the most flirtatious he has been.

"Well, my mom is from British stock, but they gave me the middle name of Akiko, which means Fall's child."

"How many generations in the U.S. on the Japanese side?"

"I'm the third. Bridgett's all excited about the Japanese Internment camps. She's discovered the rage of racism and wants to ask my dad if he's bitter that others from Japan were interned."

"Your grandparents?"

"No. My grandmother was of Japanese descent and citizenship but married to an American and living in Hawaii. My grandpa was Hawaiian, or Polynesian."

"Wait, so you're Polynesian too?"

"Yes. Not that many were interned from Hawaii though.

"It bothers me that Bridgett is so in love with other people's pain. If she sympathized, or learned something—There's also the fact that she completely ignores anything to do with feminism and women's rights, mainly because her mother and I feel passion and rage over that topic."

"I wasn't a raging feminist myself until my daughters were born; then all the things I knew of gender inequality from the beginning of time began to upset me."

Ember thinks about his little girls until she remembers that she should be speaking. "Um, you really never guessed about Tony?"

"It never crossed my mind. I had my own sexual insecurities. I've never told Tony this, but an older cousin molested me when I was a little kid. I was too scared to tell anyone and then that same cousin approached my younger sister, and she immediately let everyone know what was going on. Pretty embarrassing. So I had some odd feelings connected to sex. Well, now I've told you. What a story for over the phone.

"Right when I got back to Colorado I had sex with a woman I dated a few times after the divorce. And it was normal. I mean it felt normal. I wanted to tell you that. I had to see. I suppose I was using her to prove something to myself."

Choosing the least sensitive part, Ember asks, "So just her and Sarah, ever?" But she is hurt. Even though at that point she didn't think they had anything, it reminds her of Horace. With whom she had a lot less, but it's painful not to be considered.

"Thank you for saying Sarah and not Tony," he says, and they both laugh a little. "Yes, that's it. I think three will be my number. I'm too old and shy to—Well."

Ember pretends to ignore that. "For me it was nine before Richard. Nine that I count. College was a little crazy. I'm glad I was wild then because now I—I was lonely before you started calling. I never guessed about Richard. I knew he was strange and could be difficult, but we had a great relationship."

"Would you have stayed together if he survived?"

"No. Loyalty isn't always wonderful. I don't think I would have been easily convinced of his guilt if he were alive though. He was charming and had manipulated me before. He would have hired expensive, clever attorneys."

Their most serious conversation eventually ends in soft good-byes.

Then when Paul calls next, during Irene's farewell party, he asks if Ember ever planned to have children.

"Once, but Richard refused, and I'm very close to his daughter. It certainly hasn't been in my thoughts for many years. After seeing Bridgett to this point I'm leery of starting over. Right now I would just—" Someone calls her name from down the hall. "The party, I forgot about the party. Will you be home later? I'll call you when everyone leaves."

"Give Irene a hug for me."

The guests are listening to Irene, who says, "I also knew when I was driving my car—I never liked to drive after Dad died. By Dad I mean Lou. Traffic changed for the worse. I did dang-fooled things, but at the last minute followed my impressions. I felt Lou sitting beside me those times.

"Once my sister Ruth and I were in Pocatello, Idaho, staying in a hotel. Ruth wasn't driving any longer even then. We went to visit one of her great-nieces and on the way back we couldn't find the hotel. We had those modernized room keys that are like credit cards and don't even have the room number on them, much less the hotel name. We knew vaguely where it was, but neither of us had a real idea. Just guesses. There was a farmer-type of old station wagon in front of us—you've seen the old ones with wooden panels that are used for hauling things? I decided to follow it when it took the second exit. Ruth was upset with me, and she got more and more panicky as we drove through the streets behind that station wagon and took the same turns it took. Eventually it led us right to the hotel and kept on going. If that wasn't direction from on high, I've never known it. All Ruth could say was, 'Well I'll be demned.'"

No one seems to need Ember, but she sits cross-legged on the floor to listen. Her chest is warm with excitement and nervousness. She can't remember what Paul looks like, but his words are still in her head.

73

"When I get down to one-fifty your mom said I could be a personal trainer. She's going to put up before and after pictures of me to inspire other people," Melissa tells Bridgett, who is squinting at a page of calculus problems.

"I thought we were going to be candy stripers."

"We are, but that doesn't pay. I can't wait to start school again in January."

Bridgett snorts. "You've forgotten what it's like. If I do all advanced placement classes while you're taking your college basics, maybe you won't be too far ahead."

"Can you do that?" Tony asks skeptically.

"Yes, my teachers said I'd be ready next term. I'm like a nerd now, Tony. There's this one really cute boy who is all serious too, and he wants to go to medical school too. All the girls like him but he's starting to like me because I'm driven. He told me before he thought I was just a pretty party girl. Can you believe he thought I was pretty, and I didn't even know?"

"Your skin is much better."

"I got stuff from the dermatologist but not the pill. Were you a virgin when you were my age?"

"Yeah."

"So were Melissa and Ember. But not Mom or Carl or my dad. What about Jill?"

Tony blushes and shakes his head.

"Is that what you wanted to talk to us about?"

"Bridgett."

"Well?"

"I planned to talk to Melissa alone first." Tony looks at his niece. "I'm moving out of Ember's apartment."

"Did she evict you?" Bridgett asks as Melissa says, "Why? Where are you going?"

"Jill has an extra room. She and I have become very good friends. I'm going to pay rent, but I wanted you to know that we've been dating."

Bridgett's eyes are wide, and Tony shakes his head at her.

"Really?" Melissa asks. "That's cool." She is seeing Jill every week, and one of the things they talk about is Tony's change. "Have you told Paul?"

"Yes. He's supposed to tell your parents before they get here. I'm not looking forward to that meeting. I think they should be alone with you first anyway. I don't want my appearance interrupting their excitement over yours."

"Wow," Bridgett says, "Tony is growing up. You can tell there's a psychologist rubbing off on him." She and Melissa laugh like that's the most hilarious thing in the world. "Do you get it? *Rubbing* off?"

"You're turning into a little smart ass."

"Mom will be home any minute. Tell us about you-know-what really quick."

"We aren't to a sexual stage yet. If we get there we'll just have to work around the obvious problems."

Melissa asks, "Won't you be worried she'll eventually dump you for a big . . ." She raises her eyebrows up and down to more giggling. This is Bridgett's influence.

"I worry about a lot of things. You know, I think the weight you've lost has come straight from your face. Your parents will be so surprised. You have your uncle's cheekbones."

"Paul is pretty cute," Bridgett says. "He needs some sun though. Ember's house is going to be so empty all of a sudden."

"Ah, Ember, the mysterious Greek princess." Tony doesn't care what he says, as long as it distracts them.

"She's not Greek."

"How do you know—what does a Greek look like?"

"You sound gay, Tony."

"Fine. I can't talk to you devils. Listen, Melissa, if you need to discuss anything with me, I hope you'll feel as comfortable calling after I move. Have your parents decided when they're coming?"

"Before Christmas. Both the houses are sold unless something goes wrong. Does Paul call you? My parents always know what's going on here before I tell them."

"Not very often. I'm going now before Vicky returns and I ruin her mood. Oh, Jill and I were invited to Christmas in Mariah, did you know that?"

"Yay," Bridgett says. "Melissa is trying to convince her parents to come too. They have to agree. And Paul. I'm going to finish the book interviews, and it will be so much fun. I'm dying to see Katherine again, even though I still hate her."

Tony kisses them both on the forehead, a new habit. As a woman he was allowed so much more physical affection than men seem to be, and he misses the nonsexual touching.

74

Frances has set today aside to reread all of Richard's letters. Ember and Bridgett are both tormenting her over them—Bridgett wants to use excerpts in her book, Ember wants something indefinable like peace.

According to the family gossip, Ember is involved in a long-distance friendship with Paul Lloyd. Frances finds herself comparing him unfavorably to her son.

Which is hard to sustain.

She liked Paul fine when they met. They didn't spend much time together, but she feels sorry for him. His daughters, his Sarah. Beyond his health, he doesn't have much. He is damaged, and Tony said their marriage was almost devoid of sex, so who knows what other problems he has. Too bad he's not a closet homosexual, then he and Tony could stay together. Leave Ember out of it.

Enough of that, she tells herself, that is a filthy way to think. She never analyzes the copulation choices of gender-correct couples. Of course now her mind wanders to an image of the other big story, this one from Ember, about Tony and Jill and a strap-on dildo. Ember didn't expect Frances to know what that was. It is hard to remember that Tony considers himself heterosexual.

She needs to clear her thoughts. After jogging slowly around the house until breathless, she goes down to the basement and puts on the first disc of the *Les Misérables* soundtrack. She will start with her trampoline routine, then get to the letters.

Her energy slows when she remembers that he won't have put dates on them, so it will be impossible to tell what order they should go in. The first one she received is still in its original envelope. It was entirely unexpected and from its tone she didn't plan on another, nor did she move it from the top of her clothes dresser (where it sat next to a framed photograph of her baby boy in his laughing father's arms) until the second arrived. After that she labeled a manila folder "Richard's letters" and put it in the top drawer of her file cabinet, the one designated to him since his birth.

When she stayed with Ember she was pleased to see that Richard had remembered everything she taught him about filing. She caught herself beaming over her lasting influence in that inconsequential area, despite the much more forcefully expressed admonition to not commit murder being blithely ignored.

She doesn't jump fast enough to sweat before she quits and goes upstairs. The cabinet is unpainted metal and rusting in some places. It was a present from Thad the first year of their marriage. She used to secretly wish it were made of wood and felt annoyed that she could never replace it without hurting his feelings.

The only envelope she saved has the same address as the place Ember still lives.

In one letter he refers to basketball—that's something she can tell Bridgett about: watching basketball with Richard. She sat in the room with him when a game was on and let her mind wander, but she found she missed it when he went to a friend's house instead. Once she turned the television on when she was alone; she can't remember who was playing, but she was sitting on the edge of the couch, a little embarrassed at having just protested a foul missed by the referees, when Richard opened the front door. He was home very early and she jumped a little, but he grinned at her and said, "Those guys were so loud. I like watching better with you." He sat down, and she didn't make another sound.

She hasn't watched a basketball game since he left home, but if only people could see how he smiled at her. How they sat side by side, silent except during commercials, grinning at each other now and then when a player performed a feat of physical grace and power. If only people could see those times . . .

His first letter, still in the hastily ripped envelope reads: *Dear Mom, I was married to Ember Akiko Oto in the Pasadena Courthouse last week. She's keeping her name at my suggestion, for who knows when it might be useful for her to have her entire identity intact. It's amazing how women are so willing and eager to permanently obliterate their previous lives forever for a shiny ring and legal certificate. I'm afraid that's why they make such easy targets for predators. They are natural victims; many of them, most of them, beg to be victimized. But they will not get this woman, my last and most favored wife. I wanted you to know that I think of you, and how you loved doctors, when I dig in my garden. If justice were a reasonable goal, I would wish you the greatest happiness. It's true I blame you for many things. Everyone blames the parents, but I believe in my subconscious: what else could a mother do? Love, Richard*

It was typed in very small, italicized script, and she knew if he sounded a certain way, then he was trying to. He did everything purposefully.

The next two pages she pulls out are wrinkled. She stapled every letter that was longer than one sheet before filing, but now she wishes she hadn't. It seems unnatural, and she's afraid someone might assume they were sent that way, which would be inaccurate. Richard claimed that popular history was based on such incorrect assumptions.

There is a pen on her reading table, and she leans across the bed for it. Richard helped her move the file cabinet into her room the year after Thad's death. It's handy when she wants to look something up in the night but unexpectedly annoying during the day, which is spent downstairs on the other side of the house. Since she quit her job at the hospital and has more time, the distance of the files from her office next to the kitchen seems oddly longer and more tedious. The negative thing about not having a set schedule enforced by work is that she finds it harder to appreciate her time, or to force it into any organized pattern.

On the front of the file folder holding Richard's letters she writes in large capitals: Staples added by his mother.

It might be silly, but she feels better.

Tomorrow she needs to finish the flyer for the Community Kitchen fundraiser, and she wants it to be perfect. Lilac agreed to offer any advice she could come up with; then she recommended Horace, the *writer*. Which reminds Frances that she needs to call him to make sure he will have time to read it over.

Katherine answers the phone and promptly asks Frances for her opinion of marriage.

"I don't know, why?"

"Horace wants to do it."

Frances considers recommending lobotomies and sterilization first, and then does.

"Yes, that's what I think," Katherine says without amusement. "But it's not such a big deal, is it? With divorce being so easy and all, it's not really like going to jail any longer, is it?"

"It's hard for some people. To leave. Having children—"

"Oh, that's unlikely. Horace is completely sterile. He was just tested a while ago."

"But why did he get tested?"

"Lilac couldn't get pregnant, and she asked him to go along. She does that kind of thing a lot."

"They seem close."

"Well now she's going to have a baby. So what do you think?"

"About marriage?" Frances asks. She already knows they love each other—or think they do, which can be the same thing for a very long time—but she isn't sure what to say besides, "If you love him and he loves you . . ."

"For a wedding present he wants me to sit down with my mom."

"Really?"

Katherine sighs. "I think he got the idea from his parents. Lilac already had them sold on Ember, who they've never even met. They imagined this poetic tale of her being the widow of the town's most notorious—well, you know—and then moving here to marry Mariah's resident genius or whatever they pretend Horace is."

"I see." Frances wishes Ember and Horace were right for each other. If they stayed in Mariah, if they had children. It would tidy everything up somehow. It's almost as if she needs it to happen, as if she aches for it.

"—sitting side by side!"

"Oh. I had to change ears, what was that?"

"Just that they were sitting side by side. Did you know that Horace thinks I'm his muse? He finally finished a short story and he says I inspired it, but I can't see how. It's like science fiction or fantasy or something. He's sent it to seventeen literary journals and most of them have turned it down."

"Is Horace there?" Frances asks.

"No, I'll leave him a note, OK?"

"Thank you. Tell me when you decide—"

"Yes, of course. Thanks for the advice."

"Oh, I—"

"Do you want to come when I talk to my mom? Bridgett is saying she's still going to put me in her book, and she will probably want more than I can remember. You can take notes."

"That might make your mother uncomfortable, and it isn't—"

"Well, I've got to go. I'll call you when I set it up, see if you've changed your mind. Bye."

Frances takes one letter to bed and sets it next to her head on the pillow. Drowsiness folds itself around her entire body. She feels too heavy to even think of moving, but her imagination won't stop producing pictures of Ember and Horace's children. They could have created a happy family.

75

Bridgett is reading her father's infamous book-length essay, *A Brief Madness: Lapses in Judgment from the Beginning of Man*, while Vicky and Ember sit with her to answer whatever questions they can. As a huge stack of over six hundred pieces of computer paper, the ridiculous thing is far longer than Ember expected.

"Isn't a brief madness one thing, and aren't lapses in judgment lots?" is Bridgett's first question, showing she hadn't been listening to what Ember told her moments ago.

"The brief madness is the period of man's existence on earth. Richard called it his working title. He didn't know what the paper's focus would end up being."

"Did you know he was writing this even before *we* were married?" Vicky asks quietly as Bridgett starts to read.

"Shhh." Bridgett frowns. "Why are there all these definitions?"

"Oh." Ember leans over the table to squint at the second page. The first is a playful rhyme she gave him. He copied it to his title page so he could read it every time he felt like working on this subject. He said it reminded him not to take things too seriously. Bridgett wasn't impressed. "He has definitions and word origins for 'justice' and 'law,' then he gives his own ideas in short paragraphs between each one."

"If she's done with that poem I want to read it," Vicky says.

"It's just a dumb jotting that he found amusing."

Bridgett opens the gigantic binder and removes the first page for her mom. "I'm never going to get anywhere if you keep interrupting," she says in a tone that's just nice enough not to cause an argument. As Vicky reads the poem aloud Bridgett starts to mumble the essay's words, until both are competing for the loudest murmur.

> *"Rejoice while you study the law,*
> *Since you're not planning your own appeal.*
> *Don't focus on ev'ry flaw*
> *This is logic here, not how you feel."*

"The first is adopted from Norman French," Bridgett reads with such mock wonder that it's clear she is aiming for a grand battle.

"Ironic," Vicky says. "Since little did you know, he really was preparing for a future appeal. Or he should have been.

> *"American justice comes down to money,*
> *We all laugh and admit that we know,*
> *But for many the mess isn't funny—*
> *We refuse to evolve or to grow."*

Bridgett sighs loudly. "*That* cheered him up? I think it's depressing. Why didn't he publish this essay thing?"

"Bridgett, as I told you twenty times, it is nowhere near finished and might never have been. Why don't you just use passages from his books in your biography? Those were very successful."

"But people already know those. I want my book to be all brand new stuff."

> *"To me ev'ry wasted life is a big thing*
> *From legal to famine to foe.*
> *Unless joy an afterlife does bring,*
> *This world is just wasteful and woe."*

"My God, Ember, I have to agree with Bridgett here. This is not uplifting."

"I was trying to rhyme. And make it fit his theme."

"We should give it to Melissa," Bridgett says. "She would make it her motto."

"Like you're not interested in despair?" Vicky asks. She looks at Ember. "She's trying to get us to take her to Indian Reservations so she can interview the residents about what the American government did to them. Then to Hawaii to ask Polynesian descendents how their way of life was changed by Christian missionaries, then destroyed by tourism. She's written down all the most pertinent, depressing points so she can rile people up efficiently."

"It's for a stupid school project," Bridgett says. "Ember, how come some people know there's a god and others don't? And how come some people say God saved them for something important when right next to them a baby was killed?"

"Um, I'm not sure."

"That's OK. Are you sending Irene's entertainment stuff today? I want to include a letter."

"You should send it separately, so it doesn't get lost within all the packaging. I'm sure she'd love to hear from you."

"I told her you're an excellent packer," Bridgett tells her mother with a smirk.

"We have been skillfully excused," Ember says.

"Have fun, you two. I'm reading about the inflicting of legal vengeance."

The original boxes for the electronic equipment are piled in Frances' former room, but they have a hard time getting everything to fit in the Styrofoam compartments. Ember is impressed when Vicky easily lifts the twenty-four inch television off Tony's makeshift shelf.

"So what's the deal with Tony and Jill?" Vicky asks. "They're such an odd couple. If Tony was really a man, the way he looks—Jill's so doughy and middle-aged. Are they just friends?"

She is squatting next to a box, fitting the squeaky padding in around the television, and staring directly at Ember with her small blue eyes. Her skin is starting to harden a little from the sun, but it's also firm and glowing.

"Oh," Vicky continues, "Did I tell you Bridgett's latest move in her search for anger? She talked to our Orthodox Jewish neighbors on the next block. We've never even met them. To be that baldly annoying isn't normal, is it? They kindly gave her the titles of some books. Not that she wants to read about it. We're a little worried."

"What about the candy striper job?"

"Bridgett's going on Saturdays. Melissa's too busy right now, and I don't think she'll be able to contribute much until she gets more weight off. Maybe viewing actual, physical pain will distract Bridgett from this morbid hobby."

"Don't worry about it. She's just curious and extra bright and having an unusual childhood."

Vicky stops moving for a long moment, then asks, "Did you always know where Richard was? I didn't. His mother didn't, at least not after he left the clinic."

"I assumed I always knew where he was, but I didn't check up on him. Imagine if I'd gone to the garden one night as a surprise."

"He would have seen headlights and covered the evidence," Vicky responds quickly. "A tarp or something. Then he would say he was just leaving and whisk you away for sex."

"With the body lying there, just under a tarp?"

"He could pretend to have forgotten something. And you'd be in separate cars, so he could sneak back."

"You thought of all this?"

"I tried to defend the idea that he wouldn't have killed Bridgett or me, no matter what happened. Then, of course, I realized that if you hadn't been out of danger we weren't either. Why are we talking about this again? I've stopped thinking of it. Why does she have to read that stupid essay?"

"She'll probably try again and again over the years, thinking it's a key to understanding him. It's good it exists. I'd rather have her search through a mess of disorganized ideas than . . . well, whatever else she might try. Is Carl going to legally adopt her?"

"He wants it to be her decision, so we won't mention it again until she asks. I feel so badly for him sometimes."

"Did you and Carl ever think of having a baby?"

"We haven't used protection for years but it hasn't happened. He wants to be a foster parent. After Bridgett goes to college."

"Did he talk to Paul or something?" Ember asks casually. "He's mentioned that too."

"I think so. I don't know when either of us has time, but we'll see. It's funny that it seems fine to put your own child in daycare but not a foster child. It's like, why do it if you aren't going to be with them all the time?"

"It should be the same way with having one's own kids. People shouldn't do it if they aren't going to be there, nurturing and making intelligent citizens."

"That's the type of thing childless people say," Vicky jokes. "Oh, you don't want any little brats, do you?"

Ember laughs, then moves to the couch while Vicky drops cross-legged onto the floor.

"We consider Bridgett yours too, you know. Not that you want her."

Ember feels a rush of companionship as they both laugh again; she decides to finally tell someone about Paul's phone calls.

76

"Do you remember when Bridgett was five and she asked Richard why he and I had divorced?"

Vicky is lying in the crook of Carl's arm, the blankets pulled up under her sweaty breasts. She can tell he is starting to drift off, and she shakes her hair a little, until the ruffled tufts tickle his face and he stirs. "Mm-hm," he murmurs peacefully.

She turns so her lips brush his chest hair, then bites softly into his skin. "Do you remember?"

"What's wrong, beautiful? Can't you sleep?"

"Do you remember when Bridgett was five and she asked Richard about divorce?"

"Don't think about that now," he mumbles. "Relax."

He was exhausted before they made love, but she needs him to listen for just a moment.

"She was visiting Richard and Ember wasn't there. Or maybe it happened before Ember, but I'm sure she wasn't there or he wouldn't have said what he did. He told Bridgett that Mommy thought he loved another lady, but it was all a mistake. 'So was the divorce a mistake?' Bridgett asks next. No, no, he says, because Mom was meant to love Carl next. He told her life was organized like that. The part about you was nice, I suppose." Carl's body jerks and relaxes; a short snore fades away. She lowers her voice, "I was worried about her before Richard and I divorced because life is worrisome. Then the divorce and me wondering what she had seen when I wasn't home—what she had stored in her little subconscious. Who knows what she might suffer, I thought, who knows what all this might have done to warp her little soul. Then Richard dies, trauma, rumors, facts. People have worse things happen in their lives, don't they?"

Vicky moves away as their damp bodies become too hot and close. Carl could hug all night, glued together by sweat.

"Of course it's worse," he whispers after a long pause.

"You're awake?"

"Mm."

"It's so much easier to work with a problem like Melissa's. Anyone could diagnose it and follow the clear steps to fix it. It's true there's underlying psychological trauma, but even that is comparatively straightforward. She was involved in an accident and feels guilt and sorrow. Or guilt blocks her sorrow—OK, it's not simple, but my part is.

"Sometimes it's a relief that we're all going to die someday and no one will remember what a mess we made."

"Don't talk like that. We've had a wonderful night."

"I know. It's just that so many horrible things can go wrong. Sex is the only time everything is consistently better than expected, but someday—"

"They make pills now," Carl says, rolling close to her again. His arm goes across her stomach, heavy and wet.

"I'm a bad mother. In books and on the news whenever people's kids and spouse die they are always sadder about the kids. Or they say they can deal with the death of their partner, but the death of their offspring is unbearable. I think it would be just as unbearable if you died."

"Neither Bridgett nor I are going to die."

Vicky sighs, exhaling frustration. "You can't control that. Anything could happen."

"I love you," he says.

77

Liora flies to California for a week of parties that will culminate in a friend's wedding, but after one night she calls and asks if she can stay with Ember.

"Thank you so much," she repeats that evening when Ember opens the door to her and the teenage cousin carrying two suitcases. "Everyone there was just too happy," she says after sending her young relative off. "I feel so old since moving. Maybe it's being pregnant. I don't even show much yet, but I'm waddling. And bulky. Also, my grandma is sick. I thought it was just the flu—dangerous enough, but yesterday she said the cancer was back. She refuses treatment, and I just got the message that she wants me to call her to say good-bye.

"Call her with me, please. It's hard to hear her; she's slurring her words now. A week ago everything was fine. I feel all panicky and depressed. Like I could save her if I were there. I keep missing my parents' calls too, so I don't know the details."

Ember dials the number as Liora recites it, thinking of how terrible death is. It's such an enemy, despite people living much longer than they used to.

The phone is answered and passed to Irene. Ember speaks loudly, pressing the receiver hard against her ear but still not understanding much. She turns the volume all the way up and makes out Liora's name.

After Liora takes the phone Ember sits close to her and listens to both sides of the conversation. It seems to be a good-bye call, and Ember would leave, but Liora is pressed against her with one hand painfully gripping her thigh.

"My first-born, beautiful granddaughter...kindred spirits... From the first time I saw your beautiful face with that bump on your head...Wanted to take the doctor...for not doing anything about it. Your Mom said its nothing, its just normal fluid, but she was wrong, you're as crazy as a...."

The joke is delightful for its surprise. Liora laughs too loudly and Irene joins in.

"I'll send you some impressions on high," Irene says later. "When you get them you'd better be impressed."

Ember leaves and paces around her bedroom until Liora comes in. Her face is wet from being washed.

"I'm so egotistical. If she has to die I want it to be while she's talking to me or with one of my letters open on her lap."

Between parties they eat the only foods Liora can stand, corn chips and fresh, thick salsa, although she says sheet cakes with light, sugary frosting are bearable too.

"The ones that taste like carpet?" Ember asks.

"Ah, but sweet, melt-in-your-mouth carpet. All the wedding parties have them, lucky me. So how was the jewelry shoot?"

"Really well. Let me show you my payment."

Liora follows Ember to her bedroom.

"Ta da," Ember says after picking up the ring from her bed stand and sliding it over her finger. "Platinum band with an original three-dimensional Li-ling dragon carved from jade attached on top. It's worth far more than I would have earned if they had any cash. I told him I would help out for free but couldn't turn this down. I hope he gets rich."

"You have such a glamorous life. I would give five years off of mine for fingers as long and thin and perfect. I can't even try it on, my hands are so swollen."

"You're still doing some theatre, aren't you?" Ember asks in embarrassment.

"Well, now. *There*."

By the time the wedding is over, she and Ember are friends, and Irene is still alive.

A week later Liora calls and says her grandma wasn't dying. "She had the flu and convinced herself it was cancer. Then her throat swelled up from the wrong medication.

"She's fine now, doesn't even remember all her farewells. Or so she pretends. I feel like I went through mourning, and now I have to get used to her being alive. Isn't that strange?"

Ember talks to Irene, whose words are perfectly clear.

"Bridgett called me before I got the flu," she says. "The poor dear was all worried because a psychic she went to—without permission—told her she would never fall in love. She said she didn't believe it but at the same time was depressed.

"I told her about when I was fourteen, a bit younger than her, and I went to a fortune-teller, a man in my neighborhood with a well-known reputation. He took my palm and looked and looked—then he hesitated and asked if I were sure I wanted to know. I said yes. He had a pained expression and asked again if I were sure. I told him I didn't believe anyway, to just go ahead. 'Well, it's not a very good lifeline,' he said. 'It's very short.' He showed me where it ended. He said it was a dramatic break, and a pity; if it didn't break, he claimed, I would have lived to be an old woman because it was strong and solid at the bottom of my wrist."

"How old was the first break?" Ember asks, feeling a little breathless.

"About thirty, thirty-five."

"Were you worried?"

"No, not at all. I never believed in anything like that."

"Well neither do I, but I'd be worried. Didn't he feel bad telling that to a little girl?"

"He was an awful fellow." She sounds amused.

Ember stops herself from saying, "*And* he was wrong!" Instead she admits, "I don't know why, but it would have scared me, especially as the years grew close. And I don't believe it either, logically, or—"

"No, no. I never worried about living a long time or any of that."

After they end the call Ember stands on the balcony watching the people on the sidewalk. Irene has done so much in her life—solid things that can be measured and counted, but most impressive are her sense of humor, her amazing intellect, and the depth of her knowledge.

If she could still see well enough to read, other than large print with a magnifying glass, she wouldn't have given up her favorite pastime, but she enjoys book tapes and the television news. She seems to know everything that is going on in the world and has detailed plans for fixing the worst of the problems although her tendency is to finish every passionate discussion with, "Well, that's up to all of you now. Thank goodness I don't have to deal with this mess."

78

Frances is here to take the notes Bridgett claimed to really *really* need, and she sees why Katherine wasn't worried a stranger would be a distraction. Veronica Van Leden cowers in her chair, tilting her head toward her right shoulder and squinting her left eye. Any light would be too harsh for her.

Katherine directs Alex and Johnny in their search for tinted eyeglasses until finally Veronica mentions the van; less than a minute later Alex presents them to her, accompanied by his own trumpeting noises.

"Mom, this is Frances," Katherine says when the glasses are in place. Veronica has straightened up and is nodding her head as she looks around the room. "Frances, my mother."

"Mom," Katherine repeats. They are sitting across from each other at the small square of a kitchen table, with the boys on either side. Frances is leaning against a tall stool off in the corner by the sink. "I'm getting married, so we need to talk about some things."

Frances sighs and lifts herself onto the seat.

Veronica is staring at Johnny with her mouth slightly open.

"I told you Johnny and I got divorced. He's more like a brother to—us."

Frances has been told that the boys sleep in a bed together, but she can't believe there is anything sexual involved.

Concentrating is difficult while on this awful stool with no back support. Her joints have been aching since last night. Normally she takes over-the-counter pain medication, but she was out of the juice that stops it from irritating her stomach. Her body has new quirks that could be normal aging or the start of any number of diseases. And her heart is skipping beats, from three times a week to seven times a day. She's thinking of going to a doctor about that.

"I'm marrying Horace—remember him?"

"Your father liked him," Veronica says briskly. "Thought himself a genius quoting Horace all the time, and even if you're not marrying the same Horace..."

"I want to talk to you about Dad. He—we were all pretending he was looking for Alyssa, but they were both dead, weren't they?"

"First they were both dead, and the church ladies started coming around. Never talked to any of us before, if you remember. Now I'm one of them and I 'come around' when someone dies. No one expects me to cook anything in *this* kitchen though."

"Remember how you were always mad at Dad because he hurt Alyssa and was a pervert?"

"Now he's dead and Alyssa is an angel. That's what they tell me."

"Exactly."

"*Then* it was all a mistake; Alyssa ran off, and Gregory went looking for her."

"That wasn't true."

"I know that. You're the one with the imagination."

"Why did you start breaking everything after Dad was gone?"

"I wasn't gonna beat on you kids, was I? Then I'd be no better than him."

"She used to hurt your dad," Johnny says. "He couldn't walk normal after she was done whipping him."

"He wouldn't stop his behavior though. I wished I'd killed him first. It was my job and doin' it sure wasn't good for you. I always stopped too soon. The church ladies think it's you who was breaking stuff. I don't know how they get their ideas!"

Katherine checks on Frances, then turns back to her mother. "Why didn't you remind me about Dad being dead? I would've believed you."

"I didn't know you'd go so far. You never seemed to like him that much. Never could tell what you were up to. You didn't talk to me, though I admit I had a temper. Alex believed you. Is this the mother of the boy you said killed Alyssa?"

Everyone turns to Frances, who feels a sickening wash of alarm. "Why didn't you call the police or social services?" They stare at her, puzzled. Frances can see breaking things, and even wishes she had something to throw right now.

"If you want a church wedding I can get it taken care of."

"Horace has a rich family. You're all invited, of course. I already asked Alex and Johnny to be my maids of honor."

"Ha," Johnny says. "We're going with Horace's offer to be ushers, thank you very much."

"Can I invite anyone?" Veronica asks.

Frances writes herself a note to ask Lilac to organize Veronica before the wedding. It will be too pathetic if Katherine's tiny family looks shoddy next to all the well-coiffed Greenes and Jeans. Veronica's hair is dark yellow and almost wet with oil. Katherine must be as big a genetic freak as tall Alex because there's no way Veronica ever had those cheekbones, or the tiny straight nose—bone structure can only be disguised with fat, and the mother is closer to emaciated than she is plump.

"Sure, just give me a number soon. We don't have a date yet; we still might go to Las Vegas or something even though I have bad memories of Nevada."

"I don't know how you get to all these places."

Frances feels the superiority of the plane traveler.

Veronica gets up and walks jerkily over to the fridge. "What do we have to offer, Johnny?"

"Do you think Horace will be satisfied?" Katherine asks Frances.

"Who in your family had red hair?"

"That would be me and my mom," Veronica says, leaning against the refrigerator door. "But mom was no beauty like Katherine. Gregory never was sure she and Alex were his children." Veronica's smile shows teeth that match her hair. "*I* don't doubt it. Katherine's small like he was, and Alex thinks the same way. Of course he sat on Alex by accident, on his head when it was still soft, so we'll never know what that did. We have some casseroles in here. Presents from our friends. Most of them are more or less—"

"Oh, no. Thank you. I just ate lunch before I came. Thank you though."

"We have to get to the elementary school to do the lawn," Alex announces.

"It was nice to meet you both." She smiles at Alex and then Johnny.

"Do you ever need your lawn done, Mrs. Dayle?" Johnny asks.

"I have someone who works on it now, but I'll keep you in mind if anything changes." She tries to do most of the yard work herself lately, borrowing a neighbor's riding mower for the back and finding it a little too noisy, but other than that enjoyable.

"Thank you for coming, Frances. I'm going to stay with Mom until the boys get back. Will you call Horace for me and tell him, please? The phone here was turned off because Alex's been tossing the bills."

"Johnny and Lyssa would have had babies by now," Veronica says dreamily. "I don't know what I'd do with Alex if Johnny left. I'd have to put him in a home. That's what my friends say. I'm a saint to take care of such a big, slow boy."

"You promised no home. I'll take care of him if necessary."

Frances doesn't think there's anything wrong with Alex beyond child abuse and everyone's perceptions. He apparently has his own business, while as far as she can tell his mother lives off church charity.

"Alex lost a lot of weight, huh?" Katherine asks as she walks Frances to her car.

"I've never seen him before, but he looks healthy."

"I was always saying he gained weight so he wouldn't be kidnapped like Alyssa."

"But Alyssa wasn't."

"Yeah. Anyway, he told me the other day the real reason was our dad hated fat people. He never bothered Alex after he started to gain weight."

"Oh, the poor boy."

"Nah, he's OK."

"Could you get him to talk to Jill when she comes down for Christmas?"

"Oh, Horace wants to know how many will be staying with us and for how long, so we can get the rooms ready."

"I'll tell him when I call. I have my mobile with me, but I thought you might not want to talk in front of your mother."

"Yeah. Thank you, Frances." Katherine grabs her hand and squints up into her face. "I know we're a mess. I've seen enough of other people's lives to be clear on that. If I were ugly it would be a lot worse for me."

"Just don't take advantage of your prettiness. I know you like to put on a show now and then."

Katherine sighs.

"What do you think about Horace's parents?" Frances asks.

"It's hard to tell them apart." She bites her lower lip when Frances laughs. "They don't look alike—"

"I know what you mean."

In her car Frances moves the rearview mirror down over her face. The smooth gray bun she has been wearing since Richard was in high school is still tidily on top of her head. Her son would make fun of women cutting their hair as it started to gray, but she knows that always wearing the same old-fashioned style is just as bad. "Good-bye heavy weight of vanity," he would say when he saw a woman in her forties or fifties adopt the new hairstyle. It was usually after a slow, subtle progression, but he always noticed.

His scorn might be part of the reason she doesn't cut hers, but in the shower the color doesn't matter. Smoothing the wet strands over her breasts reminds her of the excitement long ago with even longer hair over breasts just beginning to grow, small bumps with pointy little nipples.

That is when she still feels perfectly beautiful.

Part Five

79

Bridgett imagined that with so many relatives in Mariah it would be harder for everyone to keep track of her. She was wrong: adults seeing conspicuous Melissa automatically check for the only other teenager. It's also not fair to Melissa, who is always nice but seems to prefer grown-ups, especially Vicky.

Melissa's parents went back to New Zealand before Thanksgiving and will probably stay until March. They are both very thin, which Carl explained in private was because Melissa used to eat all their food. Another time he said they were afraid of appearing too appetizing—that made Bridgett's stomach ache from laughing.

Melissa only weighs 172 pounds now. She has lost 298 since she met Bridgett's mom. When she loses twenty-two more she will start working as a personal trainer. Everyone at the Clean Cut is counting down. In some ways she looks worse, sort of deflated, but Vicky says it would be far more dramatic if she were older. Even now she needs her breasts lifted and the saggy skin on her stomach and arms removed.

No one is allowed to eat anything fun for the holidays. Her dad's whole job is making healthy food taste good, but all they had at Thanksgiving in California were berries, tons of berries, and plain chicken. Bridgett went out with her friends the next day to the first three fast food places they saw. It was a guilty, oily, face-stuffing blur of chili cheese fries, onion rings, bacon cheeseburgers, and milkshakes.

Of course it was sort of sickening too, but the worst part happened later that night after Vicky and Melissa went to the gym, when Carl said he had a surprise for her. They went to his restaurant where his very hot assistant, Oscar, had baked her a miniature pumpkin pie—but not miniature enough.

Carl told her it was for suffering through Melissa's diet, which had recently reached a new level of sparseness. Bridgett was still so full from her cheap rebellion that she had planned to go straight to bed, but now she hugged them both and began to eat.

"I feel good," she repeated to herself as a silent mantra. They brought out freshly whipped cream. She ate slowly, smiling, making *mm* sounds. It was perfect, and the filling and crust melted on her tongue, helping her pretend she was not about to vomit.

After half was gone she asked if she could take the rest home to help her finish her horrible biochemistry homework.

"Just hide the evidence," Carl said. He winked at his assistant. Did they think she was shy about eating in front of Oscar? She was far too nauseated for embarrassment.

"Pumpkin pie is my favorite food," she said on the way home. "I'm so full but I still want more."

"A good desert can be enjoyed no matter what comes first," Carl said happily.

"Or in *spite* of," she answered.

She doesn't know why adults seem so fragile sometimes, but she has to work hard not to hurt their feelings.

80

There was a one-year reprieve after Richard's death before Frances again began receiving requests to donate baked goods to the town's twelve annual fundraisers. At first she thought the letters were a mistake; most people were unable to speak to her comfortably, so it was hard to imagine them buying her desserts. Surely neither condemnation nor doubt was conducive to good digestion.

Now two years and five months after his death, she has "been given an honor never before bestowed on a townsperson" (according to Mariah Restaurant's general manager). Her job is to make an assortment of miniature desserts. After they have cooled she wraps them in plastic then encases them in a filmy mesh lined with gold. A white and gold ribbon ties them closed with a matching card attached stating the restaurant's name, address, a gracious thank you, and most importantly, the words "Handmade Gift from the Townspeople of Mariah."

Frances isn't sure why a paycheck has made her love cooking in a way she never did before.

Her position is part of a new deal the recently elected board of supervisors for the Mariah Township has made with the restaurant: a break on certain taxes for a share of the tourist trade. The agreement is unique, as historically the restaurant has pretended the town didn't exist (and until last year it didn't—not legally).

The restaurant, with the same name as the town, is still the area's most prosperous business. Its French cuisine is famous, and visitors to the tri-state area always stop there. They never stay or spend money anywhere else nearby though, which has always frustrated the residents.

Bridgett comes into the kitchen in a nightgown that reaches her knees. "Is Melissa still asleep? Why are you smiling?"

"I was thinking about my job. Melissa was up hours ago. Your mom took her lunge walking. They headed to Horace's."

"Do you get paid in food? Hey, what are you making, hockey pucks?"

"No, I'm paid in modern currency, and these will soon be tiny layered cakes. You can try one in a minute.

"Hmm—we need to get you some new bedclothes for when you visit, don't we? That used to touch the tops of your feet." Seeing her granddaughter in her nightgown reminds her how fast the girl is growing up. Normally the child wears an unflattering white beginner's bra with thick straps. Maybe they can go shopping together, get her colorful ones with lace—although perhaps that's not a good idea. "What happened to that fellow you liked? Worthington the Third?"

Bridgett looks at the floor. "Montgomery. He's having a baby with someone. Anyway, I know who I'm going to marry after medical school. His name is Rod and even Ember thinks he's really cute. My mom likes him because he can't date till he's sixteen. We study together though."

"Is he the boy you were saying thought you were too popular?"

"No, not too popular, just not a serious student. Now I'm getting better grades than him in most classes."

They hear Ember singing softly as she comes down the stairs.

"Help me frost these, you two," Frances says.

December twenty-second is coming up soon. This is the last year she will honor what it represents, but she wants to wait until after Christmas when everyone has gone. Until then she needs to act perfectly cheerful in the hope that no one else, including Ember, remembers.

81

Tony and Jill left early to drive to Colombia, South Carolina, and pick up Irene. When asked how she was doing during a mid-morning phone call, Irene replied, "I continue to linger" before losing the connection. No one has been able to reach them since. That was nine hours ago, and those in Mariah are now waiting outside in the unusually warm winter air, dressed in their nicest outfits and ready to eat.

Ember sees Paul walking down the street with Horace, both in charcoal suits with dark gray shirts and ties, handsome and delightfully tidy. Katherine pops up between them, putting her phone in her purse. She hooks her arms through theirs, and Ember hears Frances next to her with a camera.

"They're all so beautiful. Run over there, Ember, get in the next picture."

Ember doesn't move. Katherine's dress is short and bright green, matching her shoes. In high, sturdy heels of at least five inches she seems to be dancing along, pulling the men.

"You're gorgeous," Paul tells Ember, detaching himself from Katherine. "And Frances, you look lovely."

"I'd think you were related," Katherine says. "I wonder if Rich—"

"They're here," Horace interrupts loudly. "Let's go help Irene get out."

Liora is with them, tan and round all over.

Irene compliments the suits, then says, "We were sitting in church a few weeks ago, and these five men walked in with identical black suits. They were all going up to sit on the podium behind the pulpit. I turned to the lady next to me and whispered, 'No one told me we were having a funeral.' Later she must have repeated what I said because it got around, and ever since they have been careful not to match. I felt bad for them, marching up there all proudly. I need to learn to keep my mouth shut; it's always causing trouble."

After telling this story Irene announces that she's too worn out to go to dinner. She is impossible to persuade, but it's only seven so the compromise is a short nap. Frances takes the travelers inside while everyone else wanders around trying to avoid wrinkles.

"I hope this doesn't ruin Frances' big dinner," Carl mutters.

"We'll go tomorrow if today doesn't work out," Vicky says.

"Those people are sticklers," Horace argues. "It will be an embarrassment if she changes things now."

The reservation is not until nine, but the tradition of the restaurant is to first gather in the greeting room, which Carl describes as a well-lit bar with couches instead of stools, for hours of hors d'oeuvres and drinks.

"Ember," Melissa calls from inside. "Bridgett wants you. She's in the basement."

Melissa is standing on the stairs looking healthy and seventeen. Her hair is still short, but she now has it cut professionally. She's wearing a long silk skirt and blue sleeveless blouse. "Come on," she says.

They walk down the stairs next to each other, with Melissa muttering that Bridgett is having a nervous breakdown.

"I found something," Bridgett says when she sees Ember. "It's a doctor talking about how children can behave with bad intentions despite a normal environment and upbringing. This was in my dad's stuff, written by Dr. Filler; he worked at the Grangage Psych Hospital for Children. My dad seemed to think *he* was the subject. He wrote notes all over the margins. Then there's this other book saying everything Dr. Filler wrote about his patient was completely wrong. They don't agree on whether a person can be born evil."

"Bridgett, calm down. Take a deep breath. I'll read the books if you'd like, but experts are always disagreeing on everything."

"Then how can we know?"

"We can't."

"How can we know what Dad experienced?"

"We can't. There's no way to ask him now. It's just—who is more important to you, Bridgett, your father who ended lives, or your mother and Carl? And all your grandparents? Why don't you learn about their histories? What about your friends Melissa and Katherine and your boyfriend and medical school—and aren't you going to save more people than he killed? What's more important to the future, why he did what he did, or what you're going to do?"

Bridgett doesn't answer for a moment, and their breathing is loud and awful in the enclosed space. "Murderers do more evil than any other person does good. Most doctors don't personally save anyone. And for the families of the dead women—for them what he did is more important than anything."

"I'm sure it is, but you haven't told me, what's more important to *you*? Trying to trace Richard's downfall—letting his actions control your life too, or—"

"You wanted to know. You and Mom both."

"Yes, yes, it's frightening someone we all loved was so hideous," Ember says dismissively. "But look at all this research. Richard was obsessed with understanding his own brain, but he couldn't figure it out. Leave his mind alone. It was a miserable place."

She long ago planned out what she would say to help conclude Bridgett's pursuit, but nothing sounds convincing in this damp concrete room. Her throat itches and she coughs.

"You know, I worry about these things too, and I just want to hide away, alone. If only I could read his mind, I think. I can't trust my judgment." The girls are staring at her, interested. "Yes, I'm referring to Paul, but not just him. And not just with relationships.

I start to feel confused and guilty and as if the world is out of control, just like you do. The other day I was wondering what I could be certain of, what single thing, and I said to myself, jokingly, 'At this moment, I am alive.' And surprisingly, it felt good." She takes each girl by a hand and pulls her toward the stairs. "Try it. At this moment I am alive."

"Whatever," Bridgett says.

"At this moment I am alive," Melissa repeats obediently.

"Oh, that's convincing. You two are dorks."

"At this moment, I am alive!"

"It doesn't have to be said aloud. Probably you need to come up with your own anyway. Something that makes you feel like there's this small calmness inside, attaching you to the earth."

"I feel it," Melissa says.

"Ass kisser."

"No, really. It's like taking a deep breath and letting it out." She does so, loudly. "But more permanent. And you can't argue with it, so it makes you . . . quiet, maybe. In your stomach. Know what I mean?"

"Yes, now up you both go. I'm sure everyone's waiting."

Bridgett's brand new black and white striped outfit is dusty and wrinkled, but her mother doesn't say anything. Vicky has her hand lightly on Carl's arm as they all walk in a large group to Mariah's Restaurant. Carl is talking to Liora, but Vicky holds them back and waits for Ember to step next to her. The teenagers are far ahead already, singing, "At this moment, I am alive!"

"She needs time to think some things through," Ember says quietly.

Vicky is about to ask more when Carl swings her sideways and swoops her down into a low dip.

"See," he tells the pregnant and worried Liora. "She still bends over backwards and her baby is fifteen."

82

"So what did you really think of our restaurant?" Horace asks Ember, who is lying on her stomach having her back rubbed by Paul.

Katherine, in her role as instructor, keeps repeating, "If she's not moaning you're not doing it right."

"It was really built up," Horace continues, "and after being in Pasadena . . ."

"Horace," Katherine scolds in a singsong voice. "It's her *tension* that's built up. You're not helping. Now Paul, your first job is to figure out where Ember carries her stress. Neck, shoulders, and lower back are the most common. Horace is lower back, I'm neck."

"No, no, I loved it," Ember tells Horace, lifting her head only to have Katherine push it down again.

"She's not moaning."

Horace doesn't imagine Ember to be much of a public moaner, and he has other evidence of her quietness in private as well—he was about to knock on the door of Paul's room late last night when he heard suspicious rustlings and loud breathing. A couple of hours later Paul and Ember left together, and when only Paul returned Horace greeted him in the entryway.

"I wondered about you two," Horace said.

"We're in awkward stages yet."

With Katherine it is always noisy, energetic, and the opposite of awkward.

"I loved her before we were ever intimate," Paul adds, "but that part of it's been hard."

"You mean sex?"

"Yes. With Sarah, it was—different. And I imagine Richard was—talented."

When Horace was sure they were discussing Paul's sexual technique in the dark at four in the morning, he felt he could offer advice. After dating girls and women much less take-charge and ardent than Katherine, he knew some handy warm-up strategies.

"Backrubs. Katherine's great. Ask for tips with Ember there—then you'll have an excuse to rub her. When you get comfortable with that, go for oral sex—the best aphrodisiac in the world."

"Unless you've never done it," Paul said glumly.

"No wonder Tony got a sex change. Just kidding, man. You've never licked any pussy? Damn. What about the other way around? Hey, rotten luck you had marrying a man. I was wondering though, shouldn't she have been a lesbian? Since now she's a 'straight' guy?"

"I don't get it either. As a man she likes women, which is more than I wanted to know."

They laughed and shushed each other until they passed Tony's room. Two people were snoring loudly and one was making spluttering noises.

"That hasn't changed," Paul said, before they parted comfortably at his guestroom door.

Now Horace watches Paul clumsily moving his hands around and considers a career as a sex counselor.

"Oh there!" Ember says suddenly, with Paul pressing the heel of his hand into her lower back. "That feels good."

Paul flushes and focuses too intently on the area until Ember squirms.

"No, no, no!" Katherine says as he jumps to her shoulders. "You forgot the ass! If there's tension in the lower back, there's tension in the gluteus. Come on, this is the area for the squeeze, the piano, the dig—go for it!"

Horace motions Katherine to follow him out of the room. She doesn't know this is an exercise in intimacy rather than an official lesson. The other two probably won't take off their clothes and start dancing, but they might as well have the option.

83

Irene finishes reading Bridgett's book and sits quietly with her hands resting on top of it.

Nothing is more important than family, but she has left hers at a vital moment. Eventually they will find out she should have started another course of treatment months ago. Her sons and their wives have been known to pry confidential information from her doctors in the past, but she tricked them this time. They are convinced all is well.

And Liora was restless. Why, Liora is carrying her first great-grandson, to be named Daniel Lou Dark Church. "Dark" is Liora's husband's surname. They like "Dark Church" for poetic reasons, she supposes, although she doesn't think the woman's surname should be last. It's just not respectful to her husband.

Liora is convinced Irene will live to see the baby's birth. The younger woman believes this desire should overpower her grandmother's immediate need to be with her husband again. Irene understands how the dear girl feels, but she already loves baby Daniel; she doesn't need to see him.

Then there's Tony, in love with a good strong woman.

They are all doing what is right for them.

Everyone will be surprised when Irene's book comes out next fall. She even posed for the exact cover photograph she desired: an old woman lying in a coffin winking up at the camera. That was a little too thrilling. She is glad she will be cremated.

"Irene?" Bridgett asks shyly.

"Yes, dear. I finished your book. It was quite exciting. Are you going to write more—do more interviews?"

"I don't know. I was thinking maybe . . . Maybe I'm done?"

"Do you mean you no longer need to write about your father?"

"Maybe. You're right, though, it was a need. I thought it was for my dad, for Richard, that I was doing it. Then I hoped it would help everyone else, the whole world."

Bridgett sits next to Irene on the love seat in Frances' downstairs guestroom.

"That's a lot of responsibility for a book," Irene says.

"Well, I read it all, and I don't think it will help anyone—even me."

"It already has helped you, Bridgett. You're a different young lady than the one I first met."

"Really? Because no one else has noticed."

"You can change for the better without becoming completely grown-up. That will take at least five more years if you're lucky." Irene smiles thinking of her sons who enjoyed long, full childhoods. They are all good men, and she prays that the timely death of each parent is the worst that befalls them for decades to come.

"So can I be done?" Bridgett asks. "Is it giving up?"

"Bridgett. Dear girl." Irene holds one of Bridgett's hands between both of hers. "Being finished is never the same as giving up. It's not fair to yourself if you know you are ready, yet you don't move on."

84

If Ember hadn't been told of Horace's minor contribution to her sex life, she would have guessed from all his grinning and eyebrow raising. Her own contribution has been helping Paul express his fears, which she expected to be focused on his abusive cousin or the Sarah/Tony situation. So far he has admitted only to worries over Ember comparing him to Richard, imagining Richard in his place, and noticing his hands shaking when he puts on the condom.

Ember doesn't tell him that she sometimes fantasizes about Richard being forced to watch in impotent agony. It increases her excitement enormously but is less necessary now that Paul is comfortable with her in control. She used to wish she were more of the take-charge initiator type, and thanks to Paul's lack of experience she is changing too. They are evolving into something of a partnership.

Ember sighs and stretches, then jumps when someone pounds on the door.

"I'm sorry you're sick, but it's urgent!" Bridgett yells.

Ember didn't know she was supposed to be sick, but she lets Bridgett beg for a while longer before getting up from her comfortable position on the bed to turn the lock.

"Do you love me unconditionally?" Bridgett asks as she jumps on the mattress next to where Ember has flopped back down.

"You said it was urgent."

"That part's coming. Do you? Do you?" She leans against the pillow until their heads touch.

"There's no such thing as unconditional love," Ember says irritably.

"People say it though. Vicky says she loves me unconditionally."

"She won't if she hears you calling her 'Vicky.'"

"Answer me—yes or no."

"Would you love your mom if she cut off both your legs to use as croquet mallets? And then made fun of you for being legless?"

"She would never do that."

"But if she did."

"She wouldn't!"

"It's still a condition. You love her with the condition she never cuts off both your legs."

"She would have to become a different person to do something like that, so it doesn't count."

"So you love her so long as she doesn't become that different person." Ember laughs, amused with herself. "Or what if Carl starts poisoning people?"

"As long as he doesn't poison anyone I know."

"What if one of your married grandparents shot their spouse because they had bad, baaad breath? What if one of them was a pedophile—know what that is?"

"I don't know what's wrong with *you*."

"What if I kept giving you horrible examples of the things your loved ones might do someday? What about that?"

"You're obnoxious, Ember. Anyway, as long as they didn't do anything to me personally I could probably find a way to keep loving them. Or I could love the part of them that wasn't crazy."

"That's not unconditional though."

"So do you love me unconditionally if I don't cut off anyone's legs?"

Ember groans. "That's a condition, Bridgett, and conditions rule out unconditional."

"Did you love Dad unconditionally before you found out?"

"That doesn't make any sense."

"He told me once that you and I were the only ones he would love no matter what. Do you think he expected us to feel the same?"

"Well, it was easy for him. How could either of us have competed with his surprise 'condition'?"

"Does it mean he would still have loved us if we turned him in to the police?"

"People can make mistakes and have dark and dirty secrets and still be loved—even if not forgiven, but that's not the case for me with Richard. You can make your own decision."

"What if there was something wrong with his brain? Like he couldn't help himself?"

"All human traits could be described as something wrong with the brain. I just wish I could tell the murdering bastard to his face that I don't love him anymore. There, I called your dad a murdering bastard. Do you still love me?"

"You're really strange today. Hey, why do people have to be *in* love all the time anyway? Is that the whole goal of life? After people have sex does life become worthless without it? And don't tell me about the companionship and support, it has to include sex, doesn't it? No one's happy otherwise. They can't just have friends and do stuff."

"Love with everything included has its uses."

"But you realized Dad was a different person post-humorously, didn't you?"

"Posthumously. Yes."

"I have an announcement I want to talk to the whole family about right now. Everyone else is ready."

"Why don't you tell me first as a rehearsal?"

"Please. They're all out back. Waiting."

In the bathroom Ember uses eye drops and brushes her teeth, then looks in the mirror. She doesn't remember her face being so long and plain, but otherwise it's familiar. One of those surfaces she knows well enough to judge without concentration.

A backyard meeting seems a little insensitive. Ember watches herself shrug before turning off the light.

85

Tony stands with the other ten adults on the back patio watching Bridgett with her blue plastic box as she rocks back and forth from toe to heel, grinning proudly.

"Did you catch a toad?" he teases, embarrassed at her lack of self-consciousness. Paul claims this is what Tony acts like sometimes: an obnoxious teenager.

Bridgett calls for silence and then stares at the ground, suddenly shy. "Please follow me, everyone."

The sky is clear but the wind is fast and cool. Ember folds her arms across her chest, and Tony and Liora stand close on either side of Irene. The adults look wary; no one has been informed of the child's plan.

Vicky whispers to Melissa, who shakes her head. Katherine shudders and wraps both arms tightly around Horace's waist.

The bushes Richard grew to hide his garden were ripped out during the investigation, but Bridgett goes to the area where they used to stand. A dark green tarp spread over a small mound causes hesitation; she gestures them on, waiting until they have gathered around her.

"In this box," she says, opening the lid, "is the biography of Richard Earle Dayle. All the notes, the tapes, the printout, and the computer back-up disks. I wiped it off the hard drive so this is every last thing. I've been talking to people about the best way to deal with my dad's death. I'm sure a lot of the world wishes he had never been born—"

"Then we wouldn't have you," Vicky says.

Bridgett rolls her eyes at this interruption. "You'd have other kids."

"I wouldn't," Carl says. "I never wanted kids until I met you."

Bridgett blushes.

"My announcement is that I'm done with the biography and with analyzing Richard's life."

She pulls the tarp away to reveal her book's grave. Irene starts the rest of them clapping as the box is dropped into the hole. With Carl's help Bridgett pushes much of the displaced dirt on top of it.

"We'll have the lawn looking normal tomorrow," Carl promises Frances.

"I'm not done." Bridgett takes a deep breath. "I want Carl to adopt me. If he still wants to."

Tony feels Irene falter as Bridgett and her parents hug to more applause. He bends down to steady her, but her head droops. He lifts her up and cradles her body in his arms.

Liora is holding her grandmother's hand and their eyes meet.

"I'm closing mine now," Irene whispers.

Tony and Liora stand still for a moment, so quiet next to the noise of the others. Then without alerting anyone else, they move with Irene toward the house.

86

Frances stops outside the open door to her room. A light is on and she thinks the shifting on the bed is probably Ember, who went upstairs long before the others retired. Paul announced casually that he would head over to the boarding house alone since Ember wasn't feeling well. Bridgett hinted that he should play nurse and was directed to help her parents with the dishes.

Frances' light knock doesn't receive a response, so she peeks through the crack between the wall joints and sees Ember sitting in a slump with papers spread between and over her outstretched legs. "Ember?"

"You scared me."

Frances shuts the door softly after entering, then twists the lock on the knob. "So you found the letters." She prevents herself from apologizing for only sharing the first one.

"There's no way to tell the order without dates. Is counting what he disliked?"

"He liked the Roman numerals lesson, until he was chastised for using them in math problems. He kept saying they meant the same thing as other numbers and why did they teach them to him if he couldn't ever use them again?"

Ember taps the fingertips of both hands together rapidly. "He was so passionate, so grand, when explaining away the use of dates. Have you ever met a person who is panicked by the dark or heights and so they make self-deprecating jokes? That's what he was like."

Frances lies down on the very edge of the bed closest to the door, propping her head up with all three pillows.

"It's ludicrous, but am I right? He used disdain to hide an extreme fear? Of dates?"

Frances doesn't answer but folds the top pillow in half under her neck. It feels luxuriously comfortable until the pile slips and has to be readjusted.

"He disliked getting in trouble, being told he was wrong.

"One of Irene's sons picked her body up. He and Liora are having it flown out tomorrow. Jill had to get back so she went with them to Atlanta."

"How's everyone else?"

"Sad. That was good news about the adoption though, even if it's symbolic. Carl was her father as soon as he met her. If people could meet parents like they do soul mates . . . "

"You know, these letters are mainly about the big stuff—his books, his interviews, the famous people that called him. Did he tell you I did all his research?" She sighs. "It's hard to imagine now how I had the time, but I used to sleep six solid hours a night and then go all day without a break."

"But you sleep twelve to fifteen hours in a row *and* take naps."

"I have trouble staying awake now, but I had the research and outlines for six of his future books completed before he died. He never gave me public credit; I suppose because he was the genius that made it all new and interesting. He could have researched himself, of course; he did before I met him."

"That's a lot of work you did."

"I sound bitter, but I'm not—not about that. That was my choice. It felt like I was working with him, part of the project."

Frances reaches over to stroke one of the beautiful hands.

"I want your approval for something," Ember says, "but first I have to insult you by asking, did you or anyone you know of ever abuse him mentally, physically, or sexually?"

"No."

"Did you know what he was doing in your backyard?"

"No. I was terrified he would bury one of his friends, but I assumed I'd know about it right away."

"That's kind of funny. But how could he never have told anyone? He must have felt nervous or desperate. At the very worst he would want to brag."

"Maybe he was too ashamed."

Ember sighs. "Thank you for answering. Now for my favor: I'm going to write these biographies—well, five of them. Richard's publisher is interested although who knows what type of marketing they'll attempt. But I will publish them under my name only."

"OK," Frances says after a moment. "How can I help?"

"By telling people I did all the research. That Richard hadn't written the books already. You might think you can't know that, but you'll be able to tell he didn't write them. I've only just started the first, so it will be a while."

"I'll be glad to do so, but is this really what you want—to write biographies?"

"I want to write *his* biographies—the ones he chose for himself. He took my job, and I'm going to take his. He expected me to preserve his reputation as a historian, but instead I am going to take it from him. I'll replace him."

"Ember, I'm delighted to see you so driven, but you've told Bridgett that Richard is dead, and that she needs—"

"Yes, and I'm glad that—"

"You know what they say about revenge: it's never satisfactory. I'm afraid it might be even less so, if safer, when the person you want revenge on is dead. I'm worried about you. I don't want you to be eaten up by this. Or to waste your life."

"Yes, those are good points, and I've considered them all."

"Plus you don't really believe that—"

"This makes me happy, and I'm already doing it. Will you help out by reviewing my first chapter when I finish?"

Frances nods, deciding this isn't something she will worry about. Writing a biography is very time consuming, and if Ember doesn't enjoy it, she will move on to another activity soon enough.

87

Richard had felt nauseated for the last few days, with a cough, and he suspected a bad cold or the flu had already infiltrated his immune system. He could picture the thick goo spreading about slowly and sneakily, soon to invade his head. The description amused him, so earlier he had jotted it down for Bridgett. She wouldn't be allowed to come over for even a brief visit if there was the possibility of contamination.

He hadn't mentioned his symptoms to Ember since he planned to go out in the middle of a wet night. It wasn't raining or overcast but still heavily moist.

Even now he could reach the phone in his pocket and dial 9-1-1, but he was unable to stand up and unable to lift the shovel. For he was on his knees using his hands like limp paddles. He started to pile dirt onto the women, but they were so big—mammoth mounds of useless cloth and skin and hair and bones.

If he could make it the few feet to his Mercury Montego, with its headlights reflecting through his broiling skull, he could leave this place. He should have stopped before lifting Cynthia from the trunk, which was already too difficult. A hole for one was prepared days ago, but even that space had vanished. Either someone filled it in or he was on the wrong plot.

He was dizzy, which made it hard to concentrate on anything but the terror gripping his internal organs. Never before had he smelled one rotting, but today it filled the car when he was driving, and made him careless, impatient.

The stench was all around, even when he buried his nose in the dirt or covered it with his shirt.

Going to prison because of the flu would be ridiculous, especially since Ember insisted he get the damn shot.

When his hands were on the second woman's neck he felt a pain radiating from his own neck to his teeth, and now it was back in his right shoulder, which was almost numb from being pressed under the weight of the rest of his body.

To be caught when alive or caught when dead, those were his options. He would accept death if the bitches were just buried.

It was frustrating how misunderstood his actions would be, inaccurately labeled as compulsory. He sought the perfect accomplice. Women moments from sex were the best listeners, and once dead they were entirely relieved of the need to divulge what they heard.

He used to go to bars, the loudest and the busiest, but years ago in another town he was casually questioned about a missing woman, a woman going through a divorce, whose husband was convicted when they never found her.

Of course prostitutes would have been easier, more anonymous, but they often came with trouble. And it was unbearable conversing with the ignorant or the stoned.

For a while he had tried it the complicated way, in the back of a van, but women disappearing from parking lots made the news.

Never over two a month. That gave him time and space. At three-feet deep there was room for more adults than he could get away with burying, and twenty-four a year was his maximum.

He found that walking around Hollywood and smiling shyly at women, especially sad or lonely ones, often led to conversation. He parked on the street, sometimes circling around for forty-five minutes to find a spot, and then spent hours wandering among tourists in the dark before someone, always a local, wanted to go for a drive. After she was in the car it went quickly. The romantic garden, the stars so much brighter on the outskirts of Santa Monica than under the garish, unfeeling neon in Hollywood. They would stand outside, sometimes sit on the hood, and look upward.

He would have his hands on her, gentle yet ready, since a quick thinker might try to run. In less than five minutes he was able to tell her all he needed and could end it precisely as belief turned to fright. It was the way he spoke. He was always regretful in a teasing way and started with the first woman before summing the rest up. A punch to the temple subdued her if necessary, then a rough twist with one hand at the mouth and the other on the base of her skull. Or a long squeeze with both hands around the neck, although he preferred to use her scarf or bandana—if only both weren't rare in Southern California! Once he used a belt, but it took so long from start to finish that he ended up badly scratched. His grip was weak despite the regular hand exercises he did.

A room would be nice, and the time to make it worthwhile, but long ago he became aware that none of that was sustainable. There were many adventures and sickeningly close calls he would have enjoyed reviewing with later women, but time for dwelling on those was rare. It was best to speak and act quickly.

He liked to have someone know things. That was his weakness. Although being caught like this, he might as well have left these last two alive. Cynthia with the hair was useless; she sensed something before he spoke. In retrospect it would have been better to let her loose, but she was such a disappointment. And afterward it was a mistake not to take the time to bury her immediately; he lifted her into his trunk instead. He was feeling desperate by the time he saw Summer crying against her car in a parking lot. Something about finding out her fiancé wasn't a virgin. He sat on her in the garden, to be safe, but she was too shocked to cause a fuss. There was a sash at her waist, decorative yet strong.

He never wanted his own family to contend with this. He was not delusional; he knew what it would do. It was easier to die than have Ember insisting he was innocent as her trust and love slowly dissolved.

He was sure now it wasn't the flu.

88

Randall Murphy calls Ember with the warning that an attorney is planning a press conference. "I don't have details, but it would be smart for you to be in town." Thankfully no one mentions Richard's birthday on December twenty-second; she prefers to spend that alone.

Horace's delight over his story's upcoming publication in the March edition of *The Way Things Aren't*, a journal of fantasy and political comedy, has been distracting everyone. It pays fifty dollars and a six-month subscription. "I'll sign everyone's copy for a nominal fee," he jokes. "You'll each have to buy the issue so they'll be impressed that my name raises sales."

"Maybe Lilac will take care of any leftovers," someone says.

"She and Katherine are the only ones who read it before I sent it in. It's based on Kathy, but I'm dedicating it to Lilac—at least in theory since they don't give me a dedication page."

"Let me come," Bridgett whispers urgently in Ember's ear, her breath hot and heavy with chocolate pudding. Everyone has been told that a pipe burst in the condo's wall.

"I'll miss you," Paul says. "Call if you need help."

He holds on to her hip bones and pulls her belly up against his. She tilts her head back to see his face.

He is moving to Pasadena with his sister's family and trying to decide on a new career plan. She has been insisting that she doesn't want academia in her life again. "Go into plumbing! You could charge hundreds of dollars for something that takes fifteen minutes to fix!" she teases, hoping he will decide to teach.

"This is a new romance," she tells him now. But with every good moment she is tempted to invite him to stay with her.

"Frances is showing me how to make crème brûlée," he promises.

"We've got to get going," Katherine says. "I have your luggage." In her excitement to be Ember's chauffeur, she loads the car and rushes the goodbyes. It's not until they are five miles away that Ember learns her driver is newly licensed. However, Katherine has been pestering to talk to her privately, which handily prevented the others from tagging along.

"Do you have a family? Besides the people here," Katherine asks as she steers, looking at Ember far too long.

"Of course."

"What would they do if you decided not to have kids?"

"At this point they wish I'd never married, so I'm not a good person to ask. My parents have a couple of grandkids already; they're not too worried. You're lucky Lilac is pregnant."

"They're obsessed with Horace's offspring. Really obsessed. They care more about how I look than my personality. They want baby brunettes and redheads, and redheads with olive skin, and brunettes with blue eyes."

"Isn't Horace unable to reproduce?"

"*They* don't know. I consider it a selling point, but they'll think it's tragic. We're sure they'll force us to try every fertility treatment invented. It'll be awful."

"Doesn't he have a real medical problem?"

"He doesn't have a vas deferens, the thing that carries the sperm around. Basically it's a natural vasectomy."

"Then it doesn't sound like there's much anyone can do."

"They can still get sperm out in surgery, and then use other crap to get it in me. It's not as hard as if the woman has fertility problems, but considering I don't even want kids... What sucks is that Horace doesn't care either way. He'll go through with it if I want to, and he won't if I don't. But I need him to insist to his family that not doing it is *his* idea. I'm not interested in any of it. And we'll be living right here in the same town."

"You could move."

"That's impossible. He owns a house here, his family throws him tidbits, I'm able to do odd jobs." She groans. "We'd never survive anywhere else."

"Just pretend you're trying to get pregnant, then when it never happens they'll get used to the idea. Or even fake getting the treatments."

"Oh, fine then," Katherine says. "I was hoping you'd come up with the perfect statement to get them to fuck off." She sighs. "Well, I guess that might work. As long as it's *his* fault. They adore him. Do you know the story of how he and his sister were conceived?"

"Yes, Vicky told me. It's true?"

"I guess. I was wondering if they'll drudge up someone who looks like Horace and present him to me."

"Do they want the genes reproduced, or just grandchildren?"

"Who can tell? If they ever find out about *my* genes—"

"Katherine! They don't know?"

"If they remember the story they haven't made the connection. I told them my family is all out west, and of course gave my mom's last name, but as the news of our wedding spreads I'm sure someone will tell. It's going to be a disaster. They are constantly talking about their excitement over meeting my dear widowed mother and two brothers. The Greene-Jeans think I was estranged from them until Horace brought us back together. Frances told me she almost asked Lilac to beautify my mother for the wedding. Luckily my family is used to pretending. They have the idea I'll be rich once I'm married. Typical white trash." She laughs and turns the radio to a music station with loud static.

On the plane Ember finishes rereading an English translation of *One Hundred Years of Solitude*, then tries to figure out how to pronounce French words using a guide Bridgett gave her.

"Welcome back," Sammy says as she stumbles into her building. "You have timing! Reporters have been trying to break in since yesterday. The police were by moments ago to shoo them off. Get some sleep and don't worry, I'll keep 'em out."

Her apartment is chilly, but of course there's no water damage. She wonders why she didn't just admit that she wanted to go home. But Paul would have been hurt (he probably is anyway), and the expense was embarrassing. "It's only eight days," Vicky would have said. "How about we promise to leave you alone?" Even Frances might have been upset.

They never once turned on the heater when Richard was alive, but it gets colder now, and she goes for eighty degrees.

She calls Horace's and Tony answers. "Everyone's on a picnic," he says. "I came back to fill the water jug. I hope your house is OK. Listen, there's been some media action down here. I guess yesterday a former patient—some man from the Grangage Institute—sold a story to a tabloid."

"Why now?"

"Don't know. Suddenly everyone cares again. A famous true crime writer has been trying to contact Vicky. One of her fans, a victim's family member, suggested Richard as a subject. She won't do it without the family's consent."

"Good."

"She's known to be fair. She won't work on a case that's still open, and she's not sure this one has been closed satisfactorily."

"Well then."

"Horace has read her and thinks it would be better if she wrote it than anyone else."

"Or he just wants to make an industry connection."

"OK, I admit it—I've read her too. She's really thorough."

"Maybe Bridgett can dig up her paperwork and donate it."

Ember ends the call and plays her answering machine. Every message is from a journalist. It's a relief to live in a guarded building, but she still feels harassed. After shutting herself in the office, she immediately wishes she hadn't. If she allows this eerie feeling to make her paranoid she might end up incapable of opening the door. Then she will have to sleep in here, on the floor or in her chair.

"Reporters aren't known for breaking into houses and torturing people," she teases herself in a whisper. "I lived with a killer, and I'm more worried about camera and microphone wielders than I ever was my husband."

She starts to read Richard's *A Brief Madness* essay and thinks irritably that it's still the dullest, most disorganized mess she has ever come across. Not that she can blame him, he never expected anyone besides her to read it in this condition. She skips around and finds a description (and translation) of some Latin transcripts from a medieval Court of Common Pleas. They seem to have been chosen haphazardly—perhaps all he could find from that time period. She helped him research the Code of Hammurabi. She tries to locate it in the largely inaccurate rough index and wakes up with her head on the desk.

After checking the locks and turning the heat down to seventy, she goes to the bathroom to wash her face and rub in moisturizers. Before getting in bed she looks at the clock; it's only ten p.m. No one else has called in the three hours she has been here.

The police surround a house in her dream, a house in which she is sitting, waiting to be arrested. Finally she wakes up to the doorbell. Her clock says four and it's still dark.

She tiptoes to the peephole. "Stop pushing that damn thing," she says when she sees Tony. She undoes the locks and lets him in. "What are you doing here? What's going on? How'd you get in?"

"The guard remembered me."

"Great."

"No, they've been keeping people away all night." He shuts and locks the door.

"Why are you here?"

"We found out what's been getting the buzz going again. Some attorney has been announcing all over the place that he has a sealed letter left by Richard, to be opened on the second birthday after his death. Tomorrow."

"He would have been forty-five. I'm sure he wasn't expecting death when it happened though. He wasn't expecting to be caught, ever. He wouldn't write a public letter."

"It's for you, but this asshole lawyer wants free advertising. I guess Richard's solicitor died and this guy inherited all his cases."

"Why haven't I been contacted?"

"You were publicly invited to his office tomorrow. So is the media. The Law Offices of Brighton and Isserman. Frederick Garrison is the name of the guy advertising the letter."

"I don't have to open it in front of them, do I?"

"No, but we contacted Jill, and she called an attorney friend to meet us there in case there's any trouble. At first Frances, Bridgett and *everyone* else was planning to fly up here and go with you, for support, but Jill suggested that would just draw more attention to us. Would you rather Paul had come? I used every argument I could think of to talk him out of it. All the way to the airport. We all went, all nine of us, because up until the moment the ticket was purchased we weren't sure what our plans were. Do you mind we didn't call you? Frances was worried you wouldn't get any sleep if you knew, and tomorrow will be—"

"Tony, calm down. I'm glad you're here. I'm going to take a shower."

She stays under the water for a long time; she wants to be very clean for whatever happens.

Will Richard be admitting what he expected no one to know whenever it was he wrote this letter? She did wonder how someone with his obsession for biographies could stand to leave a large part of his own life undocumented—and with no one to record it for him. Maybe he wanted it to be about the other person he was, the writer, the teacher, her husband.

After putting on lotion that smells like raspberries, she plucks a few stray hairs from her eyebrows. The mirror keeps fogging over where she wipes it, so she finally leaves the bathroom with a towel wrapped around her head.

She sits on a barstool and watches as Tony's arm muscles ripple in his attempt to open one of Frances' tightly sealed jam jars. The lid begins to turn, and she thinks of how easily he could strangle someone.

Always able to fall asleep, now she feels the need urgently. For once she has let herself become so exhausted that she can no longer control her thoughts.

There are still people she knows that are alive; those are the ones she will think of. It's three hours later in the south, and even though they don't call, she knows they are waiting.

At eight Tony dials Ms. Martinez, Jill's lawyer friend, and makes plans to meet at Garrison's office in an hour. They will take a taxi.

Ember is numb with anxiety. She dresses in dark gray slacks and a matching dress jacket. Her shoes are boots "for walking quickly and possibly kicking," she jokes to Tony, who is in a suit. She has never seen him so handsome and formidable. "When I first met you, you were just a girl, and look at you now, all grown up into a man," she tells him. His laugh is loud and cheerful, but he stops it abruptly. "Should I wrap a towel over my face?" she asks. She can't make him relax again, but he'll be a good bodyguard.

Tony lifts the curtain over the balcony window, pauses for a moment, and steps quickly away. "I wish we had a better plan for getting there. The taxi is going to be mobbed."

Ember calls her renewed buddy Randall, who sends Boxer down as a driver. When Boxer sees Tony in a suit, he returns upstairs to change out of his sweats.

"I feel like a mafiosa or a rap star," she says with Boxer back and looking as professional as Tony. They are standing nervously, doing some shuffling, trying to avoid sitting and wrinkles.

She and Tony wait in the lobby as Boxer leaves unmolested. His car is parked on a street nearby.

He pulls up to the gate too quickly, forcing people and news vans to move. Stopping directly in front of the entryway, he turns the car off. After opening the passenger side door he stands in front of it, preventing anyone from entering the walkway. Tony and Ember hurry; her name is called out and there's a lot of noise. She gets in the car and Tony sits next to her. Boxer runs around the back and jumps in, bumping people as he drives away.

"That went well," Boxer says. "You were saying the press was invited into the law office?"

"Her attorney limited it to two television crews and three newspaper reporters. I guess Garrison had already spoken with them. However, Ms. Martinez said they will merely get to see the letter exchange hands, no one can force Ember to open it in public."

There are even more people in front of the plain brick building containing the law office. Boxer moves his car slowly through the crowd until he touches the curb. He turns the ignition off and faces them as more than one person bangs on the door. "Don't make eye contact. Don't look directly at anyone.

"I'm going to get out, open the door for Tony, then we will walk on either side of you. I'll come back and move the car after." He flinches as someone hits it hard.

"I'll get it fixed," Ember promises, but he's already outside.

Tony and Boxer move confidently as they walk to the building. From of the corners of her eyes she can see them on either side of her, looking around in all directions. She feels guarded from an assassin's bullet, unless the shooter is waiting on the roof or inside the building. Don't smile, she tells herself.

Police officers are in front of the doors, but they let the two of them in while Boxer hurries back to his car. Ms. Martinez is waiting and introduces Ember to Mr. Garrison, sounding as if the former has been her client since birth. All Ember later remembers about her is a brown dress.

Mr. Garrison keeps glancing at Tony as if to ask, "Does he have to be present?" Ember wonders if the lawyer is worrying his bright blue pinstripes won't photograph as well as Tony's dark suit. Boxer enters and stands with them.

"In a few minutes, Ms. Oto, Ms. Martinez and I will enter the room where the press is set up, you gentlemen—"

"They will be coming with me," Ember says.

He nods. "I will remove the letter from the safe, say a few words, and you can then decide if you will open it—"

"As we discussed before, my client will either be left alone in the room with the letter for as long as she likes, or she will read it later in the privacy of her own home."

"If she's left alone will she read it here?"

Ember wonders if he planned to shock her on camera with the news, and then embarrass her into cooperating.

They walk to the back of the building and enter a room with a bare desk and a safe, obvious on the otherwise blank white wall. Three cameras are set up, each with an operator and interviewer, and the small group of foldout chairs is also full. It seems like a larger crowd than Ms. Martinez promised.

"Thank you all for coming. I am pleased to introduce Ms. Ember Oto and her attorney, Ms. Martinez. Mr. Isserman was in Richard Earle Dayle's service for only this one task, which he clearly wanted kept separate and confidential from his other affairs. On Mr. Isserman's death, I took over his clients with continuing needs. One was Mr. Dayle, who nearly a year before he died wrote a letter to be presented to his wife on the second birthday after his death. He mentioned he might update the letter at a later date. If his wife died before or at the same time, the letter was to be destroyed. I will now open the safe, no longer in general use, but into which I moved the letter yesterday for convenience."

He types numbers into a keypad, and after opening the safe takes out a stiff manila envelope a little larger than a sheet of paper.

"The outside says, 'To Ember, my love. From Richard. The seal glued over the entire flap will have to be cut. I'm sorry you must ruin the picture because it and the negative no longer exist. Bridgett took this, catching us unaware.'" Mr. Garrison holds it up. "I don't know if you can see clearly, but the seal has been created with a photograph of the couple reading on a couch. It would be difficult to replicate."

Mr. Garrison is next to Ember, but the letter is in his far hand. He turns toward her, about to make the presentation, and she snatches the envelope away, holding the picture side against her chest with both arms crossed over it.

Ms. Martinez helps Tony and Boxer clear the room; somehow they know she will read her letter before leaving the building. She barely hears them as they promise to stand outside the two doors for as long as she needs. Boxer hands her his keys, and she holds them in confusion until she notices they are chained to a small knife. Both doorknobs have simple push locks, which make her feel truly, safely alone.

She sits in a front row chair and places the envelope on her lap. She will read it in a minute. She is still smiling, and her face doesn't want to stop, so she ignores it and starts to slice delicately along the seam at the bottom. It amuses her that the paper inside will drive thousands into energetic speculation.

Richard has already made a mistake: since she didn't know which photograph would be used, some diabolical person could have replaced it with another. Not that she believes this occurred.

Maybe he will apologize to the families of the victims. Ember knows that is what she wishes for, although it's unlikely. It probably won't help the bereaved feel the slightest bit better, but she wants him to have felt regret. To know he at least thought of those who suffered, or even better, that he felt terrible for his actions.

Maybe he will even declare her completely ignorant of his crimes. That would be nice as well. If he does both those things she will at least be able to love the Richard she thought she had.

89

"Ember," Tony says quietly. He almost laughed at first, seeing her long body curled into the fetal position on the otherwise bare desk, but minutes have passed and she still hasn't responded.

"We've got to go, Ember," he says more loudly. "Boxer is waiting out front in the car."

When her eyelashes slowly move he puts one hand under her shoulder and the other on her arm and helps her sit up, noticing the papers held against her chest.

"I don't want to leave this room right now," she says, the left side of her face chafed by the hard wood. "I can't deal with everything out there."

"I know." Tony touches her reddened cheek.

She shivers and stands. He presses his palm lightly against the back of her head. She looks up as he leans in. Her lips are cold, and when she doesn't push away he places his other hand on her waist. As he moves his tongue into her mouth she turns her head a little, then he feels her tongue on his, circling and tasting. He would rather suffocate than separate, but finally a need to breathe forces their heads apart, and they stare at each other.

Anticipating horror, he doesn't know what it means that she smiles, and then laughs softly until he laughs back.

"How did you get in the room?"

"Credit card."

As they walk to the door Tony remembers for the first time today that he isn't a normal man. Has Ember forgotten as well?

The hall outside the room is empty, but Mr. Garrison was wandering around the entire half hour Ember spent alone in the office, so Tony is not surprised when the attorney appears just as they approach the building's front doors.

Ember has grabbed Tony's hand and is squeezing it hard as they move outside, guarded from the shrieking press by numerous police officers. Before the doors shut she turns to Mr. Garrison, who is standing in the entry, and pushes the papers into his hands.

"Take them!" she shouts.

Seconds later they are in the car, and two officers wave it forward. Tony sits in the back holding Ember tightly, knowing he only has a few more minutes.

He sucks in the scent of her hair as she whispers, "I gave the letter to him. Why should I have to be chased around and tormented for something like that?"

"You shouldn't, of course not," he murmurs. "Ember? I'm—I—I worry about you."

"Thank you." She takes a loud breath. "And you love Jill, and I love Paul. I do love Paul."

Tony moves the corners of his lips up: "Good."

"No excuses though."

"No excuses." And he pulls away a little, so they aren't touching, but keeps smiling. "Now for the less important stuff."

"Yes," she says.

"I think you have a sleeping disorder."

She laughs loudly, and Boxer looks back at them. "Good news about the letter?" he asks.

"Well, it will be news. Let's see, how did he put it? He mentioned how much he loved me, then listed the top choices for his biographer. He suggested it would be best if I never marry again, to give him more dignity in future editions."

The car is silent, and then they hear Tony's phone vibrating against the keys in his pocket.

"Of course he didn't know how infamous he would be or that others besides me would care what was in the letter."

"Then why did he think his life would make any sort of biography?" Boxer asks irritably. "Without the murders he didn't do anything worth reading about, did he? He was an interesting guy to talk to, and Russell thought he was hilarious, but that doesn't make him special. I'm never going to have a book written about me, and I was way more famous in my football days. More famous than him alive at least."

Ember coughs. "He thought his books, the biographies he wrote, would make him famous. He had a lot of fans that wanted everything he produced, and he was sure his style would eventually receive more merit among serious scholars."

"What about the sealed envelope and all that?" Boxer asks.

"He didn't want those greedy attorneys to steal his biographer," Tony comes up with after a pause. Ember's glance is appreciative.

Boxer pulls up to their building, and they wait for a police officer to motion them to get out. Only one or two journalists are still around.

"Garrison must be giving the press conference of his life," Tony says.

"Do you think he'll attract clients from it?" Ember asks without much curiosity.

"He sure had an ego," Tony says, patting Sammy on the shoulder when they get to the door. "And I'm talking about Richard."

They thank the officer that escorted them to the building.

"I'm too tired for the stairs today," Ember says.

Tony puts his arm around her in the elevator but somehow isn't surprised to see Paul when the doors open on Ember's floor.

"Are you all right?" Paul asks, and she nods. "Boxer called Russell after he dropped you off." He pulls her against him. "That attorney had just finished reading the letter on television, and they were replaying the bit with you leaving the building, and then turning and shoving the envelope into his face. He said, 'Ms. Oto has apparently trusted me to share this with the public.' Are you really all right?"

Ember nods again. Her face is against Paul's shoulder, and she's staring at the floor. Lifting her eyes she looks at Tony and they grin at each other. "Has the analysis started? Did they have psychiatrists and criminologists standing by?"

"Not yet. Your hair hid your face for the few seconds the cameras caught," Paul says, running his hands over it. "So the reporters were speculating over your reaction. I'm sure they'll squeeze as much out of that as they can. All the old information and pictures will be reviewed."

"Maybe we'll get lucky and a celebrity or two will overdose after divorcing for the fifth time," Tony says, trying to keep some of her attention.

"Wouldn't it be easier to give a statement and get it over with?" Paul asks. "You used to have that publicist. She might be able to help you come up with something."

"They wouldn't be satisfied."

"It would help though," Tony says. "It's too bad that asshole Garrison had to make nothing into a news story. Maybe you can add a jab at him. Do you even have a reaction though? Shock, disgust, horror—"

Ember laughs. "Well, it wasn't that dramatic. I didn't expect anything about the murders. I did think it might have to do with the biography. That he suggested I never marry again to leave him with a . . . uh, a more impressive reputation throughout posterity? That was a little much."

"But if you didn't know about the murders?"

"Then the letter wouldn't have been as important to me—and everyone else—and I probably would have understood. He was obsessive on the subject of biographies." She steps away from Paul and puts a hand on the doorknob. "I was never going to pressure anyone to write it. I decided that before he died. It would have been different if someone had offered or asked, then I would have helped all I could. The writers he wanted were his friends, you see, or at least former students, and asking for something like that would have been embarrassing."

"So Boxer was right?"

"I expected someone to volunteer, if he lived long enough. I just wouldn't have pushed."

"What about his last book, the one he wanted you to publish?" Paul asks.

"Oh, yes." She looks at Tony. "That was mentioned in the letter too. His essay, *A Brief Madness: Lapses in* blah blah blah. I found that request quite unbelievable. The manuscript will never be publishable. Never."

"Well," Tony says after a moment. "I think you're exactly—"

"He expected me," Ember interrupts loudly, glaring between Tony and Paul at the elevator door, "to spend the *rest of my life* editing that monstrosity of an essay and forcing it through publication." Her voice has risen to a yell and starts to crack as she adds, "All the while arranging and finagling and probably marketing his biography through its multiple editions. Until the one set to go out after my death, where I make sure they will add the inscription: His widow never remarried but devoted the rest of her life to promoting his great legacy.

"And this worthy person murdered a huge number of strangers after plotting—ha, get it?"

Ember laughs and then begins to cough as though she is choking. Tony tries to distract her, "That's not—"

"It was that letter," she says. Then more quietly, to Paul's chest, "Ever since his death I've been trying to reconcile the Richard I loved, who was so good to me, with the one who murdered women. *Women.* As if that's not enough, I always feel like adding that they were innocent, loved, loving, talented." She stops for a few seconds, gazing at her hand gripping the doorknob. "But after I read his letter, then sat there for a while, then read it again—he wrote some lovey-dovey things that I didn't repeat to you, Tony, but it wasn't very long. I'm not sure how many times I read it, but afterward, staring at the words on the page until they were a blur, I saw him clearly. He was obsessed with his genius but uncaring about the right to life. This probably doesn't matter and won't make any sense, but even his love for me was because *he* loved me."

"It matters. He was your husband."

"But he's not just my husband anymore. He belongs to the people whose chance at life he ended. He belongs to everyone he hurt that's still around to feel anything, and everyone who was scared, sad, depressed, and angry just hearing the stories. I've been trying to love who and what I thought he was, but I can't any longer. It's too hard. And I do have a message for the world." She glances at Tony and gives him a small smile, then looks straight at Paul. "I'm going to get married."

"You are?" Paul asks.

After a silence, Tony says, "If you say yes."

"Me?"

Lightly Tony jokes, "You have my permission."

Paul doesn't take long to come up with a response: "Ember, I don't want to live in this building, but I would love to marry you and visit every evening from my apartment up the block."

Ember laughs and then Tony does too.

"It might just be possible to convince me to relocate."

"I'm going to see what Boxer is up to," Tony says, moving toward the stairwell at the end of the hall. "Thank him for his help with everything."

"I just want to be married by a judge," Ember is telling Paul as he hugs her tightly.

"Fine with me."

"Jill has a friend, a retired judge," Tony can't resist adding. "It would be easy to arrange."

"Or we can go to Colorado, where my family is."

Tony pushes open the door to the stairs, pausing for a second in case they decide to say anything else to him. When he glances back they are entering her place.

He jumps as he turns to the stairs and sees a person leaning against the wall.

"Jill." Tony stares at her. "You look great. I didn't recognize you."

"He finally notices," she says, staring off to the side. "So it sounds like they're planning on marriage. That will make quite a statement after the letter begging her not to: I don't think so, Richard, you asshole."

"She's pretending to be shocked by his callousness," Tony says, "but she's hated him for a long time."

Jill nods. "Revenge marriage. Oh well, there are worse reasons to wed—or so I assume."

"What have you been doing to yourself? You look really healthy."

"And thinner."

"Much thinner."

"I quit drinking. A month ago."

"I did notice you were no longer running around naked when I got home from work. I kind of missed that."

"Sober I realized how awful I looked. Maybe I'll start doing it again now. The running around, I mean."

"Good," he says. He traces his hand down her ribcage.

"Tony, are you ready to try out our belt—I mean that harness thing?"

"Ah, the plastic penis. I don't know. Are you?"

"I am," she says. "Tonight."

He kisses Jill, her lips large and soft.

Touching Ember had been exciting; he felt like he was conquering an ideal. He presses Jill against him. While her hot tongue is in his mouth, he can forget what his body is missing.

She didn't spend her girlhood fantasizing about ending up in such a strange relationship either. And if she has stopped drinking herself into a coma every night, which must be true since all the puffiness is gone, it is only Tony who is lacking.

Jill turns her head away. "So did you get to be the rescuing hero?"

"I guess."

"Are you done with all that now?"

He wants to say he is sorry but decides not to risk it. He nods instead. "I'll stop working every night if you're going to be conscious."

She traces a finger over his lips. "We're not so strange," she says.

"Except that you can read my mind."

"Oh, that's easy. You're a man, aren't you?"

It's awkward, but they hold hands all the way down the narrow stairs, bumping into the walls and laughing.

CPSIA information can be obtained at www.ICGtesting.com
Printed in the USA
245049LV00001B/27/P